KRAKEN BAKE

Other Epikurean Epics by Karen Dudley

Food for the Gods

KRAKEN BAKE

by Karen Dudley

RaveN
STONE

Kraken Bake
copyright © Karen Dudley 2014

Published by Ravenstone
an imprint of Turnstone Press
Artspace Building
206-100 Arthur Street
Winnipeg, MB
R3B 1H3 Canada
www.RavenstoneBooks.com

Turnstone Press gratefully acknowledges the assistance of the Canada
Council for the Arts, the Manitoba Arts Council, the Government of
Canada through the Canada Book Fund, and the Province of Manitoba
through the Book Publishing Tax Credit and the Book Publisher
Marketing Assistance Program.

This novel is a work of fiction. Names, characters, places and incidents
are either the product of the author's imagination or are used fictitiously,
and any resemblance to actual persons living or dead, events or locales, is
entirely coincidental.

Printed and bound in Canada by Friesens for Turnstone Press.

Library and Archives Canada Cataloguing in Publication

Dudley, Karen, author
     Kraken bake / by Karen Dudley.

(An epikurean epic)
ISBN 978-0-88801-466-5 (pbk)

        I. Title.

PS8557.U279K73 2014   C813'.54   C2014-901388-4

KRAKEN BAKE

"Come, Hermogenes! I am feeling remarkably optimistic today. After all, the early bird gets the worm."

"Not so lucky for the worm though, is it?" My disciple yawned as he stumbled behind me, his curly hair tousled and his chiton askew.

"Ah, but we are the birds in this scenario," I reminded him. "Early and swift—at least we would be if you would pick up your feet. Come, come!"

Hermogenes mumbled something under his breath, though he did endeavour to increase his pace.

We had left the house early, even before rosy-fingered Eos, goddess of the dawn, had begun to lighten the sky. My goal in doing so was to procure not a lowly worm, but some form of fresh fish at the market—an item which these days was about as rare as a three-tentacled squid. It was a chilly morning, the air holding a hint of the winter damp to come, but the newly risen sun was burning off the fog, promising at least a sunny day, if not a particularly warm one.

I strode briskly down the Panathenaic Way, Athens's main artery, with Hermogenes lagging behind me. Few were on the road at this hour, so we swept easily past the Painted Stoa (where, later in the day, philosophers would gather to pontificate), and past the Altar to the Twelve Gods (which stood at the entrance to the Agora and from which all distances in the civilized world were measured), before plunging into the labyrinthine streets and alleys that made up the market proper.

The sounds of the Agora were muted as shopkeepers went about their preparations for the day. People were speaking in lowered tones, the way they do before the sun is high. A donkey bell clanged mournfully. Off to my right, there was a sudden shout of laughter, quickly smothered.

The haze of cook smoke mingled with the dissipating fog, bringing with it the smell of spiced sausages. Hermogenes's nose began to twitch at the tantalizing aroma, but just as he opened his mouth (probably to importune me for a breakfast sausage or two), the bell sounded the opening of the market.

With this herald came the first of the merchants crying their wares.

"*Krayken*! Fresh today!"

"Get your *krayken* here!"

"Kebobs! *Krayken* kebobs! Grilled while you wait! Hot and tasty *krayken* kebobs!"

With each shout, my sunny mood darkened.

"*Krayken!*" one overly enthusiastic fishmonger bawled, jumping in our path and shoving a platter of his odiferous wares under our noses. "All cuts! From mantle to tentacle tips! Some *krayken* for you, my friend? Eh? Best quality!"

I glowered at the man's pronunciation of the word and waved him off with a snap of my wrist. Gesturing Hermogenes onwards, I stalked past the first of the fish sellers' shops.

"*Krayken, krayken*, and more sodding *krayken*," Hermogenes grunted sourly as he perused the stalls.

That was too much! It was one thing to hear the word coming from fishmongers. Quite another to hear it from the lips of my own disciple.

Thoroughly exasperated, I stopped and turned to confront him. "It's kraken," I corrected sharply.

"Beg your pardon, Chef. I forgot."

"Indeed. Perhaps it would be easier if you remembered that it rhymes with smackin'." I raised one eyebrow and flexed my hand.

Hermogenes gave me a crooked grin and ducked his head in a more sincere apology. "Sorry, Chef. I'll try to remember for next time."

"See that you do," I told him testily, pulling my cloak more tightly around me.

In fact, most of Athens referred to the creature in the same way, incorrectly pronouncing it *Kray*-ken, to rhyme with bacon. That they did so because of my archrival—a jumped-up taverna cook from Sicily—went a long way to explaining my implacable intolerance of the mistake.

A week or two after kraken had made its first appearance on the market, Mithaecus the Sicilian had devised what he'd called a "secret blend of spices" which he used to coat the kraken meat before bunging the lot into a hot oven to bake. The so-called "Kraken Bake" coating was more salt and pepper and stale barley bread crumbs than anything else, but the Athenians gobbled it up like it was ambrosia, and virtually overnight everybody started saying *krayken* rather than kraken.

To make things worse, word had gone around that Kraken Bake was so easy to prepare, even the simplest house slave could manage it (which was unsurprising given the quality of The Sicilian's culinary talents). Gossip had it that Mithaecus was raking in a fortune by selling packets of the coating at hugely inflated prices.

Now that was more than I could stomach.

The Sicilian had been the green mould on my cheese since I'd first landed in Athens. From the beginning, he had slandered me, ridiculed my cooking, and tried to bribe food sellers to offer me inferior goods. Normally, such behaviour would hardly have been enough to inconvenience me. I was, after all, a celebrity chef. At my level, one could expect a certain degree of envy from those less gifted. But in the past summer, Mithaecus had taken his petty rivalry to new depths, and as a result of his jealous machinations, I had lost all my contracts during the city's most important festival, my friends' livelihoods had suffered much the same fate, and a ruthless business associate had beaten up my fifteen-year-old disciple so badly that the scars were still visible on his face. My career as a chef had come dangerously close

to ending then and there. Had it not been for the decisive reso-
lution of certain unfortunate events, followed by the concerted
efforts of friends both high and low, I would have found myself
run out of town, ending my days slinging stew in Corinth or
baking peasant loaves in one of the colonies.

No, I did not care for The Sicilian, nor he for me—particularly after I had (most uncharacteristically) lost my temper and
punched him in the face, flattening his noble Grecian nose into
something resembling an ill-risen barley roll. It had been a small
act of revenge—one that did not even begin to pay him back for
his malicious actions—but since then, although we studiously
avoided each other, our rivalry had escalated to new and lofty
heights. Matters between us were far from resolved, and every
utterance of the word "krayken" served as a pointed reminder to
me of our unfinished business.

Scant weeks before, few in Athens had even heard the word
"kraken," let alone had the opportunity to mispronounce it. It
was a word from the distant past, something more tall tale than
truth.

Kraken were monsters of the sea. Enormous, multi-tentacled,
terrifying creatures, they formed the base of Poseidon's muscle
whenever he took it into his head to release a spot of terror on
an offending kingdom. The last time he'd sent one out had been
when the ancient land of Troy had refused to pay the god for
building their city's walls. Granted, he had been forced into the
labour as punishment for revolting against Zeus, but it had been
unwise of the Trojan king to refuse to cough up his wages. It was
the legendary Herakles who had eventually taken out that beast.

Nobody had any particulars about why a kraken had been released this time around. All that was known was that this new kraken had been slain by a young fellow named Perseus, and although his name was now on every tongue, nobody in Athens had ever heard of him before. Not until a supply ship had come sailing up to the docks of Piraeus, its holds bulging with kraken meat.

According to the sailors from this first ship, Perseus hailed from some backwater village in the colonies, and he had in his possession any number of wondrous items. Dockside gossip was rampant.

"Wotcha know, 'e's got a magic sword …"

"An' sandals wif wings on 'em …"

"An' an invisible 'elmet!"

"Invisible? 'Ow d'you know it's invisible if you can't see it?"

"Woll … I know 'e's got a magic sword. I 'eard about it from a sailor what seen it hisself. Used it to off th' kraken, din't 'e?"

Despite the conflicting reports regarding his magical accoutrements, all of Athens agreed that this Perseus had to be a hero of most impressive stature, as even the legendary Theseus would have been daunted by a calamari writ so large. How a mere mortal had managed to dispatch the creature was the subject of much speculation in the Agora. But dispatch it he certainly had, for the fish sellers' stalls groaned under the weight of it, and soon Athenians were flocking to the marketplace to line up for the rare treat. For the next few days, the blue-tinged cooking smoke that customarily hung over the city bore a distinctly fishy odour. Kraken steaks were best when grilled on a brazier.

More details came with a second heavily-laden supply ship.

"I 'eard tell 'e used 'is magic sword to kill Medusa, and then it were Medusa's severed 'ead 'e used to kill th' kraken …"

"Medusa! One o' them Gorgones sisters? Wif all them snakes fer 'air?"

"Wot? That one what'll turn you to stone if you so much as look at 'er?"

"The very one!"

"But if 'e used 'er 'ead, why din't th' kraken get turn't to stone, then?"

"Dunno, do I?"

"I 'eard maybe it was on account of it bein' supernacheral and all. Great tentacled bastard just up and died instead o' gettin' petreefied."

Kraken kebobs became all the rage.

And there was still more kraken to come. It seemed the usual flesh-eating scavengers of the sea did not much care for kraken. Neither did the other benthic denizens, for fishermen throughout the Aegean complained bitterly of their poor catches, blaming it on the lingering presence of the dead sea monster. The beast had clearly been far larger than anybody had guessed, and kraken meat, it appeared, did not rot. Large pots of tentacle stew simmered in kitchens throughout the city.

A third supply ship brought with it, in addition to more kraken, the "why" of it all. According to this ship's captain, the sea monster had been terrorizing the far-off kingdom of Aethiopia, whose queen had boasted that her daughter, Andromeda, was more beautiful than the Nereides. The Nereides were water nymphs, the good-time girls of Poseidon's court, and he was inordinately fond of them. Queen Kassiopeia really ought to have known better than to offend Poseidon—indeed, I could have given her an earful on the consequences of doing so if she'd bothered to ask. But the insult was issued, and a much angered Poseidon released his oversized pet on the kingdom.

"Would'a meant the end of Aethiopia, that's for sure," the captain told his rapt audience, which that day included Hermogenes and me. He paused and drained his wine cup. The taverna owner was quick to refill it. "But then the oracle of Ammon came a'calling," the captain continued after taking another healthy drink and wiping his mouth with the back of his hand. "Tipped off the king and queen regarding a certain loophole in the works. Told 'em the land could be saved, if they offered up their own daughter to the kraken ..." he paused and lowered his voice, "for its tea."

The crowd gasped in horror, but I was less shocked than most by the revelation. After all, being served for dinner wasn't exactly a new concept for me.

Suffice it to say that Andromeda's parents proved about as loving as my own father had been. And it was while she awaited her gruesome fate, chained to a rock by the sea and generously sprinkled with seasoning, that our man Perseus just happened to pass by, spied the girl and fell instantly in love with her. All this just as the many-tentacled kraken arrived on the scene in search of its snack. The quick-thinking hero, who had the Gorgon's head handily stashed in a pouch at his side, pulled out the vile thing and waved it at the oncoming sea monster, killing the beast, saving both girl and kingdom, and thereby earning the undying gratitude of her not-so-loving-but-still-very-wealthy parents.

Some people have all the luck.

After that, the tales about Perseus got more fantastical with each passing day.

"'E's another one of Zeus's brats, yeah? They say 'is mum's quite a looker ..."

"I 'eard Father Zeus came to 'er disguised as a golden shower, 'e did ..."

"An' 'e's got a flyin' 'orse ..."

"Bollocks! Never 'eard of no flyin' 'orse ..."

"It's true! I 'eard it meself from a sailor who knew a bloke what saw it ..."

"I still say it's bollocks!"

By the time a fourth ship arrived in Athens, sales of kraken had begun to fall off rather noticeably. I learned quickly to get to the market by first light, as all available fish—and there weren't many of these—were snapped up by early shoppers longing for the taste of something other than the ubiquitous kraken. Despite the fact that the creature had been dispatched in such a distant locale, ocean currents had steadily steered its remains towards Athens, hence the dearth of any other fish in the Agora. I strongly suspected the hand of Poseidon at work in this. He had never quite forgiven the city for snubbing him and selecting Athena as its patron god, and, as Dionysus had once observed, Poseidon could be a right vengeful bastard.

The entire Peloponnesus had been hit hard too, according

to the ship's captain. This news gave Athenians some smug satisfaction—at least they weren't the only ones suffering—until the captain mentioned that the Spartans were treating it as a sort of challenge. For weeks now, they had been eating nothing but kraken, believing that doing so would confer upon them all the might of the slain beast. At this news, Athenians once again stepped up to their dinner plates. After all, if their archrivals the Spartans could eat nothing but kraken, so could the Athenians, though *they* would do so with the style and verve for which they were so justly famous. Overnight, new recipes and methods of preparing kraken began circulating around the Agora.

A fifth supply ship arrived.

Even with the new recipes, Athenians soon wearied of the unending kraken. And by the time a sixth and seventh supply ship unloaded their unwelcome cargos, people had already started turning to anything else that was edible for relief. Even the lowly sprat—long considered a peasant food—saw a surge in popularity among those who had never before allowed such a humble fish to pass their lips. And Hermogenes reported seeing two men actually come to blows over an anglerfish. It was undergrown, not terribly fresh, and it was missing most of its tail, which is the only part of that particular fish worth consuming. Athenians, it seemed, were getting desperate.

Still feeling hopeful, Hermogenes and I now continued past the fish sellers' stalls, stopping only when we reached Krysippos's little shop. I had always found Krysippos to be one of my more reliable vendors of seafood, providing me with the highest quality fish or eels at consistently reasonable prices (well, they were reasonable after some prolonged haggling). In the years I had lived in Athens, he had rarely failed to meet my demands, or my exacting standards. But today the pale fish seller slouched dispiritedly behind an untouched display of kraken, his normally crisp blue-and-white-striped awnings drooping in the dampness. Frowning, I scanned his wares for something—anything—other than kraken. A futile effort. It was clear from his demeanour he had nothing else to offer.

"Some *krayken* for you, my cook friend?" he asked without much enthusiasm.

I pursed my lips at his pronunciation and sighed inwardly.

"I have fine steaks, and stewing meat, and even some tentacle tips today!" Krysippos said, gesturing to the silvery mounds of blue-tinged kraken meat. He'd begun to perk up the longer I stood there, his pale hands rubbing against each other, his pallid face lighting with hope.

"All very fresh," he assured me, as if kraken was ever *not* fresh. "Verrrrry tasty!" He smacked his lips noisily.

I looked again at his displays. For the wealthy shopper, there were platters of thick cut steaks and delicate, thinly sliced fillets pounded flat for frying. Bowls of tentacles—considered a delicacy among the cognoscenti—glistened in the early-morning sun, their suckers a darker shade of blue than the meat. For less refined palates there were strips of the rubbery fin, and chunks of meat, likely from the mantle, which were said to make an exceedingly flavourful stew if simmered long enough.

Krysippos was still extolling the virtues of his merchandise. Moved by the note of desperation in his voice, I opened my mouth to ask for a couple of steaks. Kraken was the last thing I wanted, but Krysippos had always been good about selling quality products to me and I felt sorry for his lack of custom.

"I can even throw in some Kraken Bake, eh?" Krysippos dropped his voice conspiratorially. "It cooks up like that!" He snapped his fingers. "No fuss, no bother, and—" he lowered his voice even further, "—*no problems!* Eh? What do you say? I can sell it to you cheaper than Kleisthenes, that miserable old fart-sucker!"

I scowled, furious now, as well as insulted. "I don't use Kraken Bake," I enunciated coldly. "And no, thank you. I don't want any *kraken.*" I emphasized the correct pronunciation of the word. "Hermogenes! Come!" I stalked away, my back rigid, my face dark with anger.

As soon as we'd moved out of earshot, I stepped close to one of the plane trees that lined the market and turned on my disciple.

"What have you been saying?" I hissed, grabbing the back of his neck.

He squeaked and tried to shake his head. "Nothing, Chef! I haven't said a word! Honest!"

"Then how did Krysippos know? Who told him? Was it you? I know how much you like to gossip!" I punctuated each question with an angry shake.

"It weren't me," Hermogenes cried. "I wouldn't do that, Chef! I wouldn't! Not to you!"

I paused. Hermogenes had flushed with self-righteous indignation, the scars on his right cheek dark against his skin. At the sight of those scars, my fury suddenly bled away. I released my grip on him.

"I'm your *disciple*, Chef," Hermogenes said earnestly. "I would never say anything about … that."

I let out my breath in a long sigh and patted his shoulder in apology. "I know," I told him. "I know."

"I think it's just gotten 'round. I mean, you're the only chef not serving kraken at the symposions. People are bound to talk, aren't they?"

I slumped against the tree. "Not that there have been many symposion feasts to prepare." I sighed, disheartened.

"There've been enough," my disciple said bracingly. Easy for him to say, he wasn't trying to save money for his own house. "And you'll see. There'll be more. Your roast lamb's a right treat, it is."

I looked down at my sandals and scowled. My roast lamb had almost been my downfall thanks to the pox-ridden Sicilian.

"And what about Anacreon's job, yeah? That's only a few days from now. All his rich mates'll be there, and they'll all be—"

"Expecting some stunningly original—not to mention succulent—kraken dish."

Hermogenes hesitated. "Well … you'll just give 'em something better, won't you? Besides, everyone's sick to death of sodding kraken. You know they are! They'll be over the bloody moon to have a change of pace. You mark my words, Chef, we'll be seeing more contracts out of that one."

He nodded once to emphasize his point before stroking his newly sprouted beard in what he clearly believed was a wise and sage manner. The beard (if a few hairs could actually be referred to as such) was a wispy, sparse sort of thing, but Hermogenes was inordinately proud of it. He had even taken to referring to it in the third person, almost as if it were a separate entity.

His encouragement cheered me. I pushed myself off the tree and allowed Hermogenes to adjust my cloak.

"Of course, if you'd just let me smarten you up a bit …" he began, tugging at the folds of my himation.

"No, Hermogenes." I held up my hand. "We've been through this before. I am not letting you tart me up like some flute girl."

"It's not about looking like a flute girl, Chef! It's about establishing your style."

"I'm a chef. I don't need a style. My cooking is stylish."

"But you aren't, are you?" he said, throwing caution to the wind. "I'm sorry, but you need … a brand."

"A brand," I said flatly.

"To identify you! It's like when people see a bloke in a piss-coloured chiton and they know right off it's Mithaecus."

"If you think I want to be compared to Mithaecus—"

"There's no comparing you to that wanker!" Hermogenes interrupted hotly. "But he's got a brand, hasn't he? Something that people recognize."

"I am *not* wearing a yellow chiton—"

"But, Chef—"

"Enough!" I cut him off with a sharp gesture. "I refuse to discuss this any further. Come, obviously there are no fish to be had today, so all we can do is hope something comes in for Anacreon's symposion—and for all those future contracts you say will arise from that." I didn't necessarily believe in the rosy future my disciple was painting. Still, I would throw myself on a red-hot brazier before I ever conceded the ground to Mithaecus. "In the meantime, we're going to need some cheese and lentils for our dinner tonight."

The morning shoppers were out in force now. I made a survey of the stalls of the other fish vendors, but, like Krysippos, they had nothing to offer but the same wide platters of silvery blue meat, the same deep bowls of plump tentacles. The sellers themselves all bore the same hopeless expressions on their faces as they wiped already spotless counters and rearranged already neatly piled meat. Even the vile Kraken Bake, it appeared, was no longer enough to entice Athenians to eat more of the stuff.

I inserted myself into the press, not even bothering to glance back at Hermogenes. I knew what I'd see—my disciple and former slave scuffing his feet glumly, fingering his nascent beard and pulling a face at the thought of choking down yet another piece of cheese or another spoonful of lentils.

I sympathized with the sentiment. Lately, at odd times of the day, I'd found myself fantasizing about a plate of scallops lightly poached in wine and herbs, or a thick-cut tuna steak, crisp and sizzling on the outside, the pink flesh tender and flaky on the inside, or perhaps a cuttlefish stewed in its own ink, the sauce dark and smoky rich and ...

"The beard could murder a fish right about now," Hermogenes groaned.

I roused from my momentary reverie.

"Indeed," I said in a brisk tone. "But it seems 'the beard'—not to mention the rest of the city—is not yet done with the kraken."

"I'd say the ruddy kraken's not done with us." Hermogenes pulled a sour face. "Better to have just let it have a go at Aethiopia, if you ask me. I mean, what did those chuffing buggers ever do for us anyways?"

He ducked away from my automatic slap, though the reprimand was half-hearted and Hermogenes knew it. My disciple was only saying what most Athenians were already thinking.

"Here." I paused and counted out a few coins into his palm. "Go and buy the lentils. I'll see what the cheese sellers have today. I'll meet you … " I paused.

"Back at The Herms?" my disciple suggested quickly, naming an area in the northwest corner of the Agora.

I gave him a steady stare.

In actual fact, there were Herms all over Athens. They marked roads, crossroads, and entrances, each of the rectangular columns possessing an erect phallus halfway up and the head of a smirking Hermes perched on top. The corner known as The Herms was simply where an inordinate number of these statues had been situated. They marked the entrance to the Agora proper, and many people touched them in passing for luck. The Herms were also where, not coincidentally, the horse trainers often passed at this time of the day.

"Fine," I relented with a long-suffering sigh. "But don't spend too much time ogling the horses. And mind you get the lentils uncooked this time!"

"No worries, Chef." Hermogenes grinned crookedly at me.

Then he popped the coins in his mouth and scampered off, darting between larger, more slow-moving shoppers and scattering a flock of speckled geese, much to the intense irritation of their owner. My disciple appeared to be heading in the direction of the gymnasium.

I shook my head and made a mental note to have a word with him about carrying out his tasks promptly. And while I was at it, I reminded myself to purchase a small pouch for him in which to carry his money. Most Athenians carried their spare change in their mouth, a practice that had always struck me as somewhat unpleasant. It was time Hermogenes was broken of that particular habit. And perhaps if *he* were to find himself on the other side of his present obsession with makeovers, he would not pester me so much about having a—what had he called it?— ah yes, a *brand*.

I knotted the strings of my own money pouch and repositioned the still empty basket under my arm, then I began to make my way purposefully through the crowd and over to the shaded section of the market where the cheese vendors set up their stalls.

The Athenian Agora was a bustling place, alive with activity at all hours of the day and night. Hoplites in heavy armour practised their battle formations alongside food sellers grilling dodgy sausages. Perfume makers boiled roses beside limed and dusty stone masons chipping away at their latest commission. And everywhere packs of low-born children scampered about, constantly underfoot, their bright eyes always searching for the opportunity to snatch a plum or a loaf of bread from an unwary merchant.

In front of the law courts, speech writers rubbed elbows with Thessalian witches, the former ready to help less articulate men defend themselves in court, the latter offering curse tablets, should that help prove ineffective. The air was thick with the smell of spiced stews simmering on outdoor cookstoves and shaven-headed slaves too long from the bathhouse. Greasy smoke rose from the sacred flames of a thousand small sanctuaries and shrines, while little owls flew and defecated where they would, secure in their protected status as Athena's sacred bird. It was dusty, noisy, and often very hot.

There were few places I loved better.

That morning, a wizened little prune of a merchant was trying to wrangle a peacock back into its carrying cage. I stopped to lay a wager on the outcome. The bird won, naturally (peacocks are notoriously feisty, ill-tempered creatures, though they do roast up a treat), and I came out of it a few obols richer. I dodged around a herd of squealing pigs, waved off a shabby-looking seer who wanted to interpret my dreams, and paused to listen to Hadinos, the market crier, call out the news of the day.

Hadinos was an extremely large man, as tall as a Macedonian, with the shape of a pithos, one of those bulk storage containers used for shipping. He had a voice that had, in the past, carried easily across many a battlefield and could now boom effortlessly over the noisy cacophony of a busy market. But Hadinos had nothing of interest to call today, merely some details about a

lawsuit between Anacreon and Hyperbolus, and the announcement of a minor religious festival. I moved on.

I stopped only once for any length of time, and that was
to examine some strands of saffron that had come all the way
from Thera. Such luxuries were beyond my present reach, but I
took careful note of the stall's location in the event my fortunes
should improve.

And then I was under the yellow and orange awnings of the
cheese shops.

I am inordinately fond of cheeses—both for cooking and
consuming—and I lingered a while, examining what was on
offer. There was much I could not afford. Sheep's milk cheese,
goat's milk cheese, pots of salty curds, cheeses rubbed with olive
oil or herbs and spices, leaf-wrapped wheels of harder cheeses
carefully aged in caves or special ripening rooms. I finally settled on a small pot of soft goat cheese, haggling with the shopkeeper until the price was more reasonable. I had never seen the
fat cheese vendor before, but his cheese was white and creamy
and he assured me that his impressive girth was due primarily
to the superior quality of his product.

I was on my way back to The Herms, and had just stopped at
a pretty flower seller's stand to have a closer look at her selection
of violets, when Hermogenes came pelting up. His dark curls
were wild, his cloak was bunched over his shoulders, and he was
panting as if he'd just run from Marathon itself.

"Chef!" he gasped. "Amazing news!"

I caught his arm. "Lower your voice!" I commanded. "People
are staring."

"But, Chef," he said, his tone somewhat more modulated. "I've just seen—"

"The athletes at the gym?"

My disciple harboured a not-so-secret dream of being an athlete himself one day. Technically, he was a free man now instead of a slave, and therefore he was eligible to compete in athletic competitions, but his improved status had done nothing for an exceedingly underdeveloped physique. Oh, he was quick enough on his feet (when sufficiently motivated), spunky (when the situation warranted it), but his most outstanding acrobatic talent was the possession of an overly glib tongue—particularly when he was in disgrace.

He flushed at my words now, having the grace to at least look sheepish. "Well, yes, but after that—"

"Let me guess, the chariot racers?"

"No! I didn't have time, did I?"

"Astonishing."

"I was at the notice boards. You know, by the Heroes?"

The Monument to the Eponymous Heroes was a marble podium topped by bronze statues of the ten heroes whose names represented the ten tribes of Athens. Any proposed legislation, any decrees or other announcements, were posted along the marble base, making the monument the official information centre for the city (gossiping slaves being, of course, the unofficial centre).

I had not thought to peruse the notices today. As a foreigner, I was not from one of the ten tribes, so most of the legislation and decrees did not concern me. And besides, the monument was on the opposite end of the Agora from most of the food sellers' shops.

"What were you doing at the other end of the market?" I demanded with some irritation. "If I recall, you were to purchase some lentils."

"Che-ef!" he wailed softly. "Just listen to me. Please!"

I set down the bunch of violets I'd been considering. "Fine. Tell me this amazing news then."

"There's to be a match," he informed me breathlessly.

I sighed. "Hermogenes, I know you're a free man now, but really, you'll never win an athletic competition. Most of those athletes have been training since they were small boys."

"No, Chef. No, you don't understand! It's a *cooking* match. It's for chefs!"

"What?" I steered him towards a quieter part of the street. "What are you talking about?" I asked intently.

"Are ye not wantin' me violets, then?" the flower seller called out.

"Not now," I barked, then softened it with a smile when I saw the disappointed look on her face. "Maybe later."

I turned my attention back to Hermogenes. "Now, what's this about a cooking match?"

"It's true! City council's come up with the idea. They're calling it the Bronze Chef. Notice said they're to pick four chefs to compete, and it don't matter if you're a foreigner!" Hermogenes's eyes were bright with excitement. "It's like a play almost. With sponsors and everything! It's to be held at the end of the month, and first-place winner gets a *thousand* drachmas! And a full set of bronze knives. And some olive oil—the good stuff! Like they give to the athletes for prizes!"

"Did this notice say what the rules are?"

Hermogenes nodded enthusiastically. "All you have to do is come up with a meal made with a theme ingredient. It has to be in every dish, and it's secret, so you won't know what it is till the competition. But that's dead easy, is that! We do it all the time, depending on what's good at market!"

I turned and started walking toward home, the violets forgotten. "Ah, but 'we' haven't been selected as one of the chefs yet, have we?"

Hermogenes danced along beside me. "You will. You'll see! All we have to do is put your name in. You're the best chef in the whole bleedin' city. Who else are they going to pick?"

"Mithaecus." I managed to say the name without spitting on the ground, though it was close.

It quelled him, but only for a moment. "So, he'll be the one to beat! And won't you enjoy wiping the floor with that dirty great wanker! I tell you, Chef, you'll be chosen for sure. You watch. It'll be The Lydian against The Sicilian battling it out in Kitchen Theatre!" He let out a loud *whoop* and punched the air.

"In *what*?"

"Kitchen Theatre," he informed me with a gap-toothed grin. "The whole thing's to be set up in the Theatre of Dionysus. So everybody can watch. It's to be a two-obol entrance fee, just like for a play. It's perfect! They'll be carting in all the food and pots and dishes and such. Everything the chefs'll need."

"I see." I kept walking.

A few steps ahead of me, Hermogenes was engaging in some kind of victory dance, chanting and flinging out his shopping basket.

"Did you remember the lentils?" I asked him.

He looked at me blankly.

I sighed and kept walking. For the first time, my disciple seemed to realize that I did not share his enthusiasm.

"But, Chef," he began hesitantly. "You don't seem very excited."

I shrugged.

"Think about it!" he urged. "We'll find a high-end sponsor, someone really posh. You'll make pots of money! You'll be famous! A man in demand! I can hear it now: The Prodigious Pelops and his talented disciple the Hamazing Hermogenes."

I raised an eyebrow. "Hamazing?"

He waved his hand airily. "I couldn't think of a word that started with 'h.' Don't worry, I'll come up with something better."

"How about the Hubristic Hermogenes?"

He grinned, but it faded when he looked at me. "Seriously, Chef, this could be it."

"Hmmm," I said noncommittally.

"Hmmm what? That's a great opportunity, that is!"

"Perhaps," I said. "But according to the rules, this secret theme ingredient must be present in all the dishes."

"So?" Hermogenes said, mystified.

"So, if you sat on the Athenian city council, what ingredient would you choose?"

Hermogenes opened his mouth to reply, but I continued before he could say a word.

"Why do you think they created a competition like this in the first place? And why now? Think about it. The whole city is sick to death of eating kraken, but there's no other fish to be had. When was the last time we saw an eel or even a nice sea bass?"

Hermogenes crinkled his nose. "Weeks, it's been."

"Exactly. Weeks. And now nobody wants to eat kraken any more because nobody knows what to do with it any more. So if you were a member of the Council and there was an unending glut of kraken on the market, you would probably hold a competition to see if you could encourage people to eat more of it. And if that is, in fact, the case, then the secret theme ingredient would have to be ..."

"Kraken," Hermogenes finished, his shoulders slumping dejectedly.

"Kraken," I agreed. "And that, my young disciple, is where we have a problem."

Chapter 2

"Piss, shit, damn, bugger, and fuck!" I swore. And then feeling that it wasn't quite enough, I repeated them all again, adding another "fuck" for good measure.

"You've not got enough wine in it," Dionysus said, waggling a helpful finger at the blackened mess on Gorgias's kitchen brazier.

"What?" I snapped in what was, perhaps, not quite the tone one ought to use when addressing a deity.

The god of wine and festivity bunched his bushy eyebrows together and gave me a reproving look.

"What do you mean?" I rephrased it, modulating my voice, though I scowled as I shook my singed fingers.

"You didn't put enough wine in, did you? That's why it flares up like that." He nodded sagely, his curled beard bouncing a little with the gesture.

"It sat in wine all night!" I protested.

"It did?"

"Yes!" I held on to my temper with no small effort. "I marinated it in wine just like you told me to do. And I *stewed* it in wine yesterday just like you told me to do. And I *pan-fried* it in wine the day before that. Just like you told me to do. The wine is not bloody working!"

Dionysus tugged thoughtfully at his beard as he leaned back on the kitchen stool. "Bollocks," he cursed, almost absently. "That's my sodding uncle for you, is that. Spiteful, fishy-arsed bastard. You should've just shagged him and been done with it, yeah?"

"Oh, right. Forgive me for not being in the mood after my father killed me, cooked me, and served me up to you lot for tea. Not to mention the fact that Poseidon was like a brother to me."

"We *did* remake you," he reminded me, peering into the wine krater to see if there was anything left in it.

"And you did such a bang-up job that your randy old Uncle Poseidon got all hot and bothered for me. Oh yes, thanks awfully."

"We made you good at cooking too, didn't we?" Dionysus added, frowning his disapproval at the empty wine krater, which obligingly began to fill itself. The apple-kissed scent of rich Thasian wine filled the air, a vintage vastly superior to the one that had been in the krater before.

I paused. It was true that my impressive culinary skills had first manifested after I'd emerged new and improved from the stew pot.

"Look," Dionysus began as he poured us each a large cup of

deep red wine. "Don't take it so personally! I know you practically grew up with him, but it's different for gods. I doubt he ever saw you as his baby brother, no matter what you might have thought at the time. Besides, Poseidon's always been one for thinking with his cock. You're hardly the first lad he's fallen for and, as sure as Hephaestus gets up and scratches his great hairy arse in the morning, you won't be the last."

"Then why hasn't he moved on already?" I demanded hotly, ignoring the proffered cup. "It's been years since I turned him down. *Years!* How long is he going to hold a grudge?"

Dionysus shrugged before swallowing a long drink of his own wine. "I've told you once and I'll tell you again," he said, belching into his beard, "he's a right vengeful old bastard."

"Vengeful? Great Zeus and Hera! It's getting so I can't even drink a cup of water without wondering what it's going to do to me! My washing water's always either ice cold or so hot I damn near scald myself. Fountains mysteriously dry up when I go to use them. Mud puddles appear out of nowhere just as I'm about to take a step. I can't poach anything in water anymore because the water will either boil away in a puff of steam or suddenly become so tepid as to completely ruin whatever I'm trying to cook!"

"Wine's better for poaching any road," Dionysus interjected. "Quite a bit tastier, if you ask me."

"That's not the point!" With some difficulty, I hung on to the last shreds of my temper. "The point is Poseidon is making my life miserable with water. I tried sacrificing to him—you know I did! And it didn't make a speck of difference. Thank the gods he can only kill with salt water, or I'd've been sent swimming down the Styx months ago."

"You're welcome."

"What?"

"You said 'thank the gods.' For the salt water bit. I was just saying you're welcome." He gave a mock shudder. "I wouldn't want to be stuck in the underworld if I were you. They're not much on parties down there, are they? Not with Hades such a boring old git." Dionysus held out the wine cup again. "Here, you look like you need a drink."

"What I need," I said, gritting my teeth, "is to be able to fashion this bloody kraken into something even remotely edible so I can win the sodding Bronze Chef competition and waltz home with a thousand drachmas to my name. Not to mention trounce Mithaecus by proving once and for all who is the superior chef, and thereby depositing his sterling—and, I hardly need add, undeserved—reputation straight into the latrine to fester like a month-old turd."

"Whew!" Dionysus wrinkled his divine nose. "There's a mental image, eh? Bit crude for you, isn't it?"

"I'm desperate," I told him through clenched teeth. "The social graces are starting to fall to the wayside."

The god of wine looked unconcerned. "I told you," he said, offering me the wine cup again. "Don't worry. Hermes and I are on the job, yeah?"

I stared at him for a moment, then, deflated, I sighed and sank onto a stool.

There really was no getting away from my past. Oh, I could

blame Poseidon all I liked, but the truth was, my problems had begun with my own flesh and blood. With my father.

Tantalus had been King of Sipylus in Lydia. The man had it all: wealth, kingdom, offspring, gods for friends. But of course, none of that was quite enough for old Tantalus. He took it into his head that he ought to be resting on his laurels on Mount Olympus with the rest of his divine chums. And when the invitation for this was less than prompt in coming? Well, suffice it to say it did not sit well with him at all. Almost overnight, the gods became *deus non grata* in his eyes, and to make a long story short, he stole from them, he lied to them, and finally he invited them all for tea. But instead of serving scones and cheese, he served them ... me. His own son. In a fit of sheer breathtaking hubris, Tantalus decided to test the gods' omniscience by chopping me up, simmering me in the stewpot, and dishing me up on his best dinnerware.

But gods are not easily fooled, and never by such as Tantalus. He was confronted and punished (one does not, after all, "test" the gods), and Dionysus and Hermes talked the others into reconstituting me (Hades had been against it, but he was outvoted). There was the small matter of a missing left shoulder (it had been accidentally eaten by Demeter—an honest mistake, given that I happened to be an exceedingly tasty stew at the time) but Dionysus and Hermes addressed this as well, arranging for an ivory shoulder to replace the old one. And ever since these events, the god of wine and the god of messages had taken it upon themselves to be my unofficial guardians. To make it all up to me, as it were.

Most recently, they had vowed to help me build a name for myself after I moved to Athens to become a celebrity chef (though their help consisted largely of turning civilized symposions into drunken orgies). It was a promise I often hoped, rather than thought, they would forget. But beggars, as they say, cannot be choosers, and there was a possibility they could be helpful to me with this business with Poseidon. Besides, as I had admitted to Dionysus, I was becoming desperate.

"Then help me now," I pleaded, ignoring my misgivings. "Your uncle is clearly playing games with me. I can't cook kraken to save my life—him and his sodding supernatural sea creature! I suppose I should be grateful I've been able to cook the ocean fishes, though I'm sure this must be due to some obscure divine law. Either that or plain oversight on his part."

Glumly, I accepted the wine, wincing as my burned fingers gripped the cup. I took a deep drink.

"The point is," I continued, "I'm fast running out of ideas. But I know one thing for certain. I cannot allow that Sicilian swine to win the Bronze Chef and walk off with *my* drachmas. And if the secret ingredient is kraken, I won't win unless I can find a way to cook the bloody stuff."

Dionysus drained his cup, smacking his lips in appreciation. "Leave it with me," he said kindly. "I'll get Hermes on it. He's the expert in this sort of thing. I mean, he's the chuffing god of messages and language and the like. He should be able to come up with some useful information—something that'll help you fry up a bit kraken, at any rate."

Stretching, he pushed himself to his feet and gave a mighty

31

yawn. "I'm sure it has somewhat to do with wine," he mused, rolling his shoulders back. "But let me see what I can sniff out."

"I'd appreciate that," I told him, rising to my feet as well to escort him out.

He paused by the front door and turned back to me. "Look, the Oskhophoria's coming up, so don't be surprised if I check out for a bit. I mean, it *is* the most important festival of the year, what with celebrating the vine harvest and all. The mortals expect a good party, and I'm the god to give it to them, aren't I? Last year I lost track of the whole month!" He smiled in fond remembrance, then he shook it off. "But I won't forget about your problem. Promise! And in the meantime, you keep your pecker up, yeah? None of this doom and gloom and rotting turds rubbish." He gave me a friendly clip on the shoulder.

I tried not to wince. For some reason, Dionysus always managed to hit me on my ivory shoulder. "I'll see what I can do," I promised with a tight smile.

I was already regretting my request.

Hermogenes arrived back from his errands shortly after Dionysus left. I wasn't sure how the god did it exactly, but he always seemed to drop by when nobody else was about. Just as well, really. Few knew of my connections with the higher entities and, for various reasons, I rather liked it that way.

"What happened, Chef?" Hermogenes demanded, wrinkling his nose as he came into the kitchen. "Are you okay?"

"I'm fine," I replied more testily than I'd intended. I was trying to soothe my burned fingers in a bowl of water. The water, fresh and cool from the hydrias, had gone uncomfortably warm as soon as I'd poured it into the bowl.

Hermogenes looked from me to the contents of the brazier and back again.

"The kraken?" he asked.

"Of course it was the gods-cursed kraken!" I snapped. "What else would it be?"

Hermogenes tugged unhappily at his facial hair and went over to poke at the charred bits of prime kraken steak still on the brazier. "Ares's great hairy bal—" he began, choking it off as Gorgias's daughter, Ansandra, came skipping into the kitchen.

Ansandra was a cute little thing who had just turned ten the previous month. But with this great life change had come a brand new attitude, or perhaps it was just an intensification of the old one.

"*Ooooo,*" she exclaimed. "Is Pelops burning dinner again?"

Hermogenes slid her a black scowl.

"Yes, Pelops is burning dinner again," I answered sarcastically, turning to look at her. "And if you don't march yourself right out of here, I'll toss that fat bird of yours onto the grill to make up for it."

As usual, Ansandra was cradling her pet quail, Kabob, a veritable lard ball of a bird who adored Ansandra and despised me (probably because, in addition to naming him, I'd also dispatched more than a few of his relatives to their fiery fates).

Of Ansandra herself, the kindest thing one might say about the grubby chiton she wore was that it was cleaner than her skinned knees, though the same could not be said of her hands.

Her cinnamon-tinged curls were her best feature, but they had long since escaped the clutches of the neat braids that Irene had foisted upon her that morning, and her hair stuck out like a dark aureole around her head.

She was unfazed by my threat. "He wouldn't do that to my snookums," she cooed to the quail, who was too stuffed with seeds to do more than blink up at her. "No he wouldn't, not to my little Boblet. My little cutie-cue."

"Try me," I said under my breath.

Hermogenes hid a smirk.

"What's burning, then?" Gorgias demanded coming into the kitchen. "Smells like a monkey's arse in here."

"Da-ad!" Ansandra protested. "That's gross!"

"Well, it's true, isn't it?"

"How would I know *that*?" She rolled her eyes expressively.

"You should show more respect to your old dad," he told her with a severe look.

"Really? Apparently my old dad goes 'round sniffing monkeys' bums. Does Zeuxo know you do that?"

"Ha. Ha. Don't you have some weaving to do?"

"Ha. Ha," she replied in exactly the same tone. In her arms, Kabob gave a little chirp, as if adding his two obols' worth.

Gorgias gave the quail a quelling stare.

"And besides, Dad," Ansandra continued, serious now. "It's mean. You shouldn't say stuff like that." She dropped her voice to a whisper that carried easily across the room. "Pelops is having trouble with the kraken."

"What? *Again?*" Gorgias's eyebrows shot up.

That was the last straw.

"Out!" I ordered, pointing towards the door. "Both of you!"

"But—"

"No buts! Out of my kitchen!"

"Actually, it's *my* kitchen," Gorgias said meekly.

"Out!"

They went out.

Silently, Hermogenes began the task of cleaning up the mess of extra-crispy kraken. I watched him for a few moments, then inhaled a deep breath and let it out slowly.

Technically, Gorgias was right. It *was* his kitchen. The whole house was his, from the andron where we ate our dinner to the dark, cool storerooms, to the wooden balcony and staircase that led to the second-floor bedrooms. The upper story overlooked a south-facing courtyard with several cushioned benches, a fine household altar, a lush herb garden and a cheerful patch of pink geraniums. It was a warm, comfortable house, and despite the fact that I had been both stranger and foreigner, Gorgias had opened its doors to me when I first arrived in Athens and offered me a home. I probably shouldn't have been ordering him out of his own kitchen. That I did so was a measure of the level of my disquiet.

The gods of wine and messages and oceans were not the only ones attempting to affect the course of my life. Hera, queen of the gods, goddess of the starry heavens, women, and marriage, also had what some might have called "issues" with me.

One of these issues was named Mithaecus. Nobody had been more surprised than I to discover that The Sicilian was one of Hera's special protégés. Of course, it hadn't stopped me from popping him in his beaky nose (though, in the heat of the moment, I confess I gave little thought to his divine patroness). I'd had ample reasons for my action—my grievances against Mithaecus were numerous and just—but gods do not always see things the way we mortals do, and I'd been informed that Hera was not pleased with me.

The second and undoubtedly larger issue was named Tantalus, for it had recently been revealed to Hera that my father was, in actual fact, one of Zeus's sons. The other gods had known it for years and had managed to keep Hera in the dark, but Hephaestus, god of fire and metalworking but not (apparently) teetotalling, had gotten into his cups during a family get-together and let it slip. Hera was … unhappy.

Not surprisingly, Zeus's wife did not look kindly on her husband's transgressions, but in order to preserve whatever marital accord remained, she generally took her anger out on the object of his lust—or on the resultant offspring—rather than on her husband. The problem in my case was that Tantalus, safely immured in the underworld where he was suffering a well-deserved everlasting torture for the stew incident, was decidedly out of her reach. I, however, was not. According to Dionysus, Hera had not yet openly sought revenge for either the blow against her protégé Mithaecus or the more egregious sin of my being her husband's illegitimate grandson. But the girl I loved with all my heart was set to marry my best friend, and I had a nasty suspicion the goddess of marriage might have had a hand in that.

If Zeuxo had accepted any man other than Gorgias as her husband, I would have fought for her, but I loved Gorgias like a brother, and he and his daughter had become my adopted family. Zeuxo was kind, beautiful, intelligent, and talented. How could I deny Gorgias that? A rhetorical question. But as the date of their nuptials drew closer, I found my mood souring, a state of affairs exacerbated by my continuing failure to make something—anything!—edible out of the omnipresent kraken.

"He's right, you know. It reeks something awful," Hermogenes remarked, screwing up his nose in distaste as he worked at scrubbing the brazier clean.

"I know," I said with a bitter sigh.

Hermogenes paused, then. "Any idea what went wrong?" he ventured.

Frustrated, I threw my hands in the air. "The coals were perfect," I told him. "I had the steaks marinating all night, then I dried them with a cloth so they would brown properly. I barely seasoned them. All I did was rub in a bit of oil and salt. A recipe worthy of Mithaecus himself!" I flared my nostrils in distaste.

"It should have worked, that," he mused, tugging again at his beard hairs.

"Of course it should have worked," I snapped. "And yesterday's tentacle stew should have worked, and the kabobs the day before! But they didn't, did they? And now the bloody steaks flare up as if they're on a bloody bonfire. I tell you, Hermogenes, it appears to be a sad but inescapable fact that any kraken I prepare is destined for the midden."

Hermogenes was silent for a moment, then he sighed heavily.

"Bollocks!" he said crossly, unconsciously echoing the wine god's earlier comment. "At this rate, we've no sodding chance of winning the Bronze Chef."

"At this rate" —I grimaced—"we'll be lucky to have dinner."

Together we finished scraping away the blackened remains of the stinking mess. As Hermogenes left to dispose of it on our rapidly growing midden heap, I pulled more kraken from the ice pit and grimly began assembling the ingredients to start all over again. My second attempt proved just as successful as the first.

We ate cheese and lentils again for dinner.

Chapter 3

When the month of Hekatombaion, with its Great Panathenaea, had finally passed, I had been exceedingly grateful. The events of the Panathenaic festival had been disastrous—for my reputation, for my savings, and for the city. The city had recovered. Gorgias and Hermogenes assured me that my career—and my savings—would follow suit.

But Metageitnion had passed too, its hot hazy days spinning themselves out with little evidence of this promised revitalization. Gone too was Boedromion, the month named in honour of Apollo's incarnation of Boedromios, The Helper in Distress. I had clients, but I needed more money. And my reputation, I felt, was not what it ought to be, especially considering the inferior quality of most of the other chefs in the city. I needed to prove myself better than The Sicilian and, perhaps even more importantly, I needed to augment my savings so I could move out before Gorgias brought a saffron-veiled Zeuxo home. I did not want to live with them once they were married. Clearly, I was in some distress, and so I offered prayers and sacrifices to Apollo Boedromios. But although he was supposed to lend a hand in times of trouble, the god of healing, music, and prophecy ignored all my entreaties.

I cannot say I was entirely surprised.

Apollo was usually a nice enough god. Fond of poetry and song and fine foods and, as it turned out, quite at home with disguises and very fond of one particular elusive, violet-eyed hetaera. In the guise of a wealthy Athenian, he'd hired me to find her. That I had failed in the quest had nothing to do with my own efforts. But try explaining that to a god.

It was now the first day of Pyanepsion, a month named after the boiled beans that the legendary Theseus had offered Apollo upon his return to Athens after slaying the dread Bull of Minos.

"Cheer up, then," Gorgias said to me at breakfast that morning. "Any month named after summat to eat has to be a promising one for a chef."

We were ensconced on the cushioned benches in the small courtyard which was normally the sunny centre of Gorgias's house. There was little warm or genial about the place today, however. Euros, god of the east wind, had blown into town the night before, wild and unruly and clearly spoiling for a fight. He'd brought with him the cooler temperatures and watery sunshine of autumn, and both Gorgias and I had our cloaks wrapped tightly around us against the chill.

I shrugged at my friend's words, picking morosely at a dish

of indifferent olives. Normally, I would have agreed with him. Everybody likes beans, and Pyanepsion boasted no fewer than eight festivals, many of which were held to celebrate the harvest (bean and otherwise). It was usually an excellent month for a chef, as citizens endeavoured to outdo each other with the sumptuousness of their festival feasts. But with little available at the market besides kraken and few who were still thankful for its bounty, this month's harvest festivals did not promise much in the way of lucrative opportunity for one such as myself.

"What have you got on for today?" I asked, changing the subject.

Gorgias was dressed for work. Both his himation and the tunic he wore underneath it were old and stained. He was shovelling his breakfast into himself with single-minded intensity, stoking up for the labours of the day.

"Big order came in yesterday," he said around a large piece of barley bread. "Grills and cookers and the like."

"Someone remodelling their kitchen?" I inquired without much interest.

He shook his head. "City council's ordered them for this Bronze Chef match. Paid up front and everything." He took another huge bite of bread. "It's a good bit of coin. It'll come in handy, that. You know, for the new wife."

The new wife.

My stomach gave a familiar twist. Carefully, I set the bowl of olives down beside me.

"Indeed," I managed to say through a throat gone suddenly tight.

Gorgias did not notice.

In fact, Gorgias was completely unaware of my feelings for his bride-to-be. The only person who knew anything about it was Hermogenes, and him I had sworn to secrecy.

"Order has to be filled quick-like," my friend continued blithely. "I've already set Strabo and Lais to mixing the clay." He named two of his slaves, huge ox-like men who possessed barely half a mind between them and weren't entirely sure what to do with even that much. They were, however, very strong and, as long as they had proper direction, very good with all things clay-related.

"And Ansandra's right in there with them like a dirty tunic," a voice behind me interjected disapprovingly.

"What, again?" Gorgias exploded, spraying bits of his last mouthful across the courtyard. "Bollocks!"

The owner of the voice came out of the shadow and into the weak sunlight, reproach written all over her thin-lipped face. In the past I had been the sole recipient of such a look— I had, in fact, privately dubbed her The Gorgon. However, Irene's opinion of me had quite noticeably mellowed in recent months and, despite her technical status as slave, she now saw fit to bestow her censure on all and sundry members of our small household, depending on her mood and regardless of their standing. These days, I only called her The Gorgon on special occasions.

"What you're thinking, letting her run about like a dirty little street urchin, I'll never know." Irene began tearing into Gorgias with such enthusiasm, I half expected her to step up and box his ears. "It was bad enough when she was just a girl. But she's almost a woman now, isn't she? And out there right now as we speak covered in filth and consorting with slaves! What your new wife will have to say about that, I can't even imagine. Why, if *I* had the rearing of her ..."

Irene was *supposed* to have the rearing of her—at least in the six years it had been since Gorgias's first wife, Helena, had succumbed to plague. Irene and I had had our differences in the past, but even during our least friendly times I'd always acknowledged the fact that she kept the household running with little more than a will of bronze and a fist of iron. It was not entirely her fault that Ansandra had managed to elude both will and fist with a combination of charm, guile, and an extremely overindulgent father—one who was now paying the price for his lack of restraint.

"You know, I *am* the master here—" he began hotly.

"And what of it?" Irene cut him off with a withering look. "Imagine! Letting her run about like a nasty savage. People are going to think she's Thracian. Bad enough when she was out and about with this one." With a sharp gesture, she indicated Hermogenes, who had just joined us in the courtyard.

Hermogenes and Ansandra had been great friends before he became my disciple. Now he no longer had the time to play Greeks vs. Amazons.

"But he's growing up and taking his responsibilities more seriously, isn't he? Even if he does look shamefully disreputable what with the scar that pox-ridden Meidias saw fit to put on his face last summer, not to mention that scraggly weed he calls a beard. If you ask me, he ought to just shave it off and save us all the sight."

Hermogenes squawked in protest, his hands flying up to cover his chin protectively.

But Irene had turned her attention back to Gorgias. "And where does that leave your Ansandra, I ask you?" she demanded. "Playing about at being a potter, if you please! Keeping company with the likes of Strabo. And Lais! What kind of prospects will she have if word gets out? I'll tell you what kind of prospects—"

"Enough!" Gorgias thundered. "Enough. I'll speak to her this instant."

"You see that you do," Irene snapped back, unimpressed. "And don't you go letting her run circles around you. Honestly, the way that girl wraps you around her little finger fair makes my hair stand on end!"

She would have kept haranguing him, but Gorgias was already beating a hasty retreat. Irene sniffed pointedly at his rapidly departing back before turning her attention to me.

I eyed her warily. When Irene was in full Gorgon mode, as she was now, one could never anticipate what she might find fault with.

But it seemed she was not irked with me today.

"I went to the Spring House for water this morning," she said calmly, her whole demeanour changing dramatically. "There's a man set up in the Agora. A hunter. Right between the meats and the cheese. You know, by that cheese vendor's shop, the grimy one who peddles The Sicilian's Kraken Bake. But that hunter—and a fine big strapping lad he was, too—he had hares for sale, didn't he?"

"Hares?" I perked up, my mind jumping ahead to one of my few contracts, a symposion feast I was to prepare for Anacreon two days hence. I had already ordered a suckling pig for the event, but I had not yet decided upon the other meat dishes, dictated as they would be by market availability and freshness.

"They'd make a lovely stew," Irene was saying with a nod. "Or roasted up on a spit with a bit of oil and salt. Tastier than any kraken, that is. I hear Anacreon's fond of a bit of rabbit now and again. And these were nice and plump, too, all fattened up for winter. Not like those scrawny beasts that Dromon carries. Hardly worth the effort of cooking, if you ask me. But these ones won't be lasting long. Not with the market the way it is these days. Nothing but blue flesh and tentacles wherever you look. I've never seen the like! But a nice bit of rabbit? That would go down a treat—and it'll fill out your menu for you, too. Anacreon's to have Pythagoras at his symposion, isn't he?"

"Uh, I believe so," I said, mystified as to why the philosopher's presence was important.

"Well then, you won't be able to serve beans, will you?"

"Excuse me?"

"Pythagoras won't eat beans, Chef," Hermogenes said around a mouthful of olives, having started in on the dish I had laid aside. "I thought I told you that."

I turned to glare at my disciple. He'd picked up Gorgias's leftover bread, and was breaking off large chunks and cramming them into his already full mouth. My scowl deepened.

"In fact, you did not," I replied, not bothering to mask my irritation. "I was planning on serving several bean dishes in honour of Pyanepsion. What on earth does Pythagoras have against beans? Is he troubled with wind?"

Hermogenes shook his head, struggling to swallow. "Not hardly," he managed finally. "Barmy old bat thinks we started out as beans, doesn't he?"

"I beg your pardon."

"He thinks we live and die over and over again," Irene explained. "Have you not heard him banging on about it? You can hear him most days if you've the stomach for it. Over by the Painted Stoa where all the other 'thinkers' are, as if the rest of us haven't got a thought in our heads, and them so caught up in all their so-called philosophizing that half of them don't bathe near as often as they ought and you can smell them clear across the market."

"Pythagoras?" I reminded her.

"He thinks we come back as a different living thing each time we die," Hermogenes answered for her. "Reincarnation, he calls it."

I stared at them for a long moment. "And he thinks we begin this ... this spiritual journey as *beans*?" I said at last.

Hermogenes shrugged and stuffed another olive in his mouth.

"From what I hear, he won't even touch them," Irene said.

"And he gets right put out if they're served for dinner," Hermogenes added. He chewed his olive and gave me a crooked grin. "Probably afraid someone'll tuck into his rellies or something."

Irene snorted.

My frown deepened. "What in Hades is he doing accepting dinner invitations during Pyanepsion, then?" I demanded of no one in particular. "And you!" I rounded on Hermogenes. "You're supposed to keep me informed of these things!"

My disciple recoiled a little, the bread he'd been about to consume arrested on its journey to his mouth. "I'm sorry, Chef!" he said, not quite as contritely as I would have liked. "I am. It won't happen again."

I drew in a breath to chastise him further, but before I could say anything, Irene broke in.

"You've not got time," she advised. "Not if you're wanting any of those hares. As it is, you'll have to nip over smartly before they've all been sold."

"Right." I pushed myself to my feet with alacrity. "Thank you, Irene. I appreciate the information. Hermogenes, get the carrying baskets." I cleared my throat ominously. "We shall discuss your communicative skills as we walk."

The hares were fresh, fat, and almost sold out by the time Hermogenes and I arrived at the Agora. The hunter was right where Irene had said he would be, his makeshift stall set up on a tattered orange blanket beside Kleisthenes's cheese shop. Without hesitation and despite Hermogenes's elaborate facial contortions, I promptly bought up the rest of the man's stock, much to the dismay of the handful of shoppers that had gathered behind me. I haggled, of course, but there was too much at stake for me to hold out for a really good bargain.

I supervised Hermogenes while he arranged the hares in our

carrying baskets. By the time he'd positioned them to my satisfaction and covered them carefully with a cloth to protect them
from the dust of the road, the hunter had dumped the coals from
his portable brazier and was rolling up his now empty blanket,
whistling happily to himself the entire time. Hermogenes, however, was less than cheerful.

"Great Zeus and Hera, Chef," he grumbled sourly as we
moved off. "You didn't need to pay that much! You could've
talked him down a bit."

"With five other men breathing down my neck? Don't be
absurd."

Hermogenes grunted in undiluted disgust. "Still. You're not
bloody made of money, are you?"

"I'm hardly on the verge of scouring the riverbanks," I replied
tartly, referring to the old men one could often see combing the
grassy banks for snails because they couldn't afford anything at
the market.

"But Anacreon's not about to pay premium prices just for a
bit of bunny—even if one of his guests has got a bee up his bum
about eating beans."

"Oh, I think he will," I told him with a confident nod. "I've
got an idea for a new dish, and even Anacreon won't balk at paying extra for it."

"Really?" Hermogenes perked up. "A new recipe? What's in
it then?"

"Hares," I told him uninformatively. "And some other things
that I won't go into just now." I swept a significant glance over
the crowds around us.

"Ah," Hermogenes breathed, eyes darting around suspiciously. "Smart, Chef. Very smart."

"Now come. Hares and suckling pig are all very well and good, but I'd like to round it out with some fish—if we can find anything decent."

"Not likely, is it?"

"No," I agreed with a grimace. "But nothing ventured, nothing gained. We shall make our offerings to Tyche along the way and see if we can't coax her into better spirits."

"Seems to me she's already chuffed." Hermogenes indicated our happily laden baskets, though he followed this by adding in an undertone that was almost, but not quite, inaudible, "Even if you did pay too much for 'em."

"Then let's ensure she stays that way," I replied, ignoring his last comment. "We'll stop at the sanctuary first, then we'll go 'round and see what the fish sellers have to tempt us with today. If nothing else, we're out of kraken again."

"Again?" Hermogenes's eyes flew to my face and he opened his mouth to blurt out some ill-conceived comment or another, but one sharp glance from me and he controlled the urge, contenting himself instead with a wisely discreet nod.

He was starting to learn, this disciple of mine.

For some weeks now, I had been making almost daily offerings to the goddess of success and prosperity. My favourite sanctuary was a small affair, tucked between the Stoa of Zeus and the Temple of Hephaestus in the northwestern corner of the Agora. It was not the most popular of Tyche's shrines, being entirely too close to the various foundries that surround the temple of the metalworking god. At times, the black smoke and choking stink could be quite unbearable. But the shrine boasted an exceedingly fine marble altar, and it was quieter there than at other, larger sanctuaries. When a man prays for success and prosperity, he does not necessarily wish for others to know he is not already in possession of these fortunes.

Before entering the tiny sanctuary, we paused by the stone basin to wash our hands. The scrawny priest nodded his recognition. In charge of keeping the sacred flames burning, the man had been tending the sanctuary ever since I'd begun making offerings there. Given his underfed appearance, I often thought that he might do better to make a few offerings of his own rather than merely supervising the efforts of others. But he never spoke to me beyond the ritual greetings, and I kept my thoughts on the matter to myself.

The goddess's altar was stained dark with the blood from countless sacrifices, and sundry rude clay figures cluttered its surface, along with the charred remains of burnt bones and goat hair. I had not brought a sacrificial animal today, contenting myself instead with a few grains of incense for the sacred fire and a small amphora of Chian wine for a libation. Last week, in one of his more expansive moments, Dionysus had let slip that Tyche was fond of the grape.

"Some might say," he'd imparted in a confidential undertone, "even a little overly fond, if you take my meaning, yeah?"

Quite a statement, coming as it did from the god of wine and festivity.

Never one to ignore a handy tip from an inside source, I'd promptly purchased the rather pricey Chian, reasoning that Tyche might appreciate the vintage, an unusually fine one from an area that generally produced superior wines.

I tossed my frankincense into the fire and, with its pungent scent still in my nostrils, I poured the rich red wine onto the ground, humbly asking the goddess for her favour, and praising her for her grace and virtue (without, of course, mentioning her propensity for drink). When I'd finished, Hermogenes stepped up to make his own small offering, a colourful bunch of fall wildflowers which, as he remarked to the priest, must be pleasing to the goddess both for their beauty and their fragrance.

Ritual completed, we reclaimed our baskets and strolled back into the bustle of the Agora. My steps were lighter than before, buoyed by the feeling that somehow the morning had improved in some small manner—an impression that was confirmed when several positive omens presented themselves. The most significant of these came in the form of a flock of little owls, which everyone knows are sacred to Athena and are therefore always considered the best of signs. Roosting among the colonnades of the Stoa of Zeus, the small speckled birds suddenly took wing as we passed, fluttering up into the sky on our right—the side associated with good fortune. And Hermogenes, after complaining of an itchy right hand, found a silver drachma in the dust, scuffed and worn but still valuable.

Perhaps Dionysus had been correct about Tyche and her fondness for wine.

Indeed, it was as though the goddess of fortune had thrown

a warm and friendly arm around us, for no sooner had I exchanged greetings with Krysippos the fish seller than providence presented itself once again in what seemed at first glance to be a distinctly unprepossessing form.

He was shaven-headed and shifty-eyed, his demeanour one of slyness and cunning. So unremarkable was he from most other slaves at the market that I never would have noticed him had not Krysippos displayed an instant, marked interest in his presence. Bearing a cloth-covered basket, the man slunk up to the fish seller's counter and immediately Krysippos excused himself, mouthing profuse apologies to me even as he ushered the man behind the cloth that hung at the back of his stall. In his haste, he did not quite draw the curtain closed behind him. Through the gap in the drapery, I saw the slave carefully set down his basket—a large woven seagrass affair—and I watched as Krysippos tweaked up one corner of the covering. His fish-belly-white face turned pink, then white again, and he nodded once. There was a clink of coins, then the slave turned and sloped off into the crowd.

Hermogenes and I exchanged a long look, but I quickly schooled my expression back to boredom as Krysippos returned and stowed the basket under the counter. He rubbed his pallid hands together, barely able to contain his excitement.

"Special delivery?" I asked with feigned indifference.

His face split into a wide grin, creasing his watery blue eyes into slits.

"A *very* special delivery," he said. "Today the Lady Tyche smiles on you, eh! I hope you have brought your silver owls.

What I have in that basket will cost them all, but oh, my cook friend, it will be worth it! You'll see! You'll see!" He rubbed his hands together again gleefully.

"Indeed?"

"The finest! A miracle! Would I, Krysippos, lie to you? Never! And certainly not about such fortune. It has been months—*months!*—since I have seen such a thing. Why—"

"Show me," I commanded, my curiosity whetted by his evident excitement. "I wish to see this miracle which will take all my owls."

He stooped down and hoisted the basket to the countertop with a grunt. There was a dramatic pause, then he whisked the cover off with a flourish. Hermogenes and I leaned closer, blocking the sight from any other interested shoppers.

It was not the ubiquitous kraken, though I'd guessed that from Krysippos's reaction. Instead, in the basket were a dozen fat fish.

"Striped red mullet," Krysippos told us, dropping his voice to a hushed, almost reverent, tone.

Striped mullet! I bent down and examined the fish closely, greedily. They were about as long as my forearm, rosy in colour, with a rich golden iridescence. Their bodies were rigid, scales tight, eyes clear and glossy. There was no hint of sliminess to them, no clouded eyes, no odour of decay. They smelled like the open ocean, and all the shades of sunset were reflected in their scales.

Krysippos watched me silently, hand over his heart, as if paying homage to the fish.

"I don't see any stripes, me," Hermogenes remarked.

The fish seller's eyebrows snapped together and he scowled blackly at my disciple. "Fool! Ignorant boy! Everyone knows striped red mullets lose their stripes the deeper they swim. And these" —his voice softened again and he smiled down at the fish with tender fondness—"these beauties come from the very depths of the Aegean."

"How did you come by them?" I inquired. "Nobody has anything but kraken these days."

"Ah, my cook friend," Krysippos began reeling me in, "now that is a story in itself …"

By the time we stepped away from the fish seller's stall, we carried, in addition to our hares, a dozen red-gold fish, several blue kraken steaks, and not a single silver owl. The mullets had been hideously expensive. In truth, I could not really afford them. But …

"Anacreon will pay through the arsehole for them," Hermogenes said gleefully, echoing my own sentiments, though in decidedly cruder terms.

"I'd prefer to get the coins from his hand," I said dryly.

Hermogenes chuckled, too delighted at the find to be cowed by the mild reprimand.

I was pleased myself. It appeared Tyche had, indeed, appreciated my offering. It had been such a long time since I'd seen any kind of mullet at the Agora—let alone a striped red mullet (which, truth be told, I had never actually seen before). In the brief moments since I'd purchased them, I had already decided upon and discarded half a dozen different recipes for them. None seemed worthy of such fish.

Perhaps just a generous pinch of sea salt, a sprinkling of oregano, and the lightest touch of olive oil. Yes, that would enhance the delicate flesh without overwhelming—

"Oof! Have a care, luv!" A voice broke through my epicurean reverie. "Watch where you're putting those dirty great feet."

I blinked and looked down.

Her form was short and stout, a bit like a sausage—if sausages were prone to wearing phallic-shaped jewellery and dressing in nausea-inducing colours. Today's chiton was an unfortunate green and orange concoction, livened up with a wide necklace of bronze penises—the latter looking uncomfortably like a string of trophies slung around her neck.

"Pharsalia!" I exclaimed, my face breaking into a broad smile at the sight of one of my staunchest friends and Athens's number-one bread dildo baker.

"Oh, it's you, is it?" she said, squinting up at me in the midday sun. Her dark eyes crinkled with pleasure. "Didn't know who was trodding on me toes. And here it's me second-favourite chef."

"Forgive me." I offered her my arm. "My head was in the clouds."

She giggled girlishly and took my arm in one meaty hand.

"And what do you mean, your *second*-favourite chef?" I demanded, pretending outrage.

She slapped my shoulder playfully. My ivory shoulder. Why did everybody always hit my ivory shoulder?

"Oooooo, listen to you!" She batted her lashes at me. "And what would my Castor have to say if he knew you were chatting me up?"

I grinned and sketched a gallant bow. "He would say I have impeccable taste," I replied.

Out of the corner of my eye, I could see Hermogenes making a face, but Pharsalia chortled and whacked me again.

Castor the Macedonian was as tall as Pharsalia was short and four times as hairy. He could probably have squished me like a wine grape had he been minded to do so. But despite his great size, he was as gentle as a new lamb, and even if he didn't like me (which he did), he would never hurt one of Pharsalia's friends.

"And where are you off to on this fine morning?" I asked her.

"It's where I've been, luv, it's where I've been. It's that time of year, isn't it?"

"What time of year?"

"Thesmophoria, of course!" She clucked at my ignorance. "Time to be making me sacrifices to Herself."

"Ah." I nodded, enlightened—though not by much.

The Thesmophoria was an annual festival held in honour of the goddess Demeter and her daughter Persephone. It was strictly a women-only affair, and although the men of Athens were expected to cough up the cash to finance it, any attempt to spy on the proceedings was forbidden by order of the goddess of grains herself. As a result, few men knew much about it—beyond that it appeared to be a sort of fertility celebration and, for some unfathomable reason, required women to prepare for it by abstaining from all manner of sexual activity. A sort of universal "that time of the month," as it were. But Athenians were nothing if not philosophical, and so the men of Athens, rather than rail at this enforced abstinence, instead took the opportunity to enjoy manly pursuits without female interference. I, myself, had contracts for two symposions during the festival, both with requests for additional wines as well as for various tasty but gas-producing foods such as beans and cabbage, dishes that were, for obvious reasons, seldom popular with the ladies.

"You've been up to the Eleusinium, then?" I guessed, naming Demeter's most popular sanctuary in Athens.

"Started out as soon as it were light enough." Pharsalia nodded. "I brought a nice suckling pig and three baskets of me bread dildos. Fresh this morning, they were. Demeter ought to be pleased."

"I'm sure she will be," I told her.

"The priestesses were chuffed well enough," Pharsalia said, a proud smile dancing on her lips. "Gave me the contract for the Thesmoi, didn't they?" she confided. "First time I've ever been honoured."

"The Thesmoi?" I inquired, raising one eyebrow.

"For the Stenia."

At my blank look she *tsk*ed. "Sometimes I forget you're from away. The Stenia's the first of the women's festivals, the one right before the Thesmophoria. And to celebrate it proper-like, they need offerings. Breads and pigs and whatnot. The breads are always shaped like cocks. Or snakes. Either one'll do."

"I see," I said. "And so you've been hired to make the, uh, phalluses for this year's Stenia?"

"And the snakes, luv. Just as easy to make a bread snake as a bread dildo, isn't it?"

"I never thought about it before," I told her honestly. "But in this, I defer to your superior experience. Well, congratulations! That's excellent news. I imagine the temple pays quite well."

"Enough to keep me in pretties for some time, ta very much." She caressed her gleaming necklace.

"I'm sure your jeweller will be delighted," I told her gravely.

We were strolling along the Panathenaic Way, which led from the Dipylon Gate to the Acropolis, bisecting the market's central square in the process. Its surface was packed gravel, which ought to have been durable enough, but instead always seemed in constant need of renewal. Even now, I could see the work crews beginning to spread yet another layer of the stuff.

On our right was a bronze statue of Herakles. He was posed with the skin of the dreaded Nemean lion draped over his head and shoulders, but the birds had been roosting on him again and the slaves in charge of such matters had not yet gotten around to cleaning him up. As a result, poor Herakles's trophy was now white with droppings, giving it a decidedly hoary appearance, and diminishing somewhat the impressiveness of the hero's victory.

To the left of the splattered statue, a pock-faced juggler had just set down a basket of bronze knives and weighted cloth balls. Pharsalia touched my arm and we stopped to watch him.

"Step right up, citizens and free men!" he cried, a powerful voice belying his stringy and somewhat frayed appearance. "See the most awesome feats this side of Mount Olympus! The Great Galinthius will astonish you! He will entertain you! He will make your head spin with balls, knives, aaaaaaaannnnd … *flame!*"

A small crowd started to gather around us. As the Great Galinthius began tossing his multi-coloured balls in the air, he continued to call out, promising to delight our eyes with his amazing skills.

"Have you heard the news about Perseus, then?" Pharsalia inquired, her eyes following the trajectory of the juggling balls.

"Perseus?"

"You know, him what offed the kraken."

"I rather suspected that was the Perseus you were talking about," I told her dryly. "I've not heard any news. Why? Has he slaughtered something else now?"

"Not hardly! He's coming to Athens!"

Just then, two of the juggler's balls collided mid-air. The green ball shot off to one side, plopping to the ground beside Hermogenes's sandalled foot.

"Sorry! Sorry!" the Great Galinthius cried. "My apologies! A momentary aberration!"

Under any other circumstance, Hermogenes would have awarded the man a withering glare, if not a scathing insult. But Pharsalia's news had effectively distracted him from anything so inconsequential. In fact, I doubted he had even been aware of the near miss. He was gazing up at Pharsalia, his mouth gaping like a freshly caught catfish, an impression enhanced by the scraggly strands of his facial hair.

"Really?" he breathed. "Perseus? He's coming here? To Athens?"

"Truly."

His face fell. "Ah, you're joking. You *must* be joking."

"Cross me heart," she assured him solemnly. "Heard it meself this morning, didn't I? Up at temple. He's set to arrive any day now. Him and his so-called flying horse—if there really is such a thing, which I have me doubts."

"What brings him to Athens?" I inquired. "Surely we have no monsters here for him to slay."

I must have sounded a bit snarky because Pharsalia flashed me a reproachful look. "Have you never wanted to see a hero, then?" she inquired. "To see the lad behind the deeds? It's not all about killing beasties, is it? There's appearances and processions …"

"He's on a victory tour?"

"'Course he is. Just like Jason did a few years back—and Odysseus before him. It's tradition, isn't it? A tour across the whole of Greece. It does regular folk like us good to have a peek at something larger then us selves." She nodded once as if to emphasize her point.

"And you said he's bringing his horse?" Hermogenes interjected. "You're sure about that? The *flying* horse?"

Pharsalia smiled at him. "That's what I heard, luv."

Hermogenes had gone all starry-eyed at the thought, but he was quickly brought back down to earth when the juggler fumbled his balls again. With a startled squawk my disciple ducked out of the way, a cloth ball narrowly missing his head. The Great Galinthius's skills were proving as patchy as his appearance.

"A thousand apologies, citizens! A mere miscalculation. A … a side effect of the warm-up, I assure you! It, uh … happens all the time with these cloth balls. Inferior workmanship. From

Corinth, you know. Now the bronze knives, my friends ... ah, the bronze knives are an entirely different story!"

I looked at Pharsalia, and at her quick nod of agreement we began to weave our way back through the crowd. It seemed wisest to leave before the Great Galinthius could incorporate knives into his act.

"And what about you, then?" Pharsalia asked as we started down the street once more. "How's the chef business coming along?"

"Slowly," I admitted candidly. Pharsalia knew all about my trials of the previous summer, having been adversely affected by them herself.

"Ah, don't you worry your great kind self about it," she said, giving my arm a comforting squeeze. "Bronze Chef competition ought to sort that for you."

"Hmm," I said.

There was a cry behind us as a less forward-thinking spectator was clipped with a flying knife. If nothing else, the Great Galinthius appeared quite skilled at apologizing.

"Fond of a bit of kraken, are you?" Pharsalia asked me, indicating my market basket (and pronouncing it correctly, may the blessings of all the gods be on her head).

I glanced down. The red mullets were carefully wrapped in leaves, hidden from sight, but I had been less assiduous with the kraken, and its blue-tinged flesh was peeking out from its wrappings.

I made a noncommittal noise.

"You know, my Castor's a right master with kraken. I could

have it every day for tea and still look forward to kraken for sup-per. A rare treat it is, the way he makes it. As tasty as success and as tender as an untried youth. Mmmmm." Wiggling her ample hips, she smacked her lips and cackled lewdly.

"Then I take it he'll be entering the Bronze Chef competition?" I asked politely.

"My Castor?" Her painted eyebrows rose along with her voice. "The Bronze Chef? Not likely, luv, is it?"

"But the 'secret' ingredient is sure to be kraken."

"Oh, I'd have to agree with you there. What else would they have, what with all the fish stalls groaning under the weight of the sodding stuff? And the fish sellers groaning on account of nobody wanting to buy it. But that competition, it's a bit out of Castor's league, don't you think?"

On any given day, when he wasn't haunting Pharsalia's bake-shop, Castor could usually be found in the Agora near the statue of Athena Ergane. It was there that the lesser chefs of Athens—tavern cooks, really—waited with their ladles and spoons to be engaged by clients too impoverished or too ignorant to know any better. Castor was a nice enough chap, but he was not a good chef—though I would never have said such a thing to Pharsalia.

"He's a decent enough cook," I lied.

"Oooo, listen to your sweet self! My Castor's a great kind man, and he knows how to please a woman even better than one of me multigrain dildos, but even I know he's not exactly Bronze Chef material, is he?"

"He's a nice fellow," I said, not wanting to agree with her, although I did.

But Pharsalia saw through me. "Don't get me wrong, luv, he suits me discerning palate just fine. And if he's not got the makings of a top chef, well, who's to say that's a shame, eh?"

"I'm glad he makes you happy," I said sincerely. "Though you know, all the bachelors in Athens have been crying into their wine cups ever since you took up with him."

Pharsalia chortled and smacked me on the shoulder. My shoulder was getting quite a workout today. I tried not to wince.

"And what about you, then?" she asked fondly.

"What about me?"

"Who's your sponsor? You know, for the Bronze Chef?"

"I haven't put my name in yet." It came out more flatly than I'd intended.

Pharsalia looked at me in dawning astonishment. "You *are* entering, aren't you?"

"I haven't decided," I replied evasively.

"What!" Her voice rose in disbelief. Several other pedestrians looked over in interest. "Not decided?" she exclaimed in a lower tone. "Go on with you! 'Course you should enter! Bloody Mithaecus had his name in before the paint was dry on the notice. Not enter, indeed! Whatever gave you such a notion?"

I glanced around before answering. Hermogenes was scuffing along behind us. In the distance, I could hear the Great Galinthius still crying out apologies. Nobody was close enough to overhear our conversation.

"It's the kraken," I admitted moodily. "I just can't cook the bloody stuff."

She was silent for a moment, then, "Ah, so there's truth to that, is there?" she said, her voice softly sympathetic.

My face burned as the import of her words sunk in. Did all of Athens know of my difficulties?

"Hardly believed it when I heard," Pharsalia continued. "Thought my Castor was having a bit of a joke when he told me. Imagine! *You* having trouble cooking up a spot of sea monster!"

"Oh, it's true enough," I confirmed sourly.

"So, what's the problem then?" she asked.

I scowled down at my feet and considered how best to reply.

The special relationship I had with the gods was not something I generally noised about. In fact, nobody else in Athens knew anything of it, with the exception of Gorgias and Hermogenes, and they only knew part of the story. When Gorgias had first offered me a place in his home, I had told him about my past—indeed, it would have been unthinkable to do otherwise. Gods, I'd informed him, had frequently been house guests in my childhood home. Without going into tedious detail, I'd also told him that I'd left due to an unpleasant situation involving those same guests that had resulted in my acquisition of an ivory shoulder. Despite the visible proof of this, Gorgias had not really believed the more divine elements of my tale—until last summer, when Dionysus and Hermes had popped around.

At first he'd thought they were acquaintances of mine. The kind of friends who show up unannounced, drink your wine, make free with your slaves, and leave their smelly sandals in the middle of your vestibule. But over the course of their visit, it had become apparent that these were much more than just fun-loving chums. In fact, Gorgias had grown quite wild around the eyes when he'd realized their true nature. Although we'd talked about it immediately after the fact, he had studiously avoided the subject ever since. I wasn't sure what he believed now.

As for Hermogenes, he knew that Poseidon had some sort of personal vendetta against me, but he didn't know why.

Nobody knew that I'd failed Apollo. Nobody knew that Hera was displeased with me. And certainly nobody was aware that Zeus had enjoyed carnal relations with my grandmother. When one was so intimately connected with such powerful—and potentially capricious—beings, one was very careful to keep it on the quiet side.

"It's complicated," I said finally.

Pharsalia gave me a quizzical look. "Well, don't go taking this the wrong way, luv, but if the kraken's giving you so much grief, you might want to have a word with my Castor about it. Thinks very highly of you, he does. He'd be more than happy to lend a hand."

Behind me I heard the hiss of Hermogenes's indrawn breath. From anyone else, such a suggestion would have constituted a deadly insult. I tried to hide my own reaction to her offer, but Pharsalia knew me too well.

"Now, don't go getting your cock in a knot, luv," she said, her voice sharp but kind. "You and I both know he's not a patch on you in the kitchen, but he *can* cook up a bit of kraken a right treat—better than any I've tasted. And with all the kraken in this city, I've had plenty of opportunity to taste me fair share."

"Thank you," I said, trying to sound grateful.

"You just think about it," she said with a decisive nod, then she tugged my arm so I bent down towards her. "It can be our little secret," she breathed into my ear.

I straightened without replying.

"Besides," she continued in a more normal tone of voice, "who wants to see that poxy Sicilian mince off with all those drachmas, eh? And it's not just the money, is it? We'll have half the city turning out for that match. You mark me words, whoever wins the Bronze Chef will be famous—and so will his recipes. Think about that!"

Hermogenes coughed—a noise that sounded suspiciously like "I told you so." I scowled at him. He glared back, unrepentant.

"Put your name in," Pharsalia advised. "And win the sodding match. Beat that stupid sod of a Sicilian at his own game. Show him once and for all who's the 'Phidias of the kitchen' 'round here." She gave my arm another little shake for emphasis. "Put your name in, luv," she said again. "You *need* it."

A Taste of Lydia

PELOPS'S HARES IN WINE

---

* 1 large hare, skinned, dressed and cut in 8 pieces
* Salt and freshly ground pepper, to taste
* extra-virgin olive oil
* small chunk of salt-cured pork belly (pancetta), chopped finely
* 4 shallots, chopped
* 2 fennel bulbs
* 3 garlic cloves, halved
* 1 cup white wine
* 18 black olives, pitted
* Fennel leaves, chopped, to taste

---

1. Wash the hare pieces and pat dry. Sprinkle with sea salt and pepper.

2. To prepare the fennel, remove the tough core, separate the stalks and cut them in small slices. Chop leaves and set aside.

3. In a medium-hot pan, heat a splash of olive oil and fry the hare pieces on both sides until well browned. Remove the hare pieces from the pan and set aside. In the same pan, add more olive oil and briefly fry the pork, shallots, fennel

slices, and the garlic over lower heat. Add the wine and stir, scraping up the bits from the bottom of the pan. Return the hare pieces to the pan and add the black olives. Cover and cook over low heat for a few minutes.

4. Transfer to an ovenproof dish and bake, uncovered, in a medium-hot oven for one half hour. Adjust the seasoning and transfer to a hot serving platter. Garnish with the chopped fennel leaves.

Chapter 4

Anacreon's bean-free symposion came off beautifully. The striped red mullets ensured the success of the feast—indeed, how could they not have done so?—and my Hares in Wine was also particularly well received.

Nobody in Athens could cook hare really well. Most chefs tended to smother it in gluey sauces, adding either too much cheese or too much oil, as if preparing some sort of weasel. Smarter chefs merely roasted the animal, sprinkling it only with salt and taking it from the spit while still a little rare. I, myself, had prepared many hares in this fashion. My new recipe, however, was infinitely better. Well-browned meat, slowly simmered with wine, fennel, olives, garlic, and salt-cured pork belly. It was both unique and succulent, the meat so tender it practically melted in the mouth in a luscious medley of flavours. A truly inspired dish.

But although the tips had been fairly generous, and many had offered extravagant compliments on both the hare and the rare red mullets, not a single guest had inquired as to my future availability. Pharsalia's words kept running through my head. She was right, of course. If I wanted to prove Mithaecus the lesser chef once and for all (and if I wanted to increase my savings in any sort of substantial way), I needed to win the Bronze Chef competition. Decisively.

And so, early that morning I was back in the kitchen, uncharacteristically ill-humoured and short-tempered, attempting yet again to fashion something digestible—let alone palatable— from the gods-cursed kraken.

I was suffering from the effects of the previous night. I rarely drank when on contract, but Anacreon's poorly ventilated kitchen had been stiflingly hot, and the wine had helped ease my parched throat. In hindsight, perhaps I had taken a little too much of it, for I'd woken late with a dull headache and heavy, bloodshot eyes.

Thus far, the events of the day were doing nothing to lift my spirits. My washing water had dried up before I could do more than dip my fingers in it. I'd had a row with Irene about the state of the storeroom (she thought it was too messy, I couldn't find anything when she "organized" it). And over breakfast Gorgias had talked of nothing but his wedding plans. Should they be married on the full moon, or wait until the following day? Which musicians ought to be secured for the procession? What should they sacrifice to Hera and Peitho, the protectors of the marriage bed? And did I think a wedding cake made of sesame and honey would be an appropriate enough symbol of fertility, as Zeuxo did not care for the more traditional date cake?

I did not want to think of Gorgias's marriage bed. Or of Zeuxo's fertility.

And when I finally escaped to the kitchen, it was only to find that fully half my kraken, which had been purchased only the day before, had become slimy and foul smelling, this despite having been stored in the ice pit overnight. By all accounts, kraken was not supposed to turn, but the meat smelled so much like, as Gorgias had so colourfully put it, a monkey's arse, that I was forced to dispose of most of it on the midden.

So when my disciple came stumbling back from his errands in the Agora, eyes practically bulging from his head, market basket notably empty of the items I'd sent him for, babbling nonsense about horses with wings, my reaction, perhaps, could be excused.

"But Chef, it's true!" he cried wildly, hand going to his now disarranged hair. "It's true! I've never ... I've never seen the like! You've got to come! I ... I never would have believed it myself!"

I had not struck him hard—a mere smack upside the head— but it was unlike Hermogenes to remain uncowed by such a reprimand. He grabbed my arm and began pulling me towards the front door, and that, too, was most unlike him. Something certainly had him in a state. I resisted for another moment, then relented, allowing him to lead me from the house. The whole time he was gasping out his news.

" ... and it landed right in the Agora! White like a cloud it is, with silver wings and gold hooves! I saw it clear as day! And

Perseus himself riding on its back! You won't believe your eyes! And when it flies ... it's like ... colours ... and ... rainbows ... and ... and Chef, you've got to hurry!"

He tugged harder, practically dragging me through the muck of the dark, narrow streets that lay between our house and the marketplace.

"Have a care, Hermogenes!" I admonished as he pulled me right through a reeking pile of refuse. My sandal had squelched down unpleasantly into the mess and I paused to scrape it clean.

"But we've got to hurry!" He danced impatiently from one foot to the other. "What if we miss it!"

"The man's come to visit Athens," I said reasonably, giving my sandal a final scrape. "I'm sure we'll get another chance to see his horse."

But by this time, Hermogenes's excitement had communicated itself to me, and when I resumed walking, it was with a much quicker pace. Until now, I'd had grave doubts about the existence of this winged horse, putting any accounts of it down to wild exaggeration or, more likely, an involvement of alcohol, but Hermogenes seemed so very sure of what he'd seen—and there was no wine on his breath. He dashed ahead, urging me to hurry.

By the time we got to The Herms at the entrance to the Agora, a crowd of people had already gathered. Far too many people. Had the entire city turned out to see this alleged flying equine? Spectators stood crammed together, slaves and citizens and freemen. There were even women in the crowd—and not just peasants and flute girls either, but Athenian matrons and daughters, lured from their protected rooms and courtyards by the spectacle.

Armed with the single-minded determination only a horse-obsessed lad could possess, my disciple began pushing against the crush of people. To no avail. Nobody was budging and, in fact, several of them cuffed Hermogenes quite unceremoniously as he tried to shove his way past them. I followed in his wake at a more leisurely pace as he tried first one route, then another. But after a fat man's foot came down hard on my instep and an elegantly dressed matron gave me a pointed and none-too-gentle jab in the ribs, I called a halt.

"Enough, Hermogenes. Enough. We'll never get through."

"But Chef!" he wailed. "The horse!"

I was about to turn around to seek a less crowded vantage point from which to view this famous horse when my attention was caught by a small feminine figure. She was pushing determinedly past slave and citizen alike, attempting to extricate herself from the crowd. For that alone she would have stood out, for nobody else showed the slightest inclination to quit the Agora. But despite the air of expectant excitement that surrounded us, her face wore a sour look of exasperated annoyance, and I saw her scowl as she squeezed past a tight cluster of merchants. And then her eyes met mine and I felt a shock of ... *something* run through the length of my body.

She was short and dark, her hair long and unfashionably straight. She carried no sunshade, her tanned skin completely exposed to the rays of Helios. I never would have given her a second glance were it not for her eyes. Blue as the Aegean, faintly streaked with white and green, they had all the searing fire of lightning, a quality made even more striking by her darkly tanned face. At once I felt as though I knew her, though I was, in the same moment, equally certain I did not. Surely, I would have recalled those eyes.

We stared at each other for a long moment. I opened my mouth to speak, though I had no idea what I might say to her. But whatever words I was about to utter were lost in the collective cry of the crowd. A flurry of arms suddenly shot in the air, pointing to the sky. I caught a flash of white out of the corner of my eye. Almost reluctantly, I pulled my gaze away from the blue-eyed woman and looked up.

A horse had taken to the air.

On golden hooves, it galloped on ... nothing. Its blinding white coat stood out in stark relief from the deep blue of the autumn morning sky. Sunlight glinted off silvered wing tips as they rose and fell. One powerful downstroke. Then another. The creature's broad wings lifted it easily above the gasping crowd. My mouth fell open at the sight, the woman and her eyes utterly forgotten in the sheer wonder of it. Of a winged horse.

The creature turned, wheeling and diving, playing for the crowd, cantering on the morning breeze. Only then did I become aware of the man on its back. He was dressed in a white-sleeved chiton, the sort of garment a charioteer might wear. He had a brown satchel slung across his shoulders and his long hair was as golden as the hooves of his steed. He smiled and waved, urging the horse to greater and greater feats, swooping straight down, pulling up at the last moment, laughing in exhilaration as the crowd cried out. Several young girls swooned. Wherever the horse passed, a rainbow lingered in the sky. And as the pair passed directly overhead, it seemed to me that the beast's snowy coat was shot through with all the colours of the world.

The man and horse were circling lazily over the crowd now, their passage changing the very tenor of the day. Sunny yellow, delicate rose, ocean blue, and spring green danced across the sky, casting ripples of colour over upturned rapturous faces. Each time the pair angled toward the sun, sharp shards of light flashed off the creature's wings, piercing the eye through with brilliance. My eyes were watering, but I was unable to look away. I couldn't even blink.

And then the man leaned forward and spoke something in the horse's ear. The horse shook its mane, sending a rainbow splash across the sky. They began a spiralling descent, dipping closer and closer to the ground, until, at last, they dropped from view. My sigh was echoed by a thousand throats.

I was still looking skyward, though there was nothing to see, when I gradually became aware of an insistent tugging on my arm. I looked down to see Hermogenes. His dark eyes were shining.

"Chef?" he said. And it was a question.

"Breathtaking," I told him honestly. "Simply breathtaking."

Chapter 5

nd they say he's been all over the whole of Greece—"
... Hermogenes's eyes were shining.

"On holiday with his mum and sister before he marries the Princess," Irene added, her own eyes no less sparkly. "Though why he'd want to put *that* off, I couldn't tell you—"

"... and he's named his horse Pegasus—" Hermogenes broke in.

"If I were set to marry royalty," Irene continued over him, "you wouldn't find me traipsing about around the countryside—"

" ... and it can fly for *hours* without a rest!"

"Ah well, there's nowt as queer as folk, as they say. I tell you, it minds me of a time when—"

" ... and he's to stay with *Archestratus!* "

"Really." It was the first interest I'd shown for the past half hour.

After witnessing the remarkable flight, Hermogenes had wanted to follow Perseus and his marvellous steed, but with the Agora virtually impassable due to the crowds, we'd had no choice but to return home. Rain clouds had moved in and the day had turned bleak and cool, almost as if the winged horse had taken all sunshine and warmth with it when it had landed. And ever since we had settled in the cloudy courtyard, lit braziers surrounding us for warmth, Hermogenes and Irene had been vying with each other to assault my ears with every scrap of gossip about Perseus, his horse, his family, his horse, his assorted heroic feats, his horse, his taste in clothing, and his horse. Hermogenes had even managed to find out what he and his horse had eaten for supper the night before (suckling pig and sea buckthorn leaves, respectively).

"How long is Archestratus to host him?" I questioned, pulling my cloak tighter against my chest. In truth, the braziers did little to dispel the chill of imminent rain. "Tell me more of this."

Hermogenes flashed a triumphant glance at Irene, who sniffed and looked away.

I waited with studied patience.

"He's to stay with him the whole time he's here in Athens," Hermogenes began, grinning crookedly at the look on my face. "*And* I heard there's to be a special symposion in his honour."

"Well, there'd have to be, wouldn't there?" Irene interjected.

Hermogenes scowled at her interruption, but nodded. "Right. To celebrate his victory over the monsters. And who better to host it than Archestratus, eh?"

"The man's as rich as Midas—" Irene broke in again.

"—and he knows how to put on a right proper do," Hermogenes added. "Everybody says so. Sophocles even wrote a play about one of his feasts a few years back, but the actors were total shite—from Boeotia, you know—so nobody went to it."

"Really," I said again, stroking my chin.

"He's to have his symposion the same night as the Proerosia," Hermogenes was saying. "You know, the first fruits festival."

"The one that's held up at Eleusis?"

"That's right. Archestratus's wife comes from an old farming family, so she and her daughters'll be out of town. Guess he figured he'd have his party without the wife coming 'round to put a damper on things."

"He's not got a wife," Irene interrupted scornfully. "She died in the plague, didn't she?"

"That's not what I heard, me. And besides—"

"Well, you heard wrong then."

"*I* heard wrong!"

Hermogenes and Irene began bickering. I frowned thoughtfully, their voices fading into background noise.

Archestratus and Perseus.

I had not yet had the pleasure of cooking for Archestratus, although before The Sicilian had near ruined my reputation I had had high hopes of just such an honour. Indeed, any chef would have considered it a coup.

Archestratus was a decidedly political animal, at various times holding the office of basileos, archon, magistrate, polemarch, and probably several others I couldn't begin to name. But in addition to being both politically active and extremely wealthy, Archestratus was also acknowledged as one of the city's few true gastronomes. I had not heard this business about the play before, but I did know the man was passionate about his victuals. With a citizen of his standing hosting a guest of Perseus's stature ... well, suffice it to say the possibilities were very interesting indeed.

Irene and Hermogenes were still arguing. A late bee droned hopefully through the fall garden, buzzing from plant to plant in a vain effort to recapture the bounty of summer. Kabob was rustling about in the leaf litter. I went back to my ruminations.

If Archestratus was planning a celebratory symposion in honour of his exalted guest, then he was going to need a chef. And who better than the greatest chef in Athens? But how best to secure the contract? Presenting myself uninvited at the door would be both boorish and humiliating. And Archestratus, travelling as he did in the uppermost levels of society, had not yet experienced a meal that I had prepared, so he had no idea of either my identity or my talents. How, then, to introduce myself to him?

If Hermogenes had his way, I would prance about the Agora in some brand-coloured chiton. I shuddered at the mental image this produced. But the more I thought about the contract, the more I lusted after it. To be the one chosen to cook for Archestratus *and* Perseus! It would certainly destroy The Sicilian's overinflated opinion of himself. And if, in addition to this, I were to win the Bronze Chef competition? Why, my victory over him would be assured.

Archestratus and Perseus. I chewed the inside of my mouth

as I mulled it over. There might, I realized, be even more to this than the prestige of cooking for such an illustrious visitor (and trouncing the daylights out of Mithaecus). Potential sponsors might also be on the guest list for such an important dinner party—wealthy, powerful men who would be only too agreeable to having their name associated with a Bronze Chef competitor. I decided I would do much to be named chef for this symposion. It was entirely possible I might even wear a chiton of Hermogenes's choosing.

Hermogenes and Irene were on about something else now. It took a moment for the import of their words to filter through my consciousness.

"Aye, no wonder he's so handsome, then. And so skilled with the sword too, to be taking on the kraken and the Gorgon."

"I could've probably taken on all three Gorgons and still—"

"You? You couldn't kill a wood tick if it went burrowing in your armpit!"

"Well, if I was the son of Zeus—"

"Don't tell me that old wheeze is still going around the Agora," I interrupted, allowing a note of scorn to enter my voice. "Perseus the son of Zeus?" I rolled my eyes.

Hermogenes paused, exchanging a puzzled glance with Irene.

"But … it's true, Chef. Perseus is the son of Zeus," he replied diffidently.

"And I suppose it's 'true' that Zeus visited his mother as a golden shower too." I sniggered at the thought. "Really, Hermogenes, when I said I wanted you to keep me informed, I was speaking of fact, not fiction."

"But, Chef, Father Zeus has acknowledged him."

"You know, a good disciple knows the difference between information and gossip and—*He did what*? When?"

"He acknowledged him. The other day, at the portico of Zeus Eleutherios. Perseus was there making an offering, and all of a sudden, lightning started flashing in the sky."

"It's almost winter." I waved it off, unconvinced. "A thunderstorm at this time of year can hardly be considered a sign."

"It is when the sky's clear blue," Hermogenes shot back. "And when an eagle flies overhead right after. And when the whole shrine suddenly starts glowing and smelling like flowers—roses!—even though everybody knows roses don't bloom in the fall and marble shrines don't go about glowing at *any* time of the year."

I closed my mouth on my next retort and reconsidered. It did sound as though Zeus was having a bit of a word.

"And the priests say there's to be two new constellations. One in the shape of Pegasus and the other in the shape of Perseus, himself! We should be able to see them tonight—so long as the clouds clear off in time."

Perseus was getting his own constellation? He wasn't even dead yet!

"Why didn't you tell me he was Zeus's son?" I demanded testily.

"I thought you heard."

"I heard nothing of this!"

"Sorry, Chef."

"How many times do I have to say it? You're *supposed* to keep me informed!"

"I'm sorry," my disciple said again, contritely. "Honest! I thought you knew. And why does it matter so much?"

I didn't answer him. Frowning, I pulled at my lower lip, plunging again into deep deliberation.

So, the famous Perseus boasted immortal kin, did he? Well, he wasn't the only one. I was Zeus's grandson, and if Perseus were, indeed, the son of the great Sky God, then I might just be able to take advantage of that.

Over the last several months—ever since The Sicilian had almost ruined my reputation—I had often considered quietly informing the Athenians of my extraordinary heritage, reasoning that if others knew of my divine connections, few would hire Mithaecus over me. The only thing that stopped me was the same reason I had not trumpeted the news from atop the Acropolis as soon as I'd first set foot in the city. It could be summed up in a single word: hubris.

Hubris. Exaggerated pride and self-confidence. It had been my father's downfall. I was determined that it would not be mine. By telling the world of my grandfather, especially when my motivation was, essentially, a selfish one, would I not be committing the same sin? I was not certain, but knowing that my father was trapped in the underworld for all eternity, I had not deemed the risk worth taking.

But if someone *else* were to inform the people of Athens of my family connections? Say, someone of Perseus's stature? Ah, now that might just work in my favour—as long I had the opportunity to inform *him* of our shared blood. Which brought my thoughts full circle right back to Archestratus's symposion.

It would be my first best chance, an ideal venue, really. I could picture it now—the end of a superb feast, the guests reclining gracefully against the cushions of their dining couches, replete with succulent foods and sublime wines. And me, modest and blushing ever so slightly, escorted into the andron amidst a shower of gushing praise and silver drachmas. Naturally, I would be presented to the guest of honour. And it would be then, while we were exchanging pleasantries, that I would let slip—oh, so casually—that we shared a common relative. Ah yes, I could see it now. He would smile in delight, perhaps even take me into a warm embrace, kiss me on both cheeks and introduce me to all present as kin. Word of my Olympic connections would fly through Athens faster than the little owls that flitted about the city. The contracts would come pouring in. Superior sponsors would line up outside my door in the hopes of obtaining the honour of my representation at the Bronze Chef competition. Mithaecus would be yesterday's catch.

I sighed happily just thinking about it.

But again, how best to secure this all-important contract? I frowned and rubbed the side of my nose pensively. For a moment—a very brief moment—I considered asking Dionysus and Hermes for aid. After all, they had offered to lend a hand on numerous occasions, and it would be nothing for them to put a good word for me in the right ears. But the gods' help was sometimes a double-edged knife, and, too often, their mildest interference had a nasty habit of heading sharply southward—especially where these two gods were concerned. Besides, it was the eve of the Oskhophoria. Men would be busy preparing the grape-laden vine branches to parade through the streets while they sang hymns of the harvest, and I suspected Dionysus had already begun "celebrating." No. I was far better off trying to secure the contract on my own first. I could always ask Dionysus to lend a hand if that didn't work—after he sobered up, of course.

"Just try it then, and we'll see how far you get!" Irene flared before flouncing out of the courtyard.

I looked up and blinked at her retreating back, unaware of what had transpired to send her off like that.

"Barmy old cow," Hermogenes muttered under his breath. "If she'd just—"

"Enough!" I made a chopping gesture with my hand. "Never mind Irene! There are more important concerns. Hermogenes, I need that contract."

"What contract?" he asked blankly.

With an effort, I refrained from boxing his ears. "The contract for Archestratus, of course!" I said through clenched teeth. "For this symposion to be held in Perseus's honour. I need it."

His eyes widened at my intensity, but he took a deep breath and thought for a long moment, blowing out his cheeks like a pufferfish. "Do we know anybody who knows him?" he asked finally. "Archestratus, I mean."

I shook my head.

"And you've never cooked at a symposion he's attended?"

"No."

He tugged on his chin hairs for a moment. "Okay," he said. "Okay. The beard's got an idea."

I gave him a flat look, which he ignored. Glancing around the garden, he leaned close and lowered his voice. Why he bothered to do so, I was uncertain. If one did not count Kabob or the still hopeful bee, we were the only two in the courtyard. My disciple's eyes had taken on an unsettling intensity.

"It's an idea I've had for a while, me," he said. "I haven't wanted to say anything because ... well, it didn't seem like the right time, did it? But this, this is perfect."

The sky darkened, heightening the drama of the moment. Hermogenes lowered his voice further. I had to lean in close to hear him.

"I call it ... direct marketing."

I sat up again and shot him a skeptical look. "Direct *what*?"

"*Shhhh*," he admonished, casting another significant look around the empty courtyard. "Direct marketing. It's a way of selling yourself. You know, by letting the right people know how brilliant you are."

"If you think I'm standing in the market by Athena Ergane with all those tavern cooks—"

"Don't be daft!" he said scornfully before remembering who he was speaking to. He flicked a uneasy glance at me and hastened to continue. "I mean, you're better than any of those tossers, Chef! By a long shot! You don't belong there. No, what I'm proposing, like, is for you to prepare some food. A delicacy. Like some of them red mullets."

"What good does that do me?" I demanded, mystified. "I've no contracts."

"Not now, Chef. But say you cook up the rest of those mullets.

Do 'em up a right treat, eh? Like you did for Anacreon. We'll get a nice dish at the market—one of those red figure jobs—and we'll arrange the fish on it with sauce and the like. Maybe even a bit of greenery to fancy it up. And then as soon as it's done, I'll nip over to Archestratus's house and present it to him. As a token of your esteem, see?"

"A gift?" I said doubtfully, though the possibilities were already presenting themselves to me.

"He couldn't help but be impressed!" Hermogenes clapped his hands together, dark eyes shining at the thought. "A tasty fish like that? At a time when anyone would give his left bollock to have something other than kraken at table? And those mullets!" Hermogenes rolled his eyes and pretended to swoon. "Like ambrosia they were! You and I, we know you're the best chef in the city. We just have to let Archestratus know it! And what better way than to let your cooking speak for itself, eh?"

Give away my striped red mullets?

It had been difficult enough to part with half of them for Anacreon's symposion, though the tips had made the sacrifice bearable. But to give the rest of them away? Without any sort of payment?

"One taste of those fish, and he'll be yours!" Hermogenes pressed. "He'll be beside himself! And when it comes time to decide which chef to hire for his symposion, you can bet your hairy arse he won't be thinking about The Sicilian and his piss-coloured chiton!" He paused, and his eyes went starry as another thought occurred to him. "And just think, Chef," he breathed. "You'll be able to meet *Perseus*!"

The rain had started falling now, a few fine drops spitting down on us. The longer I considered Hermogenes's idea, the more I liked it. I wanted—no, I *needed*!—this contract. And if truth be told, I also wanted to meet the great Perseus—and not only because I hoped he would publicly acknowledge our relationship. Perseus was half divine, as opposed to my one quarter. He had slain both kraken and Gorgon. The only beasts I had ever killed were sacrificial animals for feasts and a nest of cockroaches that had once taken up residence in the storeroom. I trod the narrow streets of Athens on foot, cooking for men wealthier than myself, while Perseus rode a winged steed across the civilized world, slaying monsters, winning princesses, and having constellations awarded him. How often did lesser folk (even if they were only *slightly* lesser) have the chance to meet an achiever of such impressively heroic deeds?

And so, although it would pain me to give such superior fish away, the rewards could prove more than worth the loss. With such a treat, Archestratus could not fail to be impressed with my culinary skills. A single taste of my striped red mullet, and he would have no choice—indeed, no other desire—but to hire me for Perseus's victory feast.

"We'll do it," I decided, jumping to my feet. "Today. Right now. Go to the market and see what kind of platter you can find. Try to get one with a fish design. Red figure, if we've the coin for it. If not, make sure the quality is impeccable. Remember, the plate is part of the gift, it needs to be elegant. I'll start the fish."

I strode to the kitchen and retrieved my money pouch while Hermogenes donned his cloak and collected his carrying basket.

I passed him a handful of coins, but before he could dash out the door, I gripped his shoulder in approval. "An inspired idea, Hermogenes," I told him. "Well done, my disciple. We'll soon have these Athenians eating from our palms!"

He turned to go, a wide grin splitting his face, but then he hesitated.

"Chef?"

"What is it?"

"Have you … have you thought about what you'll do with the kraken?"

"The kraken? What kraken? I thought we were cooking red mullet."

Hermogenes's happy smile had dimmed. "I didn't mean for marketing. It's just … well … for the contract, yeah? When you get it. I mean, they're bound to want a bit of kraken for the feast, aren't they, Chef?" he said carefully. "Seeing how Perseus killed it and all."

And with those words, my disciple burst the bubble of my shining future.

The kraken.

All my elaborate plans began to deflate. In the excitement of Hermogenes's new marketing idea, I had not thought about what would happen once I did secure the contract. Of *course* Perseus would want to eat the kraken at his victory feast. The man had killed it single-handedly, after all. But in order for him to eat the kraken, I would have to prepare the kraken, which meant that unless Perseus liked his kraken burnt to a crisp and smelling like the nether parts of a primate, there was little chance any feast I cooked for him would prove the rousing success I needed it to be.

I gritted my teeth, my hands at my side clenching and unclenching. The temperature had plummeted and the rain was coming down in earnest now, the icy drops drumming a staccato against the roof tiles.

No. I gave myself a mental shake. I could not—I *would* not—let Poseidon win this battle!

"Let's secure the contract first," I told Hermogenes with a confidence I did not feel. "We'll worry about the kraken later."

Chapter 6

Despite my brave words to Hermogenes, it was impossible for me to refrain from thinking about the gods-cursed kraken. My apprentice was often mistaken about many things, but in this, he was correct. Should I secure this all-important contract, I would have no choice but to serve kraken at the symposion. Any other chef would do so (*they* did not have any difficulty with it), which meant that somehow I was going to have to come up with a way of preparing the miserable stuff. After I waved Hermogenes off, I let out my breath in a frustrated sigh and withdrew to the kitchen.

Think! I admonished myself. *Think.*

I racked my brain, but it seemed I had already tried every manner of preparation known to man or god. Poaching, boiling, searing, simmering. With wine, without wine. Once, out of desperation, I'd left it raw, slicing the blue meat as thin as

I could and seasoning it with oil and vinegar. The result had sent Hermogenes dashing to the privy where he had heaved up the contents of his stomach so forcefully that he'd remained pale and greenish for the rest of the day.

No, if there was a solution to my dilemma, it continued to elude me, and I stood scowling in the doorway to the kitchen as I thought about it, waiting for my eyes to adjust to the dimmer light.

But kraken would not be the only dish on the menu, I reminded myself. At a feast honouring such an exalted guest, one would not dine exclusively on kraken, even if that guest *had* been the means to its untimely end. This meant that other dishes—dishes not involving sea monsters—would have the chance to shine. And therefore so would I.

I could be very good at shining when I put my mind to it.

My resolve thus renewed, I began to lay out the tools of my trade, lining up my bronze knives beside the cutting board, setting a large frying pan on the brazier to heat. I felt remarkably calm now, as if the whole prospect of cooking for Archestratus was somehow fated. It was as though Tyche herself had stepped into the room, the horn of Amaltheia tucked under her arm and overflowing with good fortune. While Hermogenes trolled the rain-swept Agora for the perfect serving platter, I started to prepare the last of my precious fish.

A fact that seemed to escape most of the other chefs in Athens was that red mullet (striped or otherwise) is a fatty fish. As a result, these lesser chefs tended to fry it in over-greased pans. Imbeciles. Mullet had to be cooked in such a way that the fat beneath the skin was released, maximizing the flavour by frying the skin to a delicate crisp in its own fat. Furthermore, the mullet's flesh is firm and translucent, with a profound taste of the open sea. One would not want to overwhelm such a delicate sensation with an overabundance of seasonings (unless, of course, one's name was Mithaecus, in which case one would probably obliterate the taste of the poor fish with a greasy mess of old cheese, dried spice and young wine—either that or dredge the thing in Kraken Bake). No, a mere sprinkling of sea salt, a touch of fresh oregano, the lightest brush of olive oil, and the striped red mullet would be divine.

Some late greens would complement the fish nicely, I decided. Wilted first, then tossed with olive oil and vinegar and sprinkled with lightly toasted sesame seeds. The tangy bitterness of the greens would enhance the sweetness of the mullets' succulent flesh. And on the side, artfully arranged, thin rounds of barley bread, rubbed with garlic and olive oil and toasted over the flame until crisp and golden. It would be a dish worthy of the gods themselves.

Or a hero.

Hermogenes returned, shaking the rain from his cloak, just as I was taking the bread from the flame.

"Show me," I ordered, though the light in his face already told me he was pleased with the purchase.

And so he ought to have been.

Round, and easily as wide as my forearm was long, the platter was the very latest in dining fashion. Three red fishes, each one striped, each exquisitely rendered, swam on a black background, head to tail around the dish. The rim had been edged with a curling pattern of breaking waves, and in the very centre of the dish, which was indented to capture juices from the food, a sea urchin had been painted, its spines radiating outward like a star.

"It's *perfect*," I told him, greedily tracing the designs with my fingertip. "Just perfect! But it must have cost a fortune."

Hermogenes's proudly beaming face took on a puzzled expression.

"It didn't," he assured me. "Not really. I bought it off some wine seller. Cost everything I had in me pouch, but it should've been a lot more. Nice dish like that? He said he'd brought it in special for some tosser who up and changed his mind. That's why it was so cheap."

I raised one eyebrow skeptically. "A wine seller?"

Wine sellers did not normally peddle crockery.

Hermogenes nodded. "I'd just done a quick run through the pottery shops," he explained. "I hadn't seen much I liked and I was about to turn 'round and have another go when I spied one of The Sicilian's poncy-arsed assistants. He was sure legging it somewhere in an awful hurry. Dirty great wanker was up to something, all right. Sly and sneaky-looking he was, so I followed him and—"

"Hermogenes." I sighed. "I've told you to stay away from Mithaecus's disciples. I appreciate the loyalty—I really do!—but nothing good will come of our respective disciples brawling in the street."

"I never!" he protested, quickly hiding one hand under a fold of his chiton.

I stopped him with a gesture. "Please," I said. "I may be a foreigner, but I'm not a total idiot. I've seen your scrapes and bruises. I know how you're getting them—and it's *not* from watching the chariot racers practise."

Hermogenes looked down, but not before I saw his resentful scowl. I waited.

"So anyhow," Hermogenes said after a moment, "I was, uh … walking … over by the Tholos, when I saw this plate propped up on a counter. On display, like."

"At a wine stall?"

My disciple nodded.

"What did the seller look like?"

Hermogenes lifted his shoulders. "Big. Curly beard. Jolly sort of bloke. Real jolly, if you know what I mean."

I arched my brow in inquiry.

"I think he'd gotten into his stock," Hermogenes explained. "Right pissed to the gills, he was. Anyway, his shop's snugged right up between the Tholos and the Bouleuterion." He shrugged again. "He seemed to recognize me, but I can't say as I knew him."

"Ah," I said, nodding in understanding. The location of the wine stall told me all I needed to know—as did the condition of the vendor.

Most wine retailing establishments were located in the opposite corner of the Agora from the Tholos and the Bouleuterion. The two municipal structures were where Athens's city council met to debate sundry issues and, as these debates were facilitated by the contents of a wine stall, my old friend, the god of wine, had cannily set up shop between the buildings.

So, Dionysus had sold Hermogenes the fish platter, had he? He had promised to watch my back. And despite the distractions of his vine harvest festival, it appeared he intended to keep his word. Briefly, I wondered how he'd known of my need for such a serving dish, then I dismissed the thought with a shake of my head. He was a god, after all. He could probably keep tabs on just about anything if he put his mind to it.

"But, Chef," Hermogenes was saying, "as soon as I saw them fish on the plate—and stripy ones, like the mullets!—I knew it was the one."

"Indeed." I clapped him warmly on the shoulder. "Good job, Hermogenes! Quite excellent! Now go and dry off. And do your best to clean up, too. We can't have a scruffy-looking messenger, can we? I suppose I cannot convince you to shave?"

He gave me a look of pure outrage.

I suppressed a sigh. "Never mind," I told him. "Go and clean up. I'm almost done here."

By the time Hermogenes returned to the kitchen, unshaved, but freshly scrubbed and decked out in his best tunic, I was just arranging some final sprigs of oregano over the fish.

"I did me best to smarten up, but you know I'll be right soaked as soon as I—" he began, before breaking off with a gasp. "Chef!" he breathed, then fell silent as he contemplated the full effect of my offering.

To this day, I cannot say what inspired me to do what I'd done. Perhaps some deeply buried artistic impulse. Or maybe just a longing for the warmer days of summer. Whatever the origin, the results were exquisite, if I do say so myself.

The fish were golden and perfect, left whole for best effect, with a reduction of wine and vinegar drizzled over them in stripes. They rested on a bed of glistening greens, the toasted bread rounds arranged artfully around them. I'd sprinkled lightly browned sesame seeds over the wilted leaves, and here and there I had placed two thin wedges of sweet apple, each cut to look like the wing of a butterfly.

On the head of each fish, just over the eye, was one of the tiny cucumbers so new to Athenian gastronomy. I had sliced each as thin as papyrus, fanning out the slices so they resembled a flower. Clusters of blood-red pomegranate seeds added a splash of colour to the dish.

It was summer on a platter.

"Chef, I've never seen the like!" Hermogenes said in a hushed tone. "How did you ... what gave you ... nobody's ever done anything like this before. Nobody!" He looked up at me, his gaze unabashedly admiring. "Them flowers! And the butterflies! That's ... that's *inspired*, that is!"

"Let's hope Archestratus agrees with you," I said briskly, though I was touched by his approbation.

"He will," Hermogenes assured me. "He *has* to!"

The fish were still steaming, their herb-scented fragrance setting our mouths to watering. I covered the dish carefully with an oiled cloth and settled it at the bottom of a sturdy carrying basket. Then, with an admonition to refrain from further altercations with Mithaecus's disciples, I sent Hermogenes back out in the rain to present the gift to Archestratus with my deepest and humblest compliments.

Hermogenes's direct marketing idea worked far better than either of us could have anticipated. Archestratus took one look at my gift and secured my services on the spot.

I had three days to prepare a symposion feast worthy of a hero.

Chapter 7

I don't know why you're so being so stubborn about it, Chef!"

"No, Hermogenes!"

"But it makes sense!"

"No."

"Che-ef! The direct marketing worked like a charm! Even you've got to admit that."

"And your point is?"

"My point is, maybe this idea's a good one too, yeah?"

"If you think I'm going to go prancing around in a brand-coloured chiton—"

"I don't think you could ever *prance*." A new, softer voice entered the argument. It was light and playful, amusement warming its tone. I knew that voice.

I heard it every night in my dreams.

Arranging my features to show nothing more than pleased

surprise, I looked up from the Anatolian hazelnuts Hermogenes had just cracked open and I was sifting for stray shells. Zeuxo stood in the doorway to the kitchen, sunlight from the courtyard illuminating her perfect form.

I wouldn't like to say that I had been avoiding Zeuxo since her engagement to Gorgias, but I must admit that I was, whenever possible, going out of my way *not* to see her. It was cowardly, perhaps, but I tried to be much occupied whenever she dropped by, or (even better) out on some urgent errand. Still, I could not escape her entirely, and at the sight of her now, my heart constricted painfully. I swallowed and managed a welcoming smile.

"Exactly what colour is 'brand'?" she inquired, venturing further into the room. "And why on earth would you want to wear a chiton in it?"

I cast a withering look at my disciple. "Ask him," I drawled, picking out a fragment of nut shell from the bowl. "He's the makeover marvel."

"I see," Zeuxo said, turning to Hermogenes, one elegantly shaped eyebrow arching up in inquiry.

With Zeuxo's attention now transferred to Hermogenes, I paused to drink in the sight of her. An unusually beautiful woman turned flute girl turned fiancée of my best friend, her eyes were as lovely as a goddess's, her skin was as pale as moonlight, and her mouth—ah, that mouth, that luscious, tempting mouth!—while too wide by conventional standards, tended to quirk up charmingly on one side whenever she was amused.

Hermogenes was telling her all about brands. Zeuxo listened to him with grave interest, her lips twitching upwards as he warmed up to his subject. But as Hermogenes continued to speak, trying to impress upon her the importance of a chef having a unique and recognizable look, Zeuxo cocked her head to one side.

Great Zeus and Hera, was she actually considering his words?

When Hermogenes had finally finished, she was silent for a moment, then, "It's not a bad idea, Pel," she conceded, turning her doe-eyed gaze back to me. "You could use a little sprucing up."

"*Sprucing up!*" I protested, hurt. "What's wrong with how I look?"

"Nothing," she assured me solemnly, but her mouth was trying to sneak up on one side again and I knew she was laughing at me.

Then her expression sobered. Thoughtfully, she tapped her bottom lip. Her head had tilted to one side again. "But in all seriousness, your clothes are a bit … uninspired, aren't they? Maybe you *would* look better if you polished things up a bit."

The words were scarcely out of her mouth when Gorgias strode into the kitchen. He'd been in his shop all morning— probably working on all those grills and cookers for the Bronze Chef competition. His chiton was fastened at one shoulder, exposing an impressive if somewhat hairy physique. I was suddenly aware of my own, less impressive musculature—clad as it was in its "uninspired" clothing.

Zeuxo awarded Gorgias a warm smile (probably admiring his broad shoulders).

"Who needs polishing up, then?" he asked curiously.

Ansandra and her quail had trailed in behind him. "Not me!" She was quick to deny it, though she was in her usual grubby state. From the look of her, she'd been mucking about in the pottery shop all morning too.

Gorgias went straight to Zeuxo and dropped a kiss on her forehead. I swallowed and looked away, catching Hermogenes's quickly sympathetic glance as I did so.

"Not you, pet," Zeuxo assured Ansandra, though if anyone had asked me, I would have said that Ansandra's chiton was in far greater need of a "sprucing" than my own. "It's Pelops."

"What's wrong with Pelops?" Ansandra asked, her eyes as bright and curious as her quail's.

"Absolutely nothing," I said firmly.

"Hermogenes thinks he needs a brand, and I agree," Zeuxo answered, ignoring me. "I mean, look at him!"

Four sets of eyes—five if you count Kabob's—turned as one to stare at me. I squirmed under their regard, suddenly aware of my tunic, threadbare, splotched with cooking stains, and sporting several small burn holes from yesterday's kraken disaster.

"I'm cooking," I said defensively. "Nobody cares about how I dress!"

"Not now, maybe," Zeuxo agreed. "But what about when you're out on contract?"

"I have a nice chiton!" I protested.

"I've seen your 'nice' chiton," she said mildly, somehow inserting a wealth of uncomplimentary meaning into the soft-spoken words.

"It's not a very nice one, is it?" Ansandra remarked to her. Which was rich, coming from her.

Hermogenes was looking from one to the other, trying not to smirk.

I turned to my friend for support. "Gorgias! Lend me a hand here."

Smiling, he shrugged, raising his arms up. "Don't look at me," he rumbled. "I know shite about fashion."

I narrowed my eyes at him. "Traitor."

"Just give it a go, Chef," Hermogenes urged. "That's all I'm asking."

"It can't hurt," Zeuxo said.

"It'll be fun!" Ansandra enthused, then she paused and frowned. "Well, just so long as *I* don't have to weave the cloth for it," she amended.

"No," Zeuxo agreed with a slight shake of her head. "He'll need to go to Cato's."

"Cato's? Cato's Chitons?" I objected. "Are you joking?"

"That poncy little tosser'll bleed him dry just for a bit of cloth," Gorgias observed, finally siding with me.

Zeuxo's eyes flashed fire. "You'd rather see him tricked out in some cheap market stall rag?" she inquired dangerously.

Gorgias was quick to back down. "Uh, no! 'Course not," he mumbled. "You know best about such things, dear."

Zeuxo rewarded him with a smile. Gorgias grinned back at her fatuously.

"If Pelops is trying to establish a look," she explained in a milder tone, "a brand, as Hermogenes calls it, then it needs to reflect who he is. The best chef in Athens ought to be dressed by the best clothier, and that's Cato."

And all five of them were looking at me again. Kabob fanned his wings, flipping them onto his back with a "that's that" sort of chirp.

There was a pause, then I threw my hands up in surrender. "Fine! Fine. I'll get a new chiton. A *brand*."

"From Cato's?" Hermogenes pressed.

I scowled at him. "Yes, from Cato's."

"And maybe you could try curling your hair," Ansandra added.

That was too much.

"Out!" I pointed an imperious finger at the door. "Out of my kitchen! All of you. How can I cook when you're cluttering up the place? I have a feast to prepare, you know. Out! You, too, Hermogenes. Out. Go … go pick some herbs."

"Which ones?"

"I don't care. Just go. No, wait. Better still, go to the market. We need walnuts for the pastry, and you can have a look at the dessert grapes while you're there."

As they filed out, I overheard Hermogenes berating Ansandra.

"You can't be doing that," he told her reproachfully. "It's too much, too fast!"

"But his hair's so straight! He'd look cute with curls."

"I know! But it don't matter, do it? You can't go overwhelming him like that. He'll dig in his heels like a bleedin' donkey, and you won't budge him for love or coin. Trust me. With the Chef, you have to … well, you have to finesse him, like. Give him a chance to get used to the change. And when he has …"

There was a pause. They were almost out of earshot, but Hermogenes's final words drifted back to me.

"*That's* when you move on to the next thing," he said with a determination as unshakable as it was disturbing.

While Hermogenes was at the Agora, I made a pact with myself.

In the ice pit were six of the nicest kraken steaks available. I was going to try one more time to prepare them. One more attempt to produce something edible with them. If I failed, then I would admit defeat. I would commission Castor to prepare the kraken dish for Archestratus. It went against everything in my being, but Poseidon was leaving me little choice. Castor's kraken was highly unlikely to be the tastiest in the city. But it was sure to be more flavourful than anything I could produce, and he was the only chef I could trust to help me.

Having another chef prepare my kraken would be humiliating (which was probably the sea god's point, damn his fishy eyes) but not impossible in this instance. An arrangement like this could only work for a symposion. I could never, for example, pull off such a stunt at the Bronze Chef competition. And the whole enterprise would have to be carried out with the utmost secrecy—I could only imagine what The Sicilian would say if he were to find out.

Another chef preparing his krayken? Ah, but what can you expect from such an unimaginative, uninspired man? Hardly better than a taverna cook, really. It's astonishing he's come as far as he has.

The thought was almost enough to make me reconsider. But Pharsalia, and therefore Castor, held no love for Mithaecus. I knew they could be discreet. The Sicilian would hear nothing of it from them.

But first … first, once more into battle against the kraken.

Chapter 8

Hermogenes! Get those pastries garnished!"

"Yes, Chef. Right away, Chef."

"You! Are first tables cleared yet? Why are you shaking your head like that? What does that mean? Does that mean no?"

"Sorry, Chef! I didn't—"

"Get in there! Get those tables cleared away. I don't bloody care if the slaves haven't finished the leftovers yet. I'm not being paid by slaves, am I? Hermogenes?" I spun around, peering through the bluish haze of cook smoke. "Hermogenes, where are my servers?"

"Servers! Halia! Nysa! Manes! To the Chef!" Hermogenes roared over the noise of the busy kitchen. His face was red and shining from the heat. He paused to dash the sweat from his brow. "Second tables are ready to go!"

There was a flurry of activity as the servers dodged nimbly around bustling kitchen slaves and lined up in front of me.

"You, take the cheeses in first. Where are my figs—ah, here they are." I motioned another server to the platter of grilled figs. "Put these in front of your master. And you." I pulled the last server forward. "You'll take the pancakes. Put them in front of Perseus. I want the platter turned this way, so it'll be easier for him to pick them up. Come back immediately. There's more. Hermogenes, haven't you finished with those pastries yet?"

"They're done, Chef."

"Well, get them on a plate! Come on people, move! The feast's not over yet!"

And then it came. Before I'd had a chance to stop and catch my breath. Even before all the second tables had gone in. It came.

"Yer wanted in the andron, Chef," one of the servers said diffidently. "They're all asking for yeh. And they're wantin' more wine too. They're out again."

Finally. The summons I had been waiting for all evening. I paused and took a deep breath through my nostrils, letting it out slowly as I smoothed my hair back.

It was time to meet Perseus, Hero of the Aegean.

All of a sudden, I found myself inexplicably nervous, my hands trembling ever so slightly. I tried to shake the feeling. I hobnobbed with gods, surely I could converse with a hero? Ah, but I wanted something from this particular hero, and I wasn't entirely sure I was going to get it. I stiffened my resolve, reminding myself that I was a prince by birth and the best celebrity chef in Athens through talent and skill. Even the great Perseus ought to be proud to call me kin.

And then Hermogenes was at my side, brushing at my chiton, tweaking its folds back into place. It was not a new chiton—I had not yet had time to get to Cato's—but Irene had scrubbed the garment to within an inch of its rather threadbare life and set it in the sun all afternoon to brighten.

"Well, I guess that's as good as it's going to get," Hermogenes muttered unhappily, standing back to examine his handiwork. Then, realizing that he'd spoken aloud, hastened to add, "But you look ace, Chef. Truly. And the dinner! It was brilliant, that. Did you see? Hardly anything come back. Dishes scraped clean, they were. And it weren't no slaves doing the scraping either." He pursed his lips and tugged once more at my chiton. Then, satisfied, or perhaps just resigned, he flapped his hands in a scooting gesture. "Go on, now. They'll be looking to tip you. Maybe Perseus'll even offer you a ride on his Pegasus, eh? Go on. Don't make 'em wait."

I quit the noisy kitchen, pausing to inhale a deep breath of the cool night air. For a brief moment, I was assailed by doubts. Part of me had wanted to succeed as a chef based on my own merits rather than on who my relatives were. I glanced up, noting the cluster of new stars that had appeared in the northern sky the night before. A sword-wielding Perseus held the Gorgon's severed head, while to his side his winged steed took to the air. I felt a spasm of jealousy at the sight of them, my moment of doubt dying as quickly as it had flared. I was almost as divine as Perseus was, but *I* didn't have my own constellation. No, I had Poseidon doing his level best to sabotage me at every turn. And with a god such as that on the opposing team, I needed to snap up any advantage that might present itself, regardless of my artistic integrity.

Resolve thus renewed, I began to make my way across the torch-lit courtyard, ghosting around the statues, slipping past the softly chattering dancers and flute girls who had not yet been called upon to provide their respective services. I paused again just outside the door to the andron and found myself checking the folds of my chiton once more. Great Zeus and Hera, Hermogenes had me preening like a ruddy flute girl! I frowned, then shook it off. Accolades awaited. I schooled my face into a more modest expression and then I stepped through the curtain and into the light of the andron.

Before the guests had arrived, I'd had the opportunity to examine Archestratus's dining room. Like the rest of the house, and indeed, the man himself, the andron was subdued, but exquisitely tasteful. The dining couches (nine, for each of the nine Muses) were neither too small nor too large, the cushions and coverings neither too plain nor too ornate. Silver bowls had been filled with scented leaves, while two terracotta incense burners, each in the shape of a woman's head, stood on small tables at either end of the room, ready to add their perfume to the air. A slave had been setting up the last of the oil lamps when I'd peeked in.

Now both lamps and incense had been burning all evening. The air was a trifle hot for my taste, though it was still well within the bounds of comfort. Too much heat can adversely affect one's enjoyment and digestion of fine food, and for that reason, a good host had to be cognizant of the number of guests his andron could comfortably accommodate without overheating. But Archestratus clearly knew the limits of his entertainment space, for there were only seventeen guests that evening, with the host making up the last of nine pairs.

The guests were of impeccable lineage and indisputable wealth, precisely what one might desire in a potential Bronze Chef sponsor. Hermogenes, who had seen many of them arrive, had rather cheekily described them as the "old gaffers who rule the city," and I saw what he meant as soon as I entered the room. Snowy-haired, exuding dignity and refinement, not one of them was under fifty—with the exception of the guest of honour, of course. He looked to be about ten years younger than myself, a mere youth, and he possessed the firm skin, superb musculature, and astonishing good looks of the very young, the very fit, and the very lucky. Given his divine lineage, his physical appearance was hardly surprising.

As befit his status, the golden-haired Perseus lounged in the place of honour on the first seat of the middle couch. My employer reclined beside him, with the remaining guests ranged around them, their slaves squatting on the floor behind each dining couch. I thought the guests seemed oddly ill at ease and quite a few appeared to have imbibed more wine than was good for them, but before I could think further on it, Archestratus was smiling and motioning me into the room with what appeared to be … relief?

How very odd.

"My friends and honoured guests," he began graciously, holding his hand up to halt the conversation, though in truth it was unusually quiet in the room. "Allow me to present to you the chef. Well done, Chef Pelops. Well done. Truly a marvel!"

Citizen and slave trained their attention on me. The guests tapped their hands together in applause, murmuring words of appreciation, though several of these compliments were almost incoherent, the men uttering them clearly in an advanced state of inebriation. For their part, the slaves all glared at me, no doubt unhappy at the paucity of table scraps and leftovers. I ignored them. It wasn't my fault if their masters were ungenerous—at least with their slaves. For myself, however, there were compliments and silver drachmas in equal, and satisfying, abundance.

All seemed as it should be.

And then Archestratus rose to his feet, beckoning me to his side. He, too, pressed a large coin into my hand, but as he did so, his gaze held an odd desperation. There! I had not imagined it. Archestratus *was* relieved by my presence. Almost overwhelmingly so. What was going on?

"Well done," he said again. "The hares were exquisite. The sesame pancakes delightful. I could have eaten nothing but pancakes and considered myself well fed."

He was speaking too quickly, almost as if he feared interruption. But what chef would interrupt while his praises were being sung?

"The kraken was also … good. Was that honey and vinegar you used as the marinade? How … unusual. Such an interesting way of preparing it. I never would have thought of mixing the two, and yet they came together … quite well."

Honey and vinegar?

My own battle against the kraken in preparation for this night had been decidedly less successful than that of the guest of honour—unlike Perseus, I had been defeated once again. And so, very reluctantly, I had engaged Castor for the job, giving him firm instructions to prepare the kraken as simply as possible. To avoid, at all costs, any sort of improvisation. A little olive oil, a sprinkling of salt. Nothing more. I had not mentioned either honey or vinegar. I ground my teeth together even as I continued to smile at my employer.

"And wherever did you find red mullets? Great Zeus Himself, those were a lovely treat! But my slaves tell me there's nothing but kraken at the market these days?" It was almost a question.

"Surely you would not have me divulge trade secrets?" I murmured evasively.

"Ah." Archestratus was worldly enough to be unsurprised, though he did seem a little disappointed. "But of course," he assured me. "It is a secret of chefs. Well. A fine meal! You will be hearing from me again. Often, I would say. A fine meal. I cannot remember a feast I enjoyed so—"

"Zeus Almighty! Dude, he gets the point already." A voice behind me spoke up.

Startled, I turned and found myself looking straight into the eyes of Perseus, son of Zeus. He, too, had risen to his feet, though it was not customary for guests to do so. And then he surprised me further by snatching up my hand and pumping it enthusiastically.

"Most awesome eats!" he enthused, doing nothing to suppress the loud belch that followed. "Those rabbits were epic, dude! You totally killed that meal! Never thought I'd find grindage like that in Greece."

The other dinner guests looked affronted, though whether by his ill-bred comment or his atrocious accent I could not tell. Perseus was oblivious to them.

"But ..." He paused and examined me closely. His eyes, I noted, were as golden as his long feathery hair. The strap of a rather weathered-looking brown satchel cut across his chest. "Hey, dude, you don't *look* Greek!"

"I ... I'm not." I shook my head. "I hail from Lydia. Sipylus, to be precise."

"Sipylus?" His golden eyebrows drew together. "Man, you want to go to the priests for that. Sounds like somethin' you get in a brothel." He brayed with laughter at his own wit. Several of the other guests winced at the sound.

"Huh," he mused aloud. "I never met anyone from Lydia before."

It was as good an opening as I was likely to get. I took a breath. "And yet, we share kin," I told him.

"Kin?" he asked.

Just then, the serving slaves bustled in with the last of the second tables, the wine steward and his slaves right behind them.

I was annoyed. I'd wanted the entire company to hear what I had to say, but with the advent of more food and drink, conversation had started up again around us and the room was noisy.

"Your father was my grandfather," I answered loudly.

Nobody appeared to have heard.

Perseus, himself, was silent for a brief moment as he absorbed the information, then the golden eyes widened in delight. "No way! Really? Your granddad? You're my frickin' *nephew*?"

Nephew? Somehow, I had not thought the relationship through in that manner.

Shouting with laughter, Perseus crushed me in a rough embrace. His satchel swung around to thump me in the side. "Ha! Come here and give your old uncle a hug, dude. Even though I've got to be, what, twenty, thirty years younger 'n you."

"Surely, not quite that much," I said a little breathlessly as he squeezed the air from my lungs.

But Perseus wasn't listening. "Whoa. That was epic, dude. You, like, totally blew my mind!" He put both hands to the side of his head as if to keep his brain from exploding outwards. He laughed. "I dunno why I'm so psyched. His Great Zeusness always had a thing for the ladies. I probably got nephews and nieces all over the frickin' Aegean."

Conversation still swirled around us, the other guests apparently oblivious to our interaction.

"But seriously, dude." He leaned in, smiling conspiratorially. His teeth seemed too white against his tanned face. His breath reeked of wine. "I totally thought you were going to say we were kin through my mom."

"Your ... mother?"

He shrugged. "Hey, I could roll with it. Always thought she must've been insanely hot in her day." He winked and wriggled his hips lasciviously.

I stared at him, shocked that he would speak publicly of his mother in such a way.

"Oh, yeah," he continued with the air of one telling a well-worn story. "When old King Polydektes came sniffing around, she wasn't exactly slappin' his hands down, was she? And when he sent me out for a Gorgon's head in the middle of the night?" He raised his hands in the air and shrugged. "Well, I didn't hear anybody beggin' me not to go. Still, I'm cool with it. Everything turned out totally awesome in the end. And besides, when you get right down to it ... DEAD ANT!"

He shouted the last two words, and before I could even blink in confusion, every man in the room was suddenly throwing himself to the floor.

They lay on their backs, all the dignitaries of Athens, arms and legs stuck up stiffly in the air, the folds of their chitons falling back to expose knife-sharp elbows and aging, knobby knees. As I stood there with my mouth hanging open, the golden Perseus chortled with laughter.

"Ah, ah, ah!" He waggled a chastising finger at one of the guests. "Way slow, Xenophon! Gotta live the consequences, Little Ant!" Chuckling with delight, he skipped over to the man—a thin, elderly individual still lying prone on the tiled floor—and held a brimming wine cup high above his head.

"Bottoms up, dude!" he sang out. And then as I watched,

appalled, he tipped the contents of the cup into the man's open mouth.

The man—Xenophon—choked and coughed, most of the wine running down his face and spilling on his chiton. Around him, the other guests were being hoisted to their feet by slaves whose eyes were as downcast as their mouths were strangely silent. Now I could see that several of the guests had wine stains around their necks, as if they, too, had had cups of wine poured on their faces.

Great gods, how long had they been playing this "game"?

There were a few poorly suppressed groans as everyone resettled themselves and began rearranging their chitons. False smiles were pasted gamely onto unhappy faces. And then, just as Xenophon's slave managed to get him shakily to his feet, Perseus yelled "Dead Ant" again and they were all forced to fling themselves down once more.

"Ha! Dude, I *love* being the Ant Master!" he told me, his eyes sparkling with mischief and merriment. "It's insanely cool! Can you believe they never heard of Dead Ant before?"

"Shocking," I murmured, exchanging a sidelong glance with Archestratus. He did not look happy.

It had been Archestratus's job, as host, to hire the best chef available (he had), to ensure both he and his slaves were clean and well-groomed (they were), and to provide amusements in the form of refined conversation, pleasant music, and feminine charms. He had done this as well. Even now the city's most talented dancers and flute girls waited in the courtyard to be called in, and a cithara player—again, the best Athens had to offer—had been ensconced in a corner of the andron (though he'd given up all pretense of playing, and was instead taking in the proceedings with much widened eyes).

Archestratus's symposion ought to have been one of elegant and refined entertainments. And yet, men who might have enjoyed civilized games of kottabos in their distant youth were pretending to be dead ants on the floor. All for the great Perseus, Gorgon Slayer, Kraken Killer, and Hero of the Aegean.

The entire time I had been preparing the feast, the slaves had said nothing of what was going on in the andron, but I had assumed this was because there was nothing to report. In retrospect, I should have realized that Archestratus's slaves had been unusually tight-lipped—especially when the guest of honour was a hero of Perseus's stature.

But there was nothing remotely heroic about this symposion.

I felt a surge of pity for Archestratus. It would have been unpardonably rude to refuse such an exalted guest anything, and yet, from the pinched look on my client's face, I could see that he was seriously considering doing so. His dinner party, once considered the social event of the season, would henceforth be known as a debacle, a disaster forever tied to his name.

And what of myself? How closely would the chef be associated with such a catastrophe? All too closely, I feared. My chest felt tight. The air was hot and close. Why, why had I said anything to Perseus about our shared relation? This was what I got for trying to finesse my way around the sin of hubris.

One of the guests groaned audibly. They were all going to be very sore on the morrow. The young hero, however, was oblivious to their predicament, chortling with glee as he poured wine all over another hapless "ant."

"Dude!" he shouted as I made to move off. "Where're you going?"

"I ... uh, back to the kitchen."

"Aw, don't go yet. We're just gettin' started!"

"I must," I stammered. "Forgive me. My ... my apologies."

But Perseus had been distracted. "Whoa, what do you think you're doing, Little Ant? Did I say you could get up? Oh, no, Little Ant! The Ant Master's not through with you yet!"

With the hero thus occupied, I turned and fled, the sound of his obnoxious laugh ringing in my ears. I stopped in the courtyard, pausing to take several steadying breaths.

"Are we to go in, then?"

I spun around and saw one of the flute girls, looking bored as she lounged on a courtyard bench. She was leaning back on her arms, and as I looked at her, she pouted and stretched, thrusting her impressive chest forward suggestively.

"At once," I told her. And with a snap of my fingers, I sent in all the dancers and flute girls. Perhaps they would distract Perseus from torturing his dinner mates any further. It was all I could do. It did not seem enough.

As I returned to the kitchen, only two thoughts were in my mind. The first was: what effect would this evening's events have on my career? And the second was: how, by all the gods on Mount Olympus, could I be related to *that*?

Drinking Games for Dummies

You've got your dress chiton, you've memorized your Homer, you've even got your slave fluffed and buffed and ready to sit at your feet, but how well do you know your drinking games? Don't get caught red-faced at a symposion! EUKRATES is here to help with these easy step-by-step instructions.

SCROLL #237 — HOW TO PLAY KOTTABOS

Step One: Recline on your dining couch with your slave behind you. Drink up your wine, but don't drain your kylix. You've got to have a few drops to flick in order to play.

Step Two: Using only your right hand, flick the dregs of your wine at the appropriate target (usually a bronze lamp stand with small discs balanced on poles). Be sure to remain in a reclining position! Only Spartans sit up to play kottabos. To be successful, the player must knock the discs off the stand in such a way that they make a bell-like sound. This is only possible if your wine does not break into multiple drops while flying through the air. Practice makes perfect, so be sure to try this at home a few times before you head out.

Variation #1: The target is a bowl of water with smaller bowls floating in it. In this case, the players must try to sink the floaters.

Variation #2: This variation is usually played towards the end of the evening. The targets are your fellow dinner guests. To be successful, the player must hit the target roundly, preferably in the face. It may be wise to hold back until your host announces or approves this variation. Neglecting to do so could result in fewer future dinner invitations.

COMING SOON!! Eukrates's *Drinking Games for Dummies*
SCROLL #458—HOW TO PLAY "DEAD ANT"

Chapter 9

"A chef who cooks for the great Perseus should have a nice chiton," Hermogenes observed a little too loudly. "The *nephew* of the great—"

"Don't." I clipped the word off, before adding in an undertone, "I'm not joking. The less said about that, the better."

Hermogenes fell silent. After last night, even he couldn't argue the point.

The addition of flute girls and dancers had succeeded in distracting the hero from his game of Dead Ant, although, from what the house slaves told us later, few of the other guests were in any shape to avail themselves of the ladies' charms. In fact, all of Archestratus's friends had fled the party as soon as decently possible. Most had required the assistance of their slaves to stagger out the door.

While his illustrious house guest had been busy with his

third flute girl, Archestratus, realizing who had sent in the women, demonstrated once again his refined nature by sending a slave to the kitchen to slip me another, much more generous tip. There was, however, no further mention of future contracts. I suspected it might be quite some time before Archestratus would be able to bring himself to entertain once more.

And so the next morning found Hermogenes and me strolling through the Agora, our pouches happily full of coins, looking for chitons, contracts, and the latest culinary gossip.

Athenians are obsessed with food. Nowhere is this more apparent than at the market, where one can shop for a new pair of boots while hearing all about the suckling pig that Kresilas prepared for Parmenides, who, upon tasting it, proclaimed it as flavourful as an old cloak. Or about the plump thrushes Zeno had promised Anytus, which, when roasted up, turned out to be scrawny, meatless things, air having been blown into their lungs to make them look plumper. Or about the angel shark that Lycon had neglected to skin, even though the scales of that fish are rough enough to polish wood. I listened carefully to all the accounts. When one makes one's living preparing food, one must keep track of what the other chefs are cooking—and for whom.

There was a most gratifying moment early on when I overheard a mouth-watering description of the striped red mullet I had prepared for Archestratus. I did not recognize the men who were discussing it, but it was clear from their talk that they were impressed by the ingenuity of my dish—as well as by the fact that I had managed to secure red mullet at all in this kraken-dominated market. There was no mention of the guest of honour.

A considerably less gratifying moment came when we saw Mithaecus and his sycophants by the cheese sellers' shops. The Sicilian was sporting his trademark yellow chiton (his *brand*, as Hermogenes would have it), and both he and his disciples carried utensil-laden baskets in their arms. They swept through the Agora, noses high in the air, announcing by their very body language that they were on their way to an Important Contract. I felt a sharp stab of jealousy at the sight. Despite being the superior chef, I did not have any wealthy clients at the moment. As they passed us, for a brief moment my eyes met those of Mithaecus, though I quickly averted my gaze with a disdainful sniff. I assume he did much the same. He and I had gone far beyond exchanging casual insults in the Agora. Our respective disciples, however, glared fiercely at each other until our paths diverged.

There was plenty of market gossip that morning surrounding The Sicilian and his chances of winning the upcoming Bronze Chef competition, including some speculation as to why he, apparently, had not yet managed to secure a sponsor. But there was other news about the competition as well.

"Two more chefs have now entered their names for the inaugural Bronze Chef competition!" Hadinos, the market crier, announced in his booming voice.

I touched Hermogenes's arm lightly and we stopped to listen.

"This very morning, Chef Laches of Athens has submitted his name."

Chef Laches? I'd never heard of the man. I looked at

Hermogenes for clarification, but he just shrugged and shook his head. An unknown, then, and therefore probably not a serious contender.

"And Chef Laches is not the only one to submit his name for the match," Hadinos bellowed. "Chef Mediokrates of Thebes has also put his name forward. This makes three chefs so far, but there will be many more before city council makes their selection. For those of you who do not know, there will be four chefs chosen from among the entrants. Their names will be announced five days before the match. Five judges will also be named, but the identity of these judges will only be revealed at the competition itself—along with the mysterious Secret Ingredient. The Bronze Chef competition will be held in the Theatre of Dionysus on the twenty-seventh day of Pyanepsion in honour of Persephone Chthonia, Queen of the Underworld and Bringer of Fruit."

As the crier went on to other, less interesting news, I tuned him out, turning my attention instead to the buzz of speculation that rose around us at this new information.

"That Sicilian'll wipe the floor with 'em," one voice said.

"Aye, and without a breaking a sweat neither."

After only a few moments, it became clear that most believed Mithaecus would have no difficulty defeating the new contenders, should he be selected.

"Well sure, even Mithaecus should be able to beat a chef called Mediokrates," Hermogenes observed as we moved off.

I smiled in agreement, but I must admit, it rankled that I was not in a position to submit my own name for the Bronze

Chef. If Mithaecus and Mediokrates were the best examples of the competition, then I would have no trouble at all in winning the match. If only kraken were not destined to be the "secret" ingredient!

I wrapped my cloak more tightly around my shoulders and sighed heavily.

It was while listening to the description of an uninspired feast prepared by this Mediokrates of Thebes (who had to be the most average cook in the city, judging from his menu choices) that I recalled the actions of another, far more adventurous cook, Castor the Macedonian. "Prepare the kraken as simply as possible," I had told him. I had not specified "No honey" or "No vinegar" for the same reason I hadn't specified "No goat dung." I had not thought it necessary. And while it was true that Archestratus had praised the dish, Castor's kraken had been the only plate to be returned to the kitchen unfinished. A chef knew a dish was a disaster when even the slaves did not polish it off.

Now, Castor had done me an enormous favour by preparing the kraken, but if we were ever to enter into such an arrangement again, I would need to set some very definite ground rules regarding improvisation. There was, I felt, no better time than the present for such a dialogue.

I looked around for my disciple and spied him standing beside another chef's apprentice, who had just finished scrawling "Lycon is a dirty great tosser who doesn't know a fish from his arse" on one of the walls. He and Hermogenes appeared to be having a disagreement over whether "arse" ought to have an "e" on the end of it or not. Much as I was in favour of literacy, I had more pressing concerns at that moment. I pulled my apprentice away from his debate, told him what I required, and together we began to search the Agora for the Macedonian.

We strolled past the statue of Athena Ergane, picked our way through the warren of shops and stalls in the meat and cheese sellers' sector, and finally ducked into the fragrant warmth of Pharsalia's bakery. But Castor was either having a bit of a lie-in, or he was actively avoiding me, for he could be found in none of his usual haunts, and even Pharsalia denied seeing hide or scruffy red hair of him that morning.

It was annoying, but I decided to give it up as a bad job. In the unlikely event that I decided to collaborate with him—or anyone else—again, I would just have to make it very clear that my rules were not to be ignored. Hermogenes and I purchased a couple of freshly baked breakfast rolls from Pharsalia ("Don't worry, luv, they're not dildos till they harden up"), then we set out to accomplish our other task of the day: creating my new brand.

Everything was for sale in the Agora, though not everything was worth the cost of its purchase. Nowhere was this more evident than on the Cloth Sellers Street, where one could obtain everything from the coarsest wool tunic to the finest imported linen chiton at wildly varying prices, depending upon the season, the omens, or the whim of the proprietor.

Strictly speaking, the Cloth Sellers Street was neither a street nor exclusively the domain of cloth merchants, being more of a walkway than a road, and boasting far more brothels than clothing stalls. At this early hour, however, there was little evidence of the street's second industry, as Athenians frowned on young men who visited brothels during the day. In fact, there were only two signs that the street was not devoted exclusively to the selling of clothes. The first was the plethora of small, cluttered shrines to Aphrodite and her associate, Peitho, the goddess of persuasion. The second was the prints left in the dust by the prostitutes' hobnailed boots, which helpfully read "This way for a good time."

The Cloth Sellers Street started out as a dingy refuse-filled alley on the far east side of the Agora. Stone walls were close and crumbling, stained black where countless men relieved themselves after having relieved other needs in the brothels. Here, the poorest shops stood in dank shadow. Used tunics and coarsely woven fabric were piled on rickety tables in an attempt to keep them from the worst of the excrement.

Only the most impecunious or insensible shopper would frequent this end of the district.

The quality of shops began to improve dramatically as the street wound its way into the bright openness of the Agora, spilling out into the market proper to form a statue-lined walkway. These statues were associated with the shops. Each form, from the crudest to the most polished, was lovingly washed and draped in cloth as if it were warm flesh rather than cold stone or metal. Marble gods, bronze heroes, and greying wooden statesmen all provided life-sized models for the latest in seasonal fashion.

This walkway of statues was our destination that morning. It was there that the best of the cloth sellers claimed the choicest locations—those right in the bustle of the Agora, where sunlight could illuminate their wares and fresh air could diffuse the stench of sewage, which wafted up from farther down the street. I should say that this was *my* destination that morning, as I was hoping to obtain a suitable chiton somewhere other than the overpriced Cato's.

Hermogenes was not happy with me.

"What about this one?" I asked, pausing to indicate a clothes stall that appeared to have a wide selection of fairly decent-looking chitons. These were folded and stacked according to colour, earth tones for the most part, though there were one or two that had been dyed a cheerier shade.

Few shoppers were out and about just yet—at least here on the Cloth Sellers Street—and the proprietor was lounging on a stool, sipping his morning cup of wine and chewing placidly on a heel of barley bread. To his left, a wooden statue, soft-edged and grey with age and weathering, displayed a saffron-coloured chiton. A herd of goats clustered around the wooden form, eyeing the shopkeeper's breakfast with hopeful interest. I noticed that the bottom left corner of the saffron chiton had been torn off, sampled, perhaps, by one of the hungry-looking goats.

Hermogenes, caught in the act of stroking his wispy beard yet again, curled his lip disdainfully at the sight and shook his head. "Cato's," he said implacably.

"Cato's is too expensive!" I protested. "I'm not so flush with silver owls that I'm willing to see them all fly the nest at once."

"Cato's," he insisted.

"But—"

"Cato's, Chef."

"Is that what 'the beard' says?" I inquired acidly.

"No. That's what *Zeuxo* says. And that's where we're going."

"She'd never know," I argued. "What's the difference between one of these chitons and one of Cato's—besides several hundred owls, of course?"

Hermogenes pulled his mouth to one side and scowled fiercely at me, refusing to dignify this with a response.

"And when did you start listening to everything Zeuxo says …" I began before trailing off.

I had just spied a familiar golden head emerging from one of the brothels at the far end of the street.

He staggered out from the alley, blinking up at the sky as if astonished to see daylight. Several half-clad prostitutes clung to his arms, rubbing against him like cats in heat. He cupped one's buttock in one hand and tweaked another's breast, beaming down at them all, his brilliant white smile by far the brightest thing in that dark, dank place. He appeared to have lost one of his sandals.

One of the women said something and he chortled, his obnoxious braying laugh carrying easily down the sparsely populated street. I winced at the sound. He still had his satchel slung over his shoulder and he was still wearing his dinner chiton, though even from where I stood, I could see the garment was stained and very much the worse for wear. Its owner, however, looked ready, willing, and more than able to go a few more rounds. Though the rest of Athens was already well into the day, the Great Perseus, it appeared, had not yet finished with his evening.

As he began to look around, I cursed and ducked nimbly behind the statue with the saffron chiton. Uncle or not, Perseus was the last person I cared to see at the moment. I listened, expecting any moment to hear a delighted "Dude!" echoing across the Agora. But when the sounds of morning remained muted, I peered cautiously around the statue and saw that Perseus had turned his attention back to his feminine entertainment. My shoulders dropped, and I breathed a sigh of relief.

The feeling was to be short-lived.

"Ah, Chef Pelops," a dry, dusty-sounding voice said from behind me. "Another contract, is it? Not enough dishes to go 'round? Or perhaps you are in need of more frying pans?"

I drew myself up and spun around, almost bumping into the counter of a small rental services shop. It was a tiny affair, little more than a stall really, pitifully plain with nothing of beauty to recommend it. It stood half-hidden behind the chiton-draped statue, which was why I had neglected to notice it before. If I had, I would have taken care to avoid the place—and the man who owned it. I should have remembered that Meidias possessed a perpetual lease for the spot. He'd been setting up his stall there since before I moved to Athens. I really ought to have stopped at Tyche's shrine, I thought then. It seemed unlucky in the extreme to run into both my sworn enemies in a single morning.

Meidias was one of the wealthier men in Athens, though one would never have known it to look at him or his shop. He was too mingy to pay for an attractive market stall (or a better location), and too cheap to pay for a decent slave to man it. His slaves tended to die off on a regular basis, either from ill-use and neglect, or simply because he'd purchased them discounted due to their failing health and the little time left to them. Another slave must have fallen recently, for Meidias, who was usually holed up in one of his warehouses polishing his coins, was seated behind the counter of his squalid stall, two of his less intelligent, muscle-bound goons flanking him.

His appearance was as dry and colourless as his voice. He would scarcely rate a second glance were it not for the enormous silver caduceus that hung around his neck, the symbol of trade and, not coincidentally, thievery.

Last summer, I had made the mistake of renting a set of dishes from him. I was cooking for a large symposion and found myself in need of the extra tableware. But the party had degenerated into a drunken orgy, with the participants taking it into their heads that they were on a warship in stormy seas. Believing, in their inebriated state, that they needed to dump the ballast in order to survive, they had tossed most of the household items into the street. The partygoers had survived; the hired dishes had not.

I had fully intended to pay Meidias back, but before I could do so, The Sicilian publicly accused me of sacrilege and, for various reasons, most of Athens believed his slanderous charges. I lost all my contracts and, therefore, all means to settle my debt with Meidias. He made his feelings about this quite clear by setting his goons on Hermogenes. My disciple was a slave then, with no rights of his own, and Meidias's thugs had administered a savage beating. Hermogenes still bore the scars.

"No dishes?" Meidias said now, when I did not answer.

"Perhaps some table linens, then? I have some very fine ones newly arrived from Aegypt. The highest quality, though naturally the cost of their rental reflects this."

"I don't think so, Meidias," I replied coldly. "Your prices are too high for me."

I glanced down at Hermogenes. His face had reddened at the sight of Meidias, the scars standing out vivid purple against his angry flush.

Meidias's dead eyes flicked to Hermogenes, then back to me. "The cost of doing business." He waved it off with an indifferent gesture. Behind him, his goons smirked and elbowed each other.

"I shall do *my* business elsewhere," I said, my lip curling.

"As you will," he replied with another dismissive wave. "You know where to find my shop if you change your mind."

"Yeah, right by the goat shit," Hermogenes snarled, unable to restrain himself.

The goons frowned and shifted their feet. One took a step forward, but Meidias gestured him back with a sharp snap of his fingers.

"You ought to do something about your slave's tongue," Meidias told me, his mouth thin. "It's liable to get him into trouble some day."

"I'm not a slave! I'm a free man, bog eyes!" Hermogenes flared, rising to the balls of his feet. Quickly, I clamped my hand down on his shoulder. His scrawny arms had come up, fists raised belligerently, his whole body straining toward Meidias.

But the shop owner, unimpressed, was already looking away. Sighing in boredom, he pulled out a money box from under the counter and began idly counting the coins, completely ignoring our presence.

"Come." I steered Hermogenes away firmly. I could feel him quivering under my hand. "It's not worth it."

"But—"

"No, Hermogenes."

Implacable, I continued to march him away. Past the hungry goats, past the statue in its saffron chiton, down past the other clothing shops. The morning crowds closed in behind us.

"*Chef!*" he cried despairingly.

"No," I said again.

He cursed fiercely under his breath, and I stopped and pulled him to one side, taking care not to release his arm. He kicked at the road dust in savage fury, his head lowered so I couldn't see his expression.

I regarded his mop of unruly curls for a moment, then sighed. "Look," I began quietly. "I *know* how you feel about Meidias. But this isn't the way, Hermogenes. His men are strong, and they're mean. They're both three times your size. You'd be flattened in an instant."

"So that's it?" Hermogenes spat out. He still wouldn't look at me. "He sends those dirty great bastards to beat me half to death, and you're just going to let him off, then?" Under his anger, the note of anguished betrayal was almost tangible.

"That is *not* what I said," I told him, and something in my tone gave him pause.

He stopped struggling and looked up at me. His eyes were bright with unshed tears.

I inhaled a deep breath and let it out slowly.

"I have not been in the habit of allowing lesser men to treat me or mine in such a way," I told him. "And I have no intention of starting now. I have not forgotten what Meidias has done. I owed him money, yes, but my payment was not so late—or so large—that he was justified in setting his thugs on you. He was making a point that did not need to be made, and I have not forgotten this. Indeed, I see the scars on your face every day, and I *cannot* forget. The scales of Astraia are unbalanced, and I promise you, Hermogenes, some day, somehow, I will rectify that. And on that day, Nemesis herself shall lend me strength and purpose."

For a long moment, I held his gaze without speaking.

"I promise you," I repeated.

He stared at me, his dark eyes unreadable. Then all at once, I felt the fight go out of him. His shoulders drooped, he heaved an unhappy sigh, and nodded.

Believing me.

Trusting me.

I swallowed past a sudden tightness in my throat.

"Where to now, Chef?" he asked, much subdued.

"Why, to Cato's Chitons, of course," I told him in feigned surprise.

He blinked up at me disbelief. "But you ... I thought ... I didn't ..."

"Come, come, Hermogenes," I said lightly. "You said it your-self. Zeuxo told us to go to Cato's. And we can't have Zeuxo unhappy with us, can we?"

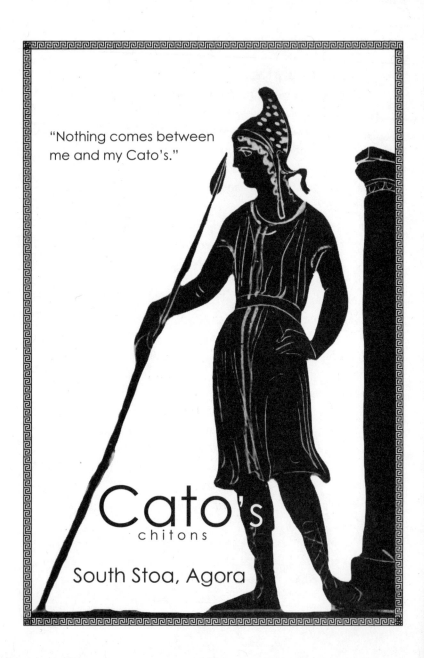

"Nothing comes between me and my Cato's."

Cato's
chitons

South Stoa, Agora

Chapter 10

Cato, according to my disciple, had never maintained a shop near the other cloth sellers, having recognized early on the perquisites of establishing a "more exclusive market presence" (Hermogenes's words, obviously). That the shop owner preferred boys over women and did not care for prostitutes may have had something to do with it too, though Hermogenes admitted that this could have just been market gossip.

"He used to be set up near the Altar of the Twelve Gods," my disciple informed me brightly. His attitude, downcast after the encounter with Meidias, was rapidly improving with the promise of a shopping excursion at the famous Cato's Chitons. "Until the South Stoa opened up for trade, that is. Cracking building, that South Stoa."

"It is lovely," I said somewhat absently. I had been distracted by the sight of a small feminine figure. She was strolling past the

South Stoa, market basket over her arm. Her face was turned away from me, but her dark hair was long and unfashionably straight, and her hands were tanned.

It was her! The woman from the Agora. The one with those remarkable eyes. But just as I opened my mouth to tell Hermogenes to wait a moment, she turned towards me and I saw only coarse features and dull, dark eyes. My shoulders slumped. It was not the same woman.

"And what a brilliant move on his part, yeah?" Hermogenes had continued, oblivious.

"It was," I murmured, not really paying attention to his words. I was a little surprised at the depth of my disappointment. I had all but forgotten the woman. Why should I be bothered by her absence now?

"He knows what he's about, that one," Hermogenes was saying. "Couldn't have picked a better spot in the whole city. And he moved the Theseus too, of course. I mean, he couldn't leave *him* behind."

I shook off my odd regret and gave my full attention to my disciple. "Indeed not," I agreed with a small smile. "What would Cato's be without his Theseus?"

Cato's bronze Theseus was one of the most noted statues in Athens, albeit more for its clothing than for the artistry that had gone into its making—though this, too, was superior. The hero of Athens stood outside Cato's shop by the South Stoa's outer colonnades, arms poised at his side, one foot slightly forward, head turned to the right as if scanning the horizon for stray Minotaurs. Every day, Cato's slaves washed and dressed him, stylishly draping his magnificent metal physique in one of the shop's finest linen chitons. Cato had been outfitting this bronze hero for years now, and any fashion trends—from colours to patterns to borders to ways of tying a belt—were first seen here. All Athenian fashionistas took their cue from Cato's displays.

Today, Theseus was sporting a pale, sea-green number edged with a darker green border. The green contrasted nicely with the burnished bronze of the statue and, as befit a son of Poseidon, the border of the garment had been embroidered in a repeating pattern of waves. The chiton was artfully tied, pinned at the shoulders with polished bronze fibulae. The cloth had been carefully arranged so that its border fell in even folds, further enhancing the impression of flowing water. And every speck of dust, every splotch of bird droppings—the bane of statues everywhere—had been assiduously wiped clean by one of Cato's many well-trained slaves. No goats would dare mill around this statue!

"Now, *this* is more the thing," my disciple breathed, openly admiring the Theseus as we mounted the steps to the Stoa.

I regarded the statue's chiton with somewhat less enthusiasm. All those waves reminded me of the open sea, and the open sea reminded me of Poseidon, and that reminded me of why I needed a "brand" in the first place.

"No waves," I said, so firmly that it checked Hermogenes's steps, though he did not tear his eyes from the statue.

But the pull of Cato's quickly reasserted itself, and he nodded absently, still drinking in the sight of the bronze Theseus. "No waves," he agreed, and we stepped into the sun-striped shadows of the South Stoa.

Cato himself greeted us at the entrance to his shop. "Good day to you," he murmured in a cultured tone of voice. "You are most well come." And with exquisite precision, he bowed his head just enough to demonstrate courtesy without fawning.

"I require new clothing," I informed him, infusing my tone with a lofty note I'd dredged up from my past. If I was going to pay a small fortune for a chiton, I wanted the best possible service. "I am looking for something subtle rather than garish." I flicked my fingers distastefully at a man strolling by in a bright yellow chiton. It was almost, but not quite, the same shade of yellow favoured by Mithaecus. "And it must be the finest quality."

"Of course, sir." He inclined his head again. The very picture of dignity and refinement.

His hair and beard were short, both combed and perfumed, the strands of white amongst the dark adding a further air of distinction to his appearance. He wore a green chiton identical to the one displayed on the Theseus, though his shoulder pins, I noted, were gold rather than bronze, and a matching band kept his hair in place. Uncomfortably conscious of my unscented hair and my own, inferior garment, I pulled my haughtiness around me like a cloak and made to sweep past him.

With a coolly professional smile, Cato ushered me into his shop between the inner and outer colonnades, refraining either through comment or glance from offering any judgment regarding my attire or my personal grooming habits. My appreciation for his discretion rose.

The front of the shop was open save for a line of small trees in painted stone pots which delineated the space. On either side of this stood a series of marble statues, all heroically proportioned men in various athletic poses, each displaying a different and exquisitely tasteful chiton.

Occupying the centre of the space was a raised dais with three dining couches where prospective clients could recline in comfort while Cato's handsome young slaves modelled the latest fashions. Bowls of fragrant flowers freshened the air, while bronze braziers, placed strategically around the couches, served to warm the space. The back of the shop was concealed behind a deep blue curtain.

I had to hide my surprise when a slave appeared at my feet and began washing them as if I were a guest at a symposion. It was not an unpleasant experience, but it struck me that Cato must have a wealthy clientele, indeed, if they expected this level of pampering when visiting the shops. And Athenians called Persians decadent! But I carefully filed the information away for further reflection. After all, it was entirely possible that some— or indeed, all—of Cato's demanding customers might be in need of the services of a fine chef. Perhaps Zeuxo's insistence on Cato's Chitons had some merit after all.

After the slave had patted my feet dry with a cloth, he led me to one of the cushioned dining couches. With uncustomary silence, Hermogenes assumed a standing position behind me, hovering in readiness should I require his assistance, though I could tell at a glance that his shrewd eyes were busily taking in all the sights of our surroundings. Surreptitiously, I ran my fingertips over the fabric on the cushions, impressed by both the softness and the fine weave. If Cato's chitons were fashioned of similar stuff, then perhaps they would be worth what I was clearly going to have to pay for them.

Cato waited until I was settled before lowering himself on the opposite couch. A slave, almost as well turned out as his master, brought us small cups of cool wine flavoured with mint and honey. A young boy brought a fruit bowl, the pears still glistening with beads of water from their washing.

"Did you have something specific in mind?" Cato inquired as I accepted a pear.

"I require several chitons," I told him. "For my professional as well as my personal wear. I am a chef."

"Please." He halted me with a warm smile. "You need no introduction."

"Indeed?" I hid my surprise behind the pear. It was sweet and juicy, perfectly ripe.

"But of course," Cato replied, allowing the smile to colour his tone. "All of Athens has heard of the great Pelops of Lydia."

"I see," I said, recovering my aplomb. "Well, perhaps all of Athens has *heard* of me, but I would like all of Athens to *recognize* me when they see me. This—" I lifted a corner of my chiton between my finger and thumb, permitting my disdain for it to show. It really was a shamefully inferior garment. I used to be a prince. When, and how, had I fallen so far? "This is not recognizable. And I'm sure I need not tell you, it is hardly the garb of a successful man."

"I am here but to serve," Cato assured me solemnly.

"Then I place myself in your most capable hands."

And so, I entered into the business of creating a brand for myself.

For the rest of that morning, I sipped Cato's excellent wine, nibbled on his excellent pears, and reclined on his excellent pillows as one after another superbly fit youth emerged from behind the back curtain to twirl past me in a veritable rainbow array of chitons.

Each chiton had to be carefully considered, its merits pointed out and debated, its deficiencies—very few of these—remarked upon. It quickly became clear that Hermogenes held definite opinions on the matter and, more importantly, that I was willing to bow to his decisions. Cato didn't bat an eyelash at this, which led me to believe that I was not the only one of his clients whose slave—or, in my case, disciple—was responsible for the task of dressing him.

By the time Cato and Hermogenes began arguing over whether a patterned border was more tasteful than a plain one, Hermogenes had emerged from behind the dining couch to better converse with the chiton seller, although, like a good disciple, he did not presume to sit in my presence.

I selected a bunch of fat grapes from the freshly replenished fruit bowl and leaned back against the cushions to enjoy them. In some ways, it felt as though I had travelled back in time, back to the days of my youth, when such pampering was part of my everyday existence. I popped a grape into my mouth and fantasized about palaces and luxury and an easier way of life.

After a while, I began to notice that although I had clearly absented myself from much of the debate, Cato kept casting sidelong glances at me. Perhaps he was merely assuring himself of my continued comfort and approval, but it struck me as a bit odd, and I found myself slightly uncomfortable under his regard, though nothing in his manner was at all accusing or threatening.

I was obliged to reenter the discussion in order to nix the gorgeous purple-red chiton that Hermogenes favoured, not because I did not care for the colour, but because the price was so far beyond my means, even a single chiton would have bankrupted me for months.

"The dye is costly," Cato explained, as a beardless youth modelled the purple outfit.

Like the others before him, the blond slave sashayed up to me like a hetaera, casting long-lashed looks my way. I ignored him as I had the other models, being far more interested in clothing than in coy youths.

"Made from the shells of a sea snail found only in the eastern Aegean," Cato informed us. "It is a highly prized colour. It does not fade, you see. In sunlight, it only becomes brighter and more intense. It takes many snails to make the dye, hence the price."

"It is very expensive," Hermogenes admitted reluctantly, though he continued to stare at the chiton with a frankly acquisitive eye.

"Perhaps," Cato conceded, stroking his oiled beard. "But you must remember, the shells of twelve thousand snails are required to colour the mere trim of a single garment."

"And I would need to cook ten times that many snails in order to afford it," I interrupted firmly before any negotiations could get under way. "Though it pains me to say it, I think we must rule out the purple."

"Of course," Cato said, without allowing his disappointment to show—something Hermogenes attempted but did not quite manage.

And so there were more chitons to consider. And more smooth-cheeked youths casting more longing glances my way. Despite the superior wine, the entire experience was beginning to become tiresome. I found myself wondering if Cato's models were instructed to moon after prospective clients, for I had never been the subject of such attentions before and I certainly did not possess the fame to warrant it now. I found it not a little irritating.

Contemplation of fame (and lack thereof) led naturally to reflection on the previous evening's events—in particular to the actions of my famous and most unorthodox uncle. Youthful exuberance was one thing, but Perseus's behaviour was quite another. How could Zeus have fathered such a lout? And what on earth had possessed me to point out our connection—in front of the entire party, no less? Cashing in on my relationship with Perseus and his divine father seemed a paltry excuse in the light of day. Could it be that foul hubris ran in my family?

I was still hoping that my ill-conceived revelation had been lost among the other concerns of the evening. It was entirely possible that the guests—and their host—had been far too distracted or too inebriated to clearly recall anything I might have said.

But their slaves will remember, an inner voice reminded me. *Slaves remember everything.*

Firmly I dismissed the thought as soon as it occurred to me. The slaves had all been far too occupied with the entrance of second tables—and with propping their masters up after several rounds of Dead Ant. And besides, none of them—citizen or slave—had treated me any differently for the rest of the evening. Surely, such would not have been the case had anyone overheard my conversation with Perseus.

Moodily, I began to fidget.

It took almost an hour longer, but Hermogenes and Cato finally settled on a chiton of Miletan wool so fine it might have been linen. It had been dyed the clear blue of an autumn sky, which Hermogenes assured me matched my eyes while providing a pleasing contrast to my dark hair. Even more importantly—at least, to Hermogenes's marketing-obsessed mind—it was a shade of blue rarely seen on the streets of Athens, as the indigo used in the dying process was a rare import from far-eastern Persia and only recently available here. If nothing else, I would stand out in a crowd, which, my disciple explained, was exactly the point.

I came to my feet and allowed them to garb me. Cato blinked in surprise when I bared my ivory shoulder, but with exquisite discretion he did not comment on it. My esteem for him rose.

The cloth was soft against my skin and I could not help running my fingers voluptuously through its sleek folds. A slave whisked away my old chiton to package it up, his nose flaring at having to handle such an inferior piece of cloth. I watched it go without regret, absently smoothing the folds of the blue chiton. Enlivening the garment was a pale cream border, finely stitched in the same blue with a handsome motif of olive leaves. This was a very fine garment, indeed. I felt like … a prince. Or, at the very least, a successful man. Perhaps even a man in demand.

"The chiton makes the man, they always say," Hermogenes observed, stroking his beard sagely as he and Cato stood back to admire their handiwork. At some point in our negotiations, his speech had taken on Cato's more refined tones, and I suppressed a grin upon hearing it.

"Truly," Cato agreed with a satisfied smile. "In my experience, the nude rarely have influence on society."

"Except, of course, as an amusing diversion for the rest of us," my disciple added.

The two of them chuckled like a pair of old cronies.

"Well, much more than clothing has gone into the making of this particular man," I said dryly, interrupting their fun.

Hermogenes flashed me an impudent grin, and Cato quickly followed with a smile, though he could not know of what I spoke. After all, murderous fathers, overly helpful gods, and divinely acquired culinary skills were not the sort of thing one discussed with one's clothier.

"Although," I conceded, "the chiton is a very fine one. Quite perfect, really."

Cato smiled again, more genuinely this time.

Entering into the spirit of it all, I ordered another identical chiton and a matching one in paler blue for Hermogenes.

"If the Chef is well dressed, then so, too, should the disciple be," I told him as he tried to protest, though his pleased blush belied any resistance he offered. "And, given Ansandra's skill at the loom, we're far better off to buy you a chiton here."

Cato murmured something about generosity and, with a snap of his fingers, directed one of his slaves to begin tallying up the cost. The total brought on a slight coughing fit, but at a hard stare from Hermogenes, I got myself under control and counted out the owls. In truth, it cost less than I had anticipated. Still, my coin pouch was a thin shadow of itself by the time I'd finished. But with every movement, the folds of fine wool brushed against my skin as softly as a woman's touch, and I could not regret the extravagance.

"May I take this opportunity to wish you all the best at the Bronze Chef competition?" Cato said as he bade me good day. "Truly, the event shall be the highlight of the season—especially with one such as yourself as a contender."

I thanked him, surprised and gratified by his well-wishing, though I refrained from mentioning that I had not yet and likely would not put my name forward for the competition— not unless, by some miracle, Poseidon and I suddenly came to terms, and I certainly wasn't holding my breath for that.

Strolling back through the Agora, I was further surprised at the number of warm greetings afforded me by men who were, at best, only casual acquaintances, some clearly even going out of their way to exchange pleasantries with me.

"Chef Pelops! A fine day to you."

"Greetings, Chef. A beautiful afternoon, is it not?"

"How well you look today, Chef Pelops. Off to market, are you? I hear a new shipment of Chian wine has arrived."

By the time a fifth man had acknowledged me along similar lines, Hermogenes had acquired a smugly satisfied smirk.

"See, Chef?" he said, fingering his facial hair yet again, though at least he had stopped imitating Cato's speech mannerisms. "What did I tell you, eh? That's what happens when you have a brand. They recognize you! Now if you'd only let me do something with your hair …"

"Leave my hair out of it," I told him severely. "There's nothing wrong with straight hair. And if you don't start leaving your beard alone, you're going to rub the poor thing right off your face."

Hermogenes lowered his hand with alacrity.

"Given that I've only just purchased the chiton," I continued, "I think it exceedingly implausible that they recognize my 'brand.' More likely word of my red mullet dish has gotten 'round."

But although Hermogenes took my advice about his facial hair, he was oblivious to my logic, and as person after person greeted me like a long-lost friend, he continued to congratulate himself on both his perspicacity and the acuity of his marketing vision.

I did not believe for an instant that a brand could become so quickly recognizable, but it was an indisputable fact that my presence in the Agora was causing a stir for *some* reason. Those striped red mullets really had been one of the best dishes I'd ever prepared. Perhaps the Athenians were finally ready to recognize my superior culinary talents. And now that I was garbed appropriately, perhaps they were ready to recognize *me*.

I stood a little taller, aware as I did so of the fine folds of my new chiton brushing against my calves. Maybe Hermogenes and Cato were right.

Perhaps the chiton did make the man.

Chapter 11

A h, you're joking!" Gorgias was incredulous.

I shook my head, grinning smugly.

"They washed your feet? Like you were some bloody prat at a symposion?"

"They did. And brought wine and fruit. Lovely pears they were, too. Ripe and juicy."

"Bollocks!"

"It's true," I assured him, tapping my lips thoughtfully. "I really must discover his fruit vendor."

Gorgias said something extremely rude. It had never occurred to me that the kraken had even had bollocks—or a specialized tentacle—let alone what one might do with such appendages. A couple of passing bread wives cackled their appreciation. Hermogenes grinned, but Gorgias ignored them all.

We were strolling through the Agora, having met up with

Gorgias on our way home from Cato's. My friend was tricked out in his second-best chiton (which was, I hardly need add, not a patch on my new one), as he had just returned from attending the Assembly.

When Hermogenes and I first spotted him, Gorgias had been much engaged in chastising a somewhat shiftless-looking young man. The reason for this soon became apparent, for as we drew nearer we could see the hangdog expression on the fellow's face and, more tellingly, the bright red smudge on his cloak.

Athenians take their democracy very seriously. When the Assembly meets, all citizens physically able to are expected to attend. Any truants, thinking to avoid the tedium of several hours of blowhards listening to the sound of their own voices, are swept unceremoniously from their comfortable perches in the Agora by council slaves wielding a rope liberally coated with red powder. The evaders' lack of democratic enthusiasm is thus evident for all to see, the crimson stain on their clothing ensuring a hefty fine for shirking public duties, as well as a scornful tongue-lashing by any who cared to administer it.

Gorgias cared very deeply about such things.

Familiar with his democratic ways, we'd waited patiently, watching as he delivered a few final, scathing remarks to the young truant, who then slunk off to lose himself in the shadows. Duty thus discharged, my friend had sauntered over to join us, a wide, white grin splitting his face. Initially, he had been effusive in his admiration of my new chiton, but his appreciation quickly cooled when he heard the details of my treatment at the hands of the famous Cato.

"Bloody wine, indeed!" Gorgias said crossly now. "All I got was water! And nobody was lurking about waiting to buff my sodding toes!"

I preened. "Well, some of us have it …"

He gave me the hairy eyeball, and I grinned, pleased to have gotten a rise out of him. He made a disgusted sound and gestured me onwards.

"Whatever were you doing at Cato's, anyway?" I asked curiously as we inserted ourselves back into the crowd and began to stroll along. "As I recall, you told me he was a poncy little tosser who would … how did you put it? Ah yes, bleed me dry just for a bit of cloth."

Abashed, Gorgias squirmed uncomfortably. "It was Zeuxo's idea," he admitted after a moment. "She wants me smartened up. You know, for the wedding."

It was a punch to the gut. Again.

"I see," I managed to say lightly. "Well, you should have come with me, you could've had your toes scrubbed."

Which distracted him neatly from the subject.

"What is it about you?" he demanded with some irritation. "I've heard of nowt but Chef Pelops since I came out this morning. What have you been up to, then, you jammy bugger?"

"Why? What are they saying?"

Gorgias shrugged. "Summat about red mullets, I think. I've been rushing here and there all morning what with one thing or another. Haven't had a moment to stop and give a proper listen, have I?"

"Ah," I nodded, stroking my chin sagely. "The red mullets.

Yes. That explains it. My reputation is preceding me. The great Chef Pelops, you see, has come up with another signature dish—a truly inspired offering that will bear my name up to the glorious heavens where it so clearly belongs."

"He's full of himself," Gorgias remarked to Hermogenes, jerking his head toward me. "Is he always this unbearable?"

My disciple assumed a long-suffering expression. "You've no idea," he said with a barely suppressed sigh. "And with hair like *that*, no less!"

I looked down my nose at the two of them.

"Mock all you want," I told them loftily. "But who was the one to get his feet washed at Cato's Chitons, despite my *straight* hair?"

"Maybe so," Gorgias shot back. "But at the end of the day, you're still a fussy little tosser, aren't you?"

"Fussy little tosser?" I pretended outrage.

He grinned evilly and gave me a friendly and none-too-gentle clip on the shoulder. Irritated, I poked him back. His smile widened and I could see him preparing to take it further. Another moment and we'd be tussling in the dust like street urchins.

"Enough!" I squawked with rather less dignity than I'd intended. I stepped back and raised my hands in surrender. "Enough, Gorgias. I paid a small fortune for this chiton, I don't want it ruined. What would ... what would Zeuxo say?"

He backed off. "She'd call the both of us a pair of dirty great gits," he admitted ruefully. "Without a speck of sense between us."

"Oh, I think she'd call us something worse than that."

He made a face, his thick, black brows scrunching together. "She probably would at that," he conceded. "She's not a girl to mind her tongue, when she's on about summat."

"Indeed." I nodded agreement, having been on the receiving end of Zeuxo's tongue-lashings.

Gorgias paused, his expression growing serious. "Did you hear that Zeno has put his name in? For the Bronze Chef, I mean."

"Ah, that wanker couldn't heat a pan of water." Hermogenes waved it off before I could respond.

"Maybe so," Gorgias agreed. "But Aristander's not so bad and he's put his name in too." He turned and gave me a frank look. "When are you going to get your name in, then? You can't be leaving it too much longer."

I grimaced. "I know!" Even I could hear the frustration in my voice. "I'm working on it. It's just … well, I'm working on it."

Gorgias nodded once, and thankfully let it drop. He paused a moment, then rolled his shoulders back. "Ah well, if I'm not going to demonstrate my obvious physical superiority, I must take me unwashed feet off to the clay pits. Speaking of a pair of dirty great gits, I've got Strabo and Lais waiting there for me now, and I'll bet you obols to owls they're lolling about with their fingers up their great hairy arses."

"I would not take that bet," I told him.

"Smart man." He laughed. "I'll catch up with you at home then, and leave you to show off your lily white toes to the masses without me. Wouldn't want to be blinded by the glow, would I? Cheers, then. Pelops. Hermogenes."

With that, he strolled off, whistling cheerfully, his step jaunty and carefree. And why wouldn't it be? The man had no worries, except perhaps for motivating his lazy slaves. He had a successful career, his own house, a daughter who loved him, and in a few short months he would marry the most beautiful woman in all of Greece.

For a very brief moment, I hated my best friend.

"And another one come in just after lunch," Irene finished.

"*Four* contracts?"

"Five, if you count the first slave, even though he didn't bring a down payment, but I count him because I've heard of his master and he's not the type to send his slave 'round if he don't mean it."

Hermogenes and I had barely divested ourselves of our cloaks before Irene had pounced upon us with the astonishing news. Bewildered, I shook my head as she began telling me again about each prospective client. Each one of high social standing. Each, it seemed, wealthier than the last. How had they all heard about my red mullet? Or was it possible Hermogenes's brand had worked its marketing magic so quickly? Five contract offers in a single day? It was unheard of.

"And a slave came 'round from that hair shop. Something about a sponsorship for the Bronze Chef."

Hermogenes perked up at this, though he quickly dropped his eyes, feigning disinterest.

"Which hair shop is that?" I inquired, settling my cloak on its hook.

"The one over by the oil sellers. You know, the one with the stupid name. Hair Today Gone Tomorrow, or some such rubbish." She snorted and stepped back to allow us to enter the hallway.

"Bloody silly name for a business, if you ask me," she said. "I'd hold out for a better sponsor if I were you, especially now that you've finally gone and gotten yourself a decent chiton." She flicked a glance at my new clothing, awarding it a sniff of approval before turning and starting down the hall. "Took herself's advice and went to Cato's, did you? Well, that ought to help bring in more custom. Not that you'll need any more help what with everyone suddenly having the notion you're Zeus's grandson—"

"What?" I choked, stopping abruptly. Hermogenes trod on my heels, but I scarcely felt it.

"Zeus's grandson." Irene looked over her shoulder and gave me a superior smirk. "Imagine! The rubbish some people believe!"

"Zeus's *grandson*?" Hermogenes squeaked.

My disciple was far from being a stupid lad. I watched his face as all the clues began falling into place for him, and I could see the exact moment when the full import of Irene's words sank in. Realization dawned, his eyes nearly bugged out of his head, and he made as if to prostrate himself on the hallway floor.

I stopped him with a sharp gesture.

Oblivious to our exchange, Irene had kept walking. "And just think! All of them coming in here hot and bothered at the thought of having the Sky God's grandson cook up a bit of supper for them. Well, I wasn't about to let on any different, was I? Not when saying so brings in that kind of custom. Five offers now and three more wanting a word with you. I'd say the kraken itself spawned me if it brought in that kind of coin. And you'd be wise to do the same. Take my advice, let them think Zeus had at your gran. You'll be set for life."

"Indeed," I said, stretching my lips into a tight smile. "Excellent advice, Irene. Thank you. Thank you for everything. Do let me know if any other offers present themselves, won't you? And now, if you'll excuse us …"

I caught my disciple by his scrawny arm and steered him down the hall, out into the courtyard and across to the kitchen where we could have at least a modicum of privacy. The entire time, I could feel him trembling under my hand.

"Not a word!" I hissed as soon as we were alone.

"But, Chef! Or … *Great Zeus and Hera*, what do I call you now? I don't know what to call a—"

"Chef will be sufficient," I interrupted him. "It is accurate, and truly it means more to me than any other title, divine or otherwise."

"So … it's true then?" His dark eyes were huge, his voice soft and full of wonder. "What Irene said? You're not just having me on?"

I released him, closing my eyes and pinching the bridge of my nose. "No. No, it's true," I sighed.

"I thought … I mean, I knew you were Perseus's nephew. You told me as much yourself last night. But I thought it were through his mum! I never dreamed it would be through his …

dad." He whispered the last word, and I had to catch his arm again before he could sink to his knees.

"Enough of that nonsense!" I ordered, shaking him to emphasize my words. "Yes, Zeus is my grandfather. Tantalus, my father, was his son. And that's how I'm related to Perseus. You'd best come to terms with it. I can't have my disciple falling to his knees every time I pass wind."

Hermogenes stared at the floor, clearly still absorbing the news. Then he looked at me. His face was screwed up in bafflement.

"Why … why didn't you tell me, Chef?" he asked.

I shrugged a little self-consciously. "It's … well, it's not something I care to noise about," I told him.

"But, Chef!" He exclaimed. "The marketing potential alone is worth a bloody fortune!"

"I'm sorry, it was—*what*?"

Pulling away from my grasp, he began pacing the room. "Bollocks!" he swore crossly, waving his arms about. "I wish I'd known before." He shot me an accusatory glare. "Why didn't you tell me?"

I glowered right back at him. Awe and reverence had certainly been short-lived.

Hermogenes continued to frown and pace, sliding me reproachful looks and muttering darkly to himself. "*Poxy close-lipped … couldn't see a marketing opportunity if it bit him on the arse … how does he expect me to work like this*?"

Through it all, I remained silent and still, letting him have his tantrum.

"Okay," he said finally, shaking it off with a visible effort. "Okay, okay." He rubbed his hands together purposefully. "No use crying over spilt wine, then, is it? I can work with this. Your new chiton is blue like the sky, so that's something. Now all we have to do is—"

"Nothing." I interrupted sharply. "We do nothing."

"With Perseus in town and everybody and their dog wanting a piece of him on account of him being ... oh, I don't know, *the son of Zeus*?" His voice rose along with his indignation.

I tried to hush him with a sharp gesture.

He lowered his voice, but not by much. "You don't want anyone to know about your rellies?" he demanded incredulously. "No one's to know you're the grandson of *Zeus*? Well, sod that, Chef! And the ox that brought it! It's too late, isn't it? They *already* know. That's an opportunity, that is! We can't just go wasting it."

"Hermogenes." I stopped him with an admonitory hand. "Hermogenes, I am not going to use this to further my career. I can't! My father was the son of Zeus and he suffered from an acute case of hubris because of it. He *angered* the gods. All of them! I have no intention of following in his footsteps. He ended badly. Very badly indeed."

If, in fact, one could describe the life of someone suffering eternal torment as "ended." Even now, years later, Tantalus stands chained to a tree in the underworld, cursed with everlasting thirst and hunger. Both food and water lie just out of his reach though well within his sight. Despite what he did to me, the thought of his punishment still made me shudder.

"But, Chef!"

"No, Hermogenes. No. Quite apart from the matter of hubris, there is another, much more difficult problem." I took a deep breath and let it out slowly. "Think for a moment, will you? Zeus is my grandfather, but Hera is *not* my grandmother. My grandmother was mortal."

My disciple closed his mouth with a snap, and for a few heartbeats there was silence as the ramifications of that sunk in. Then, "Does Hera know?" he asked intently.

I pinched the bridge of my nose. "Yes," I sighed.

He scowled to himself and started tugging on his nascent beard, his mind busily working the problem.

"Don't bother," I advised wearily. "You know how she feels about this sort of thing. Hera is a wise and fine-looking goddess, but I will do everything I can to stay on the right side of her temper." I chewed my lip for a moment. "Especially because she's already a bit miffed about Mithaecus," I admitted.

"Mithaecus! What does Hera have to do with that pox-ridden wanker?"

"He's her protégé," I told him.

Hermogenes's mouth snapped shut for the second time that day.

I tried to explain. "The way I understand it," I told him, "his mum did Hera a favour—I don't know what it was—and the long and short of it is she's been looking out for him ever since."

Hermogenes thought about that for a moment. "You probably shouldn't have smacked him in the nose then," he observed unhelpfully.

I grimaced my agreement then shrugged. "It's too late to bemoan The Sicilian's broken nose now. The thing is done and cannot be taken back. Indeed, I'm not entirely sure I would want to. It makes no difference."

"But—"

"But I cannot—and I will not—use my connections with Perseus or Zeus to further my own career, not with Hera breathing down my neck. I possess no heroic skills to defend myself, beyond my talents in the kitchen, of course, and I very much doubt they will get me very far should the Queen of the Gods decide to take serious issue with me."

"But, Chef, the whole city knows now. About you and Zeus, I mean."

"Ah yes, but I did not tell them. It's a small distinction, but a vital one. Clearly Perseus has chosen to share the details of our shared lineage. I had no control over that, and even the gods would admit it, however grudgingly. But, if I was to then attempt to capitalize on it …" I wiggled my fingers distastefully. "Then, my young disciple, the waters begin to get very murky indeed."

Hermogenes was quiet for a long while. When he finally spoke up, it was with a question I had not expected.

"Is that why Poseidon's got it in for you?" he asked quietly. "Because of what happened with your dad? Because he angered the gods, like you said?"

And just like that, I was back in the palace at Sipylus.

There were blinding flashes of light. Noise. Voices raised in anger, one apologizing over and over again. A scream of agony. Gods were all around me. I could feel them. The immense weight of their presence was pressing on me, as if the very air itself had grown heavier, more difficult to push in and out of my lungs. My bones ached with it.

I was naked, though I did not know why, glowing with some strange inner light. I lifted my arms to look at my hands. They were glowing too, almost golden. Sparkling as if the stars themselves had gathered beneath my skin. Bemused, I turned my hands this way and that, marvelling at them. They were so beautiful. My left shoulder felt odd, hot and tight. I was aware of a smell, a succulent fragrance. Oregano, garlic, pepper, olive oil. Each one separate and achingly distinct to my newly sensitive nose. There was something else in the mix. A sort of meaty odour, though I could not identify it.

For some reason, I did not wish to.

I was shaking, weak. Words were beyond me. And then, there was a pair of eyes. Greenish-grey, like a storm-tossed ocean. I could not tear my gaze away from them. They watched me with burning, unbridled desire.

I blinked and found myself back in the present again.

"More or less," I told Hermogenes.

"And he's still mad at you?"

"Yes."

"Any chance he'll forgive you?"

"No."

"So there's no point in sacrificing to him, then?"

"No."

"And the Bronze Chef competition?"

"Not likely."

Hermogenes chewed it over for several long moments. I could tell from his expression he wasn't happy. But as I watched, his eyes grew flinty and his thinly bearded chin began to thrust out pugnaciously.

"Right, then," he said, and his voice was firm with resolve. "At least I know what we're dealing with now. I'll sort this, Chef. You'll see. I'll come up with a way to make this work. We'll win that Bronze Chef match. I'm not about to let Poseidon stop us—even if he is a god."

Chapter 12

In truth, Hermogenes need not have worried about the loss of marketing potential. Athens was a city that thrived on information, and under the auspices of Hermes, god of messengers and language, she provided countless opportunities for its dissemination. Slaves were an important part of this, of course, passing on the gossip of the day to their masters, the more scurrilous the news, the better. The market crier Hadinos and his compatriots played their part too, by providing the slaves with the salacious news, if nothing else. But slaves and market criers were not the only means available for communication.

Announcements and accusations were strapped to the railing around the Monument to the Eponymous Heroes, or painted in red on the whitewashed wall opposite. Unadorned stone-carved stelae dictated new fines and laws, while other, more elaborate markers served to inform the populace of religious summons and festivals. Market stalls were festooned with notices, while ragged-edged papyrus chits blew about the streets and alleyways, news or notices of events scribbled on their worn surfaces. And everywhere, scrawled across all and sundry, regardless of its civic importance, there was graffiti.

In this manner, the name Pelops of Lydia could soon be seen all over the city.

For the first time in my career, I found myself able to pick and choose my contracts. Food vendors began offering me wildly improbable bargains just so their product could be associated with me. Offers of sponsorship for the upcoming Bronze Chef competition poured in, though for some reason an inordinate number of these were from hair shops. I suspected Hermogenes's hand in this.

Strangers began acknowledging me in the street, so they could remark to their friends in an offhand fashion, "When I spoke with Chef Pelops the other day …" There was even one oh-so-sweet moment when Hermogenes and I, surrounded by a cluster of admirers, spied Mithaecus and his sycophants sloping furtively past us on their way to whatever paltry second-rate contract awaited them. On The Sicilian's face was a discontented expression, envy and ill humour twisting his features in what was, I must admit, a most satisfactory manner.

I did not venture anywhere without my trademark blue chiton.

The only real problem with my new-found fame was that I could no longer subcontract the kraken portion of my symposion feasts—which was probably just as well, for I did not trust

Castor the Macedonian to follow my instructions. But a paucity of kraken was not an issue for my first few post-revelation clients, as Krysippos had managed to come through once more with the famous striped red mullets.

Krysippos still refused to reveal how he, alone of all the fish-mongers, managed to obtain such fishes, but I could not protest his reticence—especially after he offered me an exclusive on their purchase. It cost me a small fortune (possessing divine relatives, it appeared, only went so far), but it meant that no other chef would be able to offer anything remotely approaching the excellence of the striped red mullets. I did not hesitate to accept his offer.

With such a signature dish, the dearth of sea monster in my repertoire appeared to go unnoticed, and was perhaps welcomed with great relief. Praise and tips were gratifyingly generous, and for an all-too-brief time I managed to forget that I was still unable to produce anything edible with the kraken, that I still had not put my name forward for the Bronze Chef competition. And that I was exceedingly unlikely to ever find myself in a position to do either.

And then came the night of Meletus's symposion.

A lean, ex-military man, Meletus enjoyed fine food as much as other men enjoy cold-water enemas. Or perhaps the problem was less with the food than with the price he had to pay for it (his slave had certainly haggled like a bread wife to reduce my fee). In his youth, Meletus had distinguished himself not only in battle against the Persians, but also in several notoriously expensive symposions he had hosted in the years following his military victories. But wealth had dwindled along with youth, and although Meletus still retained his high social status, these days he held only the bare minimum of symposions in any given year.

"You should've seen what the mingy old blighter did when his youngest daughter got married," Hermogenes told me, as I was considering whether or not to accept the job. "Bought the oldest, stringiest sheep he could find for the feast—and then tried to sell the extra meat afterwards! But he buggered that up right proper when he hired The Sicilian to cook it for him." He snorted disdainfully. "That one botched the job—big surprise there, yeah?—so nobody was too chuffed about buying the leftovers."

Substandard comestibles could be explained in many ways. Possibly Meletus had not cared much for his youngest daughter. Or perhaps he did not like her fiancé. But hiring The Sicilian to cook the food showed an inexcusable lack of both taste and judgment. Almost, I was minded to refuse the contract on that basis alone. But Meletus was still extremely well connected, despite his present parsimoniousness, and my days of scant employment were not yet far enough in the past for me to forget their lesson. In addition, and perhaps more importantly, Meletus had decided that he, too, must host the Hero of the Aegean at his symposion—a fact his slave had gone out of his way to mention several times. Appearances had to be maintained, and it would have looked very peculiar indeed if I refused a contract to cook for my own uncle. And so, with some trepidation, I accepted the commission.

Striped red mullet would be the star of the feast, of course. I had hoped to serve my Hare in Red Wine as well, but the hares must have all gone to ground for the winter, for there were none to be had at the market. Instead, Hermogenes and I produced an exceedingly fine pig, stuffed with fall apples and rare cinnamon, and spit-roasted to perfection. There were honey-glazed shrimp garnished with fresh oregano, cabbage with green coriander and rue, deep-fried fritters drenched in honey and sprinkled with cracked peppercorns, and larks seasoned with thyme and baked in flaky golden pastry. It was a feast fit for a hero.

But it was not, I discovered after the meal had been consumed, entirely acceptable to his host.

"Ah, here is the chef now," Meletus said flatly, as his steward ushered me into the andron.

Thus cued, the dinner guests began to applaud. Perseus, sitting in the place of honour, was whooping like a barbarian and grinning widely. I was wearing one of my blue chitons, and I noticed several of the men casting discreetly covetous looks at it. My client, however, appeared pinched and sour, not at all in the mood to admire my wardrobe. I could tell at a glance not only that the feast had not been to his liking, but that, given my divine lineage, there was little he could say about it. Neither was sitting well with him.

"Thank you," I said to the assembly, nodding uncomfortably at Perseus, who had continued to applaud after everyone else had ceased. "Thank you. Truly, you are too kind. I trust everything was satisfactory."

It was not a question, but Meletus took it as such.

"Well," he *harrumphed* thinly, his irritation clear. "It was all quite delicious, yes. But I must say, I was surprised … perhaps even a little"—he cleared his throat again—"*dismayed* to see that kraken did not appear on your menu this evening. I believe you were duly informed of the identity of my special guest of honour?"

I opened my mouth to reply, but before I could do so, Perseus intervened.

"Whoa, dude, you're bumming me out," he protested, stuffing a fritter in his mouth. "That's my nephew you're talking to."

Meletus's face grew more pinched. The dinner guests, who had been on the verge of bestowing tips, began to fidget and shift on their couches, studiously avoiding each other's eyes, their coin-filled hands retreating back into the folds of their chitons.

Perseus seemed unaware of the sudden tension in the room.

"And besides, do you know how tired I am of that frickin' sea monster?" he demanded, shoving another fritter in his mouth and boorishly wiping his hands on the front of his chiton. "Everywhere I go, it's 'Have a bit of kraken, Perseus,' 'Let's throw some kraken on the fire,' 'Have you tried my special recipe for kraken?' Ares's balls, I've even had kraken chips! I mean, how messed up is that, man?"

He stretched, then shrugged nonchalantly. "If you ask me, dude: no sea monster, no problem."

And with that he snapped his fingers at his attending slave, who instantly presented him with the rather disreputable-looking brown satchel that he always seemed to have with him. A small pouch had been attached to its strap and Perseus took from this a large gold coin. He tossed it once in his palm as if testing its weight. And then he flipped it at me.

He tossed a coin at me.

Through the air! As if I were a beggar. Me! A celebrity chef!

Outraged and insulted, I made no move to catch it. The slaves watched avidly as the coin arced and fell. Even the dinner guests eyed its golden trajectory. The coin bounced once with a ringing clink, then it rolled under a dining couch. Nobody was gauche enough to retrieve it, though several of the slaves were clearly considering doing so. But Perseus did not notice. He had turned his attention back to his host.

"Duuuude," he said, and his tone was cajoling. "Lighten up! Dinner was awesome. Never ate pig like that before. And those pastry things? Total killer. Way better than anything Sosthenes came up with."

He rose to his feet and shook back his feathered golden hair. Pausing, he looked around, ensuring all eyes were upon him, then he opened his arms wide and proclaimed in a deep baritone, several octaves below his usual tone, "I, Perseus, Hero of the Aegean, am satisfied."

"Well," Meletus began, clearly struggling with his emotions. "Well, as long as you're happy," he said finally, managing a thin, simpering smile. "That's really all that matters, isn't it?"

Perseus nodded regally, accepting it as his due. Then he cocked his head to one side. "'Course, I'd be a lot happier with some entertainment, dude," he suggested.

"Of course," Meletus agreed quickly. "Of course. Quite remiss of me. Eudemus, send in the entertainment. At once!"

Meletus's steward nodded and left the room.

"I had to be very creative," Meletus confided to Perseus, "with all the women occupied at the Thesmophoria. Even the flute girls have gone, I'm afraid—at least the good ones have. But I've arranged for something very special. I don't think you'll be disappointed."

"Bring it on, dude," Perseus said amiably. "I'm game."

House slaves were clearing away first tables, and the dinner guests, relieved that any unpleasant conflict now appeared unlikely, began calling me over, offering coins and murmuring appreciative comments. Several of the men inquired as to my availability.

I was still making the rounds when the entertainment stepped into the room.

He was pock-faced and seedy-looking, his disreputable chiton the colour of overcooked peas. He came in juggling, his hands a blur, his eyes darting around the andron, assessing the crowd. Weighted cloth balls flew through the air around him like fat, multi-coloured birds.

"My friends," Meletus intoned, full of self-importance. "My illustrious and most honoured guest. The first of your entertainments this evening. May I present, for you, the finest juggler in all of Athens. The Great Galinthius!"

I stared. Could it be? Yes. It was the juggler from the Agora. The one who had near clobbered Hermogenes twice with his ineptitude.

"Eudemus found him in the Agora," Meletus was informing his guests. "A true virtuoso, the like of which has never—"

And just as the words left his mouth, the Great Galinthius did what I had known he would do the instant I laid eyes on him. He fumbled his balls.

"A thousand pardons!" he shouted, as coloured balls went flying off in all directions.

Dinner guests cried out and ducked instinctively.

"A momentary aberration, I assure you!" the Great Galinthius squawked, making a desperate grab for one of the balls.

He should have just allowed them to fall to the floor.

As the clumsy juggler snatched at a yellow ball, a descending red ball glanced off the back of his hand. His reflexive jerk sent the orb spinning into the air once more. It flew straight across the room to smack Meletus soundly in his disbelieving eye.

There was a moment of shocked silence. The dinner guests held their breath. The cithara player stopped playing. Slaves ceased whatever they were doing and stared. The Great Galinthius froze.

And then the Hero of the Aegean burst out laughing.

Whooping and chortling, eyes watering with mirth, Perseus smacked his thigh with one hand and pointed at the unfortunate Meletus with the other. The dinner guests exchanged quick, uneasy glances, then they too began to chuckle. The Great Galinthius smiled uncertainly.

I flattened myself against the wall, watching Meletus, wondering how he would react. How he *could* react.

He sat motionless on the dining couch, his face puce with

fury and humiliation. And as Perseus continued to point and bray, I saw realization wash over my client. There was nothing he could do. Nothing he could say now without offending his illustrious and most honoured guest.

He bowed his head for a moment, dabbing at his outraged eye with a napkin. When he raised his face again, he had somehow managed to fix a smile upon it. It was a thin, strained sort of thing. It did not, even remotely, reach his eyes.

As always, Perseus was oblivious.

"That was awesome, dude! Totally epic!" Still chuckling merrily, he put up his hand to stop a house slave who was about to clear his table away. He reached over, snagged a last shrimp, and waved the slave off. "Man, I love these bad boys!" he grinned as he stuffed the morsel into his mouth. A dribble of honey ran down his chin.

"So," the hero said, wiping his hands on his chiton with a purposeful air. "Any of you guys ever played Dead Ant?"

Chapter 13

Fortunately, my duties for the evening were at an end. I returned to the kitchen and began gathering up my casseroles and pans, grimly tossing them into the carrying baskets with little regard for their safety. The house slaves had suddenly made themselves very scarce, but I did not bother to take them to task for their lack of industry. My thoughts were otherwise occupied.

My so-called uncle had certainly not improved on closer acquaintance. If anything, he appeared even more ill-bred than I had first thought. How could he mock his host in such a fashion? How could he so completely ignore the rules of etiquette? And when had the word "dude" become an acceptable form of address?

Even when considered objectively, the Hero of the Aegean could hardly have been less heroic. Indisputably boorish, possessing the unplumbed ignorance of privileged youth, there was little to recommend him. True, he had attempted to protect me from Meletus's disapproval of the menu, but why had he seen fit to intervene at all? I'd had the situation under control. A man of Meletus's ilk did not hold sway over the grandson of Zeus. What misguided impulse had prompted Perseus to defend me? It was completely, utterly insupportable that I could find myself in the position of being *grateful* to such a creature. The gods, it seemed, would have their little joke.

Hermogenes knew something was wrong. He also knew not to ask what it was. As I've said before, he is an astute lad. Without uttering a single, ill-advised word, my disciple deftly took over the packing of our cooking implements and, in short order, he had the lot safely stowed in our baskets and loaded onto our donkey.

We quit the house with no fanfare. Indeed, any goodbyes we might have made would have been quite drowned out by the increasingly boozy laughter now issuing from the andron and the occasional shout of "Dead Ant." The autumn night was cool and still. I paused to take a deep, calming breath of it.

Meletus lived near the Diochares Gate. His was an old-money neighbourhood with large houses lining the streets and elaborately carved Herms marking each well-appointed crossroad. It was almost as far away from our house in the Kerameikos as one could get. Wearily we began our long trudge down the darkened streets and alleys, retracing our steps to the Panathenaic Way, which would see us first to the Agora and from there, home.

We did not speak.

We entered the market from the southeast quadrant. This

was the fastest route home, though it was one I generally preferred to avoid after a job. With flights of stairs breaking up all other roads traversing the area, the Panathenaic Way is the only thoroughfare open to wheeled traffic. As a result, the southeast Agora is an extremely well used locality, home to a multitude of shops and houses. It is also home to a plethora of tavernas and brothels.

As one might expect from this, it tended to be noisy there, as well as busy—especially at the hour of the night when revellers staggered from one drinking establishment to another, picked fights with men larger than themselves, or sang at the top of their lungs, their arms thrown about the shoulders of best friends whose names may or may not be recalled come morning. As we drew closer, I could see the district's torch-lit pathways snaking through the night, most terminating either in tavernas or brothels or in buildings which housed both.

Naturally, a section of the Panathenaic Way had been blocked off to be resurfaced, so we were obliged to take a detour down one of the considerably less savoury streets of the district. We tried to keep to the edges, away from the more obvious filth and the more obviously inebriated pedestrians. But due to the blockade, the route was unusually well-travelled that night, and we were obliged to pick and dodge our way around any number of obstacles.

I found myself being greeted heartily by men still sober enough to recognize my blue chiton. With a dignified nod, I acknowledged those who hailed me—notoriety was still new enough to be satisfying—though I did not stop. At the moment,

I was far too occupied with thinking unkind thoughts about the great Perseus to engage in any superficial discourse. There was, however, one individual whose greeting required more than a mere nod of recognition.

I first spotted him in front of one of the seedier tavernas. He was watching me, his entire stance one of careless ease. Ankles crossed, one shoulder casually propped against the door frame, hands toying absently with the hilt of a massive hunting knife. Torchlight played over his bald head and bulging muscles, burnishing the former with a warm glow and emphasizing the latter with shadowed relief. There was an outcry from inside and he glanced behind him, torchlight illuminating the long scar that extended down one superbly formed cheekbone. Though he was clad simply, in a tunic rather than in his usual shining bronze armour, I would have recognized him anywhere.

His attention was distracted only for a moment, then he turned his gaze again in my direction. I sighed inwardly. There was nothing for it. I would have to go to him.

"Hermogenes, take the donkey and go on ahead," I instructed, handing over the lead rope to my disciple. "There's someone I need to speak with."

"I could wait, Chef," he offered. His eyes, which only a moment ago had been heavy and drooping, were now brightly inquisitive.

"No," I told him firmly. "I won't be long. Start unpacking if you arrive home before I do—and mind you put the spices away properly this time."

"Yes, Chef." Hermogenes took the reins and began to move off, though not without casting me a curious backwards glance.

I stood, watching until he stepped back onto the Panathenaic Way. For a brief moment, I thought he was disobeying my orders, for he swung left instead of right. I squinted, prepared to deliver a sharp reprimand, then I saw the pile of crushed gravel he had swerved to avoid. The crew in charge of road surfacing must have left it there when their workday ended, heedless of any inconvenience this might cause. At times, I thought the city might have done just as well to leave the bloody road unpaved.

I waited until Hermogenes had disappeared into the gloom, then I began picking a path across the side street and over to the dingy taverna. All manner of unpleasant things squished under my sandals, my feet making soft sucking noises as I pulled them out of the filth to take another step. I amended my earlier thought. Perhaps it was just as well that at least one road in Athens was paved, regardless of the constant difficulties this caused. Wrinkling my nose in distaste, I hiked up my chiton and cloak, unconcerned at the moment with how undignified I might appear. I had paid too much for these clothes to have them ruined in such a way.

As I approached the taverna, I glanced up and spied an eagle owl perched on the roof of the building, its orange eyes glaring down sternly at the activity below. Its presence confirmed what I already knew.

"Ares," I greeted the man in front of the bar.

"Pelops." The god of war nodded briefly.

I waited, but his eyes continued to look past me, and only

then did I realize that his attention had not, in fact, been on me at all.

I turned to see what he was staring at so intently.

Further down the street, there was another taverna. Equally seedy, it too had a reputation for rough clientele and dodgy bar snacks. And at the moment, it too boasted a muscular individual leaning casually against its door frame.

Though the man appeared to be doing nothing more than enjoying an extremely large cup of wine, his was a most ferocious appearance. Red-haired and red-bearded, he towered over the darker-haired men around him. His eyes glinted oddly in the torchlight, and he clasped a large hammer, similar to something a blacksmith might wield. He held it in one hand, casually swinging it back and forth as he drank, his muscles bulging and flexing with the movement.

Ares scowled at the sight. "Who the fuck does he think he is?" he snorted.

I wasn't sure whether he meant it as an inquiry, but it is wiser not to take chances with gods and so I considered it as such. I turned my gaze again towards the individual in question. Someone said something, made a joke, perhaps, and the man guffawed loudly, spraying his wine in all directions, his hearty laughter rolling out across the night-dark Agora and undoubtedly awakening sleepers halfway across the city.

"Well," I temporized, searching for a diplomatic word to describe him, "he does look a touch … foreign."

Ares snorted. "He looks like fucking trouble."

"Surely not," I murmured. "He appears to be doing nothing more than having a drink with some friends."

"Cocksucker like that doesn't have any sodding friends."

I closed my mouth on my next comment. Clearly the god of war was in a bit of snit.

"Says he's the Mighty Thor, of all fucking things!" Ares horked and spat on the ground. "Some god from up north. Ha! What the fuck kind of bollocks name is that? He'll be fucking 'thor' after I'm done with him." He began chewing moodily on a fingernail, as if considering the possibilities.

The red-haired god continued to carouse with his mates.

"Goat-fucking tosser," Ares griped. "Thinks he can piss on my turf! I could take down that red-bearded bastard with my fucking eyes closed."

"Well … go to it," I said recklessly, then immediately regretted the impulse. I had nothing against the northern stranger. Just because I had had a bad time of it this evening was no reason to wish the same on someone else. But before I could retract my words, Ares had straightened and pushed himself off the door frame.

"Cheers. Don't mind if I fucking do." He stretched his neck to one side, then the other, gave me a cocky grin, and began to swagger off. But before he had taken more than a few steps, he paused and turned back to me.

"All right, then?" he asked, as if the thought had just occurred to him. "Haven't seen you about much. Some stupid tosser trying to fuck with you?" He sounded almost hopeful.

Yes, I wanted to say. *Perseus, so-called Hero of the Aegean.*

Take the bastard down for me. But better sense prevailed and I swallowed the words before they could emerge. I shook my head regretfully.

"No," I lied. "Everything's grand."

"Ah." The god of bloodlust seemed a bit disappointed.

Then the red-bearded god's drunken laughter boomed out once again, and Ares brightened. He rolled his shoulders back and turned again towards his quarry.

"Well, you know where to find me, yeah?" he tossed over his shoulder as he moved towards his target. "Give a shout if you need some heat."

"I will," I called. "Thanks."

I watched after him, morbidly curious to see would happen when the two gods met. With grim purpose, Ares stalked down the narrow street. He held up his right arm and the eagle owl swooped down in eerie silence to land, curved talons digging deeply into his master's skin. Ares did not flinch, nor did he take his eyes from the laughing god.

But before the god of war got halfway down the street, a smaller, stockier figure peeled away from the shadow of a Herm and made a beeline for him.

"And where, by all the Twelve Gods and their hairy armpits, do you think you're off to?" the shorter figure demanded.

Surprised, Ares rocked back on his heels as the smaller man confronted him. The eagle owl let out a startled *hoot*.

Appalled, I began jogging towards them, dropping the corners of my new cloak in my haste. I'd probably regret that later, but for now, speed was of the essence.

I knew that short man. I'd recognized him as soon as he'd opened his mouth.

Pisistratus, or "Piss" to his friends, hailed originally from Samothrace, though he'd lived in Athens for much of his life. A compact, heavily muscled man, he often worked as a foreman in the Agora, where he motivated his work crews with an impressive array of dire threats and colourful insults. Despite this, he had a good heart and a keen sense of justice. This past summer, he'd even helped me against The Sicilian.

He deserved better than to be pulverized by the god of bloodlust.

"It's okay, Piss!" I called out the assurance, panting a little as I skidded to a stop in front of them. "It's okay. He's a friend."

"Pelops?" Piss turned to look at me. "What are you doing wandering around this shit hole? Shouldn't you be roasting lambs or some damn thing?"

"Just passing through," I told him. "On my way home from a contract, though …" I paused, looking ruefully down at the now stained edges of my cloak, "I think perhaps I ought to have taken another route. But how is it with you, my friend? I didn't expect to see you here."

Piss shrugged. "I take on the odd job now and again. Gets pretty rough 'round here at times. Some toad-buggering shite eater starts pissing about and … well, it's bad for business, isn't it?" He slid Ares a darkly significant look. "That's why they hire me to keep the peace."

"I thought that's what Scythian Archers were for," I said, glancing uneasily at Ares. The god of war was known by many names, but "toad-buggering shite eater" was not generally one of them.

"Ah, those pansy-arsed bastards are rubbish in a fight." The foreman dismissed them with a rude noise. "Good with the bow, but when it comes to real muscle? Useless as tits on a bull."

Throughout all this, Ares stood in brooding silence. I couldn't decide if he was infuriated or simply shocked into silence by the man's temerity.

"So, who did you say your friend was?" Piss asked, cocking his head up at the god.

"Just a friend." Ares spoke before I could reply.

"Well, *friend*," Piss said pleasantly, "if you ask me, you've got blood and slaughter written all over your face and, by Hestia's tits, man, that's a bad combination—especially when you put it together with that red-bearded bastard over there." Eyes still fixed on Ares, he gestured at the red-haired giant lounging and drinking outside the other taverna.

"Now, I've had my eye on that one for days now," Piss continued. "He's big and he's tempting, I'll give you that. But he's not here looking for trouble and, as long as trouble doesn't come sniffing 'round for him, he'll have his drink and a few laughs, and he'll be off with his arm around something soft and curvy before you know it. And everything will stay nice and quiet."

Piss thumped his broad chest. "I like nice and quiet. It means I'm doing my job. And when I do my job, I get paid. When I get paid, the wife's happy. And by the Twelve Gods and their hairy pink arses, I like to keep the wife happy. You know what they say. Happy wife, happy life, eh?"

Piss and the god of war locked eyes. I held my breath, waiting for chaos to break loose. All my impulses were screaming at me to flee the coming conflagration.

And then I noticed Ares's mouth twitching ever so slightly at the corners.

I blinked, astounded. Ares was actually *amused* by this? Diverted by Pisistratus, who clearly had no idea who he was? I let out my breath cautiously and shook my head in wonder. Who could have guessed? Perhaps the god found the man's impertinence refreshing.

The eagle owl chose that moment to rear back, stretching its wings and glaring at Piss, its orange eyes and feathered horns lending it a most baleful appearance.

"Saaaay, that's a nice bird," Piss said, distracted.

The owl blinked both eyes at him and the foreman chuckled in delight. Crooning softly, Piss put his finger out and began stroking the bird's streaky plumage. I wouldn't have put any part of me within easy reach of such a wickedly sharp beak, but Piss seemed entirely insensible of any danger. The owl gave a purring sort of hoot and closed its eyes.

Ares looked wholly bemused.

"I like owls," Piss explained to us with a crooked grin. "Kept one when I was a kid. Nothing like an owl for keeping the mice down. How long have you had this beauty?"

I gazed from one to the other as Ares and Pisistratus began discussing owls, the red-bearded god and his tempting presence apparently forgotten. Talk of owls led to talk of fights, which led to stories of battles past. By the time Piss offered to buy Ares a drink, the two of them were laughing and reminiscing about war like the oldest of veterans.

They invited me to join them. I declined the offer, in part because I was spent from the day, but mostly because I had no stomach for the comparing of battle scars, which is inevitably the outcome of such conversation. Piss steered Ares to a nearby taverna, which was, I noted, in exactly the opposite direction from where the northern god was situated. I leaned against the Herm and watched as the short, stocky foreman and the formidable god of slaughter and bloodlust entered the building. I could hear their laughter even after they had disappeared into the crowd.

Still shaking my head a little in disbelief, I began gathering up the sadly stained edges of my new cloak, my fingers cringing away from the damp foulness. I hoped Irene would be able to work some magic on it. A fine garment like this deserved better than to be dragged through the odorous scum of the taverna district.

I was still fussing with my clothing when I heard a loud squelching sound behind me. I looked up just as the red-haired god strode past. Startled, I dropped the edges of my sadly bedraggled cloak. I had not seen him coming.

I gave him a wary look.

But Piss, it seemed, was correct. Far from offering me any sort of challenge, the northern god instead gave me a broad wink, breaking into loud and cheerful (though not particularly melodious) song. His war hammer swung from one arm, a smiling flute girl was tucked under the other.

I waited until he passed, then took a deep breath—a mistake, in this particular environment—and turned my steps wearily homeward. Between belligerent gods and troublesome heroes, it had been a long, long night.

Chapter 14

"Oh, Pel!" Zeuxo exclaimed, eyeing me doubtfully. "He didn't. You're joking! He laughed? At his own host? Whatever was he thinking?"

"Interesting word, that," I observed dryly. "I'm not sure his mind is capable of thought. All that fluffy blond hair, no doubt." I struck a pose and ran my fingers through my own dark, straight locks, shaking them out affectedly behind me.

Zeuxo burst out laughing, brightening the already sunny day with her merriment.

The weather had turned surprisingly decent for the time of year, and I'd arrived home from an early morning stroll to find Zeuxo awaiting Gorgias in our courtyard. At her behest, I'd joined her on the sun-warmed bench and been regaling her with tales of what the great Perseus was like when he was not at home. Zeuxo was not sure I was being entirely honest with her.

"Pel," she reproached me, though her face was still suffused with mirth. "That was unkind. And to your own uncle, too."

I pulled a wry face. "Ah, you heard about that, did you?"

"Heard about it? All of Athens is talking of how Chef Pelops is related to the great Perseus. They're even saying you're the grandson of Zeus himself. Very impressive, Pel!" Her dark eyes were warm and approving.

I gazed back at her and tried not to swallow my tongue. All these months, my lineage had been a well-concealed secret, closely guarded and private. Now, at last, it was out in the open. Now I could finally confide in her the truth of my divine heritage.

It had been difficult enough to keep such a secret from my friends—and even harder to refrain from saying anything to Zeuxo about it. Had I known it myself before Gorgias had proposed to her … but I hadn't and he had made his offer, and I'd thought that was the end of it. And yet now, on the verge of confessing all, a small, insidious voice inside me whispered that it was, perhaps, not too late for her to change her mind about her upcoming nuptials. That perhaps the grandson of Zeus would prove more appealing than a mere potter.

But, "I didn't know you had it in you, to be quite frank," Zeuxo continued, before I could say anything. "Though I suppose it was Hermogenes who came up with the whole scheme."

I closed my mouth, smothering any words before they could leave my lips.

"He's a clever lad, that one," she went on, oblivious to my consternation. "A few divine antecedents—even if they are spurious—ought to do wonders for your career. I hope you've told him it was very well done."

Clearly it had not occurred to Zeuxo that the gossip might, in fact, be truth. Was the idea so ludicrous, then? So beyond belief that the woman who knew me best in the world could not even entertain it? What did that say about me? I looked away for a long moment.

"He'll get you far," she was saying. "I mean, look what he's done with your appearance. You look quite the successful man now. The chiton is lovely, by the way. The colour brings out your eyes."

"Which is, of course, the first thing one looks for in a chef," I said with forced lightness.

"Oh, you!" She gave me a fond grin. "Here I am trying to tell you you've a keen business sense."

"No. You're trying to tell me Hermogenes has a keen business sense."

"Well, he does. But it wouldn't get him far if you weren't so talented a chef."

"And for that alone, I shall make you a very large pan of honey pastries," I told her.

She smiled at me again—that lovely, lopsided smile—and I felt my chest constrict.

"Is Perseus really as boorish as you're making him out to be?" she asked, her eyes narrowing in suspicion. "I mean, he sounds absolutely awful."

"He's probably even worse," I told her, grateful for the change of subject. "Have you not heard him speak?"

"Not a word. I've only seen him from a distance. He's very handsome," she added, almost as an afterthought.

"Well, count yourself lucky. His accent alone is enough to make Hades cringe. And he seems inordinately fond of the word 'dude.'"

"Dude?" she repeated, baffled. "Whatever does he mean by it?"

"It appears to signify a person." I shrugged. "As in, 'Dude, what are you doing?'" I attempted to imitate his accent.

"No!" Zeuxo dissolved into laughter.

"Oh yes," I assured her. "And as for his acquaintance with etiquette? Well, let me just say, it is a very distant one indeed. He wipes his fingers on his clothing. He farts loudly during dinner. And he has a laugh only a harpy would find sweet sounding."

"Stop, Pel!" Zeuxo's eyes were watering, she was laughing so hard.

"He flipped a coin at me, you know. As a tip! As if I were a beggar."

"Oh, no!" Zeuxo dabbed at her eyes with the corner of her chiton, torn between amusement and dismay. "You're not serious?"

I waved it off, though the incident still rankled. Imagine, tossing a coin at me. At me!

Zeuxo struggled to get her emotions under control. "I've heard his mother is quite refined," she said at last, though I could still hear the bubbling undercurrent of laughter in her voice. "But by all accounts his sister is as tanned as a slave." Her tone held both shock and disapproval. In Athens, for a woman to be outspoken was vulgar. To be tanned was scandalous.

But I was less concerned with the social blunders of Perseus's sister. In fact, I'd almost forgotten that the Hero of the Aegean was touring with his family.

"Well, they certainly couldn't be worse than he is," I grumped. "Unless of course they, too, happen to enjoy a round of Dead Ant now and again."

Zeuxo giggled at the thought. "What a show *that* would be!" She laughed.

Her merriment was contagious, and I found one side of my mouth twitching up in an unwilling grin.

I shook my head slowly. Really, it was too funny. Perseus was so loutish as to be laughable, but as long as my reputation did not suffer from it, why should it concern me? Even though he was kin, it was doubtful he would ever try to claim any rights based on that. And although I was currently in the unenviable position of owing him my gratitude, it was also doubtful he would ever attempt to collect on it. With all the wine he'd consumed that evening, he probably didn't even remember.

Perhaps Zeuxo had the right of it. It was a sort of entertainment—better than anything I'd seen at the Theatre of Dionysus—and perhaps I ought to just sit back and enjoy the show. With a last, rueful shake of my head, I gave myself up wholeheartedly to laughter.

"What's so funny then?" Gorgias asked, stepping into the sunny courtyard. He grinned at me and dropped a kiss on the top of Zeuxo's head. "The two of you sound like a pair of bloody geese, sitting here cackling away." He settled beside her and looked back and forth at us expectantly.

"It's Perseus," Zeuxo told him, still chuckling. "Pel's been telling tales. He sounds *awful*!"

Gorgias snorted. "Aye, I've heard he's a cack-handed bugger," he agreed. "For all his prettiness. Had Sosthenes playing his sodding Ant game, and damn near killed the old bastard with it. Up down, up down, fill you full of wine. They say the poor bugger's not gotten up from his sleeping couch since. And that were days ago."

"Why is it I'm always the last to hear the gossip, then?" Zeuxo complained. "Here I've been thinking Perseus was just lovely, and the two of you have known all these terrible stories about him."

"You're not on the circuit anymore, are you, luv?" Gorgias tucked her under his arm protectively. "Hard to hear the news when you're not out and about at parties."

"Yes," Zeuxo agreed, gazing up at him. "I suppose it is." It did not seem as though she minded.

I swallowed and looked away.

"Which reminds me," she said, straightening. Her tone suddenly became very businesslike. "We've some decisions to make about this wedding—"

"Well, that's my cue," I said, pushing myself off the bench with alacrity.

"Don't go, Pel," Zeuxo protested. "It won't take that long, and we could all have lunch together afterwards. It feels like I never see you anymore."

"We grandsons of Zeus are busy lads," I said, trying to sound jaunty, though Zeuxo gave me a strange look, so I don't know how successful I was.

"But what about the wedding?" she said. "Gamelion's only two months away. I'm sure we could use your input."

"Aye, I could use some chuffing bugger on my side," Gorgias said.

"I'm not taking sides!" I said a little too quickly.

Gorgias blinked, his smile fading.

"Your *side*?" Zeuxo inquired, her eyes glinting. "What do you think this is? A competition?"

"Of course not, dear," Gorgias hastened to soothe her. "It's just that ... well, men like to have other men about. You know, when they're making decisions about weddings and such. We can't leave it all up to the ladies, can we? We're liable to find ourselves tricked out in all kinds of fripperies."

"And here I'd been *so* looking forward to tricking you out," she told him solemnly, though her eyes had softened and her mouth was trying to quirk up on one side.

He grinned and pulled her closer.

"Look," I interrupted abruptly, my voice sounding odd even to myself. "All you need to know from me is that I'll be cooking your wedding feast. The rest is up to the two of you. Now, if you'll excuse me, I've ... I've got more important things to do."

It hurt her. I could see it in her eyes. I hadn't meant for it to come out like that. I tried to backtrack, explaining in far too much detail about demanding clients and the need to pick up more striped mullets. She refused to meet my eyes, and Gorgias watched gravely as my words tumbled over each other. I fled as soon as possible.

Heartsick, I stumbled from the house, past our Herm with his cock-eyed, sympathetic grin, and out into the grey-shadowed street. The day did not seem bright any longer. Laughing with Zeuxo, it had been easy to forget that Gorgias would be marrying her in a few months. And bringing her home to live.

My new-found fame had brought with it a plethora of new contracts, and my savings were growing, which was more than I could have said a week ago. But after I paid for supplies (the striped red mullets were hideously expensive) and Hermogenes's salary (he'd been cheaper as a slave), the amount left over would scarcely pay rent for a month on a decent house.

I needed more. And I needed it soon. I did not want to live with my friend after his wedding. There was nothing for it. If I was to move out before Gamelion, I was going to have to enter—and win—the Bronze Chef competition.

"Cheer up, then. You've a face like an empty wine cup," Dionysus observed.

The god of wine had been leaning against the counter of his stall, a cloth slung casually over one shoulder. Hermes was perched on a stool at the counter, a brimming wine cup in front of him. They'd both been picking desultorily at a bunch of fat red grapes, watching the lunchtime crowds stroll by. Neither seemed particularly hungry. If anything, Dionysus seemed rather drunk. A residual consequence of his Oskhophoria, no doubt.

Shifting my carrying basket, laden once more with the hideously expensive striped red mullets, I shrugged. "Money problems," I said shortly.

At my words, or perhaps my tone of voice, Dionysus's eyebrows rose and he straightened. Whipping the cloth off his shoulder, he gave the spotless counter a brief swipe with it, then, with a clatter, he set out a fresh wine krater and another unglazed cup. Catching up the nearest wine jug, he splashed its contents into the krater, topped it with a measure of water, and poured the lot into my cup, all without spilling a drop. An impressive feat, given the slight shaking of his hands.

"Take a load off, then," he urged, gesturing me closer. "And why don't you tell old Dr. D. all about it."

And suddenly there was a second wooden stool in front of the counter, though there had been none there before.

I regarded it for a moment, then sighed. I really should have been getting back home. I had not been entirely dishonest with Zeuxo, I did have a contract the following day, and there were things I ought to have been doing to prepare for it. But I hadn't been gone long enough for her to have left, and the thought of listening to her and Gorgias discuss their wedding plans was more than I could bear. Settling my basket carefully on the counter, I slid onto the stool and accepted a cup of wine.

"Thanks." I nodded at the gods. "Dionysus, Hermes." I saluted them with my cup before taking a long draught.

"Pelops." Hermes toasted me with an unsmiling nod.

I swallowed my wine. "Everything all right?" I inquired. If the god of wine was slightly inebriated, it was, at least, in character.

The god of trade and language, however, did not seem his usual perky self.

"His feet are sore," Dionysus told me.

"Your *feet?*" I looked down at the appendages in question. They did seem a bit puffy-looking. "What have you been doing to them?"

"I've been bloody on them all week, haven't I?" Hermes snapped. "That's what you get when you're the god of sodding messages. Take this to Boeotia, Hermes. This has to go right away, Hermes. Hermes, this absolutely, positively has to be there overnight!" His peevish tone was at odds with his cheerful garb—a blindingly white chiton with a flashy orange and purple border.

Dionysus made sympathetic noises and topped up his wine.

"I never thought about that part of your duties," I told the god honestly.

Hermes scowled and downed the cup in one swallow. "*Nobody* ever thinks about it, do they? Nobody thinks about how hard it is to run messages all day, every day. Nobody says, 'Gee, how does that poor bugger do that?' Nobody thinks about me running my sodding feet raw! Speaking of which"—he grimaced and slid off the stool—"I've got to run. *Again.* I've got another 'urgent' message to deliver for Hera—I tell you, the goddess does nothing but message all bloody day. Nobody's that important, not even Hera, and she can strike me down right here and now if she doesn't like it. At least my feet would get a rest."

He paused, as if waiting. When nothing happened, he

scowled and sighed heavily. "Well, I guess I'm off then. Thanks for the wine, D. Nice to see you again, Chef P." And with that, the sore-footed god hobbled off and was quickly swallowed up by the lunchtime crowds.

"Poor Hermes," I observed.

"Yeah," Dionysus agreed, giving his counter another wipe with the cloth. "He's always on about his feet. Fallen arches or summat. It's a bugger. Makes me awfully chuffed to be the god of wine, I can tell you that."

"How was the Oskhophoria?" I asked politely.

Dionysus blinked owlishly at me. "Was?"

"Ah. Still going on, then?"

"I don't get the question," he said, brows drawing together in a puzzled frown.

"Never mind." I waved it off, then sat in silence for a moment.

"Hey, nice kit," Dionysus said admiringly, reaching out to pinch the fabric between his fingers. "Cato's, yeah?" He pursed his lips in a whistle. "That poncy bugger really knows what he's about, don't he? Got a few chitons from him myself. Fancy ones. You know, for parties and the like. Had a new one made up for the Oskhophoria. Purple like wine. I never saw this blue colour. It's cracking."

"Hermogenes decided I needed a makeover," I told him, toying with my wine cup.

"Aye, and about time too."

"I beg your pardon?"

"You were starting to look a bit …" He scrunched up his face and wiggled his fingers distastefully. "Well, a bit dodgy, yeah?"

I straightened on the stool, offended. Did everyone in Athens have an opinion on my wardrobe?

"I mean, think about it," Dionysus continued, oblivious. "You're one of us—well, a quarter of you is—and now everyone and their chuffing dog knows it. You, my friend, need to start dressing the part. That disciple of yours, he's a smart lad. Not just a cheeky mouth, eh?" He held up his cup in a silent toast, then drained it dry. "That's a brilliant chiton, you know. Much more the thing. Matches your eyes too."

"So …" He put his cup down, laid both forearms on the counter and leaned toward me. "All Athens knows you're Zeus's grandson, you've a cheeky bugger of a disciple who is, nonetheless, a canny little bastard, you're all tricked out in a cracking new kit and, as far as I know, your feet aren't hurting you. So why do you look like some bugger's just nicked your last olive? Have you not got any contracts then?"

I ducked my head in acknowledgment. "I do," I assured him. "They've been pouring in since news of my lineage got 'round— not that I had anything to do with that," I hastened to add.

"No, no. 'Course not," Dionysus agreed quickly.

"Perseus told Archestratus, who told his slaves and … well, there it is." I slid him a wary glance, but when he didn't say anything else, I continued. "No, I've certainly been getting a lot of contracts out of it. It's just …"

"You're worried about Hera?"

"Well, I wasn't until you asked about it in that horrid, ominous tone," I told him, setting my wine down untasted. I had almost forgotten about Hera. "Why?" I asked cautiously. "What has she been saying about me?"

Dionysus flipped his cloth back over his shoulder and shrugged nonchalantly. "Dunno, do I? I've not seen her about. You ought to have asked Hermes when you had the chance. I know she was travelling for a bit. Ionia, I think. Word on the Mount is that she was trying to avoid a certain hero and his flying pony."

I blinked. It had not occurred to me that Hera would be just as unhappy with Perseus as she was with me—perhaps even more so, given that he was son rather than grandson.

"But," Dionysus dismissed it with a shrug, "that's just bollocks, is that. I've never known Hera to back away from anyone—let alone one of Zeus's, uh … relatives. No, if you ask me, it's pure coincidence, her gone off while his great golden heroship's traipsing about. She'll be back, you'll see."

"That's not very reassuring," I said with a sour grunt.

He shrugged his shoulders again. "It is what it is," he said philosophically.

Easy for him to say.

He pulled the cloth off his shoulder and gave the counter another unnecessary scrub. "So, if Hera isn't your problem, what's got you in such a snit then?"

"Oh, it's money," I waved it off moodily. "Nothing earth-shattering, I suppose. I mean, I've got any number of contracts, but …" I leaned forward, suddenly intent. "I need to win that Bronze Chef competition."

"Ah. Still comes down to that, does it?" Dionysus sniffed and rubbed his nose uncomfortably.

"I'm beyond desperate at this point. The competition is only ten days away and I haven't even put my name forward yet, let alone secured a sponsor! How can I, when every time I so much as look at a piece of kraken, it shrivels up and dies—and the blasted thing is already dead! Zeus's grandson or not, I'd be the joke of Athens if I entered the competition with that hanging over my head. And no respectable business would want to be associated with that. Haven't you and Hermes managed to discover *anything*? Something that will help me cook that gods-cursed sea monster?"

The god of wine took a deep breath and shook his head, suddenly very involved in wiping his counter. "I'm sorry, mate. The truth is, Poseidon's a right powerful bastard. When he takes a dislike to someone, he doesn't mess about. We *have* been looking, Hermes and I, we just … well, we haven't had much luck, yeah? And with the Oskhophoria going on …" He trailed off and shrugged.

Deflated, I heaved a deep sigh.

"Cheer up, then." Dionysus reached across and clipped me on the shoulder (my ivory shoulder, of course). "It's only a matter of time. Poseidon may be a great powerful bugger, but what's he got up here, eh?" He tapped his forehead significantly.

I eyed him uneasily and didn't answer. Dionysus had a nasty tendency to bad-mouth his relatives, which was fine if you were also a god, rather less so if you were not. I was in enough trouble with Poseidon without getting caught gossiping about his intellectual capabilities.

"Lotta sodding seaweed, if you ask me," Dionysus said, confirming my fears. "That's too much time under the waves, is that. Clogs up the works. And besides—"

"But what does this have to do with my problem?" I interrupted. "I don't see how this gets me anywhere."

"Maybe not yet," the god replied, unruffled. "But it means that somewhere, somehow, there's a loophole. And his great fishy-arsed self hasn't noticed it yet. All Hermes and I have to do is find it and then …" He rubbed his hands together gleefully. "Why then, Basileos's your uncle, isn't he?"

I stretched my lips into a smile, trying hard to keep my skepticism from showing. In my experience, Poseidon was not at all lacking in the intellectual department, while Dionysus? Well, suffice it to say, the god of wine often had something other than mere sea water clogging up *his* works.

"It's only a matter of time," he assured me. "Hermes is on the case, yeah?"

"And *he's* got sore feet! How is he going to discover anything when he's limping around like that?"

"Ah, give him enough time and that crafty little bugger'll sniff anything out. He's the ruddy god of wiles, after all, he's got his ways."

"True," I admitted. "But time is in rather short supply at the moment."

"Details, details." Dionysus waved it off. "I'm telling you, I'll sort it." He belched boozily into his beard. "After all, I'm a sodding god, aren't I? No worries, mate."

Unable to summon a smile, I nodded unhappily.

"So," Dionysus said, dusting his hands off as though the problem were solved. "You want me to do summat about those fish?" He gestured to my basket. "I could change them into eels for you. Or maybe a nice sea bass, eh?"

"Don't you dare touch my mullets!" I exclaimed, throwing protective arms around my basket.

"Just trying to help." The god of wine looked wounded.

"I know," I said, forcing my voice into a milder tone. "I know. I'm sorry. And thanks very much. Really. But these are special fish. Striped red mullets have become … well, a sort of signature dish for me. I'm sure a sea bass would be lovely—and I appreciate the offer, I really do!—but my clients expect striped mullets and I can't afford to disappoint them."

"Suit yourself," Dionysus said a bit coolly.

"Hey, how about some service 'round here, then?" a crotchety old man wheezed from behind me.

And all of a sudden the god of wine was very busy with customers.

The lunchtime crowds were out in force now, all of them, it seemed, in desperate need of a drink. I lingered for a while, wanting to apologize again. I hadn't meant to hurt his feelings. But when Dionysus continued to laugh and banter with everyone except me, I gave up, bade him a barely acknowledged goodbye, and headed glumly homeward.

I'd now offended my best friend, the girl that I loved, and a god. Could this day possibly get any worse?

"Dude! You're home!"

No sooner had I stepped into the house, hoping for nothing more than a little peace and quiet, than a mass of fluffy blond hair swooped down on me and I was engulfed in a bone-crushing hug. Shocked, I almost dropped my basket of mullets.

"Been chilling here forever, dude! Where've you been?"

He thumped me soundly on the shoulder before loosening his grip. He wore his brown satchel slung across his shoulder and as I stepped away from him, it swung out and whatever was in it thumped me solidly in the side.

"Perseus?" I managed at last, my voice sounding breathless.

The Hero of the Aegean chortled and threw his arms wide. His tanned face had broken into a huge white grin. "In person!"

With assiduous care, I set down my basket of fish. Straightening, I passed a shaking hand over my eyes. "But, how did … what …?"

"Ah, dude," he said, readjusting the strap of his satchel. "I couldn't be staying with strangers when I've got kin in town! I mean, don't get me wrong, Archestratus is awesome and all. But hey, you're *family*."

My thoughts were jumbled, inchoate. I struggled to form a coherent sentence.

"But … this … this isn't my house," I managed at last. "I'm really only a guest here."

Perseus waved it off. "No worries, man! Your friend, Gorgias, is one killer dude. Told us his house was our house. Said we could stay as long as we wanted. How epic is that, eh?"

"Uh ... we?" I asked weakly.

Perseus slapped his hand to his forehead. "Whoa, I forgot! You haven't even met my mom! Or my sister! You're gonna love 'em. Come on, dude. They're in the courtyard."

He spun around, yanking me unceremoniously through the vestibule and down the hallway to the courtyard. He strode through the house as if he owned the place. I stumbled after him, too stunned to do anything but follow in his fluffy blond wake.

Perseus was here? Perseus was going to *stay* here?

I stopped when we reached the courtyard, though my uncle still tugged on my arm like an enthusiastic puppy. I blinked in the late afternoon sunlight, trying to adjust my eyes to the brightness. Two cloak-wrapped figures had risen from one of the garden benches.

The taller of these came forward. "Greetings, Chef Pelops," she said, kissing me on both cheeks. "I am Danaë, mother to Perseus."

Her voice was cultured and pleasing, her movements grace-ful, and she held herself like royalty, which I belatedly remem-bered she was. I'd heard the stories circulating around the Agora. Danaë had been a princess of Argos before her father, learning that he was fated to be killed by his daughter's son, locked her away in a bronze chamber deep underground. This had not, however, stopped my ever-resourceful grandfather who, accord-ing to the stories, came to her in the guise of a golden shower.

But there was none of this turbulent history now in her serene features, and although fine lines crinkled around her eyes and mouth, she possessed a luminous beauty. I still wasn't sure about the whole golden shower bit, but it was easy to see why Zeus had been driven to some spectacular means to infiltrate her bronze prison.

Perseus had obviously inherited his exceptional appearance from both sire and dam. Unfortunately, he had inherited his manners from neither.

"And this is Nausea, dude," he announced, yanking the shorter figure forward. "My little sister."

Where Perseus was big and golden and bright, his sister—Nausea?—was small, thin, and dark, with unfashionably straight hair and skin as brown as a walnut. Seeing them side by side, it was painfully clear who possessed the divine lineage of the two. She appeared to be a year or two younger than her brother, and if he had inherited all the good looks of the family, he had also inherited all the good humour, for the young woman's mouth had a cynical twist to it and her expression was one of sullen unpleasantness. She did not look at me, instead keeping her eyes trained firmly on the ground.

"Nausea's been called up by the Dulcet Dude himself," Perseus informed me.

"Excuse me?"

"Apollo, man! You know, the god with the lyres? Naus had a dream, or a vision, or something. Seems the god of tunes is just jonesin' for her over at Delphi."

"To be a priestess," Perseus's sister said in a barely audible voice. "Not to play music."

"Right," he agreed amiably. "Anyhow, we'll be dropping her off on our way back to Aethiopia. Imagine, my baby sister at Delphi!" Perseus put his arm around her thin shoulders and gave her a shake. Although she kept her eyes downcast, her set expression was of one who had endured many such moments.

"Well, actually Nausea's my half sister, dude," Perseus amended. "Her old man was a fisherman. Sounds lame, I know, but he was a cool dude. Most awesome—for a mortal."

"And her name is Nausikaa," Danaë chided her son. "Really, Perseus, must you persist with this childishness?"

The reprimand might have been more effective had it not been delivered in such a indulgent tone.

"Mom, lighten up!" He grinned down at her. "She's my *sister*. Besides, we're all family here."

"True." Danaë smiled at him fondly before turning her attention back to me. "And let me take this opportunity to thank you for so kindly opening your doors to us."

I pounced on it. "Uh, yes. About that," I began. "You know, this isn't my house—"

"Dude!" Perseus waved his hands in the air to stop my words. "I already told you, the G-Man himself invited us to crash here."

"Where *is* Gorgias?" I asked, clinging to the idea that this was all a terrible mistake. That it could all be sorted as soon as Gorgias returned. How could he have opened his home to such a boor? Hadn't he, mere hours ago, described Perseus as a cack-handed bugger? What had possessed him to offer such hospitality?

"Next door," Perseus informed me. "He and the little dude are getting Pegasus settled."

"Your, uh … your horse?" I stammered. "Your horse is staying here too?"

"In the workshop." Perseus nodded happily. "The G-Man suggested it and I think it's an insanely cool idea. Pegasus doesn't like the city stables. He'll be way happier close to me. The little dude—Hermogenes?—he seemed super stoked about it."

I passed a hand over my forehead. "I'm not in the least surprised," I told him.

Perseus threw a companionable arm around my shoulder. "This'll be epic, dude! You'll see. Non-stop party time, eh? Uncle and nephew! We're gonna throw it down. Hey Nausea, you never said hello to my nephew."

Throughout all this, Nausikaa had kept her eyes firmly on her feet, but at her brother's behest, her mouth gave a sardonic twist and she finally raised her face to look at me.

As her gaze met mine, I felt a jolt of recognition.

Streaked with white and green, blue as the Aegean itself, her eyes stared at me. There was an unearthly quality to those eyes. I had noticed it before when I'd seen her in the Agora, though I had not known at the time who she was. Almost, I could believe there was something of the divine in her background. But no, according to Perseus, her father had been no god. Merely a simple fisherman—who had sired a daughter with the most arresting eyes I had ever seen.

"Hello," I said softly.

"Chef Pelops," she greeted me, stiff and unsmiling. She made no move to kiss my cheek or even take my hand. And although her voice was warm and rich, like liquid honey, her tone was as icy as purple-winged Boreas.

Chapter 15

It was all unravelling. All my carefully laid plans, all Hermogenes's clever marketing strategies, all my recent good fortune.

To begin with, the presence of Perseus and his family in my home was both instantly and mightily vexing. Bad enough that all the other members of the household exhibited unreserved delight with the prestigious guests. And that my disciple appeared to have forgotten he was chef's assistant rather than winged-horse handler (though I had to admit, Pegasus was quite magnificent). And that my best friend—usually a down-to-earth, no-nonsense sort—had taken to parading his illustrious house guest around the Kerameikos, ostensibly showing him the "sights" while making it clear to all and sundry that this most famous individual was residing in our humble abode.

Then, there was the Hero of the Aegean himself.

In a misguided effort to get to know his "frickin' nephew"

better, he had begun following me around, ever-present brown satchel slung over his shoulder, golden hair feathered out behind him. Mouth flapping non-stop. He was constantly treading on my heels.

"Faster, dude! C'mon, pick up the pace. Ya gotta work it to kill it."

He interfered with my business transactions in the Agora.

"Whoa. You're not buying *that*, are you, dude? That's totally random!"

He invaded my kitchen.

"Duuuude! Chill out, man. I just threw a few spices on those bad boys. You know, to punch 'em up a notch."

He even fed my cooking to his *horse*.

"Dude, relax! Pegasus totally thought your chow was, like, twenty percent cooler than anything else he's eaten!"

The only saving grace was that, between the symposions in his honour and the dinners for which I was contracted, I saw very little of him in the evenings. I even took to rising before first light in an attempt to quit the house before he got up. Unfortunately, he appeared to require very little in the way of sleep and could often be found lounging in the courtyard—on my favourite bench!—enjoying either a last cup of wine or a first one. He always greeted me in the same way.

"Yo, dude. 'Sup?"

It had taken me several days to discern the meaning of this.

As I say, all this was vexing enough—though not particularly detrimental to the aforementioned marketing strategies—but then matters got infinitely worse. Hermogenes, in one of the rare instances where he could pull himself away from the winged horse or the loving contemplation of his sprouting facial hair, brought to my attention a piece of very unwelcome news.

It seemed Mithaecus, in preparation for his likely participation in the Bronze Chef competition, had, with much grandiosity, unveiled what he was calling a new direction for his cuisine. All of Athens was talking of it; everyone, it seemed, was eager to sample it. In fact, my disciple had informed me only that morning, I had already lost out on three separate contracts because the clients had opted to secure The Sicilian's services instead of my own.

"Imagine anyone wanting to taste anything that cretin tried to prepare!" I complained to Dionysus. "*I'm* the grandson of Zeus! *I'm* the one with the gods-given talent for the culinary arts! Who is Mithaecus, I ask you?"

"Besides Hera's protégé?" the god of wine mumbled into his cup.

I waved off his remark with an irritated flick of my hand. "Please. He's no more than a jumped-up grill jockey with a handful of disciples and a few substandard recipes."

"Ha! Grill jockey." Dionysus giggled drunkenly.

The god was a little the worse for wear that day, his eyes bleary and his cheeks flushed and shining. All the grape vines in Greece must have been well and truly harvested by now, but Dionysus, it seemed, was unwilling to see the Oskhophoria end.

We were reclining on a pair of couches in the room behind his wine stall. From the outside, one wouldn't think the space much larger than a privy, but on the inside it was almost as big as the theatre that bore his name. The decor was appropriate to the sensibilities of its owner, incorporating motifs of vines and grapes and the like. It was constantly changing, though not in the sense one might expect. While a mortal man might update the look of his andron by replacing cushions and coverings, a god's idea of redecorating was considerably more exotic. For one thing, the leaves, which had been painted on the floor, fluttered restlessly as if in a gentle breeze, the play of light and shadow constantly shifting in their foliage. The wall frescoes moved as well, the painted images silently acting out various activities as if in a play. Today, no doubt in honour of the recent Oskhophoria, a group of smiling men in wide-brimmed hats was cheerfully harvesting clusters of dark grapes and placing them in painted woven baskets. One less industrious fellow reclined against his basket, nibbling a handful of grapes and goosing his colleagues whenever they passed by.

It could all be most disconcerting. Usually I refrained from looking at the walls.

"I can't understand why Athenians are so hot and bothered about him all of sudden," I continued, my eyes carefully averted from the moving frescoes. "Just the other day, it was *my* name scrawled all over the Agora, now it's The Sicilian's. How could things change so quickly?"

"Fame is a fleeting thing, my friend—even for a demi-god," Dionysus replied philosophically before tipping his head back to drain his wine cup.

"That's an understatement," I grumped. "I've barely had the chance to enjoy it, and already I'm last week's news."

Dionysus smacked his lips noisily. "That's Hera, is that," he observed, suppressing a boozy belch.

"Hera!" I narrowed my eyes. "You think she's gotten involved in this?"

"I'm sure of it. Did you not read the graffiti, then?" Dionysus asked as he poured himself another cup from his special Oskhophoria wine krater. Though the vessel was of suitably god-sized proportion and larger than any wine krater I'd ever seen, Dionysus had already replenished it numerous times during the course of the afternoon.

"No," I replied. "Hermogenes told me of it. Why?"

"Well, it seems your friend The Sicilian has been banging on about his divine patroness."

"What!" I sprayed my wine across the front of my chiton.

"Probably in retaliation against your news about your grand-dad," Dionysus nodded, passing me a cloth to wipe up.

"But … wouldn't that … is it not hubristic of him?" I demanded, dabbing at the wine stains. "Doesn't Hera mind?"

Dionysus shrugged. "She's not taking issue with it, is she? If I had to hazard a guess, I'd say it's her way of getting a bit of her own back at you."

I paused as I considered this.

"But really, Hera's only part of your problem, isn't she?" Dionysus leaned forward and selected a fall apple from the bowl in front of him.

"What do you mean?"

"I mean that, when it comes right down to it, the real trouble is there are just too many gods." He bit into the fruit, slurping the juices before they could run down his chin.

I stared at him, wondering if the god of wine had finally had too much to drink.

"For one city," he explained around his mouthful.

I still did not understand what he was trying to say.

"Think about it," he told me. "We're a jealous bunch, aren't we? Each wanting his own chuffing altar and sacrifices and prayers and the like. What's a poor mortal to do? They certainly can't go playing favourites. You never know what might come of that."

"You think the Athenians are hedging their bets?" The notion had not occurred to me. I took a thoughtful sip of wine, considering it.

"Wouldn't you?" he asked pointedly. "Here they've just spent the past few weeks praying and sacrificing to Father Zeus on account of Perseus—and by Ares's bollocks, does that boy know how to party! Ha! You should have seen us last night!" He grinned and tipped more wine down his throat.

"Athenians praying to Zeus?" I reminded him.

Dionysus wiped his mouth with the corner of his chiton. "Right, right. And sacrificing to him too! All because of Perseus—not to mention your pan-frying self. Don't get me wrong, I don't begrudge Dad his fair share, but it's only natural the rest of us should get a turn now."

"But ... are you telling me the other gods would be *jealous* of that? Of a few sacrifices?"

"And why not?" Dionysus snorted. "A few sacrifices might mean sod all to you lot, but it means a chuff of a lot more to us, doesn't it? Oh, don't you worry, you'll still have a bit of shine to your name on account of Dad," he assured me. "After all, no Athenian in his right mind would risk offending *him*. But they can't keep singling Zeus out for special treatment, can they? What about the rest of us? That sort of favouritism goes on too long and we might start to feel a bit unappreciated."

He polished off his apple in two more bites. "Numbers don't lie," he said, tossing the core over his shoulder. It disappeared in midair. "And me, I'm way down in my sacrifices this week, almost as low as Ares—and that muscly bugger's numbers always go down in peace time. But me? I should be bloody *rolling* in sacrifices this week." His tone verged on resentful. "I mean, the Oskhophoria's barely over, and you know that's the most important harvest celebration of the whole sodding year! My numbers should be climbing, and instead they're sagging like a bread wife's tits. It's hardly fair!"

I passed a hand over my brow. "You ... you actually keep track of these things?"

The god nodded. "'Course we do. I told you, we're a jealous lot. How are we to know who's trending if we don't keep score?"

He paused and leaned forward to pour each of us more wine. "I remember one year I got more sacrifices than Athena—seventy-three more!" He smiled, stroking his beard in fond reminiscence, then he snorted. "Well, it was the best grape season in memory, wasn't it? Only natural for the mortals to be honouring my outstanding efforts. But did *she* care about that? Ohhhh, no!" His voice took on a high falsetto note. "It's not fair! *I'm* the patron goddess of the city. *I* should get the most sacrifices."

He paused and sucked his wine back. "The olive harvest was

utter shite that year," he confided in his normal voice. "Worst that anyone could remember. Why, there was barely enough oil to see the city through the winter—and half of that went rancid before spring. Oh, she was right pissed off! And all because my numbers were better than hers. Aye, my friend, you ignore a god at your peril."

I could see the wine god's point, and it made me feel marginally better. But knowing that my fall in popularity was not personal did not negate the fact that my new-found fame appeared to be failing. If I lost any more custom to Mithaecus, I wouldn't have enough money to move out before Gorgias brought his new wife home. I would not—I could not!—live with Gorgias after his marriage. I chewed the inside of my cheek, thinking furiously.

"I'm going to need a new angle, then," I said finally. "If I'm to go up against this New Cuisine."

"This new what?"

"Cuisine," I explained with a sour grimace. "It's a foreign word that means cookery. That's what Mithaecus is calling his 'new direction,' though as far as I can see, the only thing 'new' about it appears to be a new way to cheat your clients." I took another sip of my wine, though I was starting to feel its effect (I had been there for most of the afternoon).

"Cheating? How's that, then?"

"Well," I began, watching as the god of wine drained his cup yet again, "according to this new philosophy he's adopted, he has rejected any excessive complication in cooking, declaring it old-fashioned and unhealthy." I wrinkled my nose in disdain.

Dionysus made a rude noise. "Pompous prat."

"Indeed," I agreed. "Still, this new direction of his cannot be much of a surprise, really. The man never could cope with anything more complicated than three ingredients. Oh, he claims that his New Cuisine uses only the freshest possible ingredients, 'preserving the natural flavours without strong marinades or heavy sauces.' But really, what chef worth his sea salt does anything else? Just because *he* routinely overwhelmed his dishes with old cheese and strong spice does not mean the rest of us committed the same crime."

I knocked back the rest of my drink and paused to inhale a deep breath through my nostrils. Dionysus tried to sit up to pour me more wine, but when that proved too much of a struggle, he collapsed back against his cushions and gave a negligent wave of his hand. My empty wine cup began to fill itself of its own accord.

"But incomprehensible to my mind," I continued, eyeing my rapidly filling cup, "are the menus, which have a fraction of the number of dishes one would normally prepare. And the portions! From what I hear, they're so tiny as to be considered minuscule."

The cup stopped filling just short of its brim. I took a quick sip so it wouldn't spill. The heady smell of violets filled my nostrils.

"Shocking," Dionysus murmured, waving his hand to refill his own cup in the same fashion.

"That's not the worst of it," I snorted, accidentally sloshing a few drops of the flower-scented wine down the front of my chiton. "From what Hermogenes tells me, he's charging *three* times what he did before! For a fraction of the food. And the Athenians are *paying* it! Each dish is barely a mouthful and—hang on …"

My eyes, which had been wandering absently over the moving wall frescoes, had suddenly sharpened on the images, bringing them into clear focus. At some point during our conversation, the painted grape harvest had given way to a painted symposion, complete with cithara players and scantily clad flute girls swaying to silent music. Serving slaves were bringing in first tables, while dinner guests clapped their hands in anticipation of the feast.

Each painted plate held barely a mouthful of food.

Outraged, I pushed myself up on my elbow. "*You've got his cuisine on your frescoes!*" I accused the god. "Look at them! There's barely enough food on those plates to feed a cat. That's The Sicilian's cooking! That's his New Cuisine! *How could you?*"

Dionysus had assumed a guilty expression. "I had to, didn't I?" he said defensively. "I'm the God of Parties, I've got to keep up with the trends."

"The trends?" I spluttered in indignation. "What trend? He just started this ridiculous business. How can it be a trend?"

Dionysus shrugged, though he avoided my eyes. "I like to be cutting edge, me."

"*Cutting edge!*"

Just then, the curtain that led to the front of the wine stall was pulled open as a figure slipped into the room. There was a flash of sunlight, and for a brief moment, the noise from the marketplace intruded, though both sound and sunlight were cut off again as soon as the curtain closed.

"Herm!" Dionysus sat up, greeting the new arrival with poorly disguised relief. "We expected you hours ago, mate. Where've you been?"

Hermes limped across the room and sank onto a couch with a weary sigh. "All over the sodding city," he replied, watching as Dionysus waved his hand to fill a wine cup for him. "My feet are bloody killing me!"

He kicked off his sandals and wiggled his toes. The scent of tree strawberries wafted over me. "I've said it before and I'll say it again, being the sodding god of messages and travel isn't all it's cracked up to be. Just look! Look at them!" The god held his feet up for our inspection. They were swollen and pink-looking. "I've near walked me bleeding soles off today."

The god of wine passed him a brimming cup.

Hermes put his feet down. "Ta." He nodded his thanks and took a long, deep drink.

"Ah, I needed that," he said finally, smacking his lips. "Cheers, D., Chef P."

"So what's had you out and about so much, then?" Dionysus asked. "Hera been messaging again?"

"No. I've been chasing down something for this one," Hermes replied, jerking his head towards me.

I bolted upright, startled almost into sobriety. "You've found out how I can cook the kraken?" I demanded.

But Hermes was already shaking his head. "Sorry," he said, not unsympathetically.

Disappointed, I fell back against the cushions, my head swimming from the sudden movement. With studied care, I set my cup down on the table in front of me. I'd had enough wine for one day.

"I still think it must have summat to do with wine," Dionysus mused, stroking his beard. "But I'm stuffed if I know how."

Hermes lifted his cup in salute, then took another deep drink. "Well, I hate being the bearer of bad news and all, but I think Chef P. might have more problems than how to fry up a spot of sea monster."

I stared at him, trying to ignore the dreadful premonition that washed over me like a cold winter rain. The frescoed figures on the wall behind him had stopped their feasting and carousing and were now clustered behind the god of messengers, watching, as if waiting on his next words.

"How's that, then?" Dionysus asked, sitting straighter. "What problems are these?"

Hermes's expression had lost its usual geniality. He looked downright sombre. "Let's just say, he might want to be avoiding any Thessalian witches," he said with an odd twist to his mouth.

In an overly dramatic gesture, the frescoes raised their hands to their cheeks in dismayed surprise.

"I don't know any Thessalian witches!" I protested, my mouth suddenly dry.

"Aye, but they know you," Hermes told me. "I've been finding curse tablets all over the city—down in wells, sunk in cisterns. Buried in graves."

The painted figures cried out in silent alarm. One of the flute girls swooned. Several of the others began fussing over her, fanning her prone body.

I suddenly found it difficult to swallow. "But ... how do you know these are directed at me?"

"Because all those tablets have your name on them, my friend," Hermes replied. "Have a look."

He reached into a fold of his chiton and pulled out a palm-sized object. I caught it as he tossed it to me.

"It looks like some kind of metal," I said slowly, turning it over in my hands. "But it's all rolled up."

I knew vaguely of curse tablets, of course, but I had never seen one. And, as far as I knew, I had certainly never been the subject of one.

"It is metal," Hermes confirmed. "Lead, hammered flat into a sheet, then rolled up and pierced with a nail. To help in the binding."

Uneasily, I regarded the object in my palm, suddenly reluctant to unroll it.

"What does it say?" I asked, almost in a whisper.

Hermes half-closed his eyes, and his voice took on an odd singsong quality. "*In the presence of Hermes, the One Who Binds,*" he chanted, "*I bind Pelops of Lydia, his tongue, and hands, and spirit, and feet. Just as this lead is worthless and cold, so let Pelops of Lydia and his deeds be worthless and cold. And for those men with him, let whatever they say and plot against me be worthless and cold.*"

By the time he had finished, every hair on the back of my

neck was standing on end. The hate, the vitriol behind this almost took my breath away.

"A lot of them were in your theatre, D," Hermes told the god of wine. "Buried in the dirt."

"*Bollocks!*" Dionysus exploded, suddenly more sober than I'd seen him all afternoon. "In *my* theatre? The chuffing nerve! That's that pox-ridden Sicilian, that is. Trying to fix the Bronze Chef match, I've no doubt."

"Mithaecus!" I mouthed the hated name, though I could not be surprised by the revelation.

"He ought to be ashamed of himself!" Dionysus continued to rail. "Using magic like that? Too mingy to go through proper channels, that's what he is! Didn't want to spend the coin on sacrifices. Rather give a few obols to the Thessalian witches, would he? The dirty great bastard! And using magic on a colleague! Aye, that shifty little tosser's really got it in for you, doesn't he?"

But another, more unpleasant thought had occurred to me. I turned to Hermes, eyeing him warily.

"It sounded like he's calling on you to, uh, render me ... well, worthless and cold," I said, hesitation making me stumble on my words.

The god of messages seemed so young, so *innocuous*, I often forgot about his darker incarnation as Hermes Chthonius, guide of the dead. He looked at me for a moment, and his dark eyes seemed to glitter strangely. A small smile played on his lips. This was a god who could pass easily from the upperworld to the underworld. A god who was powerful in both. I shifted uncomfortably, unable to look away.

"Ah, don't be worrying about that," Dionysus assured me with an airy wave. "Hermes doesn't *have* to oblige, does he? Not when the pair of you are mates. It's what you might call a conflict of interest."

"I wouldn't do that to you," Hermes confirmed, shaking his head. "Certainly not for The Sicilian."

"So I don't need to worry," I said, letting my breath out gustily.

"Oh, I didn't say that," Hermes said with a quick shake of his head. "I can bow out due to conflict of interest, but it's only a matter of time before Mithaecus and his witch friends twig to it. They'll be calling on Hekate next, and she's not nearly so chummy with you, is she?"

In fact, I had never met Hekate, goddess of magic, witchcraft, ghosts, and necromancy. A pleasure I now hoped would be indefinitely postponed.

"What should I do?" I asked. "Do I curse him in retaliation? I've seen the Thessalian witches in the Agora, over by the new Law Court. I could—"

"Best not," Dionysus cut me off before I could go any further. "Nasty things, those curse tablets. Tricky too, if they're not done right. You hire yourself one of them manky witches and you're like to find yourself in a whole mess of trouble."

"What am I supposed to do, then? Wait for Hekate to come 'round?"

"Win the Bronze Chef," Dionysus replied promptly. "That's what this is all about, isn't it?"

"And how exactly am I supposed to do that?" I exclaimed, bitterness souring my tone. I thrust myself to my feet, and took several quick strides. I stopped just short of the frescoed wall, clenching and unclenching my fists, my entire body quivering with impotent fury.

That Mithaecus would stoop to curse my name did not astonish me. I was only surprised it had taken him so long to do so. But how could I possibly defend myself against such a thing? Win the Bronze Chef competition, Dionysus said. But how could I win the competition when Poseidon would do everything in his power to ensure my failure? And whatever angle he might overlook, the curse tablets would surely address. I had witches on one side and a vengeful god on the other. My options appeared few indeed.

Hermes had risen as well. He came over and touched my shoulder gently. I glanced at him. His eyes were sympathetic.

"I am working on it, Chef P.," he told me, his voice soft. "Truly. I've got a few leads, but I don't want to say anything till I know for certain."

Wordlessly, I looked away, blinking back tears of anger and frustration. Dionysus's frescoes had resumed their interrupted symposion. Painted guests were enjoying a rousing game of kottabos, while the serving slaves began bringing in more food. The painted plates they carried were now properly laden with comestibles, not the bite-sized morsels of Mithaecus's New Cuisine. I heard Dionysus rouse from his couch.

He came up on the other side of me, so I was flanked by my two guardian gods. We stood in silence for a while, watching the happily feasting frescoes.

"I changed them," he told me, though I could see that for

myself. "Plonker's not playing fair, is he? Hiring witches and whatnot? It's just not on. I can't be supporting that, can I? So anyhoo, I changed it back. Thought you'd like it. Have a look. The dish that's coming in now? That's your roasted lamb, that is."

The painted figures smiled and applauded at the delectable sight. I nodded without saying anything.

"Look," Dionysus said, nudging me with his elbow. "I know it don't seem like it right now, but Hermes and I will get this sorted, yeah? I promise. We may be a pair of good-time gods, but we gave you our word, didn't we? And even though we might enjoy a nice party now and then, or a bit of a festival, we're not the sort of gods to go breaking our promises."

The Athenian Bureau of Scythian Archers (ABSA)

Official transcript #632

Suspect: You can't hold me here forever!

Scythian Archer #1: On the contrary. We can haul your ass up before the Areopagus if we want.

Suspect: The Areopagus? Wot? I never committed no murder! You can't take me to th' Areopagus!

Scythian Archer #1: We can do whatever we want, you little pissant! If we want to take you to the Areopagus, we can. If we want to beat you till you're black and blue, we can do that too.

Suspect: But, but…

Scythian Archer #2: Now, now. There's no need to talk about beatings and the like. We're not looking to smack anybody around.

Scythian Archer #1: Says you.

Scythian Archer #2: We're just having a civilized conversation here. Now if you tell us what you were doing in the graveyard—

Suspect: I wasn't doin' nuthin'! I wasn't in no graveyard!

Scythian Archer #1: That's it! I've had enough of this bullshit!

Scythian Archer #2: Please. You were caught in the graveyard. So why don't you tell us what you were doing, and my colleague here won't feel it necessary to … jog your memory.

Suspect: I know wot yer doin'! It's good Archer, bad Archer, isn't it? I sodding well know that game.

Scythian Archer #1: Then you sodding well know how it ends if you don't cooperate.

Suspect: Okay, okay, I'll talk. Just … don't do that again. And you can't tell nobody wot I said.

Scythian Archer #2: We wouldn't dream of it. Now, why were you in the graveyard?

Suspect: It were for me boss, weren't it? Bloke named Akrisias. 'E's one of them Thessalian witches.

Scythian Archer #2: Really. And your boss, this Akrisias, he sends you to graves, does he?

Suspect: 'Course 'e does. Graves of the restless dead. Them what died early or violent like.

Scythian Archer #2: And what do you do to those graves? Are you robbing them?

Suspect: Not hardly! It's for th' curse tablets, isn't it? They got to be buried on account of them being addressed to Hekate or Hermes. Usually 'e just has me put 'em down wells and springs and th' like. Sometimes in th' ground at th' Theatre of Dionysus. Y'know for the competitions and plays. But for the big jobs, 'e wants 'em in the graves.

Scythian Archer #2: Curse tablets, I see. And why are curse tablets buried in those graves in particular?

Suspect: 'Cause them spirits are the angriest, aren't they?

Scythian Archer #2: And angry spirits are better for witchcraft?

Suspect: 'Course they are! Th' witches channel all that anger. Brings more power to th' curse that way.

Scythian Archer #1: That's disgusting!

Suspect: It works, don't it? Curse like that might even work on a big bloke like you.

Scythian Archer #1: Is that a threat? You cocky little wanker! I'll show you a curse!

(end of transcript)

DECLASSIFIED

Chapter 16

"Excuse me, Chef Pelops!" An unfamiliar voice hailed me. "A word, if you please."

I turned and looked around me blearily. I had been drinking wine for much of the afternoon and was somewhat the worse for it.

"Yes?" I inquired impatiently, still unsure who had addressed me. "What is it?"

All I wanted to do was get home and lie down. I was not in the mood to be accosted in the Agora. Perhaps, I mused belatedly, I ought to have worn my old chiton so as not to be recognized.

A young slave stood to one side of me, his face full of eager excitement. "Chef Pelops, I'm from Curl Up and Dye and—"

All I heard was curl up and die.

"Is that a threat?" I demanded, outraged. "Who are you?"

The man took a step back, his well-oiled curls bouncing. "Please, Chef Pelops! I did not mean to—"

"What do you want?" I took a threatening step towards him. "Did Mithaecus send you?"

The man kept retreating, his hands held up as if to show he had nothing to hide. "No!" he protested. "No! I represent a hair shop! Curl Up and Dye! We're over by the moneylenders!"

I paused, allowing the thought to percolate through my wine-muddled brain. "A hair shop?" I asked finally.

The young man lowered his hands and ventured closer. "Over by the moneylenders," he said again.

"You weren't sent by The Sicilian?" I asked, still suspicious.

"No." The man shook his head solemnly. "My master sent me and he hails from Elis, though he has made a successful life for himself here in Athens—very successful! In fact, he wants to sponsor you for—"

Another offer of sponsorship? I let out my breath in an explosive sigh. With thoughts of Mithaecus and his curse tablets so fresh in my mind, for a brief moment I'd thought my ultimate fate was confronting me.

"I'm not interested!" I interrupted, rude with relief. He was just another stupid sponsor from another ridiculously named hair shop.

"But, Chef Pelops! We are a very well-known shop. We specialize in the most difficult-to-curl hair. Guaranteed results! Many of the city's finest athletes patronize Curl Up and Dye—"

"Which I find astonishing, given such a ludicrous name. Thank you for the offer, but I am not interested."

It offended him.

"Perhaps I ought to ask Mithaecus The Sicilian, then," he suggested snottily. "I've seen him. He's bound to be chosen as one of the contenders, and his natural curls would fit in much better with the mission statement of our establishment." He raked my own curl-less locks with a pointed stare.

I ignored the look and snorted inelegantly. "You do that," I told him. "I'm sure he'd love to be sponsored by a business called Curl Up and Dye." I let my voice ooze sarcasm at the name.

"I will then!" he spat.

"Good luck with that," I replied, all amiability.

The fellow made a rude gesture and turned away.

I tried to think of a suitable parting shot, but by the time I did, the slave was already long gone.

I sighed and hitched my cloak up on my shoulder, preparing to continue on my way. Another gods-cursed hair shop sponsor! I did not believe for one moment that it was coincidence. Not when the shop specialized in curls which, according to my overzealous disciple, I required to complete my "look."

It seemed I was going to have to have a word with Hermogenes. Damn him and his preposterous makeovers.

I arrived home, still a little drunk and considerably more than a little discouraged, to an exquisite smell emanating from the kitchen. I paused in the vestibule and inhaled deeply, trying to identify the different elements. Garlic, onions, thyme, leeks, wine, celery, a hint of saffron, and ... was that ... kraken? It smelled divine.

It *was* kraken!

I'd no idea Hermogenes had it in him. Could it be he was, at last, taking the initiative? If so, I might have to forgive him for the hair shop sponsors.

"Chef!" he greeted me happily when I entered the kitchen.

But it was not Hermogenes standing at the hearth and stirring the pot that sat bubbling on the gridiron.

Nausikaa spun around at Hermogenes's exclamation. Unbound, her long straight hair fell past her waist and, as she turned, it swirled around her small frame like a dark cloak. She and Hermogenes must have been laughing, for the echo of it still played on her lips, and her sea-blue eyes were bright with merriment.

I felt myself scowl. Wasn't it enough that the brother had foisted himself on me? Now I had the sister barging into my kitchen!

In actual fact, Nausikaa had not proved as ubiquitous as her brother, for the sole reason that she seldom left the women's quarters—at least I rarely saw her leave them. She joined us for meals, of course, always silent in the presence of her more boisterous sibling, and I had spotted her occasionally over at the Springhouse early in the morning, and once or twice in our courtyard as I strode past. She greeted me solemnly whenever I encountered her, but she never smiled and her eyes were usually downcast. Despite her unwelcome presence in my home, she was not nearly as annoying as Perseus, but then, she had never invaded my kitchen—until now.

"What are you doing in here?" I demanded, the query coming out more harshly than I'd intended.

Nausikaa flushed and cast her eyes downwards, all traces of good humour vanishing from her expression.

"Doesn't it smell totally epic?" Hermogenes enthused, having obviously picked up some of Perseus's unfortunate speech patterns. "It's amazing, Chef! Truly! Turns out, Nausikaa here's a dab hand in the kitchen. I've never seen anyone prepare soup quite like this before! Never! She's … she's bloody brilliant, that's what she is!"

Nausikaa glanced over at Hermogenes, a shy smile softening her features, then she turned back to the pot and gave it a stir, carefully avoiding my eyes.

Brilliant, was she? I felt a sudden stab of jealousy at his words. Ridiculous!

How could I be envious of a fisherman's daughter? I was the grandson of Zeus! A celebrity chef. A man with a brand! I was *not* jealous. Clearly, the pang I'd felt merely constituted the beginning throes of a very unpleasant hangover.

"Indeed?" I said, attempting to moderate my previous tone. "Well, it does smell rather … interesting."

"It's cracking!" Hermogenes exclaimed, a wide grin splitting his face. "Tell the Chef how you do it, Naus. Go on."

Nausikaa flicked an uneasy glance at me and cleared her throat. "It's all in the method," she began diffidently. Her voice was perhaps a shade low for a woman, but the depth of it was dark and rich and, thankfully, completely lacking her brother's atrocious dialect. "Each ingredient has to be added one at a time, and you've got to add them in a certain order or it won't come out right."

"It's my father's recipe," she added, when I didn't respond. "And his father's before him."

"You bring it to a boil after each ingredient, see?" Hermogenes said. "Then take it off the heat and add the next one. It's brilliant!" he said again, his eyes shining as he smiled at Nausikaa with evident admiration.

I felt another odd twinge and covered it by stepping closer to the gridiron.

"Is that kraken?" I inquired, peering into the pot.

"It is," she confirmed gravely. "Some tentacles, a bit of the mantle, I've even added a few strips of the fin, though I had to slice those up so they wouldn't be too rubbery." Her voice started to gain more confidence as she explained. "To make it really good, there ought to be several different kinds of fish in it—and some shellfish too." She paused and wrinkled her nose. "But thanks to my ever-so-splendid brother, there's not much at the market these days besides kraken, so I had to make do."

"What are the orange bits?" I asked curiously. "Those round pieces?"

"Carrot root. Peeled and sliced up."

"Carrot *root*? I've never heard of anyone eating the roots before."

"That's what they do in the colonies," Hermogenes informed me with the air of one who had always possessed this information, though this was the first he'd ever mentioned it. "Not just seeds and tops, they eat the whole ruddy plant—according to

Nausikaa, that is. I tried one. It's a bit strange, but Nausikaa says it'll add some sweetness to the broth. She also says you're supposed to serve the soup with a kind of sauce made from egg yolks and olive oil and garlic." He pursed his lips doubtfully.

"Honestly, it sounded a bit dodgy to me at first," he admitted, "but given what she's done so far, I'd say she knows what she's about." He nodded with a wisdom well beyond his fifteen years, and began stroking his patchy beard.

"The sauce adds a touch of richness," Nausikaa explained. "A sort of creaminess. And there's bread too. Toasted bread." She wagged an admonitory finger at Hermogenes. "You can never forget the bread. It wouldn't be right now, would it?"

Hermogenes and Nausikaa grinned at each other in mutual accord.

I stretched my lips into a smile that felt thin and forced. "Fascinating," I said coolly.

"The thing is, Chef," Hermogenes continued, "I think—and Nausikaa agrees—this would be a cracking addition to your cooking scrolls."

"Cooking scrolls? What cooking scrolls?"

Nausikaa and Hermogenes exchanged another long glance.

"It's an idea we've come up with," Hermogenes explained. "Nausikaa and me, I mean. A series of cooking scrolls by the great Chef Pelops. You could have your recipes copied out and packaged all together like."

"We thought you could call it 'How to be a Domestic God,'" Nausikaa added, her blue eyes shining.

"As a way of acknowledging your ... um ... well ..."

Hermogenes stumbled to a halt, still uncomfortable with the reality of my antecedents.

"Your unusual parentage," Nausikaa finished for him, obviously more at ease with such things.

"Absolutely not!" I exclaimed, scowling.

"It doesn't have to be called that," Hermogenes broke in, giving Nausikaa an I-told-you-so kind of look. "I know you don't think it's on, going 'round noising about your granddad. That's all right. We'll call it something else, then."

"No."

"Che-ef!" he wailed. "It's brilliant! You could—"

"I could what?" I snapped. "Publish my recipes so any average Jason could make them? And who would hire a chef when they could toss a feast together themselves?"

"You wouldn't put *all* your recipes in it," Hermogenes protested. "Only a few of the ... well, the less complicated ones, yeah? And for a kraken dish, we could use Nausikaa's soup. She's already said we can. And it'd be right popular too, what with there being so much kraken still at market."

"That Sicilian chef has his own set of cooking scrolls," Nausikaa observed.

Infuriated, I drew myself up and turned a wintry gaze on her. How dare she! How dare this person, this intruder, this *fisherman's daughter*, compare me to the likes of Mithaecus! Out of the corner of my eye, I could see Hermogenes slap his hand over his mouth.

"That ... *individual* of whom you speak," I said, my voice quiet and icy, "is little better than a two-obol taverna cook. And you think to compare me to him?" I paused and took a sharp breath in through my nostrils. "If you believe the actions of such an excrescence will make me reconsider this ridiculous, ill-conceived scheme, then you are very sorely mistaken."

Nausikaa blinked. "I … I didn't mean to insult you. I just thought it might be an idea to consider, given your troubles with the kraken."

Hermogenes's indrawn breath was audible in the silence that followed this remark.

I stared at Nausikaa icily. "And what would you know about that?" I demanded.

Bravely, she held my eyes, but her cheeks stained dark with colour.

"I'm sorry," she began. "And you mustn't blame Hermogenes! I was just trying to find out why you never serve kraken and—"

I turned my back on her.

"I will speak to you about your loose tongue later," I said to Hermogenes, who fidgeted guiltily under my glare. "And in the meantime, I will hear no more about these cooking scrolls. The entire endeavour is out of the question! I forbid it! And while you're at it, you can stop sending hair shop sponsors my way."

Hermogenes dropped his eyes mutinously.

"I will not accept sponsorship from a hair shop," I said firmly. "I will not curl my hair, and I will not publish my recipes in a series of cooking scrolls. And even if I were of a mind to do so, I would no more include a recipe for that soup"—I pointed an accusing finger at the pot—"than I would a recipe for Mithaecus's vile Kraken Bake."

"Now, that's not fair, Chef—" Hermogenes began hotly.

But Nausikaa had stepped in front of me. Though she was considerably shorter than me, she thrust her face in front of mine, chin raised high. "I wouldn't give you the recipe if you got down on your knees and begged me," she declared, blue eyes spitting lightning.

I recoiled, taken aback by her intensity.

"Hermogenes and I were just trying to help!" she exclaimed angrily. "There was no need to be so mean. Publish your nasty scrolls or don't, I don't care! But I'll never share my soup recipe with you."

"I never wanted your soup recipe," I retorted, stung.

"Excellent," she snapped back. "Because it's a family secret. You might be my brother's nephew, but you're no family of mine! And don't I thank all the gods for *that* particular blessing! Hermogenes, the soup is your responsibility now. Don't forget the bread."

And with that she turned and flounced from the kitchen, dark hair brushing my arm as she swept past. In the heavy silence that followed, the kraken soup continued to simmer fragrantly on the gridiron.

Chapter 17

It's a popular place," Hermogenes said around an overly large mouthful of breakfast roll.

"No."

"All the athletes go there."

"No."

"The beard thinks they'd be a great sponsor."

"No, Hermogenes! No. I don't care what 'the beard' thinks! As far as I know, facial hair is not sentient. Besides, I believe I made myself very clear about this. I will not have my hair styled at an establishment called Curl Up and Dye. I don't care how fashionable it is!"

"It's not the best name for a business," Gorgias rumbled his agreement. "Especially for a sponsor. Gives the wrong impression, doesn't it?"

Hermogenes fell into surly silence, biting into his breakfast roll with rather more savagery than usual.

I took advantage of the ensuing quiet to sip gingerly at a cup of water that I'd flavoured with a few strands of precious saffron. It was a more palatable cure—and certainly easier on the digestion—than the breakfast of fried canaries most Athenians preferred after a night of wine. I shuddered at the very thought. I'd woken late with a colossal headache and a distinctly unhappy stomach. I couldn't imagine consuming a fried bird for breakfast.

I had just decided to attempt a bread roll when Hermogenes broke his silence.

"Perseus was asking for me this morning," he said in an overly polite fashion. "Wanting me to lend a hand with his Pegasus today. They're waiting for me now." He paused to swallow, then added, almost as an afterthought, "If you don't mind, that is." The request was civil enough, but I caught the faint trace of sullenness in his tone—as I was no doubt meant to.

His attitude irritated me.

I set down my untasted bread roll. "If I don't *mind*?" My voice rose along with my temper. "If I don't *mind* my disciple buggering off to polish the hooves of some magical rainbow pony? Oh, why should I mind that? Going to the market by myself? Carrying everything back by myself? Preparing for my next contract *by myself*? Whatever gave you the idea that I should mind *that*?"

Gorgias, who had been reaching for the plate of rolls, paused and stared at me, bushy eyebrows scrunching together in a frown. He opened his mouth to say something, but Hermogenes beat him to it.

"I don't have to go, Chef, really." His features settled into a martyred expression that I also found most irritating. "He just asked, is all," he said. "If you're needing me, of course I'll stay."

The words *sounded* sincere enough, but I wasn't fooled by them for an instant. Gorgias, on the other hand, gave Hermogenes an approving nod before selecting a bread roll. But Gorgias was a man who liked harmony in his house—even if he had to turn a blind eye to achieve it. He gave his attention back to his breakfast, and my disciple took the opportunity to slide me another darkly resentful look.

I pulled my cloak more tightly around my shoulders—I felt chilled this morning—and glowered right back at him. Since yesterday afternoon, I had been the recipient of many such sullen and pointed glares. Clearly, Hermogenes had not yet forgiven me for dismissing his cooking scroll scheme—or his idea for a sponsor. Curl Up and Dye, indeed! There were times, I reflected glumly, that life had been easier when Hermogenes was enslaved help rather than free disciple. Mind you, even as a slave, he had never displayed much acquaintance with the intricacies of subservient deference.

Hermogenes and his marketing strategies. They would be the second death of me!

If I were to be completely honest, his concept wasn't wholly bad, at least when it came to the cooking scrolls. I had, after all, published a cookery scroll this past summer which contained my recipe for goat cheese and fig appetizers—and I'd made a tidy little sum by doing so. But the suggestion that I publish a *series,* and include another's recipe—someone who wasn't even a chef! Well, it did not bear consideration, no matter how many dark looks Hermogenes might slide me, or how much Nausikaa might sulk.

Perseus's sister had not appeared for supper the night before, pleading a sudden headache. I suspected she was just out of temper. Her soup had been irritatingly delicious.

I closed my eyes and massaged my temples, cursing Dionysus and his bottomless wine cup.

"Fine," I relented with a audible sigh. "Go and help the great Hero with his feathered pony. Go! Take your woeful face and be off with you. But mind you come back all the more eager to work. We've Parmenides's symposion to start preparing, and I've no intention of leaving it all to the last moment."

Hermogenes brightened. "I will, Chef! I won't be long. You'll see."

"Away with you!" I waved him off wearily and readjusted my cloak again. The morning was sunny, but I couldn't seem to get warm.

Gorgias regarded me sympathetically. "Bit on the ropey side this morning, eh?"

I grunted and shrugged.

"Summat the matter, then?"

"Why do you say that?" I asked testily.

It was Gorgias's turn to shrug. "Dunno. You've not seemed like yourself these days. Like you've the weight of the world on your shoulders. You're not having the same sort of trouble as you did last summer, are you?"

"No," I replied, waving it off. "No. Nothing like that. I had too much wine yesterday, that's all. Everything's grand—except for the kraken, of course. Not much I can do about that, it seems."

"Aye, that's a bugger, that is," he agreed.

We sat in silence for a while. Gorgias finished his roll and started in on a dish of olives. I sipped at my saffron water, suppressing a shiver as the icy liquid trickled down my throat. Of course, my water had gone quite cold this morning. In fact, it was almost freezing. Curse Poseidon and his poxy vengeance! Although, I reflected sourly, I perhaps ought to have been grateful that he hadn't taken it any further of late. I'd half-expected him to, but it seemed my struggles with the kraken were enough to appease him for a while—apart from the occasional tricks with drinking and washing water, of course. Silently, I cursed him again and huddled deeper in my cloak.

What was wrong with me today? I felt cold and ... *worthless?* The thought came unbidden, and all of sudden, I remembered the wording of the curse tablet.

In the presence of Hermes, the One Who Binds, I bind Pelops of Lydia, his tongue, and hands, and spirit, and feet. Just as this lead is worthless and cold, so let Pelops of Lydia and his deeds be worthless and cold.

A frigid chill washed over me. My hands and feet felt suddenly icy, as if all blood had drained from my veins. Was The Sicilian's curse taking effect? Were my deeds and my person to become worthless and cold? Had the witches realized that

Hermes would not help them and gone instead to Hekate? A rising tide of panic threatened to choke off my breath.

Don't be ridiculous, I told myself severely. It was only yesterday that Hermes had shown me the curse tablet. Mithaecus and his Thessalians could not yet have realized that Hermes would not aid them. It was too soon. Too soon for them to have sought Hekate's help. No, I was cold because I had imbibed too much wine the day before. That must be it. It was certainly nothing to do with curses. I shivered again, trying to convince myself that this was so.

"So there's nothing else, then?" Gorgias asked. "Nothing bothering you?"

What could I say? I couldn't tell him about the curse tablets. I did not want to expose my best friend to that frightening invisible world or, by doing so, give credence to my own fears. I couldn't complain about his house guests, either. How could I protest guests of such high social stature? And I certainly couldn't say anything about his upcoming nuptials with Zeuxo.

I forced my lips into a smile. "What else would there be?" I said lightly.

"Chuffed if I know," he said, pushing himself to his feet and shaking the crumbs from his chiton. "You're as prickly as a pox-ridden hoplite this morning, but I suppose that could be the wine."

"Very likely," I told him.

He regarded me for another long moment, then shrugged. "Well, that's me off to the clay pits then. But if you're ever needing an ear …"

I gazed up at him, my throat suddenly tight. "I know," I managed to say. "And thanks. I appreciate the offer."

He nodded once and with a friendly clip on my shoulder (my ivory one, naturally), he sauntered off to begin his workday.

Alone in the courtyard, I picked up my uneaten barley roll, then put it down again. I was not hungry in the least, though my throat felt as parched as summer. I poured myself another cup of water and sipped at it, trying to ignore its iciness. My stomach rumbled ominously. The day seemed overly bright, and I was seriously considering having a moment of silence for whatever had passed away in my mouth the night before.

Unfortunately, there was a bird on the roof that felt no such compulsion and it was happily warbling away in full voice. I winced at a particularly piercing note. Had it been a canary, I might have been tempted to try the Athenians' remedy for hangovers.

Leaning back against the cushions, I closed my aching eyes and turned my face up to the weak warmth of the autumn sunshine. I sat there for quite some time.

With Gorgias and his slaves gone to the clay pits, Hermogenes out with Perseus, and the ladies, I'd been informed, out at the Eleusinium making offerings to Demeter, I thought I was alone in the house. So when I finally gathered myself enough to leave for the Agora, it came as a bit of a surprise to see a figure loitering in the front vestibule.

Her blue-green eyes were guarded this morning, her mouth thin and unsmiling.

I decided on the spot to ignore her sour countenance and quit the house as quickly as possible. Assuming an air of studious preoccupation, I bade her a pleasant good morning and offered a small, distracted smile, as though my thoughts were much occupied with weighty affairs.

Nausikaa nodded in acknowledgment, but when I brushed past her and opened the front door, she made as if to follow me.

"Is there something you require?" I said, a bit of an edge creeping into my voice.

"It seems I must ask you the same question." Her voice was low, her tone expressionless.

I stopped just outside the door and turned to look at her. She was dressed in both chiton and himation, the cloak arranged for outdoor wear. A woven basket hung over her arm. Her lashes lowered under my scrutiny, and she regarded her feet intently, as if waiting for them to do something. Her mouth displayed a decidedly sardonic twist.

"What are you talking about?" I demanded sharply. "Why should you be asking me if I require anything?"

She raised her eyes to meet mine. Their blue depths were pale, unfathomable. "Why indeed?" she said lightly. "Except that my brother has ordered me to be your assistant for the morning, seeing as he has appropriated your real one. I believe his exact words were 'I need you to hang with Chef P. while the little dude and I rock out with Pegasus.'"

"You don't need to do that!" I exclaimed, aghast at the thought. "I am perfectly capable of going to the Agora myself."

"Oh, I couldn't hear of it," Nausikaa said sweetly. "Not when the Hero of Aegean himself has *ordered* me to accompany you."

"I will not have you trailing after me!"

She held out her arms helplessly. "But the Hero of the Aegean has commanded it."

"The Hero of the Aegean is an unmitigated ass!"

She awarded me a cool smile. "Nevertheless, I am merely his sister—and only a mortal half-sister at that. I have no choice." She opened her eyes wide and looked up at me with exaggerated innocence. "I cannot disobey him."

I regarded her for a long moment, eyebrows drawing together in a black scowl. Nausikaa gazed back unimpressed and obviously determined to ruin my morning.

Swearing under my breath, I turned on my heel and stormed back into the house, yanking the fine blue himation off my shoulders as I did so. I cursed aloud, not caring if Nausikaa heard me or not, damning both the boorish Perseus and his vexing sister straight to Tartarus—along with Mithaecus and Poseidon for good measure.

I hung my new himation on a wall hook, vigorously brushing off a smudge of dust with perhaps more enthusiasm than was strictly required. Then, still scowling ferociously, I began to rummage through the items of clothing which hung on various other hooks. If I was going to be shadowed by Perseus's sister, I had no wish to be recognized. My blue himation was far too memorable. My old cloak ought to be around here somewhere. Yes, there it was. Under Gorgias's dress cloak.

Grimly, I swung the faded brown himation around my body

and strode once again from the house, threadbare cloak billowing out behind me. Nausikaa followed closely on my heels.

I managed to ignore my unwanted shadow all through the dark twisting streets of the Kerameikos. I even managed to ignore her as I emerged onto the brighter Panathenaic Way which led to the Agora. But when we approached The Herms, which guard the entrance to the market, I felt a rude tug at my cloak.

"So, where shall we 'hang' first?" Nausikaa inquired in a hatefully pleasant voice.

Oh, she was enjoying this.

I drew myself up and looked down my nose at her. "*I* am going to the fish sellers," I informed her in an unfriendly tone. "Where I have an exclusive contract with one of the finer merchants for striped red mullet. It is my signature dish, you know."

"I'd heard that," she said, tapping her lip in puzzled thought. "And I've been wondering how this merchant has been able to procure striped red mullet when all his colleagues have only kraken. And at this time of year, no less. It's a bit late in the season for them, you know."

"And how would you know that?" I snapped unthinkingly.

Her eyes flashed. "Hello? Fisherman's daughter, here," she drawled offensively. "I've probably forgotten more than you'll ever know about seafood."

Unable to think of a suitable retort, I pulled my cloak more tightly around my body and stalked off towards the fish sellers' sector.

Krysippos was lounging at his stall, untouched piles of

kraken meat displayed neatly on either side of him. He was watching the crowds pass by and sipping morosely from an undecorated wine cup. Whatever vintage he was drinking was not doing much in the way of cheering him, but his pallid face brightened when I stepped up to the counter. And his watery eyes acquired a distinctly avaricious gleam when he noted my empty basket.

"Greetings, my cook friend," he boomed, looking somewhat askance at my brown cloak. "And how is the symposion business going for you, eh?"

"Busy as usual," I replied with an offhand shrug. "You know how it is when one is in such high demand. Never a moment's rest."

"True, true." Krysippos stroked his beard—a much more luxuriant crop than anything Hermogenes had yet managed to produce—and tried not to appear too eager. He completely ignored Nausikaa, who had, unbidden, joined me at the stall.

Affecting a casual air, I leaned against the counter. "Parmenides will be enjoying the fruits of my labours next," I told him. "And I hear he is *very* fond of striped red mullet."

Krysippos beamed. "Then it is, indeed, fortunate for you that you have stopped at my humble fish shop today."

"I had hoped you would say that," I murmured.

"Would I disappoint you?" He smacked himself on the chest. "I, Krysippos, the most successful fish merchant in all of Athens? Never! Striped red mullets you require and striped red mullets you shall have!"

"And yet, you have no difficulties disappointing me." A

most hated voice intruded on our conversation. "Why is that, I wonder?"

"M … Mithaecus!" Krysippos faltered. "I … I did not see you there, my friend. I—"

"You told me you had nothing but kraken today," The Sicilian observed pointedly. "You lied!"

I turned to look at my rival. His trademark yellow chiton was of a bright and vile hue, his pampered locks were curled and oiled, and his assistants clustered around him ready to brush off any lint that might mar his splendour. But while they might have been dab hands at keeping his chiton clean, there was little the sycophants could do about his nose. Lumpy and flattened, it bore small resemblance to the nose awarded him at birth and, in fact, more than anything called to mind a poorly risen barley roll. As the perpetrator of the deed that had rendered it thus, I took a moment to regard the appendage with a certain degree of pleasure.

"He did not lie," I told Mithaecus. "Krysippos has brought striped red mullets in especially for me. The fish do not belong to him. He did not have the right to sell them."

"Yes, yes. Chef Pelops is correct," Krysippos agreed with alacrity. "The fish were for him. A … a special order, you see, and—"

Mithaecus ignored the stammering fishmonger and turned to raze me with a scathing look. "Falling on hard times again, Chef Pelops?" he inquired insultingly, looking down his lumpy nose at my threadbare cloak. "Why, that cloak is really the colour of sadness, isn't it?"

His sycophants tittered.

I ignored their laughter and gave Mithaecus a tight smile. "Merely a disguise," I said with feigned indifference. "Being the grandson of Zeus can be a bit overwhelming at times, as I'm sure you can imagine." My tone made it clear that Mithaecus's ability to imagine anything was doubtful at best.

Eyes wide, Nausikaa looked from me to Mithaecus and back again. Briefly, Mithaecus returned the glance, then looked away, dismissing her with a superior sniff. I saw her flush.

"Are you feeling quite well this morning?" The Sicilian inquired, examining my face intently. "You seem a touch … peaky."

"Not at all," I told him, infusing my tone with a hearty note, knowing precisely why he was asking. "Indeed, I have never felt better."

"Ah." Mithaecus seemed disappointed.

He turned his attention back to the hapless fishmonger. "And as for you," he said, a scowl marring his brow. "A special order, was it? Tell me, if I, too, wish to place a special order, would you have striped red mullet for me as well?"

"I do not … that is, I …" Krysippos stumbled.

"I thought as much," Mithaecus snarled. "Well, you have lost my custom, sprat seller! I wish you luck with your remaining clients. Oh, and a piece of advice for you. For your own sake. Do make sure your clients pay *before* they make off with your wares."

I bristled at the implication—Hermogenes would have gone for his throat—but I would not give consequence to Mithaecus by responding to it. He was routed. It was enough. I would not descend to his level.

The Sicilian spun around, prepared to sweep off, but before he did so, he turned back to me.

"I suppose I shall see you in Kitchen Theatre, then—oh, but wait." He paused, tapping the side of his misshapen nose in ersatz thought. "You've not been selected, have you? From what I hear, you've not even entered your name." He tsked in mock sympathy. "The Secret Ingredient scared you off, hmm?" He aimed a helpless smile at his sycophants. "Ah well, some people just don't do well with surprises. A deficiency in their mental agility, no doubt."

At least my mind was agile enough to realize the Secret Ingredient was unlikely to be a surprise at all.

I shrugged nonchalantly, though it cost me much to do so. "Not at all," I told him. "The fact that I haven't yet registered is meaningless. Merely an oversight. And what of you? You've not secured a sponsor yet, from what I've heard. Having some difficulties there, are you?"

"Merely an oversight," Mithaecus mimicked my tone insultingly. Something flashed in his eyes. A sly craftiness. As if he knew something I did not.

What was he up to?

"At least *I've* submitted my name," he continued, distracting me from the thought.

I chuckled. "Surely you can't believe the grandson of Zeus would abstain from such a competition? Even you couldn't be so simple."

The Sicilian scowled. "You're not the only one with a divine patron," he snapped. "The Lady Hera, herself—"

"I've heard all about your divine patroness." I waved it off. "But you forget, Mithaecus, I am family, not supplicant. And even you must admit"—I inclined my head with false camaraderie—"blood really is thicker than water, isn't it?"

He drew in a sharp breath, what little intellect he possessed no doubt struggling to come up with some inferior insult or another. With a bored sigh, I brushed an imaginary speck of dirt from my cloak and turned my back on him. There was a strangled choking noise behind me, but I ignored it as I would the buzzing of an inconsequential insect.

As The Sicilian's sycophants urged him away, Krysippos mopped at his brow, unhappiness written on his face.

"An unpleasant sort." I wiggled my fingers distastefully as I turned to supervise Mithaecus's retreat. His bilious yellow garb was vivid against the more drab clothing in the crowd. "Certainly not the kind of clientele one would wish to court."

"Uh … no … certainly not," Krysippos replied, with none of his usual aplomb.

Thinking to cheer him up, I offered a business-like smile. "Now, about those mullets …" I said, rubbing my hands together purposefully. "I will need as many as you have. Yes, I know, I only ordered ten, but if you've got extra, I'm willing to pay top drachma for them."

The mention of top drachma was enough for Krysippos to recover much of his previous good humour. A smile returned to his lips, and his eyes took on a greedy sparkle once more.

But everything began to sour when he brought out the basket of prized fish.

"Those aren't striped red mullets!" Nausikaa exclaimed the moment he uncovered them.

I started. After the encounter with Mithaecus, I'd almost forgotten she was present. Krysippos froze, his face displaying shock at her temerity.

"What do you mean, they aren't striped red mullets?" I hissed, trying to keep my voice down.

"They're not striped!" she replied, gesturing at the fish. "You've only to look at them to see that."

Krysippos gave her a condescending smile. "My dear girl," he said, as if to a child, "striped red mullets lose their stripes the deeper they swim—"

"Bollocks!" Nausikaa said.

Offended, the fishmonger recoiled.

"Striped red mullets don't lose their stripes the deeper they swim!" Her tone was scathing. "They take on a darker colour. The other ones, the paler mullets, live in shallow, sandy waters. The stripes have nothing to do with it. They all have stripes! And look at those heads! Striped red mullets don't have heads like that. Theirs have a more sloping shape." She gestured with her hands to demonstrate.

Krysippos began to bluster.

"What kind of fish are they, then?" I demanded, mortification rendering me a touch short. Nausikaa spoke with such confident knowledge. Had Krysippos been cheating me all this time?

"Red mullets," she replied with a shrug. "Just plain red, not striped red. They're sacred to Hekate, you know."

I flinched uneasily at the name. The goddess of witchcraft and ghosts was not one whose attention I wished to attract—not with The Sicilian's curse tablets floating around the city.

"And look at them, they're larger than striped mullets, too," Nausikaa continued, oblivious to my consternation. "Almost twice as large. Have you never seen a striped red mullet, then?"

"No." The word was clipped. I was embarrassed by my ignorance, furious that she had witnessed it, and incensed that she had pointed it out so publicly.

"Well, striped red mullets are named because of their stripes," she said, her voice taking on an insultingly pedantic tone. "That ought to have been a dead giveaway for you. And the darker ones are the tastiest because they live deep and feed on shrimp. Striped mullets are better than plain red ones. If he's been charging you for striped red mullets, then you've been cheated."

Krysippos tried to rally. "It is possible ... that is ...they may be only red mullets," he admitted reluctantly. "But look at the colour of them. As red as a sunset, my friend. These are deep swimmers, indeed. Feeders on the delectable shrimp! And you won't find—"

"They are *not* deep swimmers," Nausikaa objected again.

"They're dark red!" Krysippos protested, giving her a look of pure dislike. "Just look how red they are," he appealed to me.

"They're red like that because they've been scaled," Nausikaa said impatiently. "If you scale a red mullet when it's freshly caught, it will appear redder." She turned to me. "It's an old fisherman's trick," she said. "Used against the ignorant or unwary."

I did not appreciate being called either.

Lips pursed, I turned back to Krysippos. He quailed at the thunderous expression on my face.

"I … I will make it up to you, my friend!" he blustered. Sweat now ran freely down his face, the moisture rendering his pallid skin more fishlike than usual. Stumbling into silence, he opened and closed his mouth several times, further accentuating the piscatorial resemblance.

"Perhaps you, too, have been deceived?" I suggested mildly.

He seized on it as a starving man pounces on a bread roll. "Deceived! Yes! A trick has clearly been played on us both, eh?" He mopped his face with a corner of his chiton. "Yes, a most cunning piece of thievery! To scale the fishes to make them seem redder? Despicable! I will wring the neck of that scoundrel who thinks to fool Krysippos! A terrible trick! Terrible!"

I let him rant on.

"I believe we need to renegotiate the price," I pointed out.

"Of course, of course," he assured me.

"After all, you would not want it said you cheated the grand-son of Zeus himself!" Nausikaa chimed in sweetly.

Great gods, would she insist on rubbing his nose in it? The fishmonger cast her a glance of utter loathing.

He did not even attempt to haggle.

"Now that's a better price, isn't it?" Nausikaa enthused as we quit Krysippos's stall. "And five fish thrown in for free! You know, I could prepare them for you, if you'd like. I've a marvellous recipe for raw red mullet livers on toasted bread and —"

"I think you've done quite enough for one day," I said repressively, setting a rapid pace homewards.

"What's wrong with you?"

I kept walking, not trusting myself to say anything else.

Rudely, she caught at my arm, forcing me to stop.

"Why are you angry with me?" she asked. "Did I not just save you a significant amount of coin?"

"At what cost?" I snapped. "How could you be so uncivilized as to confront a merchant in such a fashion?"

"*In what fashion*?" Her voice began to rise.

A passing citizen gave us a curious sideways glance. Nausikaa ignored him.

"What would you have had me do?" she demanded. "Allow him to cheat you? To sell you inferior fish at exorbitant prices?"

"Exorbitant prices or not, they're the only palatable fish available at the moment, thanks to your sodding brother!"

"You can't blame me for my brother's actions."

"No, but I can blame you for yours! Red mullets or striped red mullets, it doesn't really matter. They were my signature dish! After the way you spoke to Krysippos, it's doubtful I'll have an exclusive contract for them any longer. You've ensured that!"

"Don't be such a drama king! As long you want them and you're still willing to pay for them, why *wouldn't* he honour your contract? And what do you mean, *I've* ensured he wouldn't do so! If you hadn't been stupid enough to be taken in by such a simple trick, then—"

"Lower your voice, woman!" I cut her off savagely. "I will not bicker with you in such a public place."

"Fine," she flared. "Then give me my fish and I'll go!"

"*Your* fish?"

"Yes, mine. The free ones! There were five of them, I believe. You only got them on account of me. Because I know my head from my bum—unlike you!"

Furious, I yanked back the cover of my basket and plunged my hand into the pile of fish. I grabbed a handful, not even bothering to count them, and threw them in her basket.

"There!" I hissed. My whole body was trembling with rage. "Are you happy now? You've managed to embarrass me, offend a very important business contact, *and* entertain the entire Agora. I'd say your work here is more than done."

"Oh, I'm *delighted*," she assured me, her eyes flashing blue fire. "Absolutely delirious! Truly, it's been a *pleasure* spending time with you. But now, if you'll excuse me, I've a pressing matter of business to attend to. I'm afraid you'll have to negotiate the Agora all on your own now. Do *enjoy* your day, Chef Pelops!"

Chapter 18

Do enjoy your day, Chef Pelops!" I mimicked her words as I stalked through the market. "Nasty, sarcastic, meddlesome, who does she think she is? ... *It's been a pleasure spending time with you! ...* Snarky, stubborn, doesn't know when to keep her mouth shut ... *I'm afraid you'll have to negotiate the Agora all on your own ...* Nosing into things she has no business—"

One of the ubiquitous work crews was spreading a haphazard layer of gravel over the Panathenaic Way. At my passage, the slaves paused and looked up from their task, eyes glinting with bright curiosity. I choked off the rest of my tirade. I did not wish to make a spectacle of myself. True, I was less recognizable in this sad excuse for a cloak, but still it wouldn't do for Chef Pelops of Lydia to be seen ranting to himself in the middle of the Agora.

Scowling, I ducked down the first alley that presented itself and continued to pick my way home through the dingy back streets. Nausikaa's parting words echoed in my ears, accompanying me every squelching step of the way.

I arrived home, still burning with indignation, only to discover that Nausikaa was not the only member of her family destined to infuriate me that day.

She was not even the worst.

"Dude!"

Barely through the front door, I suddenly found myself engulfed in an enthusiastic hug. Feathered golden hair brushed across my face, poking in my eyes, getting up my nose. His ever-present satchel banged me painfully in the hip.

"Have a care!" I snapped, quickly swinging my fish-laden basket out of the way. Red mullets or striped red mullets, they were still my signature dish, and it wouldn't do to have them upended across the floor of our vestibule.

Perseus pulled away, blinking at my tone.

I set the basket down to one side and yanked the threadbare himation off my shoulders. "What in Hades is in that thing, anyway?" I growled, gesturing towards his satchel.

Perseus rested his hands protectively over the offending satchel. "Just some … stuff," he said evasively.

"Well, can't you keep your 'stuff' somewhere else?" I demanded. "You keep smacking people with that cursed satchel. It's dangerous!"

"Trust me, dude," he intoned with a dramatic widening of his golden eyes. "It'd be way more dangerous if I didn't have it with me."

"Fine. Whatever." I waved it off and turned away. I didn't much care what Perseus had in his pack—just as long he stopped hitting me with it. I bent to retrieve my basket of fish, then headed toward the kitchen. Predictably, the Hero of the Aegean followed on my heels.

"So how was the market, dude?"

"Fine."

"How'd you and Nausea get along?"

"Just peachy."

"So, she was a help, then?"

"Oh, yes."

"Awesome."

It did not surprise me in the least that sarcasm was lost on him.

He began to babble happily at me, telling me all about his day. He and Hermogenes had taken Pegasus northwest of the city to the Kolonos Hippios, which was where the charioteers raced during various festival competitions. Apparently, Hermogenes had been "stoked." I stopped listening almost immediately, instead busying myself with getting the fish wrapped and stored in the ice pit. Perseus kept droning on.

Once the mullets were safely tucked away, I turned my attention to the plate of cakes I'd prepared earlier. Destined for Parmenides's dinner tables, they needed only to be drenched in honey and garnished with chopped, toasted nutmeats. I took a pot down from the wall and set the golden honey to warming, my spirit soothed by the familiar tasks.

" … and then after we were done with that, we went on over

to the Bouleuterion and I put your name in for the Bronze Chef competition."

"*You what?!*" I spun around to stare at him, my mouth falling open.

"Whoa, dude! Your face looks like a beetroot. That can't be good for you."

Breathing heavily through my nose, I groped behind me for the stool, then lowered myself onto it. All the while, I did not take my eyes off my gods-cursed uncle.

"You know, once I saw a guy keel right over after he went all red like that," he blathered. "Was never the same afterwards, either. Everyone agreed. We thought that—"

"You entered my name for the Bronze Chef competition?" I interrupted. "*My* name." My voice was deceptively mild. Part of me hoped that I had misheard him the first time. That I had somehow misunderstood his words.

But Perseus flipped his sun-bleached locks over his shoulder and brayed a laugh. "Dude, you're the only chef I know. Who else's name would I be putting in?"

"I see. And did it not occur to you to consult me on this … action?"

"Aw, dude." He paused, self-consciously adjusting the strap of his satchel. "You're my *nephew*. I was just looking out for your best interests."

"*My best interests?*" I struggled to keep my voice down. I did not wish to expose the entire house to this altercation, but I was so incensed I could barely breathe.

"My best interests!" I repeated in a slightly lower tone. "Did you not stop to wonder why I had not yet put my name in myself? Did it not occur to you that, perhaps, I might have a better idea as to my *best interests* than an uncle who is ten years younger than me and has never known a moment's hardship in his life?"

Perseus blinked, only now becoming aware of my fury. His golden eyebrows furrowed slightly.

"Dude, I—"

"Where was Hermogenes during this? I thought he was with you."

"The little dude was with me," Perseus said.

"And did he not attempt to discourage you from this ill-conceived plan? How could he not—"

"Uh, dude, you're going all red again."

"*Did Hermogenes try to stop you?*"

Perseus shrugged, distracted by the plate of honeycakes. "He said something about you not wanting your name in, but—"

"You chose to ignore him," I finished bitterly, twitching a cover over the plate of pastries before he could pilfer one. "You decided to disregard his advice—the advice of my apprentice, my *disciple!*—and just jolly on with your little plan." I waved my hand wildly around.

"Dude, I told you, I was just trying to help," he protested. "The G-Man said you were needing to get your name in pronto. I mean, they're announcing the competitors the day after tomorrow. I just thought I'd save you the trouble. Besides, I've had your chow, you're a totally epic chef. Hermogenes tells me you're the best in the city. The little dude knows what he's talking about. So what's the big deal? You'll throw it down."

He offered me a blissfully sunny smile.

I stared at him for what seemed an eternity. Then, utterly deflated, I dropped my face in my hands.

Throw it down. *Throw it down?* Down the privy hole, maybe. In fact, perhaps I ought to just crawl down there myself and be done with it.

There was no way on Olympus or Earth that I could withdraw my name. On what grounds could I do so? Speculation would run rampant. My reputation would be called into question, damaged beyond repair. But how could I possibly win this Bronze Chef competition? How could I even compete in it? Poseidon would ensure my failure, I felt no uncertainty on that score. And no doubt he would do so in some showy fashion. Perhaps the kraken would shrivel in my casserole dish, or instantly rot into gelatinous goo on my chopping block. Or it would burst into spontaneous flames, wafting the vile stench of burned monkey parts over judges and spectators alike. Oh yes, the sea god would have fun with this. I would be the laughingstock of the competition, the entire city. Possibly even the whole of Greece, for the common people loved stories of spectacular failure, and Poseidon would guarantee mine was as impressive as possible. Damn his lecherous, unforgiving eyes!

And despite their assurances to the contrary, I could not believe that Hermes or Dionysus would succeed in coming up with a solution. Hermes's feet hurt too much and Dionysus was likely still drunk from his Oskhophoria. Besides, they were lesser gods up against an older, more powerful god. There would be no loopholes, no tricks, no last-minute solutions.

In six days, all of Athens would gather at the Theatre of Dionysus to witness my humiliation and defeat. Divine grandfather or no, I would be held up to public ridicule. Knowing this, how could I secure a sponsor? How could I even compete?

How could I *not*, now that Perseus had submitted my name?

I would fail. My fortunes would dwindle. Few would hire a chef who had been so discredited. Whatever savings I had managed to squirrel away would soon disappear and I would have to rely once again on Gorgias's generosity. There would be no distinguished career. No awards and accolades. No beating The Sicilian once and for all.

No escaping Gorgias's home after his marriage.

I rubbed my eyes and my fingers came away damp. There was nothing I could do now. Nothing. My name had been submitted. There was no withdrawing from such a thing. The damage was done. I felt cold. Worthless. And there was absolutely nothing I could do about it.

"You're right," I told Perseus tonelessly. "There is no 'big deal.'"

"So, you're cool about me putting your name in?" he asked, his mouth full of honey cake, which he had taken the opportunity to steal.

"Why not," I said, still in a monotone.

"Awesome!" He brightened, a broad grin, as white as it was clueless, splitting his face. "I just wanted to make sure we're cool, dude!" he said. "I didn't mean to tick you off. It's just … well, anything for family, eh?"

"Anything for family," I echoed.

His grin widened. "C'mon, show me some love." He held out a fist at shoulder height.

It had taken me a number of days to determine the proper response to this bizarre gesture, but I knew now what he wanted. Reluctantly, I extended my own fist, rapping my knuckles once against his.

"It's gonna be epic," he assured me, clipping me on my ivory shoulder with one hand as he stole another honey cake with the other. "You'll see! No worries, dude. Be happy! That's my philosophy."

"Of course it is," I muttered.

"Chef, I tried to stop him, I really did!" Miserably, Hermogenes tugged at his beard, yanking on the thin hairs so hard he was in real danger of pulling them out. "But he wouldn't listen to me, would he? And now your name's in and you've not got a sponsor and you'll have to cook the kraken and it'll burn and it's all a bloody disaster—"

"Which is why you're going to get me Nausikaa's recipe for kraken soup."

"But ... but," Hermogenes began, then flushed. "Nausikaa hates you!" he said in a rush. "Sorry, Chef, but it's true."

"Which is why you're not going to tell her it's for me."

Hermogenes closed his mouth and stared at me. His dark eyes reflected the flickering light of the single oil lamp that sat between us on the kitchen table. He had returned late from his winged horse–keeping duties, Perseus having sent him to find various rare and exotic foodstuffs that Pegasus apparently required. It was now late at night and we were the only members of the household not asleep. Well, I supposed Perseus must also be wakeful, for he had not yet returned home from his evening's revelries.

"You … you want me to spy on her?" Hermogenes asked in a small voice.

I squirmed inwardly at his choice of words. "I want you to learn how to make soup like that. Think of it as part of your training."

"But she said she'd never share that recipe with you, Chef. I heard her myself! It's just …" He shrugged his thin shoulders uncomfortably. "It don't seem right. To be sneaking it from her, I mean."

I held on to my temper with an effort. "Hermogenes, we know kraken will be the 'secret' ingredient in this competition. And each chef is allowed up to three disciples to help him. There is nothing in the rules to say what manner of help this might entail. I have no desire to take on other apprentices, and I can do everything else—design the meal plan, chop vegetables, make sauces—but you will have to deal with the actual kraken."

"But, Nausikaa said—"

"*I don't care what Nausikaa said!*" I snapped. "I care about winning this sodding match!"

I took a deep breath, trying to calm myself. When I spoke again, my voice was more temperate. "Has it not occurred to you what will happen if I should lose?" I inquired. "All our hard work, all your brilliant marketing strategies will be for naught.

Nobody will hire a chef who has *lost* the Bronze Chef competition. And you know how vengeful Poseidon is! He won't miss this opportunity to embarrass and ruin me. No, Hermogenes, if you don't cook the kraken for this event, we might as well pack up our pots and pans right now and go to Corinth! And if you're going to prepare the kraken, that means you must first learn how to cook the kraken."

In sullen silence, Hermogenes kicked rhythmically at the table leg, each thump causing the flame from the oil lamp to flicker and jump.

"There's more." I steeled myself to say the words. "I didn't want to say anything before, because I did not wish to alarm you, but it seems it is not just Poseidon who's got it in for me." Succinctly, I described the situation with Mithaecus and his curse tablets.

Outraged, Hermogenes straightened. "He never!" he exclaimed angrily. He had stopped kicking the table. "That toad-buggering shite-eater!"

"Indeed," I said. "Which is yet another reason I need to win this competition. Look, normally I would never ask you to do such a thing, but the only other cook who would even consider helping us is Castor—and obviously he cannot be trusted to follow my instructions."

My disciple scrunched his nose into a look of distaste. "Plus his kraken were shite," he pointed out.

"There is that," I agreed dryly. "Now, Nausikaa's soup was delicious—*yes, I know, that's not what I said at the time! Never mind that now!*—the fact remains the soup was tasty and, more importantly, it was *different*. That's what the judges will be look-ing for. Unusual preparation, unusual flavours. And if we can get a few more of those red mullets to add to it, the soup will be divine. We could win the whole competition based on that soup alone!"

"But what will we do about the rest of the dishes?" he argued. "We can't have a meal with just soup."

"I know," I said, scrubbing tiredly at my forehead. "And the truth is, I haven't a clue. I'll have to figure something out. But in the meantime, you're going to need to start experimenting. It'll have to be on your own, I'm afraid. If I have anything to do with the works, it won't turn out. We've Barates's symposion tomor-row, so we won't be able to do anything till that's over and done with. But first thing the following morning, I want you to go to the market. Get as much kraken as you can carry and start play-ing around. I'll make myself scarce so I won't skew your results. And if Nausikaa should happen to come 'round and give a look …" I trailed off suggestively.

Hermogenes was silent for a moment, then he gave a reluc-tant nod. "I'll ask for her soup recipe," he agreed slowly. "But I'm only going to *ask*. I don't want to be a spy, me." His chin had taken on an exceedingly stubborn line, and I knew I could press him no further.

"Fine." I gave him a tight smile. "Ask away. Just don't mention my name. Now let's get to sleep. We've a long day tomorrow."

Hermogenes nodded, then pushed himself up and headed off in the direction of the storeroom where his sleeping pallet waited. But before he left the kitchen, he turned to look back at me.

"Chef?"

"Yes?"

"Do you ... d'you really think my marketing strategies are brilliant, then?" A crooked grin had broken through his rather grim expression.

I regarded him through hooded eyes. "Yes, Hermogenes," I told him after a long moment. "Your marketing skills are truly impressive. Your branding of me, your idea for the direct marketing were nothing short of brilliant. My career has taken a decidedly rosier turn since you've implemented your strategies."

His grin widened. "So, Chef ... I know you're not much on the cooking scroll idea—and that's fine!—but d'you think we could maybe do something with your hair? Say, a coloured band to match your chiton? It doesn't have to be curls—"

"Go to your pallet, Hermogenes."

"So, that's not a 'no,' then?"

"Good night, Hermogenes."

"And—"

"Good night!"

"Good night, Chef."

Chapter 19

It felt odd to be at such loose ends.

With Barates's symposion behind me—at which none seemed to notice that they were served mere red mullets rather than *striped* red mullets—and no further contracts for several days, I would normally be at home, experimenting with new recipes or, more recently, trying to wrestle the kraken into some semblance of edibility. But with Hermogenes stationed in the kitchen and artfully surrounded by all the ingredients for Nausikaa's soup, it was desirable, if not imperative, that I be out of the house entirely.

There were many places I could go. I could, for example, visit the Theatre of Dionysus, where the Bronze Chef match was to be held. I had been to the theatre before. Built on the southern foot of the Acropolis where the slope forms a natural auditorium, it boasted the requisite orchestra as the main performing space, a wooden skene at the back where various props and sets were stored, and tiered seating for the audience. I suppose I could have gone to acclimatize myself to the idea of performing in the orchestra rather than watching from the terraced benches, but at this moment, I did not want to be reminded of the competition at all—and I certainly didn't want to enter the Theatre until the remainder of Mithaecus's curse tablets had been discovered and disposed of. Hermes had promised to do this, but given his sore feet, I did not know if he had yet accomplished the task. Best not to take the chance.

I could visit the Eleusinium, the urban branch of Demeter's main temple at Eleusis, and pay my respects to the goddess of grain and bread. But for various reasons, having largely to do with nibbled shoulders and guilt, Demeter was never in when I called. And although her priests were friendly enough, they were much given to discussions of crops and fields and manure and the like—especially during harvest season, which it was now.

I considered and discarded any number of other local attractions, from the picture gallery in the north wing of the Propylaea—a long way to go to see a few paintings if one could not also view the rest of the Acropolis, which, as a foreigner, I could not—to the unfinished temple of Zeus—again, a long way to go just to see a bunch of slaves sit in the shade and complain about the heat while their foremen tried unsuccessfully to motivate them.

Ultimately, I decided to go to Cato's Chitons to pick up my second chiton as well as the one I'd ordered for Hermogenes.

Cato had sent a slave around the day before to let me know they were ready. No doubt Hermogenes would be crestfallen to have missed the excursion, but I suspected the possession of a new luxury chiton would go a long way to mitigating his disappoint-ment. It was far more important for him to stay at home and wheedle Nausikaa's soup recipe out of her.

The Theseus wore blue today, the same sky blue of my own brand. Indeed, our chitons appeared virtually identical, right down to the creamy border embroidered with olive leaves. The only differences were in the accessories. The fibulae at his shoulders were silver (mine were bronze) and a large brown satchel had been arranged at his side. I examined this last as I mounted the first step. Made of sturdy fabric, it seemed oddly incongruent with the fine wool of the chiton. Could it be? I drew closer. Yes, it appeared to be a twin for the satchel Perseus habitually carried.

I arrived at the top of the staircase just as a pair of citizens was leaving Cato's establishment. The men sported plain green chitons of fine weave and broad, satisfied smiles. A brown strap cut across each torso. I swivelled around to watch them depart. Sure enough, each bore an identical brown satchel on his back. My uncle, it appeared, had started a new fashion trend.

"Chef Pelops!" Cato suddenly appeared at my elbow. "It is, indeed, a pleasure to see you again."

"The pleasure is all mine," I told him.

"Please, come in." He held his arm out to guide me into his shop.

Like his Theseus, Cato wore a blue chiton today, though his

border had been decorated with acanthus leaves. Still, the shade was identical to my own, though I thought privately the colour suited me better.

"I have come to retrieve my order," I told him.

I saw his eyes glance around in vain for Hermogenes, but he was discreet enough not to ask why I had come on the errand rather than sending my disciple. Likely he would put it down to eccentricity on my part.

"Of course," he said instead. "Please come in and refresh yourself while my slaves ready your package."

Once again I had my feet washed and dried. Once again I was led to a well-cushioned dining couch on which to recline while I waited. Once again I was offered bowls of fine fruits. But this time, I noted with some amusement, the slaves assigned to my comfort were female. It appeared my lack of interest in his coy youths had not gone unremarked.

Unfortunately for Cato, I was not particularly interested in his female slaves, either. Lovely though they were, it would take much more than doe eyes and voluptuous bodies to distract me from my worries. It was, however, a pleasant experience.

Part of me wondered why Cato was going to such lengths to accommodate me. The three chitons I'd purchased from him had been expensive, but not outrageously so. I could hardly have been among his more important customers. The answer to this question came with the arrival of the wine.

As the slave girl served me, Cato himself settled on the opposite couch as if we were attending a quiet dinner party for two.

The girl went on to pour his wine, though he did not, as I had, admire her form as she did so.

"I wonder if I might broach a matter of some delicacy," Cato began after we had sampled the wine (an excellent apple-kissed Thasian.)

I looked up from the glistening bunch of purple grapes which the slave girl was offering me. "But of course," I said magnanimously, curious as to what the clothier might have to say to me.

"First, allow me to wish you all success for the Bronze Chef competition."

"That is very kind of you, but I have not yet been selected as one of the four finalists," I told him, inclining my head modestly.

Cato smiled as if I'd said something amusing. "Only a matter of time, I'm sure," he murmured.

I bowed my head again before leaning forward to select a small cluster of grapes. They were plump and juicy and of superior quality, especially for this time of the year. Really, I had to find out where Cato purchased his fruit. But Cato had other things on his mind than the quality of his produce.

"*Once* you are selected," he continued, "I wonder if you've given any thought as to who might be your sponsor?"

Startled, I dropped the grapes back on the platter untasted. "You would want to sponsor me?" I inquired.

"Chef Pelops, it would be an honour." It was his turn to bow his head.

Still stunned, I regarded his well-coiffed curls. Cato's Chitons as my sponsor? I could hardly ask for a more prestigious one. None of the other chefs would have a sponsor of this stature.

Mithaecus had not yet secured a sponsor, but according to Hermogenes, who heard it at the market, the other chefs had all signed on with various discount or second-rate businesses. Places like Eryx Egg Emporium and Honest Enops's House of Hoplites. For me to sign on with Cato would be an unprecedented coup.

Chef Pelops of Lydia brought to you by Cato's Chitons.

Hermogenes would wet himself.

I looked around the shop with sudden proprietary interest. The entire place exuded ease and luxury. The best of the best. Cato's would be the perfect sponsor for me.

The clothier's head was still bowed as he awaited my response. I opened my mouth to tell him that of course—*of course!*—I would accept his sponsorship. And then I remembered who exactly he was offering to sponsor. It was not Pelops of Lydia, but the winner of the Bronze Chef competition.

Cato hoped to sponsor the chef who could demonstrate his superior prowess in the kitchen, the one who could prepare the tastiest of dishes, the most innovative of recipes—all of them using kraken. How could I do that to him? The man had shown me nothing but kindness, treating me like royalty, developing my "brand," demonstrating in the most significant fashion his confidence in my abilities. Heart sinking, I realized I could not saddle Cato with the failure I knew was in my future.

"It is by no means certain I will be named as one of the finalists," I began in a roundabout fashion.

Cato looked up at that. "I have no doubts," he assured me.

"And even if I am," I bulled on, "it is not guaranteed that I will win. If the auspices are poor … or if the judges are having a difficult day—"

"I can offer you the purple chiton," Cato interrupted.

I goggled at his generosity. I knew the cost of those purple chitons.

"You mistake me," I told him after a moment. "Though your generosity is indeed appreciated. No, I am most satisfied with my blue chiton, and I believe even Hermogenes would agree I ought to wear my trademark colour to the competition."

"I understand," Cato said gravely, clearly anticipating my refusal.

"It has nothing to do with you or your most excellent establishment. I would be happy—delighted!—to secure you as my sponsor. It's just …" I paused, not knowing what to say. I could hardly confide in him my troubles with Poseidon. "It is by no means certain I will win," I finished lamely. "It would be a risk."

Cato waved it off, almost but not quite impatiently. "There is always a risk in business," he told me. "I should never have been so successful had I not taken risks. I have heard of your reputation and I have eaten at several symposions at which you prepared the food. Ah, you did not know that, did you? Yes, it was earlier this year. A wedding feast for Clearchus and a symposion for Alcidas. Chef Pelops, I am well aware of what you are capable of. And even knowing the risks, I have full confidence in you."

What could I say?

I accepted his offer, of course, with all the grace and poise I could muster. We drank more wine and assured each other of our mutual admiration and regard. But as I left his shop and descended the stairs of the South Stoa, I cannot say I felt good about accepting Cato's sponsorship.

It was still too early for me to go home. I had been at Cato's for barely an hour, which was hardly time for Hermogenes to have finessed Nausikaa's soup recipe from her. I decided to go to the Agora. It was my favourite place in all of Athens and, although I was a frequent visitor, it was usually with some business-related purpose in mind.

Today, I would attempt to forget my troubles and simply enjoy the market. I would wander through its streets and alleys, perusing goods I could not afford, enjoying the sunny autumn day, greeting any who recognized me. Draped in my blue himation, having once again relegated the "colour of sadness" cloak to the bottom of the heap in our vestibule, I would be a man of leisure. A chef about town. I tucked my parcel of chitons more tightly under my arm. Perhaps, I thought, I might even let slip a word about my new-found sponsor.

But before I could greet friendly admirers, before I could finger expensive wares, before I could casually mention Cato's Chitons, or even be a chef about anywhere, I found myself accosted by my most unwelcome uncle.

He was loitering in front of the Painted Stoa, listening intently to the philosophers who congregated there and gnawing on a piece of meat that he'd obviously purchased from some dodgy sausage seller. I saw him before he saw me. Quickly, I tried to duck behind a Herm.

"Hey, dude!" his voice rang out. "Yo! Pelops! Wait up."

Concealing a grimace, I stopped and waited for him to catch up. "Good morning, Perseus," I greeted him, pasting a smile on my face.

"'Sup, dude?" he asked, still chewing the last bite of his snack.

"Uh, not a great deal, really. Just out and about at the market. You know how it is. Please, don't let me keep you from your lecture." I indicated the philosopher still pontificating on the stone steps of the Stoa.

The man was noticeably unwashed and very loosely circled by followers, though whether they gave him a wide berth due to his pungent ideas or his equally pungent body odour, I could not say.

Perseus glanced back and shrugged, unconcerned. "Nah, I think he's pretty much done for the day."

He spat out a piece of gristle and wiped greasy hands on his cloak. I turned, curling my lip in disgust. Predictably, Perseus fell into step beside me. I noticed he still had his brown satchel slung across his shoulders. Did he never take the thing off? No wonder the fashionistas of Athens had begun affecting the look.

"Hey, did you know we start out as *beans*?" he asked.

"And some of us never really progress beyond that," I muttered under my breath.

"What's that, dude?"

"Yes, I had heard that," I said. "Pythagoras was speaking today, was he?"

"Dude's got some strange ideas, but man, he blows my mind." He clutched his head to illustrate his point, then grinned and shook his golden hair out of his eyes. "I like those philosophers. They're kinda messed up, but they're cool."

"Hmm," I said noncommittally.

"So, where're we headed?"

"Uh, nowhere, really. I'm just … wandering around. No interesting plans at all, I'm afraid. So, if you're looking for excitement—"

"Nah, I'm good hanging with you."

Of course he was.

My uncle then began treating me to a detailed explanation of Pythagorean Theory as interpreted through the filter of his feathery-haired mind. I was still trying to think of a way to get rid of him when he let out a sudden whoop of delight and veered sharply off to my left.

"Man, I *love* this dude!" he exclaimed over his shoulders. "C'mon!"

I followed much more circumspectly.

The Great Galinthius stood in front of the bronze statue of Herakles and the Nemean Lion, his appearance as unprepossessing as ever. He was tossing a couple of coloured cloth balls in the air, though nobody had stopped to watch him. Indeed, his reputation must by then have been common knowledge, for all passersby were giving him a much wider berth than street performers were usually afforded.

Oblivious, as always, Perseus strode right into the empty circle that surrounded the juggler. The Great Galinthius brightened and began to fling his balls about with enthusiastic, if not particularly accurate, abandon. Wisely, I kept my distance.

The Hero of the Aegean guffawed and clapped, feathered hair bouncing on his shoulders as he tried to watch all the airborne spheres at once. And even when the Great Galinthius predictably clipped him with one of the balls, Perseus just laughed all the harder.

He turned to grin at me. "This dude's totally awesome!" he enthused.

I smiled and waved and continued to keep a safe distance.

Perseus, I realized, was much occupied with the juggler's performance. If I should slip off now, it was doubtful he would notice until I was long gone. Perhaps I could have my day in the Agora after all. I was about to suit action to thought and had, in fact, started to turn around when I spied Mithaecus stepping into the empty circle to join my uncle. I paused.

"Yo, dude!" Perseus greeted him with a friendly smile.

Mithaecus offered him a simpering one in return. "And how is the Hero of the Aegean on this fine morning?" he asked.

I ground my teeth at his obsequious manner and took a step closer. I noticed his flurry of sycophants prudently waiting for him beyond the Great Galinthius's range.

"Never better, dude!" Perseus beamed. He gestured to the flailing juggler. "You guys have some epic entertainment here, did you know that?"

"We're very proud of it," Mithaecus assured him, without even glancing at the juggler. "And proud of our cuisine too."

"The chow here is all kinds of awesome," Perseus agreed, ducking another ill-thrown ball. The Great Galinthius cried out an apology.

Still Mithaecus did not look at the performer. Instead, his beady eyes bore into Perseus with predaceous intensity. "Have you had a chance yet to sample my New Cuisine?" he asked him.

Eyes still on the Great Galinthius and his performance, Perseus shook his head amiably. "I don't think so," he said. "Unless you've made it for one of the symposions I've been at."

Mithaecus gave a self-deprecating chuckle. "Sadly, not yet. Athough I believe Stephanus is hosting you this evening?"

"That's right."

"Well, then, you shall have the opportunity to taste it tonight, as I am the chef for the feast," he announced, as if imparting some divine proclamation.

"Awesome, dude," Perseus told him, taking his eyes off the juggler for a moment to bestow a friendly grin on The Sicilian. "I'll look forward to it."

It was too much! I stalked into the empty space around them and caught Perseus firmly by the arm. "Look at the time," I said with false brightness.

"Really, dude? We gotta go?"

"Yes," I said through clenched teeth.

"Okay, I'm there." But before I could pull him away, he turned back to The Sicilian. "Hey, dude, have you met my nephew? He's a chef, too."

"We're acquainted," I gritted.

Mithaecus gave me a vastly insincere smile. "Greetings, *Chef* Pelops," he said, emphasizing my title insultingly. "Still feeling tiptop, then?"

"Just fine." I nodded, not trusting myself to say anything

more. Seething inwardly, I pulled Perseus into the crowd and yanked him down the street.

"Dude! Not so fast," he protested. "You're pulling my arm off."

"I'd like to board your mouth up," I shot back at him.

He stopped dead. Again I pulled on his arm, but he wouldn't budge.

"Dude, what's wrong?"

"What's wrong?" I hissed, almost spitting in my fury. "*What's wrong?*"

"Uh, you're going all red again."

"Of course I'm going red! I always go red when a member of my family starts chumming about with my sworn enemy."

Perseus looked around as if he'd somehow missed someone. "Uh, what sworn enemy, dude?"

"*What sworn enemy?* The Sicilian! The man in that vile yellow chiton! The one whose cuisine you said you were looking forward to sampling!"

"Whoa, whoa, whoa!" Perseus held up his hands. "Are you telling me that dude is your *enemy*?"

"Well, what else would you call a man who slanders you, attempts to discredit your friends, is indirectly responsible for having your assistant beaten up, and—oh, let's not forget!—has commissioned any number of curse tablets, cursing both me and mine to be worthless and cold?"

The Hero of the Aegean had the grace to look shocked.

"Dude," he said, much chastened. "I … I had no idea. That's brutal, man. I didn't even know who he was. He just came up and started talking."

I pursed my lips in frustration.

Perseus fidgeted uncomfortably, playing with the strap of his satchel. "If you want, I could jam on tonight," he offered.

"Jam?"

"Y'know, stay home. Not go and eat his food."

"No." I waved it off. "There's no point. The damage is done. At least a half dozen people overheard your conversation. By this afternoon, it'll be all over the Agora that the Great Perseus is looking forward to eating Mithaecus's New Cuisine. The Sicilian's sycophants are probably painting it on the walls as we speak." I heaved a bitter sigh.

"Uh, what's the deal on his New Cuisine?"

"Nothing. Tiny portions. Make sure you eat before you go. Come on."

"Where're we going?" he asked contritely, though he fell into obedient step beside me.

"I don't know," I said moodily. "Away from here."

We walked in silence for a while, then Perseus tugged at my cloak.

"Dude," he said. "I'm sorry. I really am. And I know just the thing to cheer you up."

"What exactly are you doing?" I demanded testily.

Perseus looked up from his crouching position. "I'm looking for something."

"In the dirt of the alley?"

"Yeah, last night I saw—oh, hey, there's one!" He pointed excitedly at something in the dust.

It was the imprint of a boot—and not just any boot—the print had been made by a hobnailed boot with the words "This way for a good time" inscribed on the sole.

"You're looking for a *prostitute?*" I exclaimed in disbelief.

"I thought it'd make you feel better."

"You thought wrong!" I jerked him to his feet, almost losing hold of my package of chitons in the process. "Really, Perseus! You need to grow up! What's the matter with you? Even if I was inclined to do such a thing, have you no notion of social mores? Visiting a brothel here in the middle of the day is considered one of the worst forms of debauchery."

"Whoa, that's random."

"Random? What does that even mean?"

"Hey, what's your problem, dude?" For the first time since I'd met him, Perseus was angry. His gold eyes flashed fire. "Here I am trying to apologize—to help you feel better!—and you're being a total downer."

A "total downer," was I? What exactly was a "downer"? Nothing good, obviously. An insult on top of all the injuries! Enough was enough. Furious, I glanced around. Perseus and I were alone in the alley.

I leaned in close to him. "You want to know what my problem is?" I demanded with an intensity that caused him to recoil. "You need look no further than your own reflection. My problem, put simply, is *you*! You barge into my home and ingratiate yourself with my friend. You subvert my assistant and leave me with your obnoxious sister in his place. You put my name in for the Bronze Chef competition without knowing—or caring!—that I will lose the match because the secret ingredient is sure to be kraken and I can't cook kraken to save my life or my reputation. You follow me around like an overenthusiastic puppy, you engage in friendly banter with my worst enemy in the middle of the Agora, and my name is Pelops, not 'Dude'!"

My chest was heaving by the time I was through.

Perseus was silent for a long while, his head lowered. Then, "I thought you and Nausea got on," he said meekly.

I sighed and scrubbed at my face. "No," I told him. "We do not 'get on.'"

"Oh." There was another pause, then he looked up, his expression chastened. "And the whole kraken thing?" he asked. "I don't get it. What's up with that? You're an awesome chef."

I sighed again. More heartfelt this time. "It's Poseidon," I told him. "Your sodding uncle. I offended the lecherous old bastard years ago, and he's got it in for me. My inability to prepare kraken is just his latest trick."

Perseus chewed his bottom lip for a moment. "I'm ... I'm really sorry, dude—I mean, Pelops," he said finally. "I'm sorry about Naus and Poseidon and all that other stuff. I'm sorry about the Bronze Chef. I guess ..." He paused and scuffed at the boot print, smudging its beckoning words. "I guess I didn't think."

"No," I agreed. "You did not."

We stood in silence for a while.

It was Perseus who broke it. "So ... what now?" he asked.

What, indeed? I had no stomach to wander the marketplace now, although I doubted if Hermogenes had had adequate time to obtain Nausikaa's soup recipe. At that moment, I did not care. I was utterly exhausted.

"Now, we go home," I told the Hero of the Aegean.

He fiddled with the buckle on his satchel. "Is that okay?" he asked with uncharacteristic diffidence. "I mean, that I come with you. I ... I don't want to barge in or anything."

I observed him for a long moment. His face was downcast, his shoulders slumped, even his feathery locks seemed droopy. He looked so young and dispirited, it was everything I could do not to feel sorry for him. I suppressed a weary sigh.

"Yes, it's 'okay,'" I replied finally. "After all, we *are* family."

HONEST ENOPS'S HOUSE OF HOPLITES

Called up for duty, but short on cash? **NO PROBLEM!**
Cuirass too tight? **WE CAN HELP!**
Shield cracked on the eve of battle? **NO WORRIES!**

Come on down to Honest Enops's House of Hoplites and browse our great selection of gently used armour and weaponry. We've got helmets! We've got greaves! We've got shields and swords! New merchandise arrives every week! No two visits are the same!

ONCE YOU'VE SHOPPED RESALE, YOU'LL NEVER BUY RETAIL!

ATTENTION VINTAGE-LOVERS!

This week's special!!

Bulk lot of 300 vintage Spartan capes and armour! Conditions vary from acceptable to poor. Some external wear. They'll go fast, so don't miss out!

You'll never find a better deal than at HONEST ENOPS'S HOUSE OF HOPLITES. HONEST!

Chapter 20

I had been drinking steadily since I got home. I knew this was probably a bad idea, but it had seemed like my best option at the time and, at this point, which was early evening, I was past caring about good or bad.

I didn't know what was more irritating. Perseus as he was before, clueless and tactless, barging in where he wasn't wanted, or Perseus as he was now, nervous and unsure, stumbling about and apologizing for his every move. I had never been so glad to see the Hero of the Aegean go out for the night—even if he was going to partake of The Sicilian's cooking.

Perseus was not the only one looking forward to an evening on the town. Gorgias, too, had a symposion to attend that night, and although he had invited me to tag along, I had refused his offer. I had not been invited, and I did not wish to be seen as the "ghost," or poor guest, of the party. Besides, I was not in the right temper to attend a dinner party.

He stopped by to see me in the courtyard before he went out.

"Sure you won't come along, then?" he asked, fiddling with the folds of his dress chiton.

I shook my head, then wished I hadn't when the courtyard swung around alarmingly.

"I'm just not up for it tonight," I told him, keeping my head very still.

I thought I'd sounded fine, but Gorgias gave me an odd look. Gathering up his chiton so as not to wrinkle it, he seated himself gingerly on the bench beside me and gave me a searching look.

I squirmed under his scrutiny. "What?" I asked finally, as he continued to stare at me in silence.

"What's the matter with you, then?" he inquired at last.

"Nothing!"

"Sod that. Is it the Bronze Chef match?"

Scowling into my nearly empty wine cup, I didn't say anything.

"The Sicilian?" he pressed. "Your uncle?"

"Yes, yes, and yes!" I burst out. "It's all of it! You *know* I wasn't ready to put my name in for that bloody competition, and yet, now I've been selected as one of the chefs!"

Hadinos, the market crier, had made an announcement to that effect just that afternoon, and the names of the competitors had been painted on the walls of the Agora shortly thereafter. There were four of us: Lycon of Seriphos, Mediokrates of Chaeronia, Mithaecus, and me. Lycon was an incompetent boob who had probably bribed the committee to get his name included (he had wealthy relations), while Mediokrates was as talented as his name implied. In fact, one could say his selection was an argument against Gorgias's beloved democratic process, for there were any number of chefs who had submitted their names who were far more skilled than Mediokrates. But Athenians are excessively fond of their democracy, and so Mediokrates had been chosen to compete. Which meant that it would really come down to The Sicilian and me.

"You'll be needing a sponsor, then," Gorgias observed. "Is that the trouble?"

"I've got a sponsor!" I snapped. "Cato offered me his sponsorship this morning."

"Cato's Chitons!" Gorgias was suitably impressed. "But ... that's good, right? I mean, Cato's, that's plum!"

"I don't know." I glowered once more into my wine cup. "It would be if I could cook the bloody kraken, which I can't. So now I have to worry about Cato's reputation as well as my own. And on top of that, the pox-ridden Sicilian's got bloody curse tablets buried all over the Theatre, and I haven't a clue what I ought to do about it."

Gorgias's expression darkened at the mention of the curse tablets. I had already told him about them. He had been quite vociferous in his condemnation of Mithaecus for resorting to such tactics. He had not, however, offered any viable course of action to deal with the situation—very likely because there wasn't one.

"And your uncle?" he asked at last. "What's he done to you, then?"

"You mean, apart from the Bronze Chef fiasco?" I blew out my breath in an explosive huff. "Look, I know you've invited him to be your house guest, but really, Gorgias, the boy has no clue, no concept, of how the real world works. I mean, Perseus was never chopped into stewing meat by his own father, Perseus was never served to the gods for tea, or had to have an ivory shoulder put in place of the old one. Perseus doesn't know what it's like having to work for a living, or to deal with a rival chef, or with gods that seem to delight in buggering up the works. No, Perseus gets riches and kingdoms! Perseus gets a winged horse! Perseus gets his own constellation! Perseus gets the girl, while I have to watch mine jolly off to marry my best—" I choked it off, realizing suddenly what I was saying. And to whom.

With assiduous care, I put down my wine cup. It teetered on the edge of the bench, then fell to the floor spilling dark wine into the packed dirt. "I … I'm rather drunk," I confided. "Truly, I don't know what I'm—"

But my friend's kind face had grown very grave. "Are you saying …" He spoke slowly. "Are you saying that you and Zeuxo …?"

"Not Zeuxo," I denied quickly. "She … I … I was always just a friend to her." My stomach clenched with the pain of saying those words. With the truth of them. "Despite what I may have wanted."

Gorgias stared at me. I could not read his expression. He was quiet for a few heartbeats. "I can't believe it," he said softly. "I can't believe you never told me."

I lifted one shoulder in a shrug. "There was nothing to tell. You got there first, and I am happy for you. For both of you." I tried to sound as sincere as possible.

I wasn't fooling him.

"Does Zeuxo know?"

I started to shake my head, then stopped when the courtyard began to spin again. "No," I said instead. "I never told her. She never knew."

There was a long silence.

"Is that why you've been so distant?" he asked at last. "I mean, we've barely seen you, Zeuxo said so herself. Even Ansandra's noticed you're always out these days."

I scrubbed at my cheek. "Partly," I admitted. "I *am* very busy, but … well, sometimes it's hard. To see you and Zeuxo. Together." I paused, uncomfortable. "I … I'm sorry."

Gorgias looked down at his hands and nodded a few times. "I'm sorry too," he said quietly. He paused to clear his throat. "What … uh, what will you do? After the wedding, I mean?"

It was an unexpected slap. Never mind that *I* did not want to stay in his house after he was married, clearly Gorgias did not want me there either. Blinking rapidly, I looked up at the sky, hurt, but not really surprised.

"I … well, I suppose it all depends on the Bronze Chef competition, doesn't it?" I paused, inwardly cursing my loose tongue. I had thought to stay if I didn't win the competition. To find some way of coping. Now that option was no longer available.

"If I win, then I'll have enough money to get my own house. If I don't …" I shrugged with a nonchalance that I knew did not fool him. "If I don't, then I'll make other arrangements, won't I?"

He nodded again without saying anything.

We sat in uneasy silence for a while.

"You should go to your symposion," I told him finally. "You'll be late."

"I don't *have* to go—" he began.

"Gorgias," I interrupted. "Go to your party. I'll be fine. Go!" I made shooing motions with my hands.

Reluctantly, he pushed himself to his feet. "You're sure, then? I could stay," he offered.

"And do what? Watch me pass out? I've already had the better part of an amphora. Believe me, I'm not long for consciousness." The last word came out slurred, as if to illustrate my point.

It may have been that which convinced him, for he did not protest further. Silently, he gripped my shoulder, and I could feel the heaviness in his gesture. Before he left the courtyard, he turned back.

"Pelops?"

I looked over at him. The stars had started to come out, but the night was moonless. He was nothing but a dark blur in the shadows.

"I'm sorry, yeah?" his voice said, and I heard the thread of sorrow running through it. "I'm sorry I didn't know."

The encounter with Gorgias had left me feeling raw. I retrieved my fallen wine cup and filled it again, spilling a fair bit of wine in the process. Part of me knew I really ought to seek out my sleeping couch, but the thought of mounting all those stairs to the sleeping rooms seemed like far too much trouble. Wine cup in hand, I slid down further on the bench until I was lying supine against its cushions. Above me the stars glittered. Perseus's constellation hung smugly overhead.

I'd finished my wine and had just closed my eyes to rest them a bit when I heard a small noise. Thinking it was Gorgias returning, I sat up quickly—a little too quickly, as it turned out. My head spun and I clutched the edge of the bench, trying to steady myself.

"Pelops?"

It was not Gorgias's voice.

"What do you want?" I said ungraciously.

Nausikaa ventured further into the courtyard. Her long dark hair hung around her like a cloak, and starlight cast her features into shadow. It occurred to me that her hair was even straighter than my own, but nobody seemed to nag at her to curl it. A pox on Hermogenes.

"I wanted to … well, to apologize," she said, interrupting my thoughts. Her rich voice was low in deference to the lateness of the hour. "I didn't mean to make you look bad in front of your business contact. I'm sorry."

I snorted noisily. "You're sorry," I slurred. "You're sorry, Gorgias's sorry, Perseus's sorry. Even the gods're sorry. Everybody's sorry."

She seemed a bit taken aback, but still she drew nearer. A night breeze brought me the scent of her hair. Some kind of flower, or maybe an herb. Whatever it was, it was surprisingly pleasant.

"Well, I am sorry," she said again. "I'm sorry you're having such trouble with the kraken and I'm sorry for being rude, too. It was inexcusable."

"In'scusable," I agreed. I leaned towards her and pointed a finger in her face. "You know, I never asked for this. For your brother. For you. For your whole sodding family to descend on my house." I gestured wildly, to take in our surroundings. "You come marching into my home and it's 'Publish a series of cooking scrolls, Pelops' and 'Don't buy those fish, Pelops' and 'Don't you even know a striped mullet from your ass, Pelops?' Well, sod that!"

Nausikaa had stiffened. "I'm sorry you feel that way," she began.

But I was on a roll. "There you are telling me what to buy and how to cook as if I'm not good enough! As if I don't have a bloody clue! Well, let me tell you something, sweetheart, Cato's Chitons wouldn't just sponsor anybody. I don't care if you *have* been called to be a priestess for Apollo. You're nothing! *I'm* the one with the gods-given gift for cooking, *I'm* the one with royal relatives, *I'm* the one with divine blood in my veins. Me! When it comes right down to it, you're just a fisherman's daughter."

She stared at me. Even in the dimness of the starlight, I could see that her face had gone very white.

I blinked owlishly at her. She kept going in and out of focus.

"Well," she said flatly, "I guess I'd rather be a fisherman's daughter than a royal ass."

And before I could formulate a suitable response, she spun on her heel and disappeared back into the gloom.

I thought about getting up and following her. Who did she think she was, calling me an ass? "Nasty, meddlesome old bat!" I mumbled to myself. "Young bat. Whatever. Ah, fuck it …"

I lay back down on the bench and closed my eyes. Above me, the stars spun, unconcerned with the cares of the mortals below.

Chapter 21

"Dude, duuude. Wake up, dude ... I mean, Pelops, Pelllops. C'mon, wake up. It's morning."

I groaned and pushed my face out of the puddle of saliva that had accumulated under my cheek. Then I cried out as I rolled off the courtyard bench and tumbled ignominiously to the ground.

"Son of a bitch!" I cursed.

Perseus's hands were on me, trying to help me up. "Whoa, dude—I mean, Pelops—be careful, man."

I sat up and waved him away crossly. "Wha—" I began, scrubbing at my face. I stopped and smacked my lips a few times, then tried again. "Whassa matter?" I managed to ask, though my voice sounded as furry as my tongue felt.

Groaning, I heaved myself off the ground, clutching at the side of the bench to steady myself and rubbing at my now bruised buttock.

"I've been thinking," Perseus said.

"Really," I muttered. "I'm astonished."

He coloured. "No dude—I mean, Pelops—for real. I've been thinking for real."

I collapsed back onto the bench and regarded him sourly through barely cracked eyes. "And what have you been thinking about?" I asked wearily. Clearly, he was not going to go away until he'd told me all about it.

"The Bronze Chef."

I opened my eyes a bit wider at that, though it still felt like I was squinting. My stomach was distinctly unhappy with me.

"The thing is, dude—I mean, Pelops—your problem isn't the competition or even the other chefs. It's Poseidon."

"Really," I drawled, looking around for my wine cup. Perhaps a bit of wine would settle my stomach. "And you came up with that all on your own?"

He flushed again, but pressed on. "The way I see it, The Big Sea Dude's trying to mess you up, and you can't return the favour because he's a god."

"Yes, so?" I said impatiently.

"So you have to work around him."

"And how do you suggest I do that?" I said flatly. "Have *you* a way of placating the sea god? Or perhaps you have some secret family recipe for kraken that will somehow allow me to prepare it?"

"Not me, dude, but I bet Proteus does."

I paused, confused. "Proteus? Who in Hades is Proteus?"

"A sea god."

"Another sea god?" I snorted in disgust. "Haven't I got enough of those buggering up my life?"

"Maybe." Perseus shrugged. "But Proteus is a different kind of god."

"Uh huh."

"No really, it's true. Most of the time, he just looks like some old dude on the beach, but he can change his shape into just about anything. And they say that if you can catch him and hang on to him while he's changing, he'll answer a question for you—any question."

"Who says this?"

Perseus shrugged again. "Everybody. At least where I come from. It's pretty common knowledge."

Any question.

For the first time since the Bronze Chef competition had been announced, I felt a faint stirring of hope. If Proteus could answer my most particular question, then perhaps all was not lost. Perhaps the Bronze Chef was still within my grasp.

"Where does this Proteus live?" I asked.

"On Pharos."

"Pharos? Near Kemet?" The brief flare of hope sputtered and died. "The competition is in four days! You're talking of a journey that would take weeks!"

"By boat."

"Well, how else am I supposed to travel? Fly?"

"On Pegasus," Perseus agreed.

I opened my mouth, then closed it again, considering his words. "You would lend me your winged horse?" I asked slowly.

"Well ..." Perseus temporized. "I'd probably have to come with you, dude—I mean, Pelops. I don't think Pegasus would take you on his own. But I'd be totally into helping you, man. With finding Proteus, I mean."

In spite of myself, I was touched by his offer.

"Thank you," I told him regretfully. "That's very generous of you. But I'm afraid it still won't help. I can't imagine even your Pegasus would be able to get us there and back again before the competition—and that's not even taking into account the time it will take to locate this Proteus."

Perseus broke into a wide grin, his teeth achingly white against his tan. "No worries, dude!" he assured me. "Pegasus can get us there and back in less than an hour. And he can find any-thing, anywhere." He shrugged. "I dunno how he does it, man, but it's totally epic."

"Really."

Perseus nodded, still grinning.

If Perseus was right about this ...

I made up my mind on the spot. "Let's do it," I said.

Perseus whooped as I pushed myself off the bench. I had to pause for a moment to let the revolving courtyard settle down.

"I've got to change and wash up," I told my uncle. "And I probably ought to eat something. You go get Pegasus ready. I'll meet you outside the workshop."

I tried to find Hermogenes before I left. It was not that I wished him to accompany us (our mission would be challenging enough without his youthful enthusiasm), but I still hadn't had a chance to tell him about Cato's offer.

The kitchen was empty. So was the storeroom. And although his sleeping pallet had obviously seen use the night before, Hermogenes himself was nowhere to be found. Belatedly, I realized that he had probably failed to secure Nausikaa's soup recipe and, as a result, was making himself scarce this morning.

It was annoying—I had been anticipating the look on his face when I told him that Chef Pelops and his team would be sponsored by none other than Cato's Chitons, and I thought it might cheer me up to feel like the hero for a change. But I was obliged to give it up as a bad job for now. Perseus and his winged horse awaited me in the alley.

Dressed in a old tunic, fed and clean, if not particularly warm—Poseidon had caused my washing water to ice up just as I poured it—I was on my way to meet them when Zeuxo confronted me in the courtyard. She was clad in a pale green chiton that morning, dark curls tumbling around white shoulders, silver earrings dangling from shell-shaped ears. A true vision of loveliness.

"Zeuxo! What a pleasant—" I began.

But she did not let me finish. "How could you, Pel?" she demanded.

I rocked back on my heels.

"How could I what?" I started to ask, instantly ready to defend myself, though I had no idea what egregious sin I might have committed. Then I realized her tone was distressed rather than accusing. Almost … sad?

Zeus and Hera, Gorgias had told her!

I shut my mouth and eyed her warily, unsure how to proceed.

"You seem … upset," I offered at last.

"I *am* upset!" she cried. "I wouldn't have thought it of you." She shook her head slowly. "Not you!"

I swallowed hard and cursed inwardly. The fool *had* told Zeuxo of my feelings for her! Why had I allowed myself to be so far gone in my cups last night? Why had I not guarded my tongue? And what had possessed Gorgias to share the information with the one person I did not wish to know it? Fools, both of us!

And yet, for all that, it hurt that Zeuxo could be surprised by the knowledge. *Upset* by it.

"And why not me?" I asked with an intensity I could not quite mask.

"Because I thought you were better than that!" she said softly. "Because I thought you were *different!*"

Different? From any other man in Athens? What man could look on her and not find her desirable? No, I was not different.

"How could any man feel otherwise?" I said, managing a shrug. Trying to diffuse the emotional impact of the moment with the nonchalant gesture.

She drew in a sharp breath as if hurt.

"I never asked for it," I told her quietly. My voice sounded tight and strained even to myself. I had not wanted Zeuxo to know of my feelings for her. Not now. Not when she was about to marry Gorgias. "And I never would have said anything—not intentionally. But I do take a certain pride in the fact that I never pushed myself forward after Gorgias—"

"No, you pushed her away—"

"—and when you … What? Pushed who away?"

Zeuxo gave me a strangely withering look. "Nausikaa, of course! And what does Gorgias have to do with any of this?"

I blinked. "Nausikaa?"

"Who did you think we were talking about? Irene?"

"No … I … uh," I stammered incoherently.

"The things you said to her last night, Pel." She tightened her lips and shook her head again. "You were rude and you were cruel."

Nausikaa? I passed a hand over my eyes, trying to recall what I'd said to Perseus's sister the previous evening. I had nothing but a vague memory of some sort of conversation with her. I had consumed rather a large amount of wine.

"She told me all about it!" Zeuxo continued to berate me. "How you threw her apology in her face. Taunting her for being nothing but a fisherman's daughter! How could you say such things? You're a good man, Pel. You're better than that!"

That was the second time Zeuxo had named me a good man. The first had been when she told me she was marrying my best friend.

"But …" I began.

"I'm a cobbler's daughter," she cut me off. "Are you going to start mocking me now?"

"I didn't mean to—"

"Have you any idea how hard her life must be? Sister to the

great Perseus. Mortal when he is half-divine. Plain when he is handsome. Never the favoured child. Always forgotten in the shadow of her more famous sibling. How difficult do you think that is for her?"

I had not thought of it in those terms. I squirmed uncomfortably. Zeuxo saw it and her expression hardened even further.

"Ah, having second thoughts, are you? A few regrets, now that you're not so far gone in drink?" Her eyes were flinty. "And were you also drunk when you set Hermogenes to spy on her? Oh yes, I heard all about that too! That was low, Pel. Very low."

"Fine! I'm sorry," I said. "I'm a total ass, all right? I'll go and apologize to her this instant."

"You can't."

"Why not?"

"Because she's in the women's quarters with Irene. Crying."

It gave me pause. Nausikaa was annoying, but I never meant to hurt her.

Just then Ansandra joined us, Kabob nestled in her arms.

"Oh look, it's Mr. Jerkface!"

I pointed a finger at her. "Now, don't you start!"

"I used to think you were nice!" she said, sounding hurt as well as angry. "And now, Nausikaa's *crying* because of you. She says she wants to leave for Delphi right away."

Kabob opened his beady eyes and let loose a series of short, shrill notes, drowning out the rest of what Ansandra had to say.

I opened my mouth to defend myself. To tell them that between Poseidon, the kraken, Mithaecus, the Bronze Chef competition, and assorted curse tablets, my life had been no picnic in the sun either. But as Kabob continued to harangue me, preventing anyone from getting a word in, I realized that even though my life had its challenges, Nausikaa had not deserved to be punished for them.

"Look," I told Ansandra once Kabob had finally been soothed into silence. "It's … it's a grown-up thing."

"Sod that!" she snorted with a sarcasm far beyond her ten years.

I tried to quell her with a frown. It did not work.

I took a deep breath and tried again. "I'm sorry, all right?" I told both of them. "Truly I am. I've behaved abominably. I thought I had reasons, but you're right. You're both right. There is no excuse for my behaviour and I promise I will apologize to Nausikaa at the very first opportunity. But right now, I'm afraid I must go out. I've got to meet—"

"So you're just going to leave her crying?" Ansandra was aghast. "Even though it's your stupid fault? Irene'll have something to say about that. She already wants to have a word with you. And so does Nausikaa's mom."

I winced at the thought. "I'm sorry," I said. "Truly. But I really do have to go."

Ansandra continued to protest, but Zeuxo had gone quiet. Lips tight, arms crossed over her chest like an avenging Fury, her expression more than made up for her silence.

I left with Ansandra's recriminations still ringing in my ears. Feeling like an utter heel, I skulked from the house with the unpalatable knowledge that every woman in it was angry with me.

Chapter 22

When I opened the front door to leave, I saw Perseus leaning casually against the Herm in front of our house. He turned and took one look at my face, then straightened. "Whoa, dude, what's the matter?" he asked

"Nothing," I replied shortly, closing the door behind me.

My uncle pulled his mouth to one side and gave a considering nod. "Women troubles," he said sagely.

"How do you know?"

"All I have to do is look at your face, man. The members of the fairer sex are totally awesome, and I, for one, would not want to be without them, but they're the only ones who can get a dude that steamed."

It seemed a remarkably perceptive observation—especially for him.

"Be that as it may, there's nothing I can do about it now," I said crisply. "Right at the moment, I've got to find this Proteus of yours. Where is your horse?"

"I got him stashed between the buildings." Perseus gestured with his well-sculpted chin. "Thought you might want to slope off without all the little neighbourhood dudes coming out to watch. They get pretty stoked, you know."

I knew. One of them was my disciple.

"Good thinking," I told Perseus as we rounded the corner. An errant gust of wind tried to snatch my cloak. Euros, the god of the east wind, was still in town and still spoiling for a fight. I pulled the cloak more closely around me and squinted against the chilly blast of dust which blew in small whirlwinds around us.

The winged horse, Pegasus, was waiting impatiently. White coat gleaming like new ivory, golden hooves sparkling even in the shadows of the dingy alley, he was a truly magnificent animal. As soon as he saw Perseus, the horse stomped his front hooves and whuffled, blowing the long mane away from his eyes. He looked disgruntled and not a little irritated. Clearly he was unused to being kept waiting in such an inferior and ignominious location.

Perseus hastened to his steed's side and began stroking the soft nose, murmuring endearments and entreaties into the pointed ears, which continued to flick in annoyance.

For my part, I hung back, suddenly apprehensive. It had just occurred to me, with rather gut-wrenching immediacy, that this creature—this *horse*—was going to leap into the air. It was going to beat its enormous, feathered wings and rise from the earth. It was going to fly aloft, as high as an eagle, soaring over city and countryside, negotiating gusty, ill-tempered winds. And I was going to be on its back.

My heart began to thump wildly and my knees started to tremble.

"Hi, Perseus!" Behind me, a high voice called out the greeting.

"Yo, little dude. How's it hangin'?"

It was one of Pegasus's many admirers, a small street urchin from the Kerameikos. Normally such boys were nothing more than a nuisance, but now I welcomed his timely interruption, taking the opportunity to inhale several deep, calming breaths.

As Perseus and the boy exchanged words, I crept a little closer, eying the winged horse, willing myself to relax. Sensing my unease, Pegasus snorted and rolled his eyes back, awarding me a distinctly superior look.

I straightened, offended. I had been killed and brought back to life! I would not be named coward by a *horse*—no matter how winged or supernatural it might be. Stiffening my resolve, I strode the remaining few steps to its side.

"We ought to go now," I said, interrupting Perseus's conversation with the urchin.

The boy gave me a filthy glare, but I ignored him and looked expectantly at Perseus.

"We gotta blast," he told the boy regretfully. "But if you could lay your hands on those seabuckthorns for Pegasus, that would be all kinds of awesome!"

"No problem, Perseus!"

"Thanks, little dude. Show me some love."

Perseus bumped fists with the urchin, then, whistling merrily, my uncle led Pegasus from the alley and out into the wider street. With an effortless leap, he vaulted onto the horse's broad back.

"Ready, dude—I mean, Pelops?" he said, looking back at me over his shoulder.

I squinted up at him, as another icy gust almost blasted me off my feet. "Of course," I lied.

The street urchin stood to one side, pressed up against a wall, finger picking absently at his nose, dark eyes watching enviously. Perseus leaned down to clasp my forearm and then, grunting a bit with the effort, he swung me up.

And I was astride Pegasus.

I'd thought a winged horse might feel different under my legs. That the huge wings might somehow impede movement or seem shaky and uncertain. But although Pegasus shifted restively under me, he felt as any other horse did. Muscular, solid, grounded.

Then he extended his wings.

I gasped as the east winds, blustery enough on their own, were suddenly magnified a hundredfold by the horse's enormous wingspan. The flanks beneath my thighs jumped and danced as Pegasus fought to maintain balance. Wildly, I clutched at Perseus, clinging on to the strap of his ever-present satchel with a white-fingered grip. Perseus laughed in delight, his blond hair whipping back to sting my face.

What in Hades was I doing? I wanted off. Now!

But before I could say anything, before I could even draw the breath with which to form the words, I could feel the muscles bunch beneath me. And Pegasus leapt into the air.

"*Oh shiiiiiiiiiiiiiit!*" I cried, not caring if the street urchin—or anyone else—could hear me.

The ground fell away dizzily, the horse bucking and tossing as the wind slammed into us from a dozen different directions. Pegasus neighed, a high-pitched, excited sound. My eyes filled and filled again, the tears whipped away by the fierce wind as quickly as they formed.

The icy gale whistled around us. My fingers ached with it. My heart hammered so furiously, I had to fight for each wind-snatched breath. Inadvertently, I glanced down and my stomach heaved as I saw the city far below us, the pattern of streets and alleys plainly visible, the jumbled mass of red roof tiles glowing like dried blood in the morning sun. I closed my eyes and swallowed hard.

"Epic view!" Perseus shouted back at me. "Check it out, dude!"

Steeling myself, I ventured a quick peek, blinking rapidly to clear my wind-burned eyes. Then I saw it.

The Acropolis. Gleaming atop a high, rocky outcrop, the temple to Athena watched over her city. There were the steep steps and the monumental gateway of the Propylaea. And the brilliant reds, greens, and blues of the temple to Athena Parthenos. Off to one side, I could even see the construction site of the still-unfinished Erechtheum.

These were sights which, as a foreigner forbidden entrance to the sanctuaries, I had never witnessed but only heard tell of.

Now I could behold them in all their grandeur. Magnificent, they sparkled in the fresh morning light, their colours enhanced by the multi-hued pastel splash from the winged horse's passage. My breath caught in my throat at the sight. We veered to one side and I gasped in delight as the rainbow wash rippled out to saturate the enormous bronze statue of Athena Promakhos, now made as small to my eyes as one of Ansandra's dolls.

And then, without warning, Pegasus plummeted.

I screamed as I felt my buttocks lift from his back. My tunic whipped around my face. My ears popped.

Great Zeus and Hera, we were falling!

Terrified, I clung to the strap of Perseus's satchel as if it alone could save me. "Grandfather! Help!" I cried, though I did not make a sound.

And then Pegasus suddenly ceased his downward plunge. I slammed back onto him with ball-jarring force.

"No worries, dude!" Perseus called back to me. "That happens sometimes."

It happens sometimes?

Trembling with fear and shock, I clenched my teeth and readjusted my grip on his satchel strap. It happens sometimes! And Perseus had not thought to warn me of it? I cursed him under my breath, wishing something would *happen* to him.

From that moment on, I refused to look down again, even when Perseus pointed out the boundary walls of the city. And the famous harbour of Piraeus. And the choppy azure waves of the open Aegean. Instead I stared with grim determination at my uncle's back, trying—and failing—to recall all the reasons why this had seemed like a good idea at the time.

"Pretty sure this is Kemet now," Perseus tossed over his shoulder as he leaned forward to give Pegasus an affectionate slap.

My uncle was better travelled than I was, so I had to take his word as to our location. In truth, I would not have said we were much past Athens, for we had not been long in the air (though my stomach had other ideas on the matter) and nothing in Pegasus's flight had seemed any different from one wingbeat to the next (though I must admit, I had not lifted my eyes to mark our progress). But it did seem that the winds had warmed—and calmed—considerably and the air *felt* different than it had in Athens. Wherever we were, clearly we were no longer in Greece.

I forced my gaze down.

Whether due to the calmer winds or to the lack of cityscape beneath us, I found I could contemplate the view with more equanimity than I had managed when Pegasus had first taken to the air. I adjusted my grip on the satchel strap and cautiously turned my head to look around.

We were over the open water on the edge of a landmass. The sea was quiet, the waters a delicate aquamarine by the shore, darkening to the richer blue of the deeps further out. The coastline was a generous stretch of buff-coloured sand that gradually gave way to scrubby, wind-stunted trees and rockier, rougher terrain.

Kemet seemed a lonely, desolate sort of place—or, at least, this corner of Kemet appeared so. There was no sign of human habitation. No sign of human activity at all. Not even a single sail bobbing on the distant sea. The sandy beach was empty, save for a single figure lying prone in the sun.

"Dude, there he is!" Perseus turned to me, his gold eyes sparkling with enthusiasm. "That's him! That's Proteus!" He leaned down to murmur something in Pegasus's ear. The horse tossed his mane and angled his wings to bring us in closer.

The sea god appeared to be enjoying a late morning snooze. Clad in a rumpled brown tunic, he looked like nothing more than an aging fisherman resting after a hard morning's labour. I would never have given him a second glance had Perseus not identified him. In fact, I was not entirely sure that Perseus was correct in his assumption—until Pegasus banked and came in for a landing.

As we glided closer, I could see the winged horse's rainbow reflection shimmer across the hot sands. And the instant the colourful ripples touched the god's sleeping body, he was on his feet and running as if his very life depended on it.

No mere mortal could have moved so quickly.

"He's getting away!" I shouted, as Proteus made a mad dash for the sea.

Pegasus veered to follow.

"Go! Go!" I cried, digging my heels into his flanks, urging him to greater speed. I couldn't let the god escape! I had far too much riding on this.

One beat of Pegasus's powerful wings, then another, and we were pacing the fleeing god. Proteus glanced up at us briefly, his face twisted in a snarl. Then he turned on his heel and dodged sharply to the left. Pegasus tried to backwing, but even I knew he would never be able to correct his course in time. Without stopping to plan, without even stopping to think, I pried my fingers from Perseus's satchel strap and flung myself from the horse's back.

I was airborne for only a heartbeat, and then I landed directly atop the sea god.

We crashed into each other, arms and legs flailing, the two of us sent tumbling across the sun-heated sands. I heard the breath go out of him in a watery *whoosh*, and I scrambled to get a grip on his writhing body. But before I could secure any kind of hold, he began to change.

I saw his features shift and flatten, and for a brief moment, I recoiled. His limbs were elongating, melding to his changing body. Scales were coming out on his skin, rippling, pulsing in time to some inner rhythm. Recalling myself, I grabbed him about the neck and tried to hold tight. His now serpent-like body twisted and thrashed in my arms.

"Hold onto him, dude!" Perseus shouted at me.

Dimly I was aware that Pegasus had landed. That Perseus now stood on the sand, his arms raised above his head as if in some bizarre supplication.

Beneath me, Proteus heaved, his coils lashing from side to side. I tried to get a better purchase on him, but his new-formed scales were slippery, and slid easily from my grasp. The giant snake slithered towards the sea. In desperation, I hurled myself upon him once again, hoping to pin him with my weight. He hissed viciously. Drops of venom spat from his fangs. I cried out as the droplets burned against my neck and shoulders.

Zeus Almighty! Where was Perseus? Wildly, I looked around, trying to locate my uncle. He was still standing on the beach, his perfectly sculpted body bent in half from the waist down. What in Hades was he doing?

"*Perseus! Help!*" I managed to cry out.

But before I could say anything else, Proteus's form began to change once more.

The change was faster this time, near instantaneous. The firm body beneath me suddenly went slack, becoming softer, almost gelatinous. A waft of putrid air washed over me. I had a fleeting glimpse of a wide mouth with dozens of glistening, jagged teeth. Then a wiry black tail slapped the sand beside me, showering me with grit. I spat to clear my mouth and held on, digging my fingers deeply into the now viscous flesh. He writhed in protest, emitting a piercing squeal.

And then he was morphing again.

The viscid body firmed and shortened, growing limbs once more. But they were not the limbs of a man. Sprouting ruddy fur, they appeared to be feline rather than human or reptile. In a heartbeat, his face had regained its human features, its expression twisted in hatred and absolute fury.

I thought I had him then. I thought my hold must be secure.

Then I saw his tail.

The thin, wiry appendage had thickened to a muscly rope. Covered in the same reddish fur of his body, it lashed back and forth like a cat's. And as I watched in horror, sharp spikes began to erupt from its flesh. The skin wept where they pushed through, blood and fluid saturating the fur and running onto the sand. The spikes grew, glistening malevolently in the bright sun.

Then Proteus cracked his tail like a whip, and a cluster of the lethal arrow-like objects spat into the air. I cried out as one of them sliced past my face, narrowly missing my eyes.

He snapped the tail again. More spikes shot out. Others pressed up from his skin, replacing those that had detached.

As the cruel projectiles flew around me, I flung myself from side to side, grunting with the effort, my fingers still clutching his writhing body.

Even as he attempted to impale me with his tail spikes, he struggled to break free. I tried to maintain my grip on him, rolling as he rolled, rising as he rose. Dodging each angry lash of his deadly tail. But I didn't dodge fast enough. Suddenly, one of the spikes cut across my arm, gashing deeply into the muscle.

"*Perseus!*" I shouted again with a despairing cry. My hands were now slick with warm blood and sweat. I could feel my grip slipping.

And then, with a colossal wrench, Proteus tore away from me. In two short bounds, he was at the water's edge.

"No!" I cried, falling to my knees.

But Proteus had already plunged into the sea. I glimpsed a smooth streamlined shape, impossibly large, then a huge silvery fish tail rose up and slapped the water's surface with a thundering crash.

And Proteus, the sea god, disappeared beneath the waves.

Chapter 23

I collapsed onto the beach, my gasping breath whistling with each laboured inhalation. I was covered in sweat and grit. Blood ran freely down my arm, dripping onto the hot sand where it was quickly wicked away.

It had all been for naught.

I had braved the skies on a winged horse, enduring both dizzying heights and terrifying winds. I had engaged in vicious hand-to-hand combat with a god who had become a giant serpent, a manticore, and a creature from nightmares. And after all that, I hadn't even uttered a single word—let alone asked the shapeshifting god my question.

Had I had the breath for it, I would have cried out in anguish. Had Mithaecus's curse tablets begun their evil work? Were my words and deeds to be cold and worthless? At this moment, they certainly felt so. I felt utterly defeated.

"Whoa, rough luck, dude," Perseus said, dropping to the sand beside me. "I mean, Pelops."

"*Rough luck?*" I repeated incredulously, flaring temper lending me the breath to speak. "Bad luck had nothing to do with it! Where were you when I needed help?"

Perseus shrugged uncomfortably. "You seemed to be doing okay on your own—at first, anyway." He began raking his fingers through the sand.

I scrambled to a sitting position, galvanized by my anger. "Then where were you when when I wasn't 'doing okay'?" I demanded. "When Proteus was—oh, I don't know—*getting away from me?* What was all that nonsense with the bending and reaching to the sky? Were you praying for aid? I saw you there on the beach. When things weren't 'okay.'"

Perseus shrugged again. A gentle breeze played with his feathered hair. "I was stretching."

"*Excuse me?*"

"Stretching, dude. You know, stretching the muscles out." His golden gaze was open and guileless.

I stared at him, my mouth agape. Somewhere in the distance, a sea bird cried, its voice carrying on the lonely winds.

"You can't just jump into an intense workout like that," he explained earnestly. "Not without warming up first. That one I was doing? I like to call it the Helios Salutation. Or sometimes just 'Yo, Helios.' It sort of depends on—"

"Warming up?" I repeated. "*Warming up!*"

"Hey, I didn't know you were going to haul off and tackle the dude," Perseus protested. "It wasn't my fault I didn't have my game on!"

For a moment, I didn't trust myself to speak. So much had depended on my getting an answer from Proteus. It wasn't just about winning the Bronze Chef competition. It was everything else too. My reputation. Zeuxo's wedding. Poseidon. My entire future.

"*Great Zeus!*" I finally spat. "I thought you were supposed to be some kind of hero."

Perseus blinked.

"What kind of hero 'warms up' before going into combat? What kind of hero holds back while someone else wrestles with a god? What kind of hero lets the—"

"I'm not a hero," Perseus denied.

"Oh, that is most abundantly clear," I retorted acidly.

Unable to bear the sight of my fluffy-haired uncle any longer, I turned my head and stared into the distance. Blood from my wound still trickled down my arm. My teeth were clenched so hard, I could feel my jaw throbbing. A warm breeze had come up. It brought with it the fresh smell of the sea but did little to dispel the icy silence that descended between us.

"Dude," Perseus began finally.

"My name is Pelops!" I snapped.

"I know! I … I'm sorry, Pelops. It's just that …"

"I've lost the only chance I had for winning the Bronze Chef competition? I'm well aware of that, thank you very much."

"But—"

"But now I shall lose my reputation and consequently any

hopes of proving myself to be Mithaecus's superior once and for all? Yes, I'm aware of that too."

"But, dude!"

"Pelops."

"Pelops, then! We can try again!"

It stopped me. I turned my head to regard him suspiciously. "What do you mean?"

The ocean breeze was blowing his golden hair in his eyes. He shook it out of the way impatiently. "I mean, if Pegasus could find Proteus once, he can find him again. "

I paused for a heartbeat.

"Truly?" I asked after a moment. "It wasn't a one-off occurrence?"

"Honest!" He nodded eagerly. "We just have to give Proteus a day or two. Y'know, to chill and forget about us, and then we'll get Pegasus to scare him up again. No problem."

I considered his words.

"The Bronze Chef competition is in four days," I reminded him.

"No problem," he said again.

I eyed him skeptically. Was it possible all was not lost?

"We can do this," he assured me as my silence dragged on.

I took a deep breath, fresh resolve stiffening my spine. I did not entirely trust my uncle, but really, what other option did I have? I would not go down without a fight. If Perseus was correct, I would find and confront Proteus again and next time ... next time I would prove victorious.

"And next time," Perseus began, echoing my thoughts, "we can warm up *before* we jump him."

I flicked him an irascible glare. "What is it with you and warming up?" I demanded. "I've never heard of a hero needing to stretch his muscles out before. Jason didn't. I'm fairly sure Odysseus didn't either—at least, not in any version of his legend I've ever heard."

Perseus dropped his gaze. He was quiet for a long moment, then, "I told you, I'm not a hero," he said. His voice was soft, almost tentative. "I ... I never was. It's a fluke."

I blinked, caught by his tone.

"What do you mean a 'fluke'?" I asked, sliding him a sidelong glance.

He didn't answer right away. Instead, he stared down at his toes, burrowing them in the warm sand. A rivulet of sweat ran down the side of his face. My injured arm had begun to throb.

I waited.

Like a child, he scooped more sand over his feet, packing it down to create small mounds. He sucked in a lungful of air and blew it out a bit at a time as if trying to decide whether or not to confide in me. Then he raised his eyes to meet mine. He was more serious than I had ever seen him.

"I mean the kraken, Medusa," he said flatly. "All of it. It's all a lie."

My mouth fell open. "You ... you did not slay them?"

He avoided my eyes, concentrating his attention on his buried feet. "Not like everybody thinks," he mumbled.

I took a long breath and let it out slowly through my nostrils. "Tell me."

The ocean wind stilled and died as if the whole world waited on Perseus's words.

He began hesitantly. "I … I was always sort of awkward when I was a kid," he admitted with a shrug. "Mom said I was all feet and elbows and knees. She said my dad—Zeus—was kinda like that too."

In fact, Zeus still possessed somewhat knobby knees, I recalled.

"I broke a lot of stuff," Perseus continued. He still would not meet my eyes. "Never on purpose. Just … I dunno, clumsy, I guess."

He took another deep breath, as if steeling himself for what was coming. "Polydektes *did* send me out to kill Medusa, that part's true. But he never thought I'd do it. He just wanted me out of the way so he could put the moves on my mom. He thought I'd get turned to stone."

A sea bird flew overhead, its shadow flashing across the sands. Without the breeze, the air had become quite warm. I felt a bead of sweat run down my back.

"So what happened?" I asked quietly.

"*I* happened," he said with a humorless laugh. "Me and my big feet. I got into the cave all right. And Medusa was there sleeping, all those little hair-snake dudes crashed out with her. And then …" He trailed off and fell silent.

"And then?" I prompted.

"I tripped over my sword." He said the words quickly, almost defiantly.

"You tripped over your own sword?" I repeated, startled.

He pulled his mouth to one side. "Yeah. The thing went flying. It's a magic sword, you know. And it's sharp. Like awesome sharp. I think Zeus might've done something to it. Anyhow, it goes soaring off and lands on Medusa. Sliced her head right off. I almost cut off my own foot too. Look, I still have a scar." He pulled his right foot out of its sandy mound and turned it toward me. There was a thin white scar line across the top of it.

Slowly, I shook my head in disbelief.

"Did you trip on your sword and kill the kraken too?" I inquired.

Perseus gave a self-deprecating shake of his head. "Nah. It was even more lame than that."

"Really."

Sarcasm was lost on him. "Yeah." He nodded. "You see, even though Medusa's head was, y'know, not attached to her body anymore, it could still turn stuff to stone."

"And you knew this how?"

"I kinda poked at the head a little. To make sure she was dead. It rolled over and there were some rats scurrying around and …"

"They were turned to stone," I finished.

"Yeah. So I knew I couldn't just leave the thing there. Plus I had to prove to Polydektes that I'd killed her. So I wrapped it in my cloak. Not looking directly at it, of course."

"Of course," I echoed.

"And by then Pegasus had sprung from her body."

"So that part is true?"

He nodded. "Yeah. Don't ask me how or why, dude. But I turned around and there was Pegasus all 'Let's rock out.' So I hopped on and we headed home."

"What happened then?" I asked, fascinated in spite of myself.

"Oh, that was epic," he reminisced with a lopsided grin. "That was really epic. You see, Polydektes had tried to put major moves on my mom, so she'd gone to the temple of Athena. For refuge, you know? He and his buddies hadn't quite worked up the nerve to storm the temple, but they were there in the palace drinking themselves up to it."

"You turned them all to stone, didn't you?" I accused him. "With Medusa's head!"

"Yeah." Perseus agreed, a sheepish grin splitting his face. "Yeah, I kinda did. You shoulda seen old Polydektes when I held it up! He was all like 'Aaaaahhh!'" He chuckled, remembering. "Made for an insanely hilarious statue, I tell you!"

I closed my eyes and shook my head.

"Well, he deserved it!" Perseus protested. "After what he tried to do to my mom? His own brother's wife! Well … they weren't exactly married, but that's beside the point. It was not cool, dude. Not cool at all."

I opened my eyes and sighed. "No doubt," I told him. "So what happened with the kraken? How did you 'kill' that?"

"It was a total accident," Perseus admitted. "Me and Pegasus were just flying around minding our own business. I didn't even know about the whole deal with the kraken and Andromeda. I had the head in a bag—y'know, Medusa's head?"

"I surmised that much," I said dryly.

"Right … well, I guess I didn't have it tied tight enough. Pegasus hit a patch of air and took a bit of a dive—you know what that's like."

I shuddered, remembering all too well.

"So, he goes down in this major dip and damned if the head didn't fall out of the sack. I tried to grab it, but I missed and it plopped down right in front of the kraken. I didn't even know the kraken was there till it went belly up. Then there was all this cheering and stuff."

"And what about Andromeda?" I asked. "Is that part true?"

"Oh, yes," Perseus nodded, colouring slightly. "She's beautiful and a princess and … well, she's going to marry me."

He sounded vaguely startled by it all.

He shook his hair back from his face and rolled his shoulders back. "But first," he said decisively, "I gotta do something about the head."

I started. "*What?* You still have Medusa's head?"

"Of course I do, dude! I fished it out of the sea. You can't just leave something like that lying around. Who knows who might pick it up."

I conceded the point, though it was difficult to imagine a less responsible person with it than Perseus.

"Where is the head now?" I asked intently.

"It's safe," Perseus assured me. "Same with the sword."

"The magic sword?"

"Yeah, I keep it stashed. I don't want anyone getting cut by accident. The thing's wicked sharp."

"So you mentioned."

"I got a couple of other pretty epic things too, you know," Perseus added after a moment.

"Oh?"

"From a bunch of nymphs who"—he blushed again—"well, they thought I was kinda hot. Anyhow, they gave me my satchel. And the sandals, of course."

"Sandals," I repeated, mystified.

"The winged sandals," he agreed.

Vaguely, I recalled the first stories I'd heard of Perseus's escapades. There had been mention of winged sandals and an invisible helmet too, if I remembered correctly.

"The sandals totally kill," Perseus was saying. "But ... well, they *really* kill, if you know what I mean."

I had a sudden and very strange mental image of murderous footwear. "I don't believe I do," I said cautiously.

"I mean, they're epic and all—c'mon dude, they're *winged* sandals! You can fly all over the place with them. But ..." He hesitated.

"But?"

"You can't control them worth stink," he admitted. "At least, *I* never figured out how to do it. Plus," he shrugged ruefully, "you know how clumsy I am. Can you imagine *me* in flying sandals?"

"Ah. Nearly broke your neck, did you?"

"A couple of times," Perseus agreed with a shudder. "I packed 'em away. If I have to fly anywhere, I'd rather go on Pegasus."

The sandals sounded more challenging than dangerous, but I made a mental note to myself to keep them away from

Hermogenes. I suspected my adventuresome disciple would be only too delighted to try out a set of flying footwear.

"Is that all?" I asked Perseus. "You've not got an invisible helmet stashed away somewhere?"

His blond eyebrows drew together in a puzzled frown. "How would I know I had a helmet if it was invisible?" he asked.

"I think it was supposed to render the wearer invisible. Not that the helmet itself was invisible." I shook my head. "It doesn't matter."

"An invisible helmet …" Perseus's golden eyes were distant and dreamy as he thought about it. "Man, I wish I *did* have something like that, dude. Old Proteus would never see us coming."

Indeed, an invisible helmet might have helped us to sneak up on the slippery sea god, but right now I was more concerned with how to hold on to him once we captured him. And for that I was going to need more powerful and much more dependable muscle than my bumbling, *un-warmed*-up uncle.

Fortunately, I knew just where to find it.

STATIOS'S SANDALS

Chapter 24

By the time Hermogenes tracked me down in the courtyard, I was still very much in recovery mode. My arm was caked with dried blood from the fight with Proteus, I was covered in a crust of sweat and sand from the same, and my face probably looked as green as cabbage from what had been a harrowing flight home afterwards.

Needless to say, I was not at my best.

"So, I had another marketing idea, Chef," Hermogenes began, as he strode into the sunlight. "What if you—*Ares's bollocks!* Chef, are you okay? What happened?"

I was attempting to bind the wound on my arm and, if truth be told, I was making a rather sloppy job of it. Bandaging one's own arm, it turned out, was an exceedingly awkward task.

"I'm fine," I told him shortly. "It's nothing."

Hermogenes came and took the strip of cloth from my

fingers, giving me a searching look as he did so. Then he deftly wrapped the bandage around my wounded arm. Happily, he did not pester me with further questions.

"I had an adventure with Perseus," I said after a moment. "It turned out ill."

"Oh," Hermogenes said, as if that explained it all.

And perhaps it did.

He finished wrapping the bandage and tied it off neatly. I thanked him, examining his handiwork closely. The projectile had cut me across the bicep. Though it was deep enough, it was not a particularly serious injury as long as I managed to keep infection at bay, but the padding of the bandage made the injury seem more severe than it actually was. I wondered if such visible evidence of heroic effort might earn me a few sympathy points with the women of the house who were, no doubt, still disenchanted with me.

"So, about my idea ..." Hermogenes began again.

There were times when Hermogenes was both perceptive and astute. This was not one of them.

I was tired, sore, discouraged, stressed, and certain unmentionable parts of me were chafed raw from sand. I wanted nothing more than to soak out my various aches in a warm bath. I already had the water for it heating in the kitchen.

"Now is really not the best time," I told my disciple, hoping he'd take the hint.

"But it's a great idea, Chef!" he bulled ahead. "Truly! You see, I've come up with a plan for a demonstration. A public demonstration. It'll be kind of like a lecture."

"A lecture?" I raised a skeptical eyebrow. "I am not a philosopher."

"No, no! Not a lecture like that. Something more along the lines of a cooking demonstration. See, we'll get you set up in the Agora with a brazier and a counter. You prepare something really cracking—maybe even those striped mullets—and you can explain as you go. You know, telling people what you're doing and why."

"Hermogenes—" I sighed.

"Think about it, Chef. At a symposion, nobody ever gets to actually see the food prepared. It's all done in the kitchen and then the slaves trot it out as if the gods themselves made it magically appear. This way you can show everybody how it's done. And how brilliant you are. It'll create buzz before the big match, yeah?"

Me cook in the Agora? Like a lowly sausage seller? I could only imagine what The Sicilian would have to say about that.

The Lydian is grilling sausages in the Agora? Obviously, he's resuming his rightful place in the world. Ah well, it was only a matter of time, really. And do you know, he actually fancied himself a real chef?

"No, Hermogenes," I told my disciple. "Absolutely not."

"But, Chef!" he wailed. "You said you *liked* my marketing strategies. Brilliant, you called them!"

"And some of them are," I agreed. "But not this one. I will not prepare food in the middle of the Agora. If people wish to watch me cook, then they can come to the match—or better yet, hire my services for the evening. I will not prepare food in front of a crowd of gawking peasants. It's a terrible idea."

"But Chef!"

"No."

"But—"

"No," I said again, annoyed. "Have you always been this obtrusive?"

"I don't know. What does it mean?"

"Pushy."

"I got worse since you freed me," he said flatly.

"Indeed. Well, no amount of pushing on your part is going to change my mind about this."

"Fine, then I guess we won't have any pre-match buzz happening."

"It appears not."

Hermogenes uttered an exceedingly frustrated sound, then, all indignation, he turned on his heel as if to stalk from the courtyard.

"Not that we'll require much in the way of pre-match 'buzz,'" I said to his back.

Hermogenes halted in his tracks and half-turned, casting a darkly suspicious look over his shoulder. His beard, I noticed, was starting to look a little thicker.

"Not with Cato's Chitons as our sponsor," I said, picking a non-existent speck of lint from my chiton.

Hermogenes did not move. I glanced over at him. His dark eyes were wide, his mouth had fallen open inelegantly.

"You'll catch flies like that," I told him.

He closed his mouth, but continued to stare at me. "Chef," he managed finally. "Is … is it true? You're not just having me on?"

"Oh, it's true," I assured him. "Cato approached me yesterday, when you were supposed to be getting Nausikaa's soup recipe. How *did* that go, by the way?"

Hermogenes's cheeks coloured. "Not well," he said, shaking his head. "But Chef! How did Cato ask you? What did he say? Tell me everything!"

I gave him a stern look for his failure to secure the recipe, then I relented and told him all about Cato's offer.

"*He offered you the purple chiton and you turned it down?*" Hermogenes was aghast. "The purple one! The one dyed with all them sea snails?"

"Yes. And yes, I turned it down," I said, annoyed at his tone, which seemed to my ears particularly unbecoming to a disciple in disgrace. "You were the one who told me I needed a signature colour. A *brand*. That's why we went with the blue chiton. Blue is my brand."

"But it was the *purple* chiton!" he wailed. "How could you have turned it down? Chef, you just didn't think!"

"I gave it plenty of thought!" I snapped, thoroughly irritated now. This was not going at all the way I'd imagined it.

"If you'd given it plenty of thought, you would have *known* to take him up on the purple chiton! It could've been your *new* look! You could have worn it for the cooking demonstration!"

"I've already told you, I'm not doing that."

"But Chef! Now that you've got a sponsor, it's *expected!*"

"Don't be ridiculous! Cato would never expect me to cook in the Agora like some second-rate chef."

"But, it's free advertising!"

"No."

"But—"

"No, Hermogenes. This discussion is closed."

My disciple threw his hands up and let out a bellow of pure exasperation. Then, with a last reproachful glare, he turned and stormed from the courtyard. The slam of the front door echoed through the house. Doubtless he had gone to walk off his blighted hopes.

I ought never to have called him brilliant to his face.

Hermogenes was angry and frustrated, but he would get over his little tantrum and would probably return with some new marketing scheme with which to trouble me. Ah well, I would deal with that when it came. In the meantime, I needed a bath and a drink, not necessarily in that order.

I quit the courtyard more calmly and certainly more quietly than my disciple had, entering the kitchen to check on the state of my bathwater. I found Irene and Nausikaa sitting on a pair of stools. They were just finishing an afternoon snack of bread and olives. I let my wounded arm drop down as if it were paining me. The wide strip of cloth was white against my skin.

"Oh, so it's yourself, then," Irene observed, her tone as flat as her regard.

So much for sympathy.

"Having a go at Hermogenes now too, are you?" she asked.

"Excuse me?"

"I heard you! The whole house heard. First you tear a strip off poor Nausikaa here. Imagine! Saying such things to a nice girl like that, and her as friendly as can be! And now you've gone and got your own disciple worked up into a rare state, and him so helpful and accommodating! Oh yes, I heard every word. Well, you might think you're the bee's knees, but if you ask me, you're nothing but a cranky old—"

"Enough, Irene!" I said, cutting her off with a gimlet-eyed stare, embarrassed that she would harangue me so in front of a house guest.

"That's exactly what I was minded to say," she said, supremely unimpressed. "Enough is enough! I'll not have this kind of trouble in the house! With all the house guests and winged horses and other shenanigans, not to mention himself's wedding coming up, trouble is the last thing we need! You've everybody on eggshells around you and it's got to stop. You can start by apologizing to poor Nausikaa."

"Please," Nausikaa broke in then. Her eyes were downcast, but her voice held a touch of firmness and there was a stubborn line to her chin. "It's all right, Irene. Really, it is. Chef Pelops shouldn't have to apologize for speaking the truth as he sees it."

"That's not what Zeuxo said, is it?" Irene sniffed. "Well, I suppose it's between the two of you then, though what herself will have to say about such rudeness, what with her set to being the new mistress, I couldn't tell you."

She rose from the stool and patted Nausikaa kindly on the shoulder. "I still say he owes you words, but I'll leave you to sort it, pet. Don't be letting him get the better of you. He's naught but a mere man, for all the gossip there is about his granddad. And mind you don't take too long either. Zeuxo"—she emphasized the name, making it sound like a threat (which it probably was)—"promised to come by this afternoon to help you with your hair."

Before Irene left the kitchen, she gave me her best gorgon glare.

I scowled back, a parting retort ready on my lips, but before I could deliver it, Nausikaa had slid from her stool, obviously prepared to follow on Irene's heels. Now that she was facing me, I noted the puffiness around her eyes, the blue of her irises made more striking by reddened rims. Her tanned face seemed splotchy and her colour was bad.

It gave me pause. She *had* been crying, and for quite some time, if the state of her complexion was any indication. Could it be *I* who had caused that?

Zeuxo had named me cruel for the things I had said to Nausikaa. In truth, I did not recall my exact words to her—did not recall much of the conversation at all—but it was clear that whatever I'd said to her, it had hit home in a fashion I had never intended.

All of a sudden, I felt like a total boor.

"I am very sorry," I fumbled. "Truly, I did not mean—"

"Don't bother," she advised, her tone expressionless. "You meant every word of it. Drink will do that to you, don't you know? It frees the social inhibitions. In wine is found true honesty."

"That's not true," I protested. "Well … it can be," I amended.

"Wine is notorious for loosening men's tongues, but I didn't mean—"

"Or course you did," Nausikaa said. Although the words sounded indifferent, I thought I detected a faint trace of hurt in her voice, though perhaps I was imagining it. She held herself with such cool dignity.

"Last night, you made it perfectly clear that I am beneath you," she said. "I am. Your father was a king. Mine was a fisherman. Your grandfather is a god who sends lightning bolts across the heavens. Mine broke his back hauling fish from the ocean. My mother is beautiful, and my brother is semi-divine. I am neither. I am not 'nothing,' as you so succinctly put it, but I am not much more than that."

"That's not true," I floundered. "You ... you were *called!* By Apollo Himself! You're to be a priestess at Delphi. Perseus told me! *You* told me!"

Nausikaa's eyelids fluttered and her gaze darkened, but she remained silent.

"Apollo doesn't just call anybody, you know," I continued gamely. "Only the special ones."

"You did not think me special last night when you were so generously sharing your opinion of me."

"I was drunk," I admitted. "I should not have said the things I did. I—"

"Have you any idea what my life has been like?" she asked with an intensity that silenced me. "I have little in the way of family, you know. My father is dead. There are no aunts or uncles or cousins. And I have few in the way of friends. I am deemed unworthy by a mother who can only see the glory of her demigod son. Mocked and teased by my much more attractive though infinitely stupider brother. I am ignored both for my intellect and my lack of beauty. Dismissed by all save those who believe I will help them get closer to my brother. Oh yes, my life has been *special*, indeed."

Unshed tears glistened in her eyes.

"And then, we came to Athens where there were any number of possibilities for me. New people, new situations ... new *family*, even if we were not related through blood. But, it seems this branch of the family has as much appreciation for me as most other people do. The only ones who have gone out of their way to be kind to me here—for my *own* sake!—are Hermogenes and Zeuxo. And Irene and Gorgias, of course."

"I'm sorry," I tried again.

But she brushed it off. "The only reason you're apologizing to me now is because Zeuxo wishes it."

Perhaps at one time that had been true. It was not any longer, but before I could deny it, Nausikaa had moved past me on the way to the door. Before she left the kitchen, she paused and turned back.

"After the things Hermogenes told me of you—your kindness, your generosity—I thought perhaps I could be your friend. He worships you, you know. But you have made it quite plain you do not wish my friendship, and frankly, Chef Pelops, I do not require—or desire—your pity. So please, do not trouble yourself with apologies. I shall tell Zeuxo you were suitably contrite and that will be the end of it."

With a swirl of dark hair, she was gone. I stood there for a long time after she left, gazing sightlessly at the empty doorway.

Chapter 25

Hey look, it's that juggler!" Perseus veered off.

There we were slogging through the Agora late at night when all I really wanted to do was go home and fall onto my sleeping couch. We were on a crucial mission, but could my uncle stay focused for any length of time?

"What are you doing?" I demanded, trying unsuccessfully to catch at his arm.

"It's that dude! The one from the symposion. I love this guy!"

"We're here to find Ares," I hissed. "Not to gape at some third-rate juggler."

"Aw, come on!" Perseus protested, slowing without stopping. "Look at the poor guy. He's down on his luck!"

And so he must have been, to be busking in the Agora at this late hour of the night. Save for a few men still carousing on the next block, the street was empty, and it was so dark one could

343

barely see the Great Galinthius's act—although perhaps that was the whole point.

"Come on, dude! I just want to give him some cash." He began fumbling in his satchel. "We don't have to stand and watch or anything."

"Fine," I relented. "But hurry up, I'd like to find Ares tonight if at all possible. The Bronze Chef match is in two days! I'm running out of time."

Perseus, still rooting in his bag for a coin, began to quicken his pace.

It was a mistake.

We were in the taverna district, on a section of the Panathenaic Way that was thick with refuse at the best of times. And with all the road resurfacing that had been carried out lately, this was not the best of times. As he strode towards the now enthusiastically juggling entertainer, Perseus stumbled on a piece of road debris.

He swore as he tried to catch his balance. A valiant effort, but a futile one. Flailing wildly, he tumbled sideways, tripping on still more debris. He had pulled ahead of me, so I was some distance from him. Not close enough to catch him up. He hit the mucky ground with a wet squelch.

Sighing inwardly, I drew closer, intending to take him to task for his clumsiness. The last thing I needed now was Perseus with a broken ankle. But he appeared to be uninjured and, even before I reached him, he was already struggling to his feet, a black silhouette against the shifting shadows of the poorly lit Way.

And then, as he straightened, I saw a roundish-shaped object detach itself from him.

I couldn't tell what it was through the gloom, but there was something sinister about it. Something not right in its form or substance. It rolled inexorably toward the unlucky juggler, and I must have had some sort of presentiment about it because my breath caught in my throat at the sight.

"*Don't look at it, dude!*" Perseus cried.

But the Great Galinthius failed to heed his warning.

Still juggling, the entertainer glanced down at the object that had fetched up against his feet. And from one breath to another, the Great Galinthius appeared to freeze solid. His airborne balls fell past motionless, insensible hands, dropping to the ground like fat raindrops.

"*What in Hades—?*" I exclaimed.

Perseus cursed roundly. "*Don't look at it, Pelops!*" he shouted.

"What is it?"

"It's the head!"

The head?

"*Medusa's* head?" I gasped. "*That's* what's in your satchel? A *gorgon's* head? *You've been carrying a gorgon's head around this entire time?*"

"Ever since I've been on tour," he admitted.

I was speechless.

I'd seen him take that satchel everywhere. Perseus had carted that snake-haired weapon all over Athens! He'd dragged it to the Agora! Taken it to symposions! The Great Galinthius hadn't been frozen, he'd been *petrified*.

"I didn't want anyone else to find it," Perseus was explaining. "You know, by accident."

By accident? Great Zeus and Hera! What if Hermogenes or Ansandra had stumbled across the contents of his satchel *by accident*?

"Zeus Above, Perseus!" I swore. "How could you be so clumsy? Didn't you have it secured? What are we going to do? We can't just leave it there!"

"I know! I'm working on it."

I ventured a cautious peek out of the corner of my eye, careful not to look directly at where the Great Galinthius stood. Perseus had knelt down, and was fumbling again in his satchel.

"No worries," he assured me, though tension thrummed through his voice. "I've got something … here it is!" He pulled a small item from his bag. Reflected light flashed briefly from its surface.

I gasped and squeezed my eyes shut. "What's that? What are you doing?"

"It's a piece of polished bronze," he answered. "If I move it just the right way, I can see the head without actually seeing it, you know?"

"And that will work?" I demanded, my voice quavering.

"It did before," Perseus said, sounding distracted. I could hear a squelching sound.

Tentatively, I opened my eyes. Through the gloom, I could see that he had risen to his feet once more. He was walking backwards, holding the piece of metal at eye level, warily picking his way past the debris that had tripped him up before. He moved slowly but surely toward the shadowy lump that lay on the road. My heart pounded unevenly in my chest. I forced my gaze down, willing myself not to look.

I stared at my feet, unseeing, and for what seemed like an eternity, I was conscious only of the sound of my own harsh breath.

And then, "There! I've got it!" Perseus exclaimed. "Don't look yet! I'm putting it back into my satchel and ... okay!" His sigh of relief was audible. "You can look now, dude."

Cautiously, I raised my eyes.

"Are you sure?" I asked, still hanging back. "It *is* secure now?"

"It's tight," he assured me.

I drew closer. "*Great Zeus and Hera!*" I swore, gazing at what remained of the Great Galinthius.

Medusa's still-potent gaze had caught him mid-fumble, his ineptitude now immortalized in a fine-grained marble more elegant than anything he had achieved in his life. His expression was one of mild surprise.

"Uh, dude, we should ... you know ... probably not stick around." Perseus fidgeted uncomfortably.

"Right," I answered, still staring in morbid fascination at the newly formed statue.

"Dude!" His tone was more urgent now. "Come on! I think the Scythian Archers are coming."

It was enough to rouse me. I glanced up and down the street. It was still empty in the immediate vicinity, but a torch-lit group was making its way towards us from further up the street.

"Let's go," I said.

Skulking in the shadows, we slunk from the scene. I wondered if anyone would remark on the statue. Or if the Great Galinthius would be as ignored in death as he had been in life. Just another one of the many stone figures that dotted the Agora, and that most people had long since ceased to notice.

It was a most ignominious end.

"What did you mean when you said this worked before?" I asked, once we'd put enough distance between us and the statue. "How many times has that ... thing gone rolling about?"

"A couple," Perseus said evasively.

"How many?" I insisted.

"Well, lemme see ... first there was that fisherman on Delos, then a flute girl in Thebes, then there were Archestratus's slaves—"

"You turned Archestratus's slaves to stone?" I demanded incredulously.

"*I* didn't!" Perseus denied. "They looked in the bag! They weren't supposed to be going through my stuff! But I found them in my room and the head was there all snaky and ..." He shrugged uncomfortably. "I had to stash 'em in the garden so nobody would know."

I gaped at him. At his audacity.

"That's why I came to stay with you," he explained. "It just ... I dunno, weirded me out staying with Archestratus. Seeing those slaves standing there in the shrubs every day all stony-looking?" He struck a pose imitating a statue. "It was kinda *creepy*, if you know what I mean."

I passed a hand over my eyes, feeling like I ought to take him to task for it, but not having the slightest idea of what to say.

"Hey, look!" Perseus tugged at my arm, gesturing to a taverna whose exterior walls were covered in erotic graffiti. Light spilled from its open doorway. "That one's open. Let's see if Ares is there."

I stared at him. "How can you jolly on after what just happened?" I demanded. "A man has been turned to *stone!*"

"You're the one who said he had to find Ares," Perseus protested.

"Yes, but ..." I trailed off, at an utter loss for words.

Perseus turned to face me, his expression sober. "Pelops," he began. "Look, I know what happened. And I don't know what to do about it. That fisherman on Delos? I tried everything to bring him back. Nothing worked. All I managed to do was accidentally break off his arm."

I winced.

"I didn't know what to do for him, and I don't know what to do for the juggler."

"We've got to get rid of that head," I told him.

"I know," he agreed miserably. "But how?"

At a loss, I scrubbed at my forehead. My immediate impulse was to enlist the help of Dionysus. A supernatural solution to a supernatural problem. There would be a certain elegance to it. But Dionysus was a terrible gossip, and if I recalled correctly, Medusa had once been Poseidon's lover. I had enough trouble with the sea god without any of this getting back to him.

Hermes? It was a possibility. He was the god of wiles, after all. Over the years, he had probably engineered any number of awkward disposals. But given how painful his feet were lately and how grumpy he'd been because of it, I did not feel comfortable asking him for any favours.

"I haven't the faintest idea," I told my uncle. "But I'll think of something."

"So," Perseus began hesitantly. "You said 'we.' 'We' have to get rid of it. Does that ... does that mean you're going to help me?"

"I will help you," I confirmed.

He searched my face, as if he didn't quite believe me, but something in my countenance must have reassured him. He brightened, his golden eyes lighting up like twin suns. "That would be awesome, dude!" He broke into a relieved smile. "Ha! I *knew* I could count on family!"

Family. Yes, we were that. By blood if not spirit.

Perseus clapped me on my injured arm. "Come on, dude, let's scare up Ares, find Proteus again, and get you your answer. And after you win the Bronze Chef, you and me are gonna get rid of this head once and for all."

"It can't be soon enough," I muttered, turning my steps to the well-lit taverna.

Ares was nowhere to be found in that particular establishment. In fact, we had to visit several more tavernas before we managed to track down the god of bloodlust and slaughter. Throughout our long search I was acutely aware of Perseus's satchel and its evil contents, and whenever light and visibility permitted, I found myself obsessively checking the knots that sealed it shut.

I had no wish to witness another petrification that night—or any other night, for that matter. The sooner we disposed of that gods-cursed head, the better.

The last taverna we tried was definitely the least savoury of the lot. Indeed, I never would have set foot in such a disreputable place, but I knew we would find Ares there as soon as Perseus pointed out the building, for the god's eagle owl was perched fastidiously on the topmost peak of the roof.

The taverna's entrance was located at the lowest point in the road, which, for a drinking establishment, was somewhat less than desirable, considering the ultimate outcome of said drink. As I feared, just outside the narrow door, a wide puddle of piss steamed in the cool night air, ready to pollute the sandals of the unwary. I avoided it by stepping on a flat loose stone, no doubt placed there for that very purpose. Behind me, there was a small splash, then a muffled curse. I glanced back and saw Perseus shaking his foot. The satchel, I noted, was still slung over his shoulder.

"Is it secure?" I asked for what must have been the hundredth time.

"You don't have to keep asking, you know," he complained as we entered the taverna.

"Why yes, I believe I do..I—"

Whatever else I was about to say was choked off as a miasma of odours suddenly assaulted my nostrils: acrid smoke from cheap oil lamps, the sour tang of painfully new wine, and too many bodies too long from the bathhouse. Some sort of meat was sizzling on a brazier, its rancid smell almost but not quite obscured by the noisome stench of the room. The light was dim, and the air thick and cloying. In the corner, a small brown dog was busily urinating on a patron too far gone in his cups to notice.

For a god, Ares certainly had appalling taste in entertainment venues.

I held a corner of my cloak—thankfully, not my new one!— to my nose and peered around the crowded room. Perhaps, I wondered hopefully, the god of war was patronizing another establishment?

Then I saw the enormous red-haired god, the one Ares had called Thor. Although Ares had ominously promised that the northern god would be "thor" when he was through with him, not only was the foreigner in no pain, he was clearly feeling quite chuffed with life. So were Ares and Pisistratus, who lounged at the table beside him. In fact, they all appeared to be the best of friends now, swilling wine and shouting with laughter as they watched the urinating dog continue his tireless work on another unconscious taverna-crawler.

"Ho! Pelops!" Ares boomed when he spotted me. "Join us!" He threw his arms wide, accidentally smacking Thor in the head in the process. The two gods looked at each other, then they shouted with laughter, hauled off and banged their foreheads together with a resounding crack, and laughed again.

For a moment, I despaired. Ares seemed in no condition to do battle with a sea god, though he was in better shape than Pisistratus, who was alternately squinting and widening his eyes as he attempted to bring me into focus.

"'Lo, Pelps," Piss slurred, trying unsuccessfully to pull himself upright. He was practically under the table.

I patted him on the shoulder and seated myself gingerly on the bench beside him. Perseus had plopped right down between Ares and Thor and was already filling a wine cup for himself. I gave him a sharp look. We were not there to carouse.

But I had misjudged him, for he filled Thor's cup as well as his own, effectively distracting the northern god's attention. I seized the opportunity.

"A word, please, Ares," I said as Perseus and Thor began an animated conversation.

"The word is 'bollocks.'" Ares snorted a laugh into his wine. The purple drink sprayed up, liberally splashing the front of his chiton, although the dark stains faded and disappeared even as I watched. Apparently even the god of bloodlust and slaughter had appearances to maintain.

Pisistratus giggled at the sight and slid a little further under the table.

"I need help," I said, then paused. "*Muscular* help."

With a small sigh, Piss put his head down on the table and started snoring. Ares, however, had straightened, his bloodshot eyes suddenly sharp and clear.

"Somebody fucking with you?" he inquired dangerously. He rolled his shoulders back and cracked his thick neck, the sound audible even over the noise of the taverna. The scar on his cheekbone had darkened ominously.

"Just being difficult," I said quickly. "It's a minor god. A sea god. Proteus. I need to catch him."

The god of war slammed his wine cup down on the table and jumped to his feet. "Let's do it!" he cried, muscles bulging, eyes sparking fire.

"Uh … well, not this instant," I said, nonplussed.

"Let's do it now!" he insisted.

I certainly couldn't fault his enthusiasm.

"We can't," I told him regretfully. "There are … other considerations."

"Like what?" he demanded belligerently.

Like finding a safe place to stash the Gorgon's head before Perseus petrified half of Athens.

Discovering that Perseus had been carting that evil thing around with him had changed my plans. Obviously, we couldn't take it with us on our quest—who knew what might happen if we did? I could hardly ask Gorgias to mind it. Ever since I had confessed my feelings for Zeuxo to him, he was barely speaking to me. Oh, he was polite enough—achingly polite—but where there had once been warmth, now there was only coolness, and I did not know what to do about it. But even if we'd been on better terms, I could not have endangered him by leaving a Gorgon's head in his care. The only solution I'd been able to come up with was to bury the thing temporarily in my herb garden. It wasn't ideal—indeed, it smacked of desperation more than anything else—but nobody puttered in that garden except me. And I could use leaf litter to hide any sign of digging from curious eyes.

"*Other* considerations," I repeated to the god. "What about first light tomorrow? Could you be ready then?"

"I'm ready now."

"Yes, but I am not. Let's say tomorrow morning. We'll meet you by The Herms."

"I don't like that little fucker," Ares complained peevishly. "Why do we have to meet by his statues?"

"Fine," I said, refraining with some effort from rolling my eyes. "We'll meet at your temple then. The new one in the north Agora."

His expression brightened. "It's brilliant, isn't it?"

"It's a lovely temple," I told him gravely.

"That little puke Hermes doesn't have a temple like that." The god of war seemed quite pleased by it.

"Indeed," I said, rising to my feet before Ares could start in on why he didn't care for the god of messengers. I had no wish to offend Hermes. He was my friend, he was trying to discover a way for me to cook the kraken, and Mithaecus had been calling on him to curse me. Although Hermes had thus far refrained from doing so due to our aforementioned friendship, I did not want to give him reason to change his mind.

"I'll see you at dawn, then," I told Ares. "Perseus and I will be on Pegasus. I assume you have other transportation?"

"I'm covered." Ares waved it off.

I started to move off, but Ares plucked at my himation.

"Are you sure we can't go tonight?" he asked hopefully, shaking out his arms and shoulders. "I could use a good brawl right about now."

I extricated my cloak from his grasp with a smile. "I'll see you tomorrow," I said firmly.

Chapter 26

"Chef Pelops!"

I rocked back on my heels. "Nausikaa!"

"I did not think—"

"What are you—"

We both broke off at the same time.

Eos had not yet dispersed the mists of night, and the court-yard was lit only by the stars. I had just finished arranging the leaf litter over the spot in the garden where Perseus and I had buried the Gorgon's head, and was on my way to meet him in the alley. I might have missed Nausikaa altogether had she been standing to one side or sitting on a bench. As it was, I had all but run into her in front of the geraniums.

"Forgive me," I said into the silence, my gaze flicking back to the herb garden. Was there any sign of disturbance? Had she seen me crouched down beside it? "I ... I did not think anyone else would be up this early. I was careless. I hope I did not tread on your toes?"

"No. No, I'm fine."

We both fell silent again.

I wanted to check the garden again, to make sure there was no sign of our clandestine activity. But I did not want to bring her attention to the area. With no small effort, I kept my eyes trained on her face. The faintest touch of rose had begun to creep into the sky. Nausikaa's features were still in shadow, but I could see the dark mass of her hair tied back in some fashion.

The silence dragged on.

Perseus had gone on ahead (to warm up, he'd told me), but he and his winged horse would be waiting for me now. I needed to go. But I found I could not quit the courtyard just yet. There were words I owed this woman. Words that were, perhaps, best said under the cloak of darkness.

"I ... I know I tried to say this to you before, but I must say it again," I began, stumbling a little on my words. "Nausikaa, I owe you an apology. I said things—cruel things!—that were not true. Things that hurt your feelings. I should never have done so."

"No," she agreed coolly.

She was not going to make this easy for me.

I swallowed and continued gamely on. "I am truly sorry I caused you pain," I told her. "It was, I know, utterly unforgivable of me. And yet—" I paused and took a deep breath. "And yet, I hope—I am very much hoping—you can find it in yourself to do just that. To forgive me."

The sky was lightening by the moment. Now I could make

out her features, though I could not decipher her expression. Was she angry? Receptive? Indifferent? I could not tell. Her blue eyes were pools of shadow.

I waited.

"Your words *were* hurtful," Nausikaa said finally, her words slow and considering. "And they did make me very angry. My brother ..." She paused, started to speak, then stopped again and sighed. "My brother has been saying thoughtless things to me my whole life. Hurtful things at times, though I know he did not always mean them to be so. He tosses off these ill-conceived remarks and apologizes for them in the same breath as if it's all a big joke. He never sees that I am not laughing. My mother smiles indulgently and I am expected to do the same—all because of who he is."

She pulled her mouth to one side in a self-deprecating smile. "I'm not telling you this to excite your sympathy," she assured me. "The truth is, it's become very easy for me to dismiss apologies of any kind. To believe the worst of people. I certainly believed the worst of you, despite what Hermogenes told me to .the contrary, which is why I didn't listen to you before. But I see things a little differently now, and so, thank you. I accept your apology."

I let out my breath in a faint *whoosh*, though I had not been aware of holding it.

"And I thank you for that," I said gravely. "I know I don't deserve it." I paused. "But, tell me ... what changed your mind?"

"Hermogenes told me all about your trouble with the kraken—and Poseidon's role in that," she replied. "I understand

now that you were struggling with your own difficulties. But—"
She paused and offered me a crooked smile. "I think it was
Zeuxo who convinced me you were serious, She said you could
be pigheaded and thoughtless sometimes, but that you were one
of the best men she knew. And that if you were apologizing to
me, it was because you truly meant it."

"I see," I said, my voice a little rough. I cleared my throat
again. "She's right, you know. I did mean it. I meant every word
of it. I should never have taken my troubles out on you the way I
did. But your brother …" I paused and sighed much as Nausikaa
had done a few moments before. "Your brother was vexing me
rather greatly."

"Oh, he excels at that sort of thing," she told me.

"Indeed," I said. "Although I must admit, he has improved
somewhat these last few days."

"His heart is usually in the right place," she agreed. "Even if
his brain is not."

I chuckled. "An apt description. But this isn't about Perseus,
it's about you. I was angry with your brother and the whole situation with the kraken, and I took it out on you. It was wrong of
me in every way. And I am very, very sorry."

A tentative smile lit her face. Her teeth were white against the
tan of her complexion. It was, I realized, an exceedingly attractive combination.

"Friends, then?" she asked.

I nodded and smiled back. "Friends."

We stood there grinning at each other. Now that it was
lighter, I could see that her dark hair had been curled and tied

back with some sort of scarf, tendrils escaping to frame her face. It was very Greek-looking, one of Zeuxo's favourite hairstyles. But I did not think it suited Nausikaa.

"And now where are you off to so very early this morning, Chef Pelops?" she asked, her voice teasing.

"Please, just Pelops," I told her.

Her smile widened. "Pelops, then. I woke early, but you look like you're going out?"

I made a face, suddenly recalling my task. "I am," I told her. "And really, I must be on my way. I'm quite late now. Perseus and I are off to find a way for me to cook the kraken and win this miserable Bronze Chef competition."

"Perseus!" Nausikaa looked startled. "You're going with *Perseus*?"

"Yes. He's told me of a certain sea god who might be able to help me, a fellow named Proteus."

Nausikaa's eyes widened further. "I know of Proteus!" She gave me a long, considering look. "You know, that actually might work. If you can find him, that is."

"Oh, we found him once already," I told her, gesturing to my bandaged arm. "I've got the wound to prove it. Now we just have to hang on to him. Look, it's a long story and I haven't time to tell you right now. But I promise I shall tell you all about it once we're back."

I was about to turn away when Nausikaa touched my arm lightly. I paused and looked down at her. By the ever-brightening light of Helios, god of the sun, oaths and the gift of sight,

Nausikaa's eyes were very blue now. As blue as the Aegean itself. She really did possess the most haunting, ethereal eyes.

"Good luck," she told me in her honey-rich voice. "If you're going with my brother, you're going to need it."

Chapter 27

It was almost déjà vu. The sun warmed my back, the wind whistled in my frozen ears, and my stomach churned unhappily. Azure waves twinkled below us, a desolate expanse of sandy beach stretched off to our right. There were a few differences this time around. Perseus no longer sported his satchel with its fearsome contents, and off to our left, pacing us in the air, was an enormous eagle owl, its flight powerful and silent.

The god of war rode on its back.

When Ares had assured me he had his own transportation for our venture, I had not quite imagined this. One would think that after all my years of consorting with gods, such things might seem more commonplace to me. But although I'd stood in front of Ares's sparkling new temple and watched as his owl grew to unnatural proportions in order to accommodate him, the whole thing possessed a distinctly dreamlike quality.

There was, however, nothing dreamlike or unreal about our quest.

Pegasus swooped down low, his wingtips brushing the foam-kissed waves. Droplets of water sprayed up to soak my legs. I could feel the winged horse's muscles shift and dance beneath my buttocks as he negotiated our passage. I clutched Perseus around the waist, terrified I might fall off my precarious perch and plunge into those endless deep-eddying depths. I had been fearful of deep, dark water ever since Poseidon had made it clear he had it in for me. Not surprising, I suppose, but as Pegasus dipped even lower, almost galloping atop the very waves themselves, I held my breath and wondered if Dionysus had had the right of it after all. If I'd just shagged the god of sea and earthquakes and been done with it, my life would have been immeasurably easier. I certainly wouldn't be clinging to the back of a flying horse as it galloped over the churning Aegean looking to trap a shapeshifting sea god.

I clenched my teeth, clung more tightly to my uncle, and offered up a prayer to any god who might be listening. Pegasus flew on, rising and falling with the waves.

Ares spotted our quarry first, reposing once again on a sunny patch of sand. For a benthic god, Proteus certainly seemed to enjoy a bit of lie in the sun. We came in from the sea, cutting off Proteus's access to escape. With a wordless gesture, Ares motioned us to the right, while he took the left.

The sea god never even saw us coming.

Silent as the night, the eagle owl glided across the shallows. Ares leaped lightly from its back onto the sandy beach. Just as silently, Pegasus landed us a stone's throw away, holding his wings up so we could disembark more easily. Perseus flowed from his back like water, landing on his feet without a sound. I tried to mimic his stealth, though I could not quite suppress a small sigh of relief as my own feet touched blessed, solid ground.

The sound was enough to rouse the snoozing god.

Proteus jumped up, eyes darting in all directions. It only took an instant for him to realize he'd been cut off.

He glared at us, curling his lip nastily. "Piss off," he snarled.

"Not bloody likely," Ares said, his lazy grin belied by a battle-ready stance.

Beside me, Perseus stood with his feet shoulder-width apart, his whole body quivering with excitement, primed and ready for action.

"My nephew here's got a question for you, sea dude," Perseus said. "Give him an answer, and you can go back to your nap."

"If you think you can just—" Proteus spat, then without warning he dove to the right. In the blink of an eye he had rolled across the sand, flowing to his feet with a speed that left me breathless.

In the same instant, Ares pounced on him like a cat.

The two gods grappled with each other, seemingly evenly matched. I balanced on the balls of my feet, ready to jump into the fight should the god of war require my aid.

I expected Proteus to change—I knew he would change!—but when he did, there were no tentacles, no claws, no spiked tails with deadly projectiles. It was no creature from nightmares that greeted my eyes. Instead, the god of war was suddenly wrestling with the most beautiful woman I'd ever seen.

Amber-kissed hair rippled down her back like liquid honey. Her skin, almost as golden as her hair, glowed in the morning sun. Long, perfectly shaped limbs lay against Ares's stronger, muscular legs. She was nude, save for an exquisite gold filigree girdle which encircled her tiny waist. Her bare breasts were thrust forward, their rosy tips tight with desire. My mouth dried to a desert at the sight.

She was Aphrodite, the goddess of love, beauty, and procreation, and she practically oozed sensuality and carnal pleasures. I could feel myself stiffen in her presence, ready to procreate right there on the spot.

"Ares," she breathed, tugging gently to pull him down on the sand with her. Her full lips were pouting. "I've missed you."

"Aphrodite?" Ares whispered, following her down most willingly.

But her glorious eyes flickered past him. "Hephaestus! No!" she cried.

Ares jumped back as if scalded.

"*Hephaestus?*" Ares scrambled backwards, whipping his head around to scan the nearby trees as if searching for the goddess's lame husband.

Hephaestus, I knew, had never forgiven Ares for canoodling with his wife and, although the god of bloodlust and slaughter was powerful when it came to combat, the god of fire and metalworking was no slouch himself in that department. But Hephaestus was nowhere in evidence. Probably because it was not

Aphrodite lying there on the sand—a fact which had momentarily escaped the god of war.

In his confusion, Ares had let loose his grip on the shape-shifting god. Fortunately, Perseus was ready to leap into the void. Doing precisely that, the Hero of the Aegean launched himself at Proteus just as the sea god regained his feet.

Clearly there was something to my uncle's idea of a pre-combat warm-up. Either that, or Perseus had been very warmed up, indeed. As he crashed into the fleeing god, the force of their impact sent the two tumbling head over heels across the sand. I ran to follow. When they finally came to a stop, Perseus had his hands firmly around the sea god's neck.

But Proteus had assumed another shape.

Her hair was titian instead of golden, the rich hue of rare cinnamon bark. Her naked body was slender rather than voluptuous, almost coltish, but possessing an innate grace for all that. She was nowhere near as beautiful as the goddess of love, but she was breathtaking enough. Lovely enough that her mother had once foolishly compared her beauty to that of the Nereides.

"Perseus?" her voice was as high as a young girl's. "You're hurting me!" Large, expressive eyes welled with tears.

"An ... Andromeda!" Perseus stammered. He snatched his hands away from her neck, holding them up as if in surrender. "I ... I'm sorry! I didn't mean to—"

Andromeda/Proteus gave an evil laugh and shoved him aside unceremoniously, her features twisting into an expression the absent princess had likely never assumed in her life. And then Proteus was up and running again.

But this time, I was there.

I tackled him without hesitation, bowling him bottom over wine krater. We landed hard, me on my left shoulder, skidding across the gravelly sands. For once, I thanked the gods for the ivory nub which afforded me some small protection from the burning grit. My torso was not so fortunate. I cried out, but did not break off my attack. I could not afford to let him get away again. This was my last chance!

Before Proteus knew what I was about, I'd seized him around his waist. He struggled, flinging himself from side to side. I clasped him tight to my body, my grip as sure as a vice. He would not get away from me this time.

It took everything I had to maintain my hold on him, especially when I felt the flesh—the very bones of him—shift and writhe under my grip.

And just like that I was holding Zeuxo.

I was surprised—and yet, not. Proteus seemed to know our weaknesses, though how he could have known about my feelings for Zeuxo I could not imagine.

Her nude body wiggled delightfully against mine. I inhaled sharply. The scent of her violet perfume enveloped me. Dark curls tumbled across my face. Her mouth, so luscious and tantalizing, quirked up at me.

"Not so tight, Pel," she said breathlessly in a way that caused my own breath to tighten in my throat.

I had never dared hold her so close before—at least, not in anything but my dreams. I would never get the chance to do so again. I held on tighter.

"Pel!" she protested.

I took a moment to appreciate Proteus's skills. He even *sounded* like Zeuxo! He had all the appearance, the sound, the very scent of her. But he had not her essence.

He was not Zeuxo.

I continued to hold on tight.

Dimly, I was aware of Ares's sandalled feet coming to stand beside us. Perseus joined him a moment later. I didn't move, too afraid to even shift my grip in case the slippery sea god wriggled away from me.

"Way to go, dude!" Perseus enthused. "That was epic!"

I gave him a smile that was mostly grimace. Despite Proteus's present feminine appearance, the god himself was no wilting flower, and it was taking all my strength to hold on to him.

"Game over, Proteus," Ares said.

"Piss off!" Zeuxo's lovely mouth formed the words, though the tone was not hers at all.

"Piss off, yourself, eel-fucker!" Ares retorted. "Rules are fucking rules, you know that. You really want to be taking this up with the Big Guy?"

Zeuxo/Proteus hesitated for a several heartbeats, then I felt the flesh shift beneath my hands again as he reverted to his true form.

I held on tight to the old man, not trusting the cunning god for an instant. But all the fight appeared to have gone out of him.

"It's okay, Pelops," Ares told me. "He knows he fucking owes you now, the tricky bastard."

Cautiously, I loosened my grip.

Proteus pushed himself up, scowling blackly at me.

I sat up, giving him some space, ready in case he decided to do a runner after all. But Ares, it appeared, was correct. The shapeshifting god stayed put, conceding total if unwilling defeat.

I stood and brushed myself off. Proteus followed suit, shaking out his sand-crusted tunic with sharp, irritated gestures.

He took his time getting himself back together: rearranging the folds of his clothing, combing the tangles out of his grey hair with his fingers, spitting to clear the grit from his mouth. When he'd finally finished, he glanced at Ares and Perseus, sniffing rudely. Then he turned and slid me a flat look.

"Well?" he demanded ungraciously. "What do you want to know, then?"

Chapter 28

"Kraken, Chef?" Hermogenes asked, staring at the coins I'd dropped in his hand. He exchanged a quick look with Nausikaa, who sat opposite him in the courtyard. "Are you sure?"

"Positive," I replied in a crisp business-like tone. "As much as you can carry. All cuts. And you'll have to hurry. The fishmongers won't be there for much longer. How much wood have we got?"

"Wood?" My disciple protested, though he was already rising from the bench. "What do we need wood for? We've plenty of charcoal for cooking."

"Smoking!" Nausikaa guessed, her eyes alight. "You're going to smoke it! That's what Proteus told you to do, isn't it?"

I offered her a tight smile. "Correct on both counts," I told her.

"Who's Proteus?" Hermogenes demanded crossly. "And why

did he tell you to smoke the kraken? And why don't I know about this? Shouldn't you keep your *disciple* informed?"

"Proteus is a sea god," I told him. "A minor one, but if you catch him and hang on to him, he is obliged to answer any question you care to pose."

Hermogenes thought about that for a moment, then his eyes widened. "You asked him how you could prepare the kraken?"

"I did," I confirmed.

"What did he say? Why the smoke?"

"He told me I had to alter the kraken's nature. By bathing it in smoke, you see, I can modify its essence, changing it from an oceanic element to one of air. In other words, I can shift its association from Poseidon, who is unfriendly to me, to Zeus, who is not."

Nausikaa's indrawn breath was audible.

"Chef!" Hermogenes gasped. "I never would've thought of that. That's … that's brilliant, that is!" His eyes were sparkling.

"It will be when we have some kraken to smoke," I said pointedly.

"I'm on it," he squeaked, his voice high with excitement.

Then he popped the silver coins in his mouth and darted down the hallway towards the front vestibule. I was about to ask him where his new money pouch had gotten to—carrying coins in the mouth was such a revolting habit!—but he was through the vestibule and out the door before I had the chance.

"Hurry!" I called. "We've got to get it all smoked by morning."

"I know!" his voice drifted back.

"And don't forget the wood!" I yelled after him.

He shouted something indistinguishable just as the front door slammed shut. Nausikaa and I exchanged an amused grin.

"He won't forget," she told me.

"I know," I said.

We continued to smile at each other. Her blue eyes danced with laughter. Such lovely, lovely eyes. When I realized I was staring, I dropped my gaze and began to fidget with the belt of my tunic.

"So what will you make with it?" Nausikaa asked in the silence which had, to my mind, become suddenly uncomfortable. "All this smoked kraken, I mean."

"Oh." I cleared my throat a few times. "I've got a number of ideas. I was thinking of a tart made with quail eggs and onion. I could chop up some kraken, add some dill, maybe even some goat cheese."

"Mmmm. It sounds delicious," she said.

"And sesame pancakes, rolled and stuffed with thin slices of kraken and thyme. Perhaps a few sautéed mushrooms too."

"Perfect," Nausikaa agreed.

"And some sliced tentacles, dredged in wheat flour and deep fried, served with a tart olive relish."

The ideas were coming fast and furious. For weeks I had been unable to come up with a single palatable recipe. Now, it was as if a dam had broken, and any number of succulent possibilities were surging forth to present themselves to me. "And then—"

"A kraken soup?" Nausikaa inquired.

I paused, eying her cautiously. "I had not ... that is ... I did not think ..."

"You did not think I would share my recipe with you?"

I was quiet for a moment, then I let out my breath in an explosive sigh. "I did not," I confirmed. "And I would not blame you in the least if you wouldn't. Not after the way I abused you."

She nodded slightly, acknowledging the unspoken apology. A small smile played on her lips. "I think the soup would be divine with smoked kraken," she told me, her voice low.

I regarded her for a long moment. Sea-blue eyes gazed back at me, clear, unguarded, and without a trace of hostility or reluctance.

Finally, I bowed my head. "Would you teach me how to make it, Chef Nausikaa?" I asked humbly. "I would very much like to prepare your delicious soup for the Bronze Chef competition."

"Of course, Chef Pelops," she replied, and I could hear the smiling lilt in her voice. "I would be happy to."

Chapter 29

All the kraken had been smoked. All the pots and pans were packed. All the utensils bundled in cloth and ready for transportation to the Theatre of Dionysus. I stood in the courtyard surveying the packages with great satisfaction. I felt better, more confident, than I had in a very long time. I was aware that I was standing taller, that my mind was sharp and clear. For the first time since I had heard about the Bronze Chef competition, I felt stirrings of excitement untempered by anxiety or doubts. At last I was going to show all of Athens just how very talented I was. At last my genius would be recognized. I would prove myself better than Mithaecus once and for all. To myself, to him, to the entire city. I just needed Hermogenes to return from the market and then we could go.

As if on cue, I heard the front door slam open.

"Chef!" Hermogenes cried. "Chef! Where are you?"

"In the courtyard!" I called. "What on earth is the matter? Why are you bellowing like an ox—great gods, what happened to you?"

My disciple, clean enough when he'd left for the Agora an hour earlier, was now scuffed and dirty. There was a shallow scratch along his right cheek, and one corner of his tunic (fortunately not his new one) was torn. I could see several bruises already coming up on his arm. He'd been fighting! On this of all days!

"Nothing!" He waved it off wildly. "It's nothing! But, Chef—"

"You've been fighting again, haven't you?" I accused him. "Hermogenes, I told you to stay away from Mithaecus's disciples! When are you going to start listening to me! I can't have you—"

"But, Chef! It's a bloody disaster!"

It was the panicked look on his face rather than his melodramatic words which gave me pause. My disciple, after all, is not widely known for his calm sobriety.

"What, specifically, is a disaster?" I inquired impatiently, trying to keep the edge from my voice.

I had sent him to the Agora on what ought to have been a simple and quick errand. I needed fresh thyme for the kraken pancakes, and Kabob had defecated all over my own thyme plants—a compelling argument for the quail's name, though I was thankful he had not exposed any evidence of my digging. Hermogenes and I had been up most of the night smoking endless amounts of kraken, and we were supposed to leave for the Bronze Chef match within the hour. We were overtired, a little stressed, and we needed to focus. We did not have time to engage in petty bouts of rivalry with inferior disciples.

"It's … it's the match!" Hermogenes stammered. "It's *The Sicilian*!"

"What about him?" I shrugged. "We knew he was one of the competitors."

"But we didn't know he were bringing his own dishes! And table napkins and cushions and—"

"*What?*"

"He got them all from that toad-buggering Meidias. All them fancy napkins from Aegypt. And the dishes!" He pulled at his hair, almost weeping in frustration. "Painted by Polygnotos himself! His high-end stuff! You've seen 'em yourself at market. There's nothing like 'em! They're bloody brilliant, they are!"

I was speechless for a long moment. Mithaecus had hired table linens? Dishes decorated by the most important vase painter in Athens? I'd thought all the tableware for the competition would be supplied. It was *supposed* to be supplied!

"Who told you this?" I demanded when I could find my voice. "Wasn't city council to provide dishes and napkins?"

"They were!" Hermogenes nodded, his face twisted in frustration. "They are. But I've seen their dishes, and they're not a patch on what The Sicilian's going to be bringing."

"How do you know? Have you seen Mithaecus's dishes?"

"No," he denied, shaking his head. "But I cornered one of his dirty great disciples behind the veg shops. I had to 'convince' him to talk, but he told me all about it."

"How did Mithaecus find the coin to pay for this?" I

wondered aloud. "Meidias's rates are bloody expensive for that sort of thing. It must have cost a small fortune!"

"It didn't cost him an obol!" Hermogenes spat out the words. "Meidias is his sodding sponsor!"

I swore long and loud.

"Chef, I don't know what we're going to do!" Hermogenes said miserably. "The match is in less than two hours! And you know I'd do anything for you, but I can't, I just *can't* go to Meidias!"

A few tears did spill over then, running down his cheeks, dampening his scar. I reached out and touched his shoulder gently.

"Hush, Hermogenes," I soothed him. "Hush. I've no intention of sending you to Meidias. As The Sicilian's official sponsor, he'd never rent anything to us anyway. And even if he wasn't a sponsor, I've no intention of hiring anything from that excrescence!"

"But, Chef," Hermogenes wailed. "Mithaecus'll have all them fancy dishes and—"

"And we will have fancy food," I told him firmly.

He closed his mouth, dark eyes gazing up at me imploringly, wanting to believe. *Needing* to believe.

"It really doesn't matter what Mithaecus serves his food on," I told my disciple. "Because we know precisely what that food will taste like. Uninspired. Flavourless. Some might even say vile. And there will be too little of it to boot, what with all his New Cuisine nonsense." I flared my nostrils in distaste.

"Now tell me," I continued. "If you were a judge, what would you rather eat? Minuscule portions of The Sicilian's substandard cooking served on the loveliest platter? Or robust servings of my own succulent concoctions presented, admittedly, on plainer ware, but exquisitely—even beautifully—prepared?"

Hermogenes shook his head. "There's no contest! Except maybe for the minuscule portions bit. That'll work in his favour, seeing as the judges won't have to choke down so much of it."

I grinned at his staunch loyalty. "No doubt," I told him gravely. "But it is a very small advantage. Now enough about the tableware. Yes, it is unfortunate we did not hear of The Sicilian's stratagems before now, but his cooking remains the same stodgy mess no matter how prettily he presents it. Come, help me load up the rest of this smoked kraken. Then, I need you to clean your face and put on your new chiton."

I gave him a bracing clap on the back. "My disciple," I said. "It is time for us to go and win the Bronze Chef competition."

The day had dawned sunny, but clusters of puffy white clouds had begun to move in, bringing a distinct chill to the air. Despite this, I welcomed the sight of them. Autumn in Athens could be very warm and we would be cooking outside in the middle of a shadeless theatre. Under such circumstances, cooler temperatures would be welcome.

For reasons having to do with social acceptability, the women of the household were not to be present to witness the competition, though they all gathered in the courtyard to see us off. They were a smiling, cheerful group, full of enthusiastic advice and warm encouragement.

Ansandra was also staying home for obvious reasons, despite

having selflessly offered her services as a junior apprentice the previous night. Gorgias had saved me from the necessity of refusing her offer by instantly nixing the idea, which had left her rather sullen. But after Kabob's morning desecration of my thyme plants, she and the bird had made themselves scarce, no doubt fearing I might add a last-moment quail dish to the Bronze Chef menu. She had not come down to the courtyard with the rest of them, but I heard a faint cooing coming from behind the second floor balustrade and I knew she was watching us.

Zeuxo had reluctantly refused to attend, despite the fact that several of her flute girl friends were to be at the match. I knew she wanted to come, but she was a soon-to-be-respectable matron, and so had deemed it wiser to remain at home. She gave Gorgias a quick embrace and bid him a warm goodbye, then she turned to Hermogenes and me.

"Best of luck, you two!" she said, touching Hermogenes lightly on the shoulder and giving me a sisterly peck on the cheek. Her mouth was quirked up in its crooked smile. "Truly, you deserve to win. The gods must surely be with you!"

I bobbed my head and smiled back.

The exchange had given me pause. While her words were invigorating enough, the kiss was oddly less bittersweet than I would have expected. But before I could think further on this, Danaë had stepped forward.

Being women of superior breeding, Danaë and her daughter were staying home as well. The rules of society in these matters had become more fluid in recent years—particularly with regards to foreign women—and I'd thought Nausikaa, at least, might venture to accompany us. But Danaë was old-school, and she refused point-blank to be seen at such a public event, or to have her daughter attend. I suspected Nausikaa had protested the decision but her mother had been adamant.

"Good fortune be with you, Chef Pelops," Danaë said formally, her cloak wrapped around her in a stately fashion.

I inclined my head, a gesture which Hermogenes attempted to imitate with somewhat less success.

It was Nausikaa's turn next. I noticed that her hair had not kept its curl, and she wore it now long and unbound like a fine linen cloak. I found I far preferred the sight of it down.

"I'll wish you good fortune too," she said with a bright smile that set her blue eyes twinkling. "But you won't need it!" She looked from me to Hermogenes and back again. "I *know* you'll win! I believe in you—*both* of you!"

She kissed each of us soundly then, and it was only with conscious effort that I refrained from touching my cheek afterward. Her lips had been so soft, and her encouraging words gave me a warm glow, like a cup of fine wine on a cold winter's day.

Irene was the last to wish us well.

Being a slave, she could have attended the match if she'd cared to pay the two-obol entrance fee, but Irene had already informed me with a pointed sniff that she had better uses for her money than to watch a bunch of poncy chefs (present company excluded, of course) prance around making food that any self-respecting household slave could prepare with greater ease, fewer dramatics, and at a fraction of the cost.

"You just see to it you beat that Sicilian at his own game," she instructed in a tone rivalling that of a hoplite drill sergeant. "If nothing else it'll save me from the dreary sight of your mopey faces if you lose."

"Yes, ma'am," I replied, refraining at the last moment from saluting.

And then it was time to depart.

The Theatre of Dionysus was situated on the southeast slope of the Acropolis, which meant we had to follow the Panathenaic Way through the winding streets of the Kerameikos, past all the shops and stalls of the Agora, and circle around the Acropolis itself. We stopped only once at my favourite of Tyche's sanctuaries to offer a sacrifice and libation to the goddess of fortune, fate, and providence. For the first time since I'd been making offerings there, the attending priest addressed me with more than the standard ritual greeting.

I had offered my sacrifice (a quail, which was not Kabob) and poured my libation (the Chian that Tyche had seemed to enjoy so much before) and was preparing to leave when the scrawny priest plucked at the corner of my blue himation.

"Go give 'em what for at th' match," he wheezed with a smile as broad as it was toothless. "Take that Sicilian down a peg, eh!"

I had no idea what Mithaecus had ever done to the fellow (no doubt he had committed some act of dinner on the man), but having a priest of Tyche on my side could only be a good omen.

"I'll see what I can do," I promised him.

We ran into Pharsalia and Castor by the Clepsydra fountain just east of the ramp which leads up to the various temples of the Acropolis. Arm in arm, accompanied by a gaggle of slaves I recognized from Pharsalia's bakeshop, the coupled hailed us merrily.

Pharsalia, boasting a breeding (not to mention a profession) even the kindest could not describe as superior, would be one of the few women attending the match. Her Theatre ensemble was a vibrant orange enlivened (though it hardly needed more zip) with a necklace of bronze phalluses. Several dozen bracelets decorated her muscular arms and erect bronze penises dangled from her earlobes.

Her advice was much the same as Irene's, if somewhat more crudely phrased.

"If you let The Sicilian win, we'll be bloody weeks with nowt to eat but his arse-burning Kraken Bake," she told me. "And I'm far too fond of me stomach for that." She paused and patted her ample belly. "Me digestion's counting on you, luv!"

"Then I can do nothing but win," I told her gravely.

She let go of Castor's arm and stepped close to give me a quick rib-cracking hug. "All right?" she murmured in my ear. "You've managed to sort your problem, then?"

"It's under control," I assured her.

"Good!" She gave me another hug, inadvertently pinching my ivory shoulder, then resumed her place beside Castor. He put his arm around her possessively. She barely came up to his hairy chest.

"Good luck, Pelops," the Macedonian rumbled, holding out his free hand.

"Thanks." I shook his hand. "I appreciate it."

"Come *on*, Chef!" Hermogenes interrupted, pulling at my arm. "We've got to get set up."

"Ooooo … yes, look at the time!" Pharsalia exclaimed quickly, gesturing up at the sun. "You'd best get moving, hadn't you? Don't want to be late, after all!"

No, I did not want to be late. I had a Sicilian to beat.

Chapter 30

Spectators had already started to gather at the Theatre of Dionysus by the time Hermogenes and I finally arrived at our destination. We were not alone, being accompanied by Perseus and Gorgias along with our household slaves, Strabo and Lais, who carried the bulk of our supplies.

As soon as we were recognized, the throng parted to make way for us, random cheers accompanying our footsteps. I scanned the faces, smiling impartially. I did not know if they were cheering for me, as one of the four Bronze Chef contenders, or for Perseus, Hero of the Aegean, who was grinning widely and waving with wild abandon at all and sundry.

Strabo and Lais lurched along behind my uncle, awkward smiles pasted on their faces, pleased but clearly uncomfortable with the attention involved in being part of our retinue. Gorgias strode by my side, equally ill at ease, though I could not say if this were due to the situation or to the wall that had sprung up between us. In fairness, he had offered no recriminations regarding my ill-conceived confession, as a lesser man might have done, but his continuing cool civility was both hurtful and wearing, and I still had not the slightest idea what to do about it.

We entered the Theatre of Dionysus via the entrance opposite the Odeon of Perikles. The Odeon was a roofed, multi-pillared structure that the famous statesman had had constructed for the Panathenaic musical contests. It was an attractive enough building, covered with timber from captured Persian warships (which, hailing from that country myself, made me somewhat uncomfortable), but it was nowhere near large enough to house a competition the size of the Bronze Chef.

The Theatre of Dionysus, on the other hand, could seat some fifteen thousand people, and even though the match was not set to start for another hour or so, the benches were almost full. Already the various food and wine sellers were out in force, their slaves wending their way through the press of people with skewers of spiced meats, baskets of fall apples, and rude clay cups of watered wine. The air was thick with the smell of grilled sausages.

"Good turnout," Gorgias remarked, taking it all in with a glance.

Hermogenes looked up at me and grinned. His eyes were bright and he hopped back and forth from one foot to the other, practically dancing with excitement. "Look at 'em all! This is cracking, Chef! Just cracking!"

I smiled at his antics, though my stomach felt suddenly

uneasy as I squinted at all the faces in the crowd. Somehow, I had not expected so very many people—and they would all be watching me cook! It had been a long time since I had been the recipient of so much public attention.

"Well, I'd best be off to find a place to plant me arse, then," Gorgias was saying as he eyed the rapidly filling sections.

There were ten sections, one for each of the ten founding tribes, but even if you were a member of that elite group you were not guaranteed a spot—especially for the most popular events. Athens was, after all, a city of some two hundred and fifty thousand people, and even if half of these were women, slaves, or foreigners (who would not get a seat anyway) there were still too few benches left for too many men. Indeed, the only people who could be certain of a seat in the theatre were the priests of Dionysus, various city magistrates and officials, and visiting dignitaries.

"Hey, they saved me a seat!" Perseus exclaimed happily, pointing at a spot on a bench front and centre. A sign had been propped up on it which read: Perseus, Hero of the Aegean.

Little did they know.

"Can you sit with me?" Perseus asked Gorgias.

Gorgias looked startled. "Not hardly," he rumbled. "Those are for important men, priests and officials and the like. Not for potters."

"Oh." Perseus's face fell. "What if I don't want to sit with a bunch of priests?" he said mutinously.

"You must," I told him firmly. "When are you going to grow

up, Perseus? You are the Hero of the Aegean. The city expects certain things of you." Really, he was such a child sometimes.

"But I'd have more fun with the G-Man," he protested.

"No doubt," I said unsympathetically. "But you're here to watch a competition, not carouse with your friends."

The Hero pulled a sour face at my words. "Okay, dude," he agreed reluctantly, scuffing his feet in the dust much as Hermogenes did when I asked him to do something he did not wish to do.

"We'll have a bit of a party after the match," Gorgias assured him.

Perseus brightened. "Awesome!" he exclaimed. Then he turned his attention back to me. "Good luck, Pelops!" he said. His grin was wide, white, and sincere. "And no worries, dude! You'll throw it down." He extended his fist towards me. "Show me some love, bro!"

I reached out and bumped fists with him, rolling my eyes as I did so. The noise of the crowd increased, and I suspected my popularity had just gone up a notch or two simply because of my association with the darling of the Aegean.

"Thanks," I told him. "Do try to enjoy the show, even if you must sit beside the priests."

Meanwhile, Gorgias had turned to Strabo and Lais.

"All right, you two, you need to help the Chef," he instructed firmly. "And then take your places in back. And don't be sloping off afterwards, either! We'll need you to haul this lot back home once the match is done."

He sounded severe, and looked the very picture of a stern

Athenian citizen giving instructions to his shaven-headed slaves, but I noticed he slipped them each a handful of coins to buy wine and sausages. A generous master, was my friend.

"Chef Pelops? Finally!" A small, fussy man, obviously some sort of official, came bustling up. "We expected you well before now," he said reproachfully. "The other chefs have been in place for *quite* some time."

I glanced back at Gorgias and he winked at me solemnly, friendlier than he had been in a long while. "I'll be off, then," he said. "May Tyche smile on you today, my friend!"

The appellation warmed me more than the good wishes. Perhaps there was yet hope for our friendship.

"Please, Chef Pelops!" the official interrupted impatiently. "This way! Come, come! You *must* hurry!"

Gorgias grinned at me, then turned to lumber off.

"Lead on," I said to the fussy official. "I'm ready."

And I was.

That is not to say that I did not feel nervous (I did). Or that my stomach did not feel uneasy at the thought of so many people watching me cook (it did). But I felt confident, secure in my abilities. With the smoked kraken, I knew I could win this competition and prove myself against The Sicilian once and for all.

The centre of Dionysus's theatre is the orchestra. A full circle paved with stone, it measures some eighty paces across, and it is here that performances of every kind take place. For the Bronze Chef competition, the orchestra had been divided into four sections for the four competitors.

A central area, to which each section had equal access, had been blocked off to form a sort of storeroom in order to accommodate the various foodstuffs that the chefs might require. Here there were wines, olive oil, herbs and onions, legumes and vegetables, meats and grains. All of the very best quality. All awaiting the skilled hand of a chef to bring them to succulent perfection—well, *my* skilled hand would do so; whether my fellow competitors were capable of such culinary magic remained to be seen. In the centre of all these ingredients was a table set apart from the others. It was covered with a red cloth in honour of the god whose theatre we were in.

Under this cloth was the Secret Ingredient.

I had checked and rechecked the rules of the competition. There was nothing to say a chef could not bring a few of his own ingredients—in fact, for the sake of creativity, he was encouraged to do so—although I do not think city council expected us to bring our own Secret Ingredient. Nevertheless, there had been nothing in the rules prohibiting it, which was why Strabo and Lais had hauled baskets of smoked kraken across half of Athens.

The quadrants had all been selected by lot, so I was pleased when the official led us to the northwest section of the orchestra. Front and centre, as it were. The judges were in the skene behind us, still waiting to be revealed, but a long table had been set up for them just in front of the first terraced bench. From there, I noted with satisfaction, they would enjoy a perfect view of my temporary kitchen.

I was vexed when I saw that Mithaecus and his bevy of

sycophantic disciples had been placed directly to our left (the unlucky side, naturally), but I decided to ignore their presence, even though they were already ostentatiously arranging Meidias's red-figure dishes and fine table linens around them. I tried not to stare at these too enviously, but I could not suppress a twinge of jealousy when Mithaecus unpacked an exquisite platter and placed it carefully in the centre of his preparation table, positioning it so the judges could best admire it.

Hermogenes, however, did not remark on the platter, being entirely too busy glaring daggers at The Sicilian's disciples, one of whom bore purplish marks from what must have been their earlier scuffle.

I forced my eyes away from Mithaecus's dinnerware, turning my gaze instead to the other two quadrants, where the chefs Lycon and Mediokrates had set up their kitchens.

"Great Zeus and Hera!" I exclaimed, as soon as I caught sight of Mediokrates. "What on Earth is he wearing?"

At my words, Hermogenes spun around, then burst into peals of laughter as he saw the unfortunate chef.

Mediokrates of Chaeronia was in full hoplite panoply. Strapped around his torso was a linen cuirass reinforced with bronze scales. Bronze greaves covered his shins, a bronze helmet with cheek plates completed his ensemble. There was even a bronze shield, somewhat dented and scratched, propped up against one of his preparation tables. He certainly looked ready for battle. He did not look as though he was ready to cook.

"It's his sponsor, isn't it?" Hermogenes chortled. "Honest

Enops's House of Hoplites! Ha! They must've made the poor blighter wear all that for 'em, Chef."

"Ridiculous!" I said, though I could not halt my own smile. "How on earth is he supposed to cook in that?"

But before Hermogenes could comment further on the unfortunate Mediokrates, a deep voice boomed out, drowning out all but the noisiest spectators. City council had secured the services of none other than Hadinos, the market crier, to announce the competitors and host the event. Already head and shoulders taller than the average man, he stood on a raised pedestal by the central table to best project his voice across the theatre.

"Chef Pelops of Lydiaaaa!" Hadinos announced with a tremendous bellow. "And his disciple The Heeeeeroic Herrrrrmogenes!"

I felt my eyebrows climb to my hairline, and I glanced back at my disciple. "The Heroic Hermogenes?" I inquired pointedly as the crowd cheered for us.

Hermogenes coloured, but did not quite manage to erase the self-satisfied smirk on his face. "I told you I'd come up with a better 'h' word, Chef," he said with an easy shrug. "And it sounded ace, didn't it?" He grinned crookedly at me.

I sighed and shook my head, waving to the cheering spectators as we strode across the orchestra.

And then we were in our section.

Each quadrant had been outfitted with the cookers and braziers and grills that Gorgias and the other potters of the Kerameikos had been so busy turning out. Each quadrant had four preparation tables, one piled with dishes and napkins, which were, I noted with some dissatisfaction, of distinctly lesser quality than the ones Meidias had loaned to The Sicilian. There were casserole dishes and pots and frying pans too, though most of the chefs (myself included) had brought their own, preferring to rely on familiar cookware for this all-important event. Lycon was the only chef who had not brought his own pots and pans, but as I mentioned before, he was an incompetent boob.

Lycon was also behaving rather strangely that morning, prancing around his quadrant and kicking up his heels like a flute girl. Every time he bent to retrieve something from his carrying baskets, he did so with his arms extended and one leg lifted coyly behind him.

"What an ass!" Hermogenes sniffed, pointing at the galloping gourmet with a disdainful gesture.

"The crowd seems to be enjoying him," I observed dryly.

And so they were. Pointing and laughing, they cheered each of Lycon's flirty kicks.

Hermogenes shook his head and snorted again. Then he began to unload the contents of our baskets with no undue embellishment.

We were professionals. It did not take us long to prepare. By the time the hour for the match had arrived, our braziers were lit, our frying pans were heating over the fire, and my bronze knives had been laid out in a gleaming row on the main preparation table. Various herbs and foodstuffs that I had brought, the fresh thyme and the carrot roots for Nausikaa's soup, were arrayed around us. The smoked kraken, however, was still in its basket, covered with a cloth to hide it from prying eyes. If Athenians wanted a Secret Ingredient, I would give them one.

"Citizens of Athens," Hadinos boomed. "It is time for the first Brooooonze Chef competition to commence!"

The crowd gave a ragged cheer, and those spectators not already in their seats hurried to find room on the benches. Hadinos waited until everyone was seated and the crowd had quieted expectantly. Then he raised his arms to the sky. I could see his bull-sized chest expand as he took a deep breath.

"I call on loud-roaring and revelling Dionysus!" he bellowed most impressively. "Come, Dionysus, furious inspirer, leader of satyrs and maenads, begot from Thunder, by gods revered, who dwellest with human kind. Come and bless this competition which is held in your glorious name!"

"All right, already. I'm here!" A familiar voice drifted out from inside the skene.

Dionysus was here?

Dionysus was one of the judges?

I felt a flush of heat that had nothing to do with fever. Why hadn't he told me he was to be a judge? Curse him! Did he not think that was pertinent information? If nothing else, it might have alleviated some of my anxieties.

"Not now, you fool!" another, equally familiar, voice hissed. "We're supposed to wait inside until they call us!"

My heart sank. I knew that voice.

Zeus protect me! Hera was one of the judges too.

There was more bickering behind the walls of the skene, but

Hadinos drowned them out as he explained the rules of the competition.

"We are here," he announced, "to witness these four chefs compete in the ultimate gourmet challenge. My friends, before you is a pantheon of culinary giants! All here today to see whose cuisine reigns supreme!"

Though I kept the smile on my face, I scowled inwardly at his choice of words. Cuisine was a term The Sicilian had come up with. Could Hadinos not have chosen another?

"The rules are simple," he continued. "Each chef has just two hours in which to prepare five dishes using our Secret Ingredient. Each judge can award up to twenty points to a chef: ten for taste, five for originality, and another five for presentation. But first, before we introduce these fine chefs to you, and before we discover the Secret Ingredient, my friends and citizens, let me introduce to you our judges!"

I craned my head to catch a first glimpse of the judges as they exited the skene.

"Who are they, Chef?" Hermogenes, too short to see over the other chefs and their disciples, tugged urgently at my chiton. "Is it anyone we know?"

"I don't know. I can't see—" And then I spotted them.

There were five judges in total. Dionysus was first out the door, followed closely by Archestratus. That was good. Archestratus was a known gourmand, and both the man and the god had previously enjoyed my cooking. Both would be sympathetic to me.

Hadinos introduced Dionysus as Bakkhos son of Astrapaeus

(no doubt an identity the god assumed when he "dwelt with human kind"). The god grinned and winked at me as he took his place at the judges' table. He was draped formally in a wine-coloured chiton. I still could not fathom how he had managed to be named judge—and why he had not told me!

The third judge was this year's Archon Basileos, a fellow named Thrasyllus, who was responsible for overseeing various civic and religious arrangements. I had never cooked for him, but given his official duties, I was not surprised that he had been named a judge. If his girth was any indication, however, he was a man who enjoyed a good meal. I hoped he would enjoy mine.

My heart sank a little when I saw the fourth judge was none other than the slovenly philosopher Socrates.

"Bollocks," Hermogenes muttered under his breath when he spied him.

I shared his sentiment.

It wasn't that I hadn't cooked for Socrates before (I had), or that he hadn't enjoyed the meal when I'd done so (he had), it was just that the man had the stomach of a goat and the undiscerning palate of a savage. He would—and did—eat everything with indiscriminate gusto, devouring the most delicately flavoured fish and the blandest barley meal with equal enthusiasm. It was said that he consumed only bread and water except when he attended a symposion, and although that might explain his appalling lack of taste, it did not make him a good judge for a cooking competition. I could not rely on his vote, for he was just as likely to award full points to a boiled egg as he would to Nausikaa's complex and succulent soup.

Socrates must have been selected by lot, I mused. He was not important enough to have been selected otherwise and he did not currently hold any public office. Damn Athenians and their democratic process!

The philosopher took his place at the judges' table with a dramatic swirl of his faded and threadbare himation. He settled into his seat, beaming around him, no doubt happily anticipating the comestibles to come.

The fifth and last judge was, as I feared, Hera herself.

The goddess of starry skies swept from the skene, her noble expression commanding reverence, draperies billowing out behind her like a soft yellow cloud. The colour, I noted, was the exact shade of Mithaecus's own garb.

Spectators began to murmur as they caught sight of her. She had chosen a form familiar to me, that of a mature woman with hair the rich brown of chestnuts and large, wide eyes. Her hair was caught up in an elaborate silver diadem with a matching yellow veil at the back, and her bearing was as regal as any ruler's. She wasn't exactly glowing, as gods were perfectly capable of doing when they wanted to appear particularly godly, but she was Queen of the Gods, and it showed.

She was not, however, introduced as such.

"And now for our fifth and final judge," Hadinos announced. "She has been hostess of some of the finest symposions in our fair city. Renowned for her intellect, she is a connoisseur of fine victuals, wines, and conversation. Named after that most beautiful goddess herself, the lady Hera of Miletus!"

Named after her? She *was* that goddess! I glanced around me, certain that someone in the audience would recognize her—or at the very least, take issue with the fact that a woman had been included in the panel of judges. But nobody seemed to recognize her, except for Mithaecus, who offered me a smug smirk when our eyes met, and nobody complained about her gender, probably because they thought she was a foreigner and therefore free of the legal restraints which might otherwise disallow her participation in public life.

It appeared I was stuck with Hera as one of the judges.

And so that made two judges disposed to be favourable to me, one unknown, one who would award full points to a boiled egg, and one judge who was actively against me. The odds were not as good as I'd hoped.

I exchanged a concerned look with Hermogenes. He could tell I was unhappy with the selection of judges, but he had not recognized the goddess and I could hardly inform him of her true identity here. There was little I could do. I was not even a citizen to complain about the council's choices.

With no little effort, I kept a pleasant expression on my face even as Hera, all warm smiles for The Sicilian, offered me only the blackest of scowls. She assumed her seat at the table, pointedly ignoring Dionysus, who sat on her left. Hera smiled at Thrasyllus on her right and began to engage him in conversation. Every so often, she glanced up and gave me a hard stare.

I swallowed and looked away.

"Citizens of Athens," Hadinos intoned. "The time you've been waiting for has finally arrived. Friends, it is time to meet your chefs and their sponsors! First up is Lycon of Seriphos, brought to you by Statios's Sandals, THE place to go for sassy, strappy, happy footwear!"

The crowd cheered as Lycon took a turn around his quadrant, kicking up his heels and waving to the audience with both hands. His "happy" sandal straps were of plaited leather, dyed a flashy bright red. Courtesy of his sponsor, no doubt. I wondered if the conditions of his sponsorship involved leaping about in such a ludicrous fashion. Silently, I thanked all the gods for Cato, who required only that I wear his superior garments during the competition.

"Chef Lycon is best known in Athens for his Bream in Cheese and Oil and his cookery scroll, Cooking in the Colonies. Please welcome Chef Lycon and his team!"

Lycon and his disciples all began skipping around the quadrant now. All four of them, apparently, wearing strappy, happy sandals, though the chef's footwear was noticeably fancier than that of his assistants. I very much doubted any of them could cook better than they could prance.

"Our second chef today," Hadinos announced, once the crowd had settled down, "is Mediokrates of Chaeronia, brought to you by Honest Enops's House of Hoplites. You'll never find a better deal for armour and weaponry than at Honest Enops's House of Hoplites. Honest!"

There was no skipping about for Mediokrates, not with all that bronze armour weighing him down. Already I could see his shoulders bowing under the weight of it all.

"He's sweating like a horse," Hermogenes observed in an

undertone. "He'll be roasting himself if he doesn't take it off. Imagine! Trying to cook in all that! Stupid sod."

"Chef Mediokrates is best known for his Cabbage With Vinegar and his Soft Boiled Eggs—"

"That must've been a stretch for him," Hermogenes murmured out of the corner of his mouth.

I suppressed a smile.

"Please welcome Chef Mediokrates and his disciples!"

Mediokrates and his three disciples gathered themselves in ragged battle formation to salute the spectators, though it was clear from their milling about that none of them had ever actually seen active duty. The disciples were, however, better off than the master, carrying only small hunting spears and lacking the heavy, bronze armour. They waved their spears gamely as the crowd cheered for them. One disciple waved a bit too enthusiastically, smacking the fellow beside him and accidentally slicing open his cheek.

There was a delay and a flurry of activity as the injured disciple was first examined, then taken from the theatre, blood still pouring down his face. Mediokrates stood uncertainly to one side, as if he didn't quite know what to do next.

While all this was happening, the spectators gossiped and drank and called for more skewers of meat. I could hear Perseus laughing with the priest of Dionysus, probably telling him off-colour jokes. The clouds were moving off and the day was beginning to feel warm. I scanned the sky, hoping to see more clouds. If the sun came out in force, it was going to get uncomfortably hot here in the orchestra.

Hadinos waited until the injured apprentice had been escorted from the theatre and much of the furor had died down. Then he raised his arms for quiet.

"Friends and citizens," he cried. "Our third chef for this inaugural competition is none other than Mithaecus of Sicily, brought to you by Meidias's U Rent It Symposion and Party Centre. Athens's largest selection of fine dinnerware and serving pieces, table linens and cushions, wine kraters and cups. Meidias's U Rent It: Reasonable rates for superior goods."

Hermogenes snorted quite audibly at this, which caused both Hadinos and The Sicilian to glance over at us. As Mithaecus's eyes fell on my disciple, Hermogenes began to pick his nose, flicking it insolently towards The Sicilian's quadrant.

"Stop that at once!" I hissed out of the side of my mouth. "It's unsanitary! As soon as we've been introduced, you'll wash your hands."

"Yes, Chef. Sorry, Chef." Hermogenes said, dropping the offending hand to his side and not sounding sorry at all.

Hadinos cleared his throat and continued. "Chef Mithaecus is best known for his famous Kraken Bake, that crunchy golden crust that locks in the juices and brings out the flavour. Kraken Bake: it's better than frying! Friends, please welcome Chef Mithaecus and his delectable disciples."

While Mithaecus and his sycophants paraded around their quadrant, Hermogenes made loud retching noises. Hera stood to applaud her protégé, causing the entire theatre to follow her example with alacrity. The Queen of the Gods was powerful as well as beautiful. Dionysus, however, endeared himself to me for all eternity by remaining seated, seemingly much occupied with addressing an urgent itch on his posterior.

Mithaecus raised his arms high above his head, bathing in the adulation of the crowd. His disciples were equally smug, casting sidelong glances our way to make sure we were watching. Hermogenes looked away and almost started picking his nose again, but after a quick glance at me, he decided to tug at his beard hairs and feign a yawn instead. The Sicilian's disciples muttered angrily amongst themselves.

Finally, Hadinos held up his arms for silence. "And now, my friends," his voice boomed out, drowning out the residual cheering, "it is time to meet your fourth and final chef for the Bronze Chef competition!"

Perseus leapt to his feet and let loose a tremendous *whoop*. Hadinos gave him a quelling stare, though I noticed his lips twitching as if he suppressed a smile. Perseus settled back on his bench, grinning unrepentantly.

"All the way from distant Lydia, Chef Pelops is brought to you by the incomparable Cato's Chitons. Chef Pelops is wearing one of Cato's own creations today. An elegant number it is, as you can see, a shade of blue not often seen on our fair streets. Cato's Chitons caters to the discerning citizen. Nothing comes between Chef Pelops and his Cato's!"

Unlike Lycon, I did not prance around our quadrant, though I did smile and hold myself very erect, the better to display my elegant blue chiton. Hermogenes was grinning ear to ear, holding out his arms to show off his own Cato's chiton.

"Chef Pelops is best known for his Roast Lamb stuffed with

Plums, which some call sacrilegious and others call delicious! He is also known for his exquisite Striped Red Mullets."

I could almost hear Nausikaa's voice correcting him. Perhaps it was a fortunate thing she was not able to attend.

"My friends, please welcome Chef Pelops and his disciple, the Heroic Hermogenes!"

Now it was the other disciples' turn to retch, though Hermogenes was far too pleased at being labelled heroic again to notice.

"My friends," Hadinos dropped his voice dramatically. "Are you ready for the tension, the creativity, the competition of … Kitchen Theatre?"

"Bring it on, dude!" Perseus shouted. "We're ready!"

Two slaves stepped up to either side of the covered table and paused, waiting.

Hadinos raised his massive arms again. "We have the ingredients assembled," he boomed. "We have the chefs, we have the judges. But there is one more ingredient for our competition … the Secret Ingredient! My friends—"

Just then, there was a disturbance at the entrance to the theatre. A cluster of men, not early enough to secure a place on the benches, had begun milling about noisily. I saw Hadinos draw breath to task them for it, and then the crowd parted to reveal a breathtaking figure.

"Sorry I'm late," she breathed, her wispy voice somehow carrying across the theatre.

Amber hair rippled down her back like liquid honey. Her skin was almost as golden as her hair, and despite the cloudiness of the day, it glowed as if in full sun. As she sashayed into the theatre, long, perfectly shaped limbs were clearly visible beneath her chiton. Indeed, the garment was so fine, it was practically sheer, and her nipples stood out in sharp relief. There was a collective gasp as every man in the theatre became instantly and insistently aroused.

Aphrodite tinkled a little laugh, all too aware of the effect of her presence. "I'm just here to watch the match!" she said with a heart-stopping smile.

Instantly a thousand men rose to their feet to offer their seat.

The goddess of love, beauty, and procreation giggled at the sight and chose a place beside Perseus, ousting the priest of Dionysus from his seat. The priest did not look unhappy at the knowledge that Aphrodite's plump posterior would rest where his own scrawny buttocks had so recently resided. Indeed the man's eyes had not left her perfect form since she had entered the theatre. Perseus seemed happy enough with the new arrangement, though he always looked like a grinning fool, so it was hard to tell. Dionysus seemed vastly amused by it all. Hera, on the other hand, glared at the other goddess.

"Don't let me delay things any longer!" Aphrodite called out, settling herself on the bench with a voluptuous wiggle.

Hadinos had fallen silent, as smitten as the rest of the audience.

My arousal had grown painful. What was Aphrodite doing here? As far as I knew, she had no interest in cooking.

If I didn't know any better, I'd have said Poseidon had arranged for her to attend, knowing full well how it would disrupt the proceedings. But Poseidon and Aphrodite were not the best of friends, and she was unlikely to do him any favours. No, she must have come of her own accord. The goddess of love was frequently in need of reassurance, and it would not be the first time she had visited a mortal event merely for the effect it had on the male population. It was, I realized, going to be very difficult to cook with an erection.

My only consolation was that Mithaecus would have the same problem.

"Uh ... friends ..." Hadinos began weakly. He paused and cleared his throat, pointedly looking away from the goddess of love. It seemed to help.

"Friends," he said again, more strongly this time. "We have the ... uh ... ingredients assembled. We have the chefs, we have the judges." His voice regained some of its former confidence. "But there is one more ingredient for our competition ... the Secret Ingredient! The theme on which our competitors will base their succulent variations! Friends and citizens, the Secret Ingredient for the first ever Bronze Chef competition iiiiiis ..."

He paused. The two slaves, who had been waiting patiently by the covered table, seized the corners of the red cloth.

And then, they whipped it away just as Hadinos bellowed, "HONEY!"

Chapter 31

Honey?
  Honey?

My body had already half turned towards my baskets of smoked kraken, my hand already reaching out to tweak the coverings from them.

Honey!

Hadinos was still talking. Something about time and rules and the competition beginning. There was a flurry of activity around me as the other chefs and their apprentices descended on the table of honey pots, gathering up the Secret Ingredient by the armload. Nobody else seemed surprised by the announcement.

I could not make myself move.

Honey. The Secret Ingredient was supposed to be kraken! Everyone *knew* it was kraken! Why else would city council create such a competition if not to use up the unending supply of kraken?

Honey! This was worse than any curse tablet!

"Chef! Chef!" Hermogenes was tugging at my chiton.

I stared down at him without really seeing him.

"Come on, Chef! We've got to get started!" He grabbed my arm, pulling me towards the central table.

I took a reluctant step. "But … but the kraken!" I objected.

"I know," he said, giving me a consoling pat with one hand while he continued to yank my arm with the other. "I know. But they've gone and changed it, haven't they? We've got to work with honey now. We'll sort it. You're good with honey!"

I took another step.

"Come on," he urged. "We'll make them sesame pancakes you always do up for the symposions. They're cracking!"

I had stopped in my tracks again. "But … what am I going to do with all this smoked kraken?" I demanded peevishly. "What am I supposed to make with *that*?"

Hermogenes was hopping from one foot to the other in frustration. "I don't know, do I?" he snapped, running a hand through his unruly curls. "But if we don't get our arses moving, I know we won't be able to make *anything* because there won't be any sodding honey left!"

One of The Sicilian's disciples ran past us then, his arms loaded with clay jars of honey, the bump in his chiton testament to the goddess of love's continuing presence. He glanced back at us curiously, then gave a nasty laugh as he saw Hermogenes tug on my arm once more.

It was enough to rouse me from my stasis (though in truth, not all of me was in stasis, certain parts of me being entirely too roused).

I straightened. "Come, Hermogenes!" I ordered, sweeping past the other chefs' disciples and elbowing my way to the table. "We've got to hurry!"

Hermogenes had been right. The Secret Ingredient table was already noticeably depleted. But it was not empty yet.

There appeared to be several kinds of honey available. Wild-flower, clover, buckwheat. There were even honeycombs, though not many left of these. I snatched up pots and bowls, tumbling them into Hermogenes's eagerly waiting arms.

I was just about to step away when I caught sight of a small decorated vessel tucked behind a larger plain pot of clover honey. I grabbed the smaller jar, beating Mediokrates to it by a heartbeat. Had he not been so encumbered with battle armour, I might not have been successful. He scowled at my triumphant grin.

Dipping my finger into the pot's contents, I sampled the golden liquid. Perfect! Honey from Mount Hymettus, the best-quality honey in all of Greece. It would make an exquisite dessert. I tucked the pot carefully in the crook of my elbow and motioned Hermogenes back to our quadrant.

The other chefs and their apprentices had already begun cooking, all in various states of discomfort thanks to Aphrodite.

For my part, I was still in shock over the revelation of the Secret Ingredient. Still half-believing that someone somehow had made a terrible mistake. I was also still quite aroused, and I silently cursed the goddess of love and her neediness.

But I am nothing if not resourceful. Ignoring my physical discomfort, I began to develop a menu based upon honey.

"So what are we going to make, Chef?" Hermogenes hissed, bouncing on his tiptoes, his eyes darting around nervously as he watched the other competitors. I couldn't help but notice that he, too, was being sorely affected by Aphrodite. "What other ingredients should I get?"

"Duck," I decided, having seen them in the larder of available foodstuffs. "We'll make the sesame pancakes like you suggested, and we'll have duck breasts covered with honey and almonds. Are there shrimp? We could make shrimp and honeycomb fritters."

"I don't know," Hermogenes said doubtfully. "I didn't see much in the way of seafood, beyond the kraken."

I grimaced at the word. "Don't bother with the kraken. I'll try to come up with something we can do with our smoked kraken. But get some greens! Let's make a side salad with a honey mustard dressing.

Meanwhile, Hadinos had been providing commentary throughout our whispered consultation. "We have quail coming out in Chef Lycon's kitchen," he announced. "Chef Mithaecus has started a pot heating with honey and what looks like rosemary. An unusual combination. He's also got a chicken out and his disciple is cutting that up right now. Eggs are being separated in Chef Mediokrates's kitchen. I'm not sure what he's planning on doing with them, but one of his disciples has just started beating those whites. That's going to be a long time before they're foamy. Off in Chef Pelops's kitchen, the chef and his disciple are ... well, they're standing there talking."

"Go!" I ordered giving Hermogenes a gentle shove. "Get duck and shrimp, if it's there. And bring back some almonds too. Let's move!"

Duck crusted with honey and almonds. Sesame pancakes drenched in warmed honey and thyme. Fresh greens drizzled with honey mustard and vinegar. What else could I make?

"Chef Mithaecus has put his assistants to washing off some scallops," Hadinos informed the audience.

Scallops? There were scallops in the larder? An idea began to form in my mind. I turned to tell Hermogenes to get some scallops, but he'd already dashed over to the tables. Unwilling to shout after him and risk one of the other chefs snatching what I wanted, I ran to the temporary larder and began ransacking through the ingredients. If Mithaecus had taken all the scallops ...

But no. There they were. A small basket of the delicate shellfish. I don't know where city council found scallops, what with all the cursed kraken, but at that moment, I did not care.

I had an idea.

"Chef Lycon has got some mushrooms frying now, though he appears to be having some difficulty with his sandals. Oh, look! The straps have come undone. Bad luck with that! Oops! And there one sandal has gone flying—ooooh, right into Chef Mediokrates's bowl of egg whites!"

The audience roared with laughter.

"Chef Lycon really shouldn't be kicking up his heels like that. Chef Mediokrates is going to have to work hard to make up the time now, but … wait a moment, Chef Mediokrates appears to be in some distress! Ouch! It seems like his cuirass is interfering with his … well, his uncomfortableness. He's unbuckling the shoulder straps now. Oh, his sponsor's not going to be happy about that, though the Chef certainly seems relieved. And here comes Honest Enops now. He and Chef Mediokrates appear to be arguing."

The buzz of the crowd grew louder as bets were placed on who would win the argument between Mediokrates and his sponsor.

I ignored it all, already back at our preparation table and pulling out the strips of smoked kraken.

"Meanwhile, Chef Pelops finally appears to be on the move in his kitchen. The Chef has a basket of lovely-looking scallops and he's pulling out some kind of meat or fish. I'm not sure what it is yet, but his disciple is running back with a whole armful of ingredi—ooooh, the Heroic Hermogenes has just taken a nasty spill!"

The crowd gasped and I spun around to see what had happened. Hermogenes was splayed across the ground like a starfish, the greens I'd asked him to gather spilled out around him. But even as I started towards him, he was already pushing himself to his feet. I breathed a quick sigh of relief. Not hurt then. Conscious of the rapidly passing time, I turned back to my task.

"What a mess!" Hadinos cried. "There's duck all over the ground and greens on top of that. It looked like Hermogenes might have been tripped by one of Chef Mithaecus's disciples. That's just not on! Chef Mithaecus had better keep a closer eye on his apprentices or he'll be disqualified."

I had started slicing the strips of smoked kraken, but I turned around again at the announcer's words. The Sicilian's disciples had tripped Hermogenes?

Furious, I aimed a scowl at Mithaecus's quadrant and glared a warning at him. He sneered back at me.

I held his gaze for long moment, then I noticed he was looking a bit wild around the eyes. *Interesting.* Was The Sicilian finding the stress of competition too challenging? Or perhaps the state of his arousal was interfering with his all-too-inferior talents. I grinned, much heartened by the thought. Mithaecus gave me a startled look, confused by my smile.

I glanced over at his patroness sitting at the judges' table. She had noticed our exchange and was giving me an icy stare. As I looked at her, she pointed her middle and index fingers to her eyes, then she turned her hand and pointed the fingers at me.

The message was clear. Hera was watching me like a hawk.

I gulped and vowed not to look in The Sicilian's direction again. If he was having difficulties, I would not gloat. If he was cheating, there was nothing I could do about it—apart from hope that the watchful Hadinos would catch him at it.

Hermogenes pelted up then, comestibles spilling from his arms.

"I rescued them, Chef," he panted. "But that toad-buggering shite eater tripped me!"

"I heard." I gripped his shoulder sympathetically.

"I'd like to—"

"No." I cut him off before he could go any further. "I'm sorry he tripped you, truly I am! But you must let it go now. We have only two hours—less than that now!—and the clock is running."

I glanced over at the water clock which had been brought into the theatre especially for the match. From a hole in the base of the first vessel, the water was flowing steadily into a second.

"We need to focus," I told Hermogenes.

My disciple's brows drew together in a scowl, then his expression eased and he heaved a great sigh. "I know," he said, displaying a maturity I would not have credited before. "But next time I run into that wanker in the Agora …"

"You have my permission to rearrange his nose," I told him.

Hermogenes grinned briefly at the thought, then he frowned again as he looked down at the jumble of ingredients in his arms. "The duck's all to cock," he told me. "And there's no more of it on the tables."

"Then let's get it cleaned off and see what we can do," I said briskly.

The duck had been washed and patted dry, more greens had been gathered, and I'd just set Hermogenes to mixing the batter for the sesame pancakes when Dionysus came sidling up to me.

The judges had all risen from their places and were sauntering around the orchestra, observing the chefs and their disciples at work. Thrasyllus and Archestratus were watching Lycon butcher a hapless cheese. Hera, of course, had not yet left The Sicilian's quadrant where she gushed with girlish enthusiasm each time

Mithaecus so much as stirred a pot. And Socrates had entered into a lively debate with Mediokrates, who leaned against his preparation table, having apparently forgotten he was supposed to be cooking. I suspected Honest Enops would be by again at any moment.

I smelled Dionysus before I spotted him, for he reeked of wine both young and old.

"Good day to you, Chef Pelops," he greeted me formally, a salutation marred by only a slight slurring.

I looked up from the duck I had started to dismember.

"Good day, *Judge* Bakkhos," I replied, and in a lower voice, inquired pointedly, "Tell me, when exactly did you discover you were one of the judges?"

"Not till this morning," he told me with an easy shrug. "Zeus called in sick at the last moment. Didn't want to go up against Hera, I suspect. Not with all the kerfuffle over Lamia."

"Over what?"

"Over 'who,'" Dionysus corrected. "Lamia. Some mortal woman Zeus took a shine to."

"*Another* one?" I asked incredulously.

My grandfather certainly had a weakness for the ladies.

Dionysus held out his arms as if to divest himself of any responsibility. It was then that I noticed the god of wine was looking distinctly the worse for wear. Bloodshot eyes, reddened nose, and breath that could fell an ox. A brimming wine cup was in his hand.

"You look a bit rough," I ventured.

He shrugged, spilling the wine down the front of his purple chiton. "Oskhophoria," he explained with a fermented belch.

"But … wasn't that weeks ago?" I asked, holding my breath until the belch dissipated. Great Zeus, how long did he intend to celebrate his vine harvest festival? At the rate he was going, next year's grapes would be ripening on the vines before he sobered up.

"Not sure I understand your point," he said, blinking at me as if the sun was hurting his eyes.

"It doesn't matter," I told him, turning my attention back to the duck I was cutting up.

Dionysus took the opportunity to peer into a pot of honey and fresh thyme warming on the fire.

"So … all right, then?" the god of wine asked with a broadly significant look.

I paused and stared back at him. "Ye-es," I drew out the word. "Why?"

He stepped closer and leaned heavily on my shoulder (the ivory shoulder, of course). "I told you it had summat to do with wine," he whispered gleefully in my ear.

"What do you mean?" I inquired.

"What do you mean, what do I mean?" he asked, then paused for a moment as if attempting to understand what he had just said. He shook it off, giving it up as a bad job. "I told you already."

"Told me what?"

He looked around dramatically, then bent his head toward mine once more. "About the kraken!" he whispered. "I told you I had the Secret Ingredient changed out for you."

"*You what?*"

"I told you it was going to be honey!"

"You didn't tell me any such thing," I hissed back. "I've not seen or heard from you in days!"

Dionysus blinked at me. "You haven't?"

"No!"

"I never told you how I got the council shit-faced during the Oskhophoria? Or maybe it was after the Oskhophoria. I can't quite remember now. But I did get them pissed up right good and proper. I told you, didn't I?"

"No," I said, unable to keep the edge from my voice.

"I never told you how they agreed to change the kraken to honey, even though Hera put up a dirty great stink about it?"

"No. You did not." I took a deep breath in through my nostrils. "Wait a moment … *Hera* was in on this council meeting?"

"Yeah," Dionysus nodded eagerly. "She and I, we've made our peace, haven't we? Oh, I know we've had our moments over the years, and she wasn't too chuffed about changing the Secret Ingredient to honey, but she kept pouring wine for me the whole time I was talking to council about it. Nice goddess that. Thoughtful like."

Thoughtful enough to get the god of wine so drunk he forgot to tell me he'd fixed the competition. I looked over at the judges' table. Hera had resumed her seat and was watching me, elbow on the table, chin resting in her hand. A wide smile split her face.

I turned back to the god of wine. "You never told me any of this," I said seriously.

"I didn't?"

"No."

He blew out his breath in surprise. "Well, bowl me over with a feather and tickle me bollocks. I *meant* to tell you."

"Thanks, awfully," I said, not meaning it. I went back to my duck and began hacking at it with a knife. I was so incensed, even the impact of Aphrodite's continuing presence had been diminished.

Dionysus stood watching in silence for a while. "Sorry about that, then," he said at last.

I shook my head once. "It's not *your* fault," I said shortly.

As one we looked over at Hera. She preened in her seat and blew us each a kiss.

"Ah," Dionysus said, understanding. His shoulders dropped. "Oh."

Indeed.

He watched me for a bit longer without speaking. Then, "Did you ever, you know … find out *how* to cook the kraken?" he inquired with a certain diffidence.

Wordlessly, I pointed with my knife, indicating the baskets full of smoked kraken.

"Oh." The god of wine pursed his lips and fell silent again.

I finished one duck and started in on another. Hermogenes was at the other prep table watching our exchange intently, his task momentarily forgotten. I gave him a stern look and he flushed and turned back to the pancake batter.

"All right, then?" Dionysus asked after a while. "I mean, with the honey."

"I've not got a problem with Melisseus," I told him, naming the rustic god of honey and beekeeping.

Dionysus waved that off. "'Course not," he said, a little too heartily. "He's a laid-back bloke. Well, guess I should let you be, eh? Let you cook in peace!"

"That would probably be best," I told him.

The god of wine turned to move off, his shoulders slumped.

"Dionysus," I said in a low voice.

He paused and looked back at me.

"Thanks very much," I told him, and this time I meant it. "I appreciate what you tried to do for me, even if it didn't quite work out."

He brightened and gave me a thumbs-up. "It'll be fine," he predicted. "You'll see! You'll smoke 'em, won't you?"

I tried not to wince at the word "smoke."

Chapter 32

By the time the judging portion of the competition took place, both audience and chefs were looking decidedly frazzled for having spent the past two hours in the presence of the goddess of love. As had been determined by random selection, Hermogenes and I were to present our dishes last. Lycon had gone first, followed by Mediokrates. Both men stumbled through their presentations, dabbing often at their sweating foreheads, trying unsuccessfully to hide the evidence of their arousal behind platters and serving trays.

As expected, Socrates awarded full points to both, but Thrasyllus, too, seemed overly generous with his points—especially given that Mediokrates's offerings looked about as flavourful as his name implied, and that Lycon managed to produce only three of the five required dishes, one of which was burned. Dionysus deducted points for this, as did Archestratus, but Hera subtracted only a fraction of the points she ought to have done. The judging appeared to be all over the place. Both chefs, however, did lose serious points for originality.

By the time Mithaecus stepped forward to serve his offerings, I did not know what to expect.

The Sicilian had better luck hiding his excitement, possibly because the exquisite quality of his dinnerware distracted the eye from any lesser sight. He and his sycophants had managed to prepare the five dishes, all of which were presented on these plates. Needless to say, the minuscule quantity of food in each portion in no way detracted from the plates' beautifully painted designs.

"The first dish I have prepared for your dining pleasure is based on the concept of my New Cuisine," he began pompously. "As you may know, my new method of food preparation is characterized by lighter, more delicate dishes. It is far more flavourful and healthier than the usual fare one might expect from more ignorant chefs." He slid a sidelong glance at me. "And if the great statesmen Perikles had not so tragically succumbed to the plague, I feel sure that he would have been among New Cuisine's most ardent admirers, for he knew me as a true proficient in the kitchen. Indeed, he once declared my cooking fit for Olympus itself, and described me as a Phidias of the kitchen—an appellation which clearly shows—"

"D'you think he's going to feed them anytime soon?" Perseus's whisper carried easily across the theatre. The crowd tittered and Mithaecus's expression darkened.

"For your dining pleasure," he repeated loudly enough to

make himself heard over the laughter, "I present to you, the most honourable judges, the first of my dishes … loukoumades!"

He motioned his apprentices to begin serving.

"That's it?" Hermogenes muttered incredulously. "After all that? Loukoumades? How is that 'new'?"

Loukoumades are deep-fried doughnuts that are drenched in honey and served to the winners of the Olympic Games. They are not "new," nor are they particularly light or delicate. I thought perhaps The Sicilian might have done something different with them, added an unusual spice or flavouring, but no, they appeared to be standard loukoumades, though, in the spirit of his New Cuisine, each judge was served only a single smallish doughnut on a very large plate. Socrates seemed particularly crestfallen by this.

Hera enthused about his presentation, of course, and as The Sicilian offered up each subsequent dish with a subservience that verged on obsequious, his eyes sought mine as if to ensure I was witness to his triumph.

But while Hera praised his presentation, even she had difficulty coming up with a kind word for his final dish, which appeared to be nothing more than his vile Kraken Bake liberally doused with honey.

Archestratus was not sparing in his condemnation of it.

"Oh, that's just vile!" he exclaimed, spitting his mouthful onto the ground and reaching for his water cup to rinse the taste from his mouth.

Mithaecus was completely nonplussed. I hid a smile behind my hand. Hermogenes did not bother with the hand.

Even Socrates, with his goat-like stomach, did not care for the dish. "Most ill-conceived," he declared, shaking his head once he'd tasted it. "The flavours do not blend at all." His words were disparaging, though I noted that he alone of all the judges had finished his tiny portion.

Thrasyllus was equally uncomplimentary and Dionysus said not a word, contenting himself instead with a revolted expression and a wave of dismissal. And so, Mithaecus was thanked for his offerings and he and his sycophants returned to their quadrant.

The god of wine was still picking the remnants of The Sicilian's food out of his teeth when Hadinos gestured me forward.

"And finally, Chef Pelops," the market crier said with a smile. "What have you prepared for us today?"

Hermogenes and I exchanged a glance. He grinned at me, his crooked smile encouraging. I smoothed my blue chiton and took a deep breath.

This was it.

"I have prepared a number of dishes for the judges today," I began, carefully keeping my tone professional without sliding into servility. "We shall start off with honeyed wine to …" I paused, as if searching for the right words, "… cleanse the palate of unwanted flavours."

Out of the corner of my eye, I could see Mithaecus glowering. Hermogenes stepped forward, serving each judge a cup of the wine.

It was a lovely Thasian with a delicate taste of apples. I'd watered it properly and added a touch of honey in which I'd simmered a curl of rare cinnamon bark. The taste was both refreshing and unusual. Finishing it off was a small skewer of honeycomb artistically placed across the rim of the cup. Hermogenes had been most impressed with this idea.

The judges were quite appreciative as well—I had been the only chef to offer wine as part of the menu—and I noticed even Hera seemed to enjoy her drink, though she frowned when she realized I was watching her.

After the honeyed wine was the first course, toasted rounds of barley bread topped with fresh goat cheese, walnuts, honey, and finely chopped rosemary. I'd wanted to make my cheese and fig appetizers, but figs were not in season at this time of the year, so I'd had to come up with another idea. The toasts were quite delicious, if I do say so myself. Archestratus devoured them eagerly.

The cheese toasts were followed by greens, served with a tart-sweet dressing made of honey and vinegar and ground mustard seeds. Then came the duck breasts, seared to perfection and topped with a golden crust of honey and chopped almonds.

And after this came my ultimate achievement.

The idea had come to me unbidden. Perhaps a gift from the gods, or perhaps merely the result of furious thinking. Whatever its origin, I was grateful.

I had taken the scallops—lovely plump fresh shellfish they were, too—and wrapped each one in a thin slice of my smoked kraken. I'd placed them carefully on the brazier, grilling them just enough to crisp up the kraken without overcooking the delicate meat of the scallop. Meanwhile, Hermogenes had poured small puddles of wildflower honey on an oiled pan and set it over the fire, watching it carefully. The heat caused the honey to thicken, darkening to a rich caramel colour, and when the pan had cooled, these honey coins were easily lifted from its surface. Working quickly, I had positioned the hot scallops on the serving plates and carefully placed a honey coin on top of each one. The heat from the scallop melted the honey enough to form a thin crust. A sprig of fresh thyme finished them off.

The judges groaned with pleasure as they bit into the morsels. Even Hera could not help licking the juices from her fingers, though I did not allow her to see me smile at the sight. I did, however, glance over at Mithaecus, who now had a face like a black storm cloud. I could not quite suppress a smirk. The crowd grew restless, jealous at the sight of the judges' obvious enjoyment.

After the scallops were the sesame pancakes and my version of loukoumades. Where The Sicilian's loukoumades had been standard (or, more likely, substandard) fare, mine were drizzled with warm honey syrup made from the Mount Hymettus honey, and served with toasted nuts and a dollop of creamy soft cheese. I had thought to dust the doughnuts with ground cinnamon bark—it was, after all, a rare and exotic spice—but I'd used cinnamon in my honeyed wine palate cleanser and I wanted to show my versatility. Instead, I garnished my loukoumades plates with chopped fresh mint to lighten the sweetness and provide a splash of colour. The flavours came together beautifully.

I watched the judges finish their meal in the full knowledge that I had well and truly outdone myself.

The five judges retired to the skene then to consult amongst themselves. Hadinos went with them. The waiting crowd shifted and buzzed, rehashing the highlights of the event, calling for more wine. The day had become uncomfortably warm.

Hermogenes stood silently by my side, watching the audience.

I touched his arm to get his attention. "Well done, my disciple," I told him with a warm smile. "No matter the outcome, I want you to know how very great an honour it was to cook here with you today."

My disciple's dark eyes shone with pleasure, and for the first time since I'd known him, he appeared speechless. And when, at last, he did open his mouth to speak, his words were drowned out by the cries of the crowd.

The judges were returning.

Now that the telling moment was upon us, my heart began pounding as if I'd run to Marathon and back. I knew I'd done my best, but was it enough? If only kraken had been the Secret Ingredient, I might have done even better! Nausikaa's soup alone would have won the competition.

What if The Sicilian wins?

It was unthinkable! Even a victory by Lycon would be more palatable than that. But surely the judges would not give the award to Mithaecus for his vile Kraken Bake and honey!

Would they?

I stood stoically, fighting to maintain an outward appearance of composure. A flush of heat stole slowly up my body. I could feel my knees trembling.

Zeus Hikesios, I prayed silently, *God of Suppliants, hear me.*

Zeus Epidotes, Giver of Good, hear my prayer. Zeus Moiragetês, Leader of the Fates, I beseech you. Please, Father Zeus, do not allow The Sicilian to win.

The judges marched across the orchestra, eyes distant, faces expressionless, giving nothing away. Hadinos had taken his position on the pedestal, head bowed, arms at his sides, waiting until the judges had settled at their table. I could sense Hermogenes quivering beside me.

In a swirl of coloured draperies, the judges resumed their seats. Hadinos waited a heartbeat, then he looked up.

"Friends and citizens," he began, lifting his arms to the heavens. "You have come here today to watch four chefs compete in the Bronze Chef competition. To see whose cuisine reigns supreme! My friends, the judges have spoken and the winner is …"

He paused and lowered his arms. "Chef Pelops of Lydia!"

Hermogenes's gasp was audible even over the roar of the crowd.

"Chef!" he squealed. "You did it! You bloody well, sodding well did it!" He was jumping up and down.

My smile was as wide as my disciple's. "No, Hermogenes," I corrected. "*We* did it!"

Hadinos was still talking, but I heard nothing beyond my name. Nothing of the breakdown of points awarded. Nothing of the list of prizes that would be mine. I was aware of Hermogenes dancing by my side. Of Perseus whooping with excitement and taking the opportunity to bestow a celebratory kiss on the goddess of love's golden cheek. And of Gorgias jumping up and down and cheering almost as loudly as Perseus. His unabashed delight for me was both gratifying and humbling.

I was also briefly aware of Mithaecus's stunned face, the whining voices of his apprentices, and of Hera's hard, angry eyes. Even without knowing the Secret Ingredient ahead of time, even without fancy dishes and table linens, even while nursing a stiffy to end all stiffies, I had proved once and for all that I could out-cook The Sicilian with my eyes closed.

As my friends came up to pound me on the back and offer their congratulations, I stood and smiled, savouring a victory that was as sweet as the Secret Ingredient.

Chapter 33

Half the Kerameikos turned out for my victory celebration, and when you added their numbers to the friends and fans who followed us home, the ensuing party was very large indeed. All the way home, Gorgias strode the streets by my side, announcing my win in a voice that could have rivalled that of Hadinos himself. Perseus hadn't stopped beaming since we left the theatre, and he punctuated Gorgias's announcements with exuberant cries of "Woo hoo!"

Hermogenes proved his heroic nature by seeing our victory olive oil home safely. I had not thought to allow anyone but myself to carry the elaborately decorated amphora, but it was good that he did so. Everyone, it seemed, wished to pound me on the back and congratulate me on my win, and had I attempted to carry the amphora, it surely would have shattered.

The women met us at the front door, having been alerted to

our arrival by all the cheering and shouting. Irene's eyes widened as she took in the crowd of people massed behind us, but Nausikaa gave a cry of delight and pushed past her, flinging her arms around me in a victory embrace.

What followed was a blur of smiling faces, thumping hugs, and heartfelt congratulations. I was aware of Zeuxo's violet-scented perfume and her congratulatory kiss pressed lightly on my cheek, but I was more aware of Nausikaa's smiling blue eyes following me. And even as I was embraced by Pharsalia followed by Ansandra followed by Danaë followed by any number of others, it seemed that I could still feel Nausikaa's slight body against mine and the soft brush of her dark hair across my arm.

"We've got a feast all ready and waiting to be served," Irene informed us, eyeing our greatly expanded retinue with some dismay. "But we weren't expecting a crowd like this! How we're going to feed everyone on what we've got prepared, I don't know."

I patted her on the shoulder. "We'll manage," I assured her.

And we did.

Pharsalia sent to her shop for baskets of bread (dildos and otherwise). A neighbour, whose family owned a farm outside the city, brought enough greens to feed an army. Pisistratus appeared with a large basket of spiced sausages. And Gorgias kindly surrendered the contents of his storeroom. Several of the neighbourhood wives and their house slaves had joined Irene in the kitchen, though my own offer to help was amiably but firmly refused.

"It's your party," Irene told me with a shooing gesture when I hesitated in the doorway. "Don't be loitering about in here. Go on and enjoy yourself, then!"

I scuffed my feet a bit, unwilling to allow strangers full run of my kitchen, but after watching the women for a while, I concluded that they knew what they were about and I should probably just take Irene's advice and enjoy the festivities.

From somewhere a pig was brought in, duly sacrificed and spitted, and set to roasting over a fire. The rich smell of pork and the sharp scent of grilling sausages perfumed the air. Our stores of wine were not large, but I'd glimpsed Dionysus carousing in the crowd and I knew the god of parties would not allow us to run low on drink. The festivities spilled out into the streets and alleys surrounding our house.

I was roundly congratulated by all, thumped on the back, kissed on the cheek, and passed from person to person until my head spun. Even the elegant Cato made an appearance, looking only slightly uncomfortable at slumming it in a neighbourhood such as the Kerameikos.

"Congratulations, Chef Pelops!" he said to me, tweaking the folds of my blue chiton back into place with a proprietary gesture. "A well-deserved win!"

"It is I who should thank you," I told him sincerely. "Had you not taken a chance and sponsored me …"

He waved it off, though he seemed gratified by my words. "Indeed, it was a risk well worth taking!" he said, then paused and offered me a little bow. "Though I must say, I never considered it much of a gamble."

He grinned then, allowing his pleasure to show. "You must come and see me when you are in need of another chiton."

"I would go nowhere else," I assured him.

Hermogenes, too, was the focus of much attention, and when at last I had a moment to breathe, I spied him in the middle of a rapt cluster of Kerameikos urchins who were listening with breathless excitement as he described the match in glorious (and probably wildly exaggerated) detail.

There was food, there was drink, and there was singing and dancing. And so I ate roast pork and stewed apples and salad and bread, and I washed it down with cup after cup of sweet wine. I sang (after I had enough wine in me) and I danced at least once with what seemed like everybody from the Kerameikos, and twice with Nausikaa, who laughed up at me as we spun around arm in arm.

I even danced with Ansandra, neat and tidy for once, who had forgiven me my harsh words to Nausikaa, just as I had forgiven her quail for defecating on my thyme plants. Ansandra's cheeks were flushed and her eyes were bright—a fact that did not escape the notice of several of the young lads from the Kerameikos. She danced with them, too, though I saw that she did so under the watchful eye of Zeuxo, who appeared ready to whisk her away if things got too wild.

Hermes arrived at the tail end of the party, limping in after dark, well after the pig had been carved and devoured.

"You're late!" Dionysus accused, pointing at him with his wine cup and spilling much of its contents in the process. "You've missed half the party!"

Hermes gave him a black scowl, though his countenance lightened when Dionysus pressed a full wine cup into his hand.

"Couldn't help it, could I?" Hermes groused. He gestured toward me with his chin. "This one's got Hera all in a right snit now, with nothing better to do than send 'urgent' messages here and there." He paused and took a long drink. "Congratulations, by the way," he said to me, wiping his mouth. "I heard you were cracking."

"Thanks," I told him, my face splitting into a wide grin. Then my smile widened still further as a thought occurred to me. "Are your feet still hurting you?" I inquired.

Hermes slid me a dark look. "Does Ares scratch his hairy bollocks in the morning?"

I ignored the unpleasant mental image. "I might be able to help," I told him. "I'll be right back."

I found Perseus surrounded by a bevy of Kerameikos girls who were tittering and whispering amongst themselves and casting soulful looks his way.

"You're going to be a married man," I reminded him.

He coloured self-consciously. "Aw, they're just girls," he said with a shrug of his broad shoulders.

The girls giggled, openly admiring the view.

"Uh huh," I said. "Come with me for a moment."

Perseus extracted himself from his disappointed fans. "'Sup, dude?" he asked as I pulled him into a quiet corner.

"Have you still got those winged sandals?" I asked him.

"Well, yeah," he said.

"Any objections if I give them to somebody?"

Perseus hesitated a moment. "Would this person be okay with them?" he asked finally. "I mean, they're kinda dangerous."

Concern? From my uncle? Was it possible Perseus was finally growing up?

"Oh, he can handle them," I assured him.

While Perseus went off to rummage through his belongings, I waited in the corner, enjoying a brief respite from the festivities. For the first time in a very long time, I felt relaxed and happy. Full of good food and fine wines, I was warm and happy, though not drunk. It was a wonderful feeling.

Perseus returned with the sandals and, showing once again an uncharacteristic maturity, he had wrapped them discreetly in cloth.

I accepted the bundle, almost dropping it when I felt the sandals move under my hands.

"Be careful," Perseus said at the same time. "They like to move around a bit."

I gave him an exasperated look and tightened my grip on the bundle. The sandals shifted restlessly as if eager to be free of their packaging.

I found Hermes alone in Gorgias's courtyard, the party having moved en masse out into the street. A single torch lit the garden. It was quiet there, though the sounds of revelry carried easily on the night air. Carefully I unwrapped the bundle.

"I've got something for you," I told him, placing the still squirming sandals in his hands.

"For me?" Hermes was thunderstruck.

The sandals' straps were plain leather, without braiding or

embellishment, but the perfect white wings on the heels more than made up for their plainness. As Hermes held them, the wings fluttered as if eager to be airborne.

"I—well, Perseus and I—thought they might help you deliver all those messages," I told him. "At least they ought to save some wear and tear on your poor feet."

The god of messages looked down at the sandals for a long moment, then he looked up at me. His dark eyes shone with boyish delight. All of a sudden, he reminded me very much of Hermogenes.

"Do you have any idea what I can do with these?" he asked, his face breaking into a wide and rather naughty-looking grin.

"It's probably best that I don't," I told him.

He flashed me another mischievous smile, then bent to fasten his new footwear. There was an odd buzzing noise, like the sound of bees. And then the god of messages was airborne.

He flung out his arms, his cloak billowing around him. "These are brilliant!" he laughed.

I smiled up at him.

"Cheers, mate!" he cried.

And with a last delighted grin, Hermes zipped up and over the walls of our house. I watched for his return, but he was gone, no doubt to put his new footwear through its paces.

Gorgias found me still staring up at the heavens.

"What have you got there, then?" he asked, looking up at the empty sky in bemusement.

"Nothing," I told him with a smiling shake of my head. "How's the party going?"

He gave me a lopsided grin. "Epic," he said.

I rolled my eyes reproachfully at his choice of words. "Not you, too!"

He chuckled, pleased at getting a rise out of me. "What *are* you doing in here, then? That's your victory party out there."

"I know," I told him. "I just needed a moment."

Gorgias settled on his favourite bench. "Take a load off," he invited.

I shrugged and sat down beside him. From somewhere he produced a couple of wine cups and a small amphora.

"It's Thasian," he told me, pouring it into the cups. "I bought it to celebrate."

I was touched. "You were that confident, were you?"

"Of course!" It was his turn to shrug. "It's you, isn't it? You're the best chef in Athens—and the best friend."

I swallowed past a sudden lump, unable to reply.

"The thing is," Gorgias pushed on, passing me a cup of wine, "you're *my* best friend, and I don't say that lightly. I know you don't want to talk about this but—"

"Gorgias—" I began, knowing what he was going to say.

He held up his hand to stave off my interruption. "No, let me finish."

I fell silent, staring down at my cup. By torchlight, the wine in it looked as black as ink.

"Maybe if I'd known before how you felt about Zeuxo, things might have come out differently," he said. "But I didn't, and they're not, and I'm sorry about that—for your sake."

He paused and took a sip of his wine before continuing. "But

I can't say I'm sorry for mine. I never thought I'd feel this way about a woman again, you know. Not after Helena."

He opened his mouth, then closed it again and sighed. I waited.

"I knew everything there was to know about that woman," he told me finally. "I knew how she thought. I knew what she'd say. I knew each mark on her body. Each scar and mole. I knew the *shape* of her. And when she died …"

Wordlessly, he shook his head. He was silent for a while, then he cleared his throat.

"Well, anyhow," he continued, "I never thought I'd feel that again. Until I got to know Zeuxo." He paused and took a deep breath. "I'm sorry you love her, Pelops. I'm sorry I didn't know. But I can't give her up. I just … I can't."

I opened my mouth, but Gorgias cut me off before I could say a word.

"The thing is," he rushed on, "I don't want to give *you* up either. You're me best friend, you bloody bugger."

I couldn't have spoken even if I tried to. I knew that Gorgias was *my* best friend, but I had not known that I was his. Unlike Lydians, Greek men did not share their innermost thoughts. They talked about chariot racing or Homer or even the latest in chiton fashions. They did not speak of friendship and feelings.

"I've lost most of my other mates," Gorgias was saying. "The wars took a few, and plague took the rest. You're the only one now. The brother I never had. And I don't want this coming between us."

"It won't," I assured him, because I had to say something. But I was surprised to discover I meant it.

But Gorgias wasn't finished yet. "Now that you've gone and won the Bronze Chef match," he continued, "I ... well, I don't want you thinking that you have to move out after the wedding. If it's not too hard for you, we'd—I'd—love to have you stay."

For the first time, the thought did not bother me.

When had that happened?

"I'd understand if you can't," he said, studiously avoiding my eyes. "Truly, I would. But you're part of the household now, aren't you? Family. I mean, Ansandra thinks of you as an uncle, and I don't know what Irene would do if she didn't have you to be ordering about. It's just ... well, it wouldn't seem right for you to go—"

It was obvious that it was Gorgias himself who did not wish me to go—and equally clear that he believed I would. I reached over and touched his hand to silence him.

"No," I told him. "It wouldn't seem right at all."

He looked at me, hope warring with doubt on his face.

"You'll stay, then?" he asked carefully, as if bracing himself for my response.

I offered him a lopsided smile. "I'll stay," I said, my voice tight with emotion that had nothing to do with grief over Zeuxo's choice. "After all, you're my family too."

Gorgias nodded once, briefly, his only display of emotion. Then he lifted his wine cup and took a long swallow. I did the same. We sat and drank for a while, comfortable in our silence. All the words that needed to be said had been spoken. There were no recriminations. No regrets. And I realized I was finally ready to be truly happy for my best friend and his new wife.

Out on the streets of the Kerameikos the merrymaking continued on.

HOW TO BE A
DOMESTIC
GOD

PELOPS'S BRONZE CHEF LOUKOUMADES

For the dough

- **1/2 cup water**
- **1 1/4 tbsp yeast**
- **2 1/2 cup flour**
- **1 tsp honey**
- **1/2 tsp salt**
- **1 tsp ouzo**
- **1 cup lukewarm water**
- **vegetable and olive oil for deep frying**

For the syrup

- **1 cup honey**
- **1 lemon, juice and zest**
- **2 tbsp butter**
- **2 tbsp water**
- **1/4 cup toasted almonds or pistachios**

To serve

- **1 tbsp Greek-style yoghurt or soft cheese**
- **1 tsp ground cinnamon or 1 tbsp chopped fresh mint**

In a mixing bowl, dissolve the yeast in 1/2 cup lukewarm water, then cover the bowl with a cloth and let it stand for 10 minutes in a warm area to allow the yeast to rise.

Add the flour, honey, salt, and ouzo to the mixing bowl and mix well. Add the remaining lukewarm water while continually mixing. The resulting batter should end up as soft and sticky dough, soft enough to be able to drop from a spoon. If it's too thick, add a little more water.

Cover the mixing bowl with a cloth and place in a warm spot to rise for approximately 1 hour or until it has doubled in bulk and has bubbles forming on the surface.

When the dough has risen, heat oil until hot, but not smoking (180C/350F) and prepare to fry the loukoumades in batches. Add enough oil (a mix of extra virgin olive oil and vegetable oil is nice) to fill at least half the deep fryer. On the side, have a small spoon and a cup with a little extra virgin olive oil. By dipping the spoon first into the cup with the oil and then into the batter, the batter will not stick to the spoon.

Carefully drop spoonfuls of the mixture into the oil and fry for 3-4 minutes or until crisp and golden-brown. Remove from the hot oil using a slotted spoon and set aside to drain on kitchen papyrus.

For the syrup: place the honey, lemon zest and juice, butter and 1 tbsp water in a saucepan and heat through. Add the toasted nuts and remove the pan from the heat.

Pour the sauce over the loukoumades and add a dollop of Greek yoghurt or soft cheese. Dust with ground cinnamon or chopped mint.

Chapter 34

Stop treading on my heels!"

"I can't help it, dude," Perseus objected. "I can't see a thing."

"Neither can I," I said. "Neither can Hermogenes. But you don't see us stepping on Piss's feet."

"Well, no, because I can't see a thing."

"If you two toad-buggering shite eaters are about finished now ..." Pisistratus suggested caustically.

"Sorry," I told him, and almost walked into his back. I apologized again. "Are we there now?"

"Close," he clipped the word off.

It was the middle of a moonless night, clouds obscuring even the negligible light of the stars. The Agora was dark, strange with shadows. At this hour, the place was empty of all but the black silhouettes of shuttered shops and stalls. Even the most raucous taverna had long since closed its doors, sending its patrons stumbling home to sleep off their various indulgences. The market was completely deserted.

Ideal conditions for what we were about to do.

"It's just around the corner now," Piss murmured.

Instinctively I glanced around, though it was so dark I'm not sure what I was expecting to see.

"Where are we going, Chef?" Hermogenes tugged on my cloak again. "What are we doing?"

"You'll see," I told him for the fourth time. "Patience."

It had been my idea, but I'd needed Pisistratus to help execute it. He knew the marketplace better than anybody. Only he could safely navigate its twists and turns on such a night. When Perseus and I had approached him and explained the situation, he had been only too happy to help, though I wondered now if he was having second thoughts. He seemed uncharacteristically quiet, with little of the good-natured bluster or recurrent swearing that I'd come to associate with him.

He hadn't said anything about misgivings, however (perhaps he was merely hungover from the victory party the previous night), and he had guided us unerringly down the maze of streets and alleys to the place where the road-surfacing crew had dropped their equipment at the end of the day. We had gathered picks and shovels, everything we needed for our task, and Piss had seemed fine with it all. Perhaps the tension was getting to him now.

"Mind the statue," he warned, reaching back with one hand to guide me around it.

I did the same for Hermogenes, then reached back for Perseus, but as my uncle grasped my hand, he stumbled, the shovel

441

that he was carrying bumping heavily into the dark shape of the statue. The shorter shadow that was Pisistratus swore under his breath and leapt back, steadying the wooden figure before it could tumble over.

"I told you to be careful, man!" he hissed.

"Sorry, dude," Perseus said apologetically.

"By all the gods' hairy arses, do you want those goat-fucking Scythians to come sniffing around?"

"I said I was sorry, dude!"

But I wasn't listening to Perseus and Piss anymore.

I recognized this spot. Even in the gloom, I recognized it. The statue only confirmed it. The figure was wooden, not stone or bronze. Perseus wouldn't have been able to budge it otherwise, not without considerable effort. This statue was old, grey from weathering, and the last time I'd seen it, it had sported an orange, goat-nibbled chiton.

I heard Hermogenes's indrawn gasp as he, too, realized where we were.

"We're here, aren't we?" he asked, a slight quiver in his voice betraying his emotion.

"This is where Meidias has his shop," Piss confirmed in an undertone.

Perseus surged forward. "Epic! Then let's get to work, dudes," he said eagerly. "I've got a powerful need to get rid of this thing."

"No doubt," Piss snorted quietly.

Hermogenes moved as if to join them, though as yet he did not know what we were about to do. I placed a hand on his shoulder to stay him.

"This is for me to do," I told him quietly. "Your task is to bear witness."

With picks and shovels, Perseus, Pisistratus, and I dug down into the Panathenaic Way, excavating a deep hole right under Meidias's austere little shop. We situated our excavation in the very front of his stall, directly under the counter. Anyone foolish or ignorant enough to step up to his place of business would be standing right over the spot.

All three of us were sweating and out of breath by the time Piss judged the hole deep enough. A light breeze had come up, blowing away some of the cloud cover. The night was still devoid of moonlight, but the stars cast a faint cold glow on our dirt-smeared faces. Hermogenes had stopped asking for clarification and I could see his face, pale in the starlight, his eyes wide pools of darkness as he watched us. Perseus was standing hip-deep in the hole when Piss called a halt to our work.

"That should be good," Piss said. "Nobody's going to dig down that far to see what's there, even if they do notice the surface has been disturbed."

I bent and offered Perseus a hand up. He grasped my forearm and heaved himself out from the hole. We stood looking down into its black depths for a moment.

"Well, no time like the present," Perseus said, suddenly very business-like. He bent to retrieve the brown satchel which he'd carefully stashed beside Meidias's stall. "Turn around, dudes."

I caught at his arm before he could lift the bundle.

"Be *careful*, Perseus," I warned him.

He shook his feathered hair back and grinned crookedly at me. "Hey, it's me!" he said.

"Oh, I know," I assured him.

I glanced at Pisistratus and rolled my eyes. He gave me a tight smile, then, as one, we turned our backs on Perseus. I bade Hermogenes to do the same. Silently, I offered a prayer to Nemesis, goddess of retribution. There was a rustle, a sickening sort of thud, then the sound of dirt and gravel falling.

"You can look now, dudes," Perseus said at last. "It's done."

I turned cautiously. My uncle stood at the edge of the hole, shovel in hand, a relieved smile lighting his face.

"Let's get this filled in," Piss said, stepping forward. "Nyx is moving on. We'll have Eos lighting the sky any time now, and we don't want to be anywhere near here when she does."

I looked up and realized he was right. It wasn't dawn yet, but it was close.

Quickly we filled in the hole, first with dirt, then with the pails of gravel we'd pilfered from the road-surfacing crew. By the time we'd finished, the sky was tinged with rose, and here and there I could hear the stirring sounds of a waking city.

By the early light, we stood back to survey our work. I was tired, dirty, and covered in sweat, but I regarded our handiwork with grim satisfaction. Nobody would look twice at the spot. Nobody would notice anything amiss. And nobody would even guess what lay hidden under Meidias's place of business.

Only then did I finally tell Hermogenes what we had done. What we had buried.

Medusa's severed head would rest here, interred in the very

heart of the Athenian Agora. Hidden from mortal eyes, it would no longer turn the unwary to stone, but here under Meidias's shop, it would cast a pall, an invisible miasma, over his affairs. His regular customers would find themselves less eager to do business with him. Potential customers would look at his stall, then glance away searching for a more prepossessing shop from which to rent their dinnerware. His dishes would crack or break, mice would get into the table linens. It would be some time before Meidias would even consider that his location might be the problem. And because he held the lease for it in perpetuity, he would not even think about spending the coin to switch to a new location—not until it was far too late. It would not happen overnight, but gradually, over time, Meidias's business would fail and he would never know why.

Hermogenes listened in stunned silence while I spoke, his dark eyes wider than I had ever seen them. When I finished, he stood there for a long moment, staring up at me. Speechless. And then, with an inarticulate cry, he flung himself at me, nearly bowling me over.

"I can't ... you did ... you did that *for me*?" He buried his face against my chest. His thin arms were hugging me tightly. I could feel the dampness of his tears through my tunic. "Thank you, Chef!" he whispered brokenly. "Thank you."

Perseus and Piss began gathering up our tools, giving us space. I held Hermogenes as he continued to cry, as all the pent-up anger and helpless frustration over Meidias's treatment of him was finally released.

"I made a promise to you," I said when his tears had quieted. "It was owed."

And so it had been.

At last the scales of Astraia were balanced. And as we walked away from our night's work, my arm resting affectionately across my disciple's shoulders, I could almost feel the hand of Nemesis, herself, patting my back and rejoicing in my victory.

"Hades's balls, that's gotta be a relief to have *that* finally sorted," Pisistratus remarked to me as we finally left the Agora.

"You have no idea," I told him with a heartfelt sigh.

"Totally," Perseus agreed.

The clouds had all moved off, and Eos had well and truly arrived. With her, the first vendors and shopkeepers had begun trickling into the marketplace. Yawning and bleary-eyed, they led their basket-laden donkeys down the Pathathenaic Way, sparing us no more than a cursory glance as they passed. I was grateful for it. Apart from Hermogenes, who stumbled behind us half-asleep on his feet, we none of us bore close inspection. I, for one, did not wish to be recognized in such a state. Even though I was wearing an old tunic and cloak, my victory at the Bronze Chef competition would ensure fame for some time. The sooner we could clean up, the better.

We had returned the shovels and picks to the work site, and although the mound of gravel there had been reduced by several basketfuls, Piss assured us that no one would notice. The area around Medias's shop had been returned to its original state too, with no evidence of the digging that we'd done. It may have been fancy on my part, but already it seemed a heaviness hung over the place, a feeling of dank and rot and things best left in the dark. Almost, I felt sorry for Meidias. Almost.

"So what's your plan now?" Piss was asking Perseus. "Got more beasties to slay?"

Perseus grinned, his teeth very white in the morning light. The sky was clear blue. It was going to be a glorious fall day. "Nah," he said with a shake of his feathered hair. "I gotta take Nausea over to Delphi—"

My stomach gave an odd lurch. With everything that had happened in the last few days, I'd forgotten all about Nausikaa and her destiny with the priestesses of Apollo. Or perhaps I had not wanted to think of it.

In the short time Perseus and his family had lived with us, Nausikaa had become an integral part of our small household. A part of my life. It seemed impossible that she could leave. It felt … wrong.

"Excuse me?" Piss was asking Perseus. "Nausea?"

"My sister," Perseus explained.

"Her name is Nausikaa," I interjected. "Really, Perseus, don't you think it's time to offer her a little more respect?"

"She's my sister," he protested.

"She's a *woman*," I told him. "She's intelligent and kind and she has feelings that you're hurting every time you refer to her by that ridiculous nickname."

Perseus looked abashed. "Really, dude?"

"Trust me."

We kept walking in silence, Perseus chewing on his lip.

"I didn't know that," he said finally. "I mean, that it hurt her feelings. I just thought it was … you know, funny."

"Not to her," I told him.

447

He fell silent again, clearly mulling over my words.

"Why do you have to take your sister to Delphi?" Piss asked after a while.

"She's been *called*," Perseus told him, his pride in her evident in his voice. He might mock her to her face, but Perseus did love his little sister. "Called by the Dulcet Dude himself. Naus—" he cast a quick glance at me, "—ikaa's going to be a priestess. She's been waiting a while now. It's time I got her over to Delphi. And then …" he trailed off.

"And then?" Piss prompted.

Perseus shrugged self-consciously. "And then I figure it's time for me to settle down."

"Athens is a pretty great city," Piss nodded. "There's a lot here a guy with a winged horse could do."

"Not Athens," Perseus shook his head again. "Got an epic fiancée waiting for me in Aethiopia."

"You're leaving?" I blurted.

Perseus turned to me, his expression regretful. "I have to, dude," he said. "Andromeda's been waiting for ages now and …" He hesitated, his mouth twisted to one side. "Well, I guess it's time I was more responsible. Y'know, grew up a bit."

I stared at him, my mouth open, surprised at how unwelcome his words were. Perseus was leaving? My interfering, idiotic, irritating uncle was … leaving?

He fidgeted under my gaze. "Hey, that whole growing up thing? It's just a theory," he said as the silence dragged on. "I could maybe … I dunno … come back to visit. On Pegasus, it'd take me like that." He snapped his fingers.

I closed my mouth. That's right. I'd forgotten about his horse's special abilities. I wasn't losing my uncle forever. Perseus would be able to visit any time he wanted to—probably more often than I might wish.

I forced a smile and reached out to clap him on the shoulder. "I'll miss you," I said around a throat that had grown unaccountably tight. And then, because I knew he'd never expect it, I followed this with, "Dude."

Piss gave me a startled look, and even Hermogenes squinted sleepily at me, but it was Perseus's reaction that I was waiting for.

He blinked a few times, as if he didn't quite trust what his ears had heard. And then, his face lit up. Eyes shining, mouth split into a delighted grin, he threw his arms around me, crushing me in a huge bear hug. "Dude!" he exclaimed. "You're finally chilling out!"

He squeezed tighter.

"Too ... hard," I gasped. "Can't ... breathe ..."

"Give him some air," Piss advised, giving Perseus a hard poke to loosen his hold. "No use cacking the man now that he's finally learned to lighten up."

Instantly, Perseus let me go. I bent over, taking a couple of whooping breaths.

"Sorry, dude," Perseus apologized. "It's just ... well ..." He threw out his arms happily. "Now I'm *totally* gonna have to come back for a visit."

Chapter 35

We were home and cleaned up. Perseus had gone to "catch a nap" before lunch. I, too, was tired with a bone-deep weariness that seemed out of keeping with what we had done. As a chef, I had often worked through the night, and I was no stranger to harder physical labour. There was no reason I should be so tired. And yet, I was. Tired and oddly saddened by the news of our houseguests' imminent departure. I felt wrong. As if reality had suddenly spasmed and was no longer quite the same as it had been before.

I wandered through the house, unable to settle down to any task. The house was almost deserted. Gorgias and his slaves were at work in the shop. Hermogenes was out having his beard curled on a well-deserved day off, and from the sounds of Irene's industry coming from the second floor—and Ansandra's whining—the two of them were taking advantage of the sunny day by scrubbing the women's quarters to prepare them for the coming winter.

I fetched up in the kitchen, thinking I might prepare something. Perhaps experiment with the mounds of smoked kraken that now filled our storeroom. But for the first time since the gods had remade me, I did not feel like cooking.

I puttered around, rearranging my stores (I would need to buy more coriander), polishing my kitchen knives (Hermogenes had left spots on them), checking on the state of my prized olive oil (exquisite, or as Perseus would have it, "epic"). Now that the victory celebrations were over, I found myself feeling a little flat about the whole thing. What had I proved by winning the Bronze Chef, after all? That I was a better chef than Mithaecus? I knew that already. Anybody who had sampled our respective cooking knew that. So what did it really mean to be acknowledged as the superior chef? Would I see more contracts from it? More money? Now that I didn't need to leave the house, that seemed a moot point. So what had it all been for? Merely a sop for my ego? If so, what did that say about me? Was I guilty of the same prideful ways of my father?

And what of Poseidon? In my efforts to win the competition, I had outwitted a god. Had it been hubristic of me to even consider doing so? I sank onto a stool and pondered the possible consequences of it. It was true I was now able to cook the kraken (provided it had been smoked first), and no doubt that greatly irritated the sea god. But the supply ships had finally started bringing in something other than sea monster, so even if I hadn't discovered this method, my inability to prepare kraken would not have had a lasting impact on my career. And kraken had not been the Secret Ingredient in the Bronze Chef competition after all, so if Poseidon's goal had been to embarrass me in front of the entire city, then this omission *might* be enough to defuse his ire.

Wouldn't it?

I chewed on my fingernail, examining the problem from all sides. But pondering got me nothing except a slight headache and a very short fingernail. All I could really do was hope that Poseidon would not see it as a victory over him. I resolved to make a large offering of flowers to Elpis, goddess of hope, as soon as possible.

Restless, I pushed myself up off the stool. And then, even though I wasn't particularly hungry or thirsty, I set out a few olives in a dish and poured myself a small cup of wine. I decided to take wine and olives out to the courtyard and enjoy the autumn sun.

Nausikaa was sitting on my favourite bench.

I stopped when I saw her. Her face was tilted up to the sun, her eyes closed as she revelled in its warmth on her skin. A piece of cloth and some tarnished jewellery were piled beside her on the bench, though her hands sat quiescent in her lap. Her hair was loose again, falling down her back and shoulders like a cinnamon-tinged cloak. It suited her in a way that Zeuxo's elaborate hairstyle had not.

Nausikaa would be leaving soon.

The thought made my throat hurt.

Suddenly, she looked up and over at me as if I'd said something, though to my knowledge, I had not.

"Pelops!" Her face brightened when she saw me, sea-blue eyes sparkling like sun on the waves.

"Hullo," I said, coming further into the courtyard. "I thought I was all alone here."

She looked down at the pile of jewellery and cloth by her side and screwed up her face. "I'm supposed to be scrubbing the necklaces," she confided. "But it seems too nice a day to work."

"There won't be many left before winter." I nodded my agreement and offered her an olive. She accepted with a smile.

"Would you like a cup of wine?" I asked. "I could get you one. It's no trouble."

"I've got some water, thank you," she said, indicating a cup by her feet.

I hesitated, unsure where to sit, but Nausikaa solved that problem for me by shoving her cleaning cloths and necklaces to one side and making room for me on the bench.

"Why don't you have a seat?" she invited. "The sun is marvellous from this angle."

I settled beside her on the bench, noticing as I did so the delicate scent of her hair.

"I assume you and my brother were successful last night?" she inquired.

"You assume correctly," I told her with a grave nod. "And I must admit, it is a distinct relief to finally have *that* out of the house."

"Try travelling with it," she said dryly.

I shuddered. "I still find it difficult to fathom how he carted that thing all over most of Greece."

"You mean without turning half the populace to stone?"

I made a face. "Yes, without doing that."

"It's not that Perseus is ill-willed. He's just …"

"Clumsy." We both said the word at once.

We grinned at each other. Nausikaa's blue eyes were crinkled with laughter. My heart gave an odd thump, and I felt the smile slip from my face. I covered it up by taking a sip of my wine.

"So, Perseus told me you'll be leaving for Delphi soon," I said, though I did not know why I was pressing the issue.

"Delphi," she echoed tonelessly. Her hair had fallen to cover her face. I could not see her expression.

"You can't ignore a calling like that forever," I told her gently.

She sat silently for a moment, her fingers plucking at the fabric of her chiton. When she finally looked up, all I saw were her eyes. Blue as the Aegean, streaked with white and green, they had all the searing fire of lightning and were shadowed with all the sadness of the world.

Concerned, I caught up her hand in mine. "What's the matter?" I asked.

Wordlessly, she continued to gaze at me, her glorious eyes filling with tears.

"Tell me!" I urged.

"I … I lied," she said finally.

"You … what?"

She pulled her hand from mine and raised her chin

defensively. "Lied," she confirmed. "I never had a vision. Apollo did not call me. I have no reason to go to Delphi."

It felt as though all the breath went out of me in a *whoosh*.

"But why?" I managed after a moment. "Why would you say such a thing?"

Nausikaa had dropped her gaze again, her mouth turned down unhappily. "To be special," she said in a small voice. "At least once in my life."

I had never heard a person sound so hopeless as she did then. Gently, I took her hand again in mine and covered it with my other. "You *are* special," I told her, pouring all my sincerity into the words. "You're clever and talented and beautiful and funny and anyone with half a mind can see that."

"You didn't see it right away."

"Clearly I was only operating with half a mind then," I told her and she chuckled in spite of herself. "I'm much better now." Somehow, my arm was now around her shoulders.

She nodded and smiled shyly up at me. "You are," she agreed.

"About what I said to you that night—"

She lifted a finger to my lips to silence me. "It's forgotten," she said. "After all, a good memory is an undesirable quality in a friend."

A friend? Was that what I was?

Nausikaa rested her head in the crook of my arm, and we sat in silence for a while.

"So …" I ventured finally. "I suppose you'll go to Aethiopia now? With the rest of your family?"

Nausikaa pulled away from me, and for an all-too-brief

moment I could still feel the warm impression of her on my body.

She regarded me with those sea-blue eyes, her expression sober. "I don't think so," she said slowly, watching my face. "I think ... I think I might stay in Athens."

My heart, which had been feeling small and pinched, suddenly gave a strange twist.

"Athens?" I managed.

"Mmmm," she agreed.

"What ... what is in Athens for you?" I asked. "For a foreigner, much of the city's amenities are off-limits, you know. And for a woman, there really wouldn't be ..." I trailed off lamely.

I do not know what my own eyes revealed, but Nausikaa's began to shine as if lit by Helios himself.

"You know," she said in her low honey-rich voice, "for a smart man, you can be awfully stupid sometimes."

And then, she was kissing me.

Or I was kissing her.

In truth, I'm not really certain who kissed who. All I knew was that her soft, full lips were pressed against mine and nothing, nothing in my life felt as right as this did.

Oh, I thought.

Oh.

FOR LEASE: stall in the Agora, Cloth Sellers Street. Former location of Meidias's U Rent It Symposion and Party Centre. All offers considered. *PRICE REDUCED!*

Author's Note

By now you've probably guessed that I like to play fast and furious with Greek myths, not to mention Greek history. What can I say? It's fun! It's goofy! It makes me laugh! Hopefully it makes you laugh too because, frankly, most of us could use a little more levity in our lives. But sometimes all this playing about can result in a bit of confusion on the reader's part—especially for those of you who might not be as familiar with Greek myth and history as I am. So, what was real? What was myth? And what burbled up from the Stygian depths of my imagination? (Did you see what I did there? I snuck in *another* reference to Greek mythology. Yes, I am a nerd.)

Ahem. So, real vs. made up... Pelops and his less-than-loving father are mythological characters, of course, as is Perseus. But although professional chefs really did exist in Periklean Athens and they were predominantly foreigners, Myth Pelops never went on to become a celebrity chef (clearly an unforgivable omission on the part of mythology). As for Myth Perseus… he did slay the dreaded kraken by waving the Gorgon's head at it, but the sea monster of mythology turned to stone instead of dying and leaving its remains for the citizens of Athens to consume. Really, where's the fun in that? Myth Perseus is also very noble and virtuous and heroic (blah, blah, blah), and although mythology doesn't say anything about it one way or the other, it is probably doubtful he ever enjoyed a rousing game of Dead Ant. You can see why I had to change things up a bit, can't you?

Oh, I played some things straight. According to the myths, Danaë was visited by Zeus disguised as a golden shower (a bit weird, I know, but there you have it), Proteus was a shape-shifting sea god who would answer any question if you could hang on to him while he was changing, and Hermes obtained his trademark winged sandals from Perseus. In addition, Medusa's severed head was said to be buried under a mound in the Athenian agora, though whether or not it was interred under the stall of an unscrupulous merchant is a detail which has been, alas, obscured by the mists of time.

In terms of history, I tried to write the period, which is around 520 BC, as realistically as possible—in so far as one can with gods and krakens and the like. There really was a Theatre of Dionysus (though to my knowledge, it never hosted a competitive cooking event), Archestratus was a real gourmand (he even wrote a gastronomic poem on where to find the best food in the Mediterranean), and Pythagoras was a real person (to which geometry students everywhere can attest). Incidentally, Pythagoras really did believe that the soul was immortal, going through a series of reincarnations beginning with ... you guessed it, beans. Seriously, you can't make this stuff up.

If you want to know more about Greek mythology and history, there are any number of excellent online and print sources. Have fun while you immerse yourself in the research! After all, you never know what you'll find. Bread dildos and reincarnation from beans are just a couple of the little gems I've discovered. Who knows what else there is out there ...

A few of my personal favourite sources (i.e., the ones that are sitting on my desk and desktop) are:

Andrew Dalby, *Siren Feasts: A History of Food and Gastronomy in Greece* (New York: Routledge, 1996).

Andrew Dalby and Sally Grainger, *The Classical Cookbook* (Los Angeles: The J. Paul Getty Museum, 1996).

James Davidson, *Courtesans and Fishcakes: The Consuming Passions of Classical Athens* (New York: Harper Perennial, 1999).

Bettany Hughes, *The Hemlock Cup: Socrates, Athens and the Search for the Good Life* (New York: Alfred A. Knopf, 2011).

Peter James and Nick Thorpe, *Ancient Inventions* (New York: Ballantine Books, 1994).

Philip Matyszak, *Ancient Athens on Five Drachmas a Day* (London: Thames & Hudson, 2008).

Peter Connolly and Hazel Dodge, *The Ancient City: Life in Classical Athens & Rome* (Oxford: Oxford University Press, 2001).

"Theoi Greek Mythology: Exploring Mythology in Classical Literature and Art." *The Theoi Project: Greek Mythology.* http://www.theoi.com/.

Acknowledgements

There are, unsurprisingly, many people to thank for their help and support with this book. There are the usual suspects: Sharon Caseburg, Jamis Paulson, and Sara Harms from Ravenstone (I know how hard you guys work, and I truly love you for it!), my fantastic editor Catherine Marjoribanks (with whom I have a deeply satisfying writer/editor relationship), my excellent writers group, Mike Friesen, Chris Smith, and Chadwick Ginther (who love my work most of the time and don't hesitate to pull the punches the other times). And, as always, there is my fabulous husband and daughter whose belief in me is both elevating and humbling.

But there are also a couple of *un*usual suspects who need to be thanked. First off is Carolyn Walton-Kay who went far above and beyond the call of friendship to ensure copies of *Food for the Gods* were in all the libraries on Vancouver Island. Who knew

461

that a pizza and a bottle of wine after a gruelling Russian exam would result in such a close and long-lasting friendship?

The second unusual suspect is Dr. Mark Lawall, a Classics professor from the University of Manitoba. To fully understand Dr. Lawall's inclusion in these acknowledgements, you have to go back over twenty years to when I was enrolled in Classical Studies at the University of Alberta. As a wide-eyed undergrad, my dream was to work at the Archaeological Institute of America in Athens. It was—and is—THE place to work if you're interested in Greek archaeology. I wanted to dig up temples and statues and pottery sherds under the Mediterranean sun (preferably while quaffing Greek wines and eating Greek foods). Obviously it didn't happen, and I went on to other things, including writing novels. Well, last fall, I got an email from Mark. He told me that a student had given him a copy of *Food for the Gods* and that he'd read it while on a dig in Rhodes. Now I thought *that* was pretty darn cool, but then he told me that his wife, Lea Stirling (another Classics professor), was also given my book by the same student. Not needing two copies of *Food for the Gods*, they gave this second copy to a friend of theirs who is no less than the head of the Archaeological Institute of America in Athens! [insert squeal here] And so, even though I never worked at the AIA in Athens, my *work* is there now. So you see, sometimes dreams really do come true—just not always in the way you might have envisioned. Thanks, Mark and Lea, and thanks to your generous student! It's been a few months since our conversation, but I gotta tell you, I'm still grinning about this.

About the Author

Karen Dudley didn't know she was supposed to be a writer, so she studied everything from Greek history and mythology to ecology to Quaternary pollen analysis. Then she wrote a short stack of wildlife biology books and four environmental mystery novels before she decided that maybe she should be writing fantasy. Having far more in common with hobbits than with elves, she is shortish, fond of gardening and fine foods, and has been known to take part in jewellery-related quests. She lives in Winnipeg with her husband, daughter, and the requisite authorial cats.

Missed the first Epikurean Epic?

Enjoy this excerpt from
Food for the Gods

Dessert was late.

I snatched up another almond, crammed it into the last date, then dumped honey over the lot before ordering a kitchen slave to finish the garnish. All that was left to do now was arrange the cakes. It only took a moment, but it was a moment too long.

"Chug, chug, chug-a-lug…"

I could hear the chanting—and a sloshing sound that could only be the wine splashing to the floor.

Quickly, I slid the final sweet triangle onto the platter. "They're ready," I told the serving girl. "Go, go! Take them in. Same serving order as first tables."

She stepped up to the tray with a perky jiggle.

"And re-pin your chiton," I added, disapproval colouring my tone. The clothing in question was slipping from her left

465

shoulder, revealing the soft smoothness of her skin, the swell of her breasts. How could anybody concentrate on food if the slaves were jiggling about in such a fashion?

"Oops," she said insincerely and shrugged the shoulder, which made the chiton slip even further.

More shouts of laughter boomed out from the dining room, mingled again with naughty feminine giggles. The serving girl winked, picked up the trays and grinned back at me with a flirty flick of her chiton.

She did not come back for the fruit bowl.

"You." I motioned to another slave. A young boy this time, with dark eyes and long lashes. "Here, take the fruit in for them. Can you carry this? Good. Set it down in front of your master. Be careful, mind!"

He did not come back either.

I'd sent in extra lamps, tasteful entertainment, and slaves to keep things clean. The last of the food had been served. I had now officially done all I could.

Weariness suddenly set in, and I surveyed the mess in the kitchen, absently rubbing my shoulder. Herakles himself might have found the task daunting. The household slaves would clean the bulk of it, but I disliked leaving my hired crockery for slaves to attend. Too often, the pots and pans ended up chipped or cracked or ...

Crash!

... even worse.

Mentally, I added the cost of a fruit bowl to tonight's mounting tally.

I was rapidly coming to the unpleasant realization that I'd made a rather strategic error when I agreed to cook for Nicander's symposion. Oh, Nicander himself wasn't a problem—the man was a fine upstanding citizen, owner of a prosperous shield factory. Any of the celebrity chefs in Athens would have been delighted to provide the culinary entertainment for his symposion. But a number of his invited guests had less than stellar reputations when it came to the sober, philosophical discussions of Homer which are supposed to make up the Athenian male's dinner party. And the gatecrashers, who'd breezed in shortly after the grilled tuna had been served, were even worse.

I took a sip of well-watered wine, sighed heavily, and began scraping off the casserole dishes. All the while trying—and failing—to ignore the increasingly raucous noises coming from the andron where the guests had gathered, ostensibly to dine.

Inviting Proteas had been Nicander's first mistake. Proteas may own one of the largest silver mines in the country, but even the slaves knew him for an ass—and the man drank like a Thracian. Including him among the dinner guests had been bad enough, but I couldn't imagine what had possessed Nicander to name him symposiarch for the evening.

Proteas as symposiarch. It would be laughable if it weren't so horribly, horribly real.

The symposiarch is the life of an Athenian dinner party. A jolly sort. The kind of fellow who keeps the conversation moving and directs the entertainment for the evening. It's his job. It's also his job to water down the wine so the partygoers don't get dung-faced, annoy the neighbours, and generally find themselves unable to converse in a coherent, philosophic manner. But while Proteas might be able to keep a conversation clipping along, watering the wine was not proving to be one of his strengths.

"We're sinking! We're sinking!" several voices cried out.

"Oi! Clear th' decks!"

"Dump the ballast!"

Great Hera! What were they up to now?

I stepped out of the kitchen and saw a dinner guest stagger across the courtyard, one of Nicander's carved serving tables clutched under his arm. I gaped at the sight—and was nearly run over by Nicander and Proteas shouldering one of the dining couches between them.

"*Wha … what are you doing?*" I demanded shrilly.

"Bloody trireme's sinking, isn' it!" Nicander explained with slurred urgency. "Mus' be th' storm. Been told t' clear th' decks!"

Trireme? Storm?

There was a crash as the small table splintered onto the street, followed quickly by the muffled thump of the couch with all its cushions and coverings. I had to dodge aside as another group of guests with another set of dining tables marched past. Recovering myself, I ducked across the courtyard, past the curtain and into the dining room. Two more couches were following the first out the door. I flattened myself against the wall and blinked to adjust my eyes.

Oil lamps flickered in the dimness, their untrimmed wicks sending black curls of greasy smoke toward the ceiling. The sweaty stench of a dozen diners had long since overwhelmed the delicate scent of the flower baskets, and the air was hot, heavy with stale perfume and the fruity fumes of wine. Only three couches remained in the room. One was vacant. On the second, a man was busily throwing up in one of the wine kraters. And on the last couch, I saw the serving girl who had disappeared earlier. She lolled against the cushions, her eyes distant and dreamy. Her chiton had slipped even further, but she didn't seem to mind. Neither did the citizen who was fondling her rosy-tipped breasts.

"Ho! Pelops!" A voice boomed out from behind me.

I started and spun around.

He was tall for an Athenian, with broad shoulders and a magnificent beard. One of the gatecrashers, I guessed. I didn't recognize him.

He leaned in close. His wine-soaked breath leaned even closer. "It's me," he hissed. "Dionysus."

It took a moment for the name to register. "*Dionysus!*"

"Shh!" He hushed me and bent his head to my ear. "I'm in disguise," he whispered gleefully. "So's Hermes."

"I, uh … Hermes is here too?"

Dionysus chuckled and gestured with his beard. "He's found love."

I glanced over at the couch. The serving girl looked very happy. And so she should. It wasn't every day a girl got to make love to a god.

"Brilliant party, yeah?" Dionysus elbowed me back to myself. "Gods, I'm good."

"*Brilliant?*" I sputtered. "They're *destroying* the place. They

469

think they're on a bloody warship. They never even touched my desserts! How much drink have they had?"

The god of wine looked affronted at my tone. "Several amphorae, I think." He belched long and loud, then offered me a blissful smile. "I may have lost track."

"*Several* amphorae!" I choked off the rest of my words.

"It seemed best," Dionysus was nodding eagerly. "We've all been told to keep an eye out for you, haven't we? You know, to make up for—" he waved his hand around airily, "—things."

I scrubbed at my forehead. My knees were urging me to sit down. "But, what … why … how did you know I was here?"

"Well, you could say … I heard it through the grapevine!" He slapped his knee and burst into peals of boozy laughter.

I managed a feeble grin. When a god thinks he's funny, you'd better think he's a scream.

Dionysus threw an arm around my shoulder and gave me a friendly shake. "Pelops, *relax!* Hermes and I just thought we'd, you know, smarten things up a bit. Help you make a name for yourself in Athens."

I dropped my gaze, certain my dismay was all too apparent. "Oh, I'll have a name for myself all right," I muttered under my breath. "Whether I'll ever have work again is another matter."

"Ah, bollocks!" Dionysus brushed it off. "You worry too much, my friend."

I should have known he would hear me.

He clapped me on the shoulder. "You should have a drink. Piss about. I promise you, by tomorrow all of Athens will know about this party. You can't *buy* publicity like this! Just look! *Look* at them!"

He spread out his arms to encompass the scene and laughed in unadulterated delight.

"Mortals are so much fun! I've got to get my lazy arse off The Mount more often. Well, must be off. Things to do, people to see, tables to toss. Cheers, yeah? *Ho! Nicander! Wait up, mate!*"

And with that, the god of wine jumped back into the fray, helpfully grabbing one end of a couch, which was making its way speedily out the door.

I bit back a string of oaths. Dionysus *and* Hermes! No wonder this dinner party had descended into chaos. My eyes had finished adjusting to the darkness. Now I could see the bowls of carefully selected fruit upended on the floor, the discarded clothing lying in wine-sodden heaps in the corners. A citizen was savouring the delights of a flute girl on a bed of leftover honeyed shrimp.

The dog was eating my pastries.

Deflated, I stared at the ruin. This dinner party was supposed to have been an important step for me. Another rung in the ladder of professional success. I was one of the best chefs in Athens. An up-and-coming foreigner with a wealth of new and interesting recipes for jaded Athenian palates. A person of importance! *A man in demand!*

Hermes lifted his mouth from the serving girl's bosom and gave me a mischievous wink. I offered him a sickly smile in return. How do you tell a god you don't need—or want—his help? The crash of breaking crockery startled me from my stasis.

My dishes!

I moved quickly then, darting around a half-clad cithara

player, stepping over another writhing couple, slipping on a forgotten tuna steak. I tried desperately to rescue my hired dishes. Dinner guests in search of more "ballast" wheeled and swerved around me, their eyes red with the wildness of wine. Another table—an elegant gem with ivory inlays—was hoisted through the courtyard and sent tumbling into the street.

By the time someone finally reported the civil disturbance and the archons arrived to investigate, a crowd had gathered in front of the house to enjoy the show and to pick through the windfall of household possessions. With the gravity that comes only after imbibing large quantities of drink, Nicander informed the officials that the trireme he was on was sinking in the storm, and that the pilot had instructed him to dump the ballast. It was a task, he explained solemnly, he had almost, but not quite, completed. And then, after imparting this information to his disbelieving, but highly amused, audience, Nicander collapsed with a small sigh into the street on top of all his furniture.

Or so I heard.

Long before the archons got there, I'd gathered up my pots and pans and what was left of the hired crockery and slipped out into the hot Athenian summer night. As I guided the mule towards home, I tried out a number of different excuses for the state of the pottery. None of them involved gods. All of them sounded contrived. When Meidias saw his dishes, he was going to be upset. He'd probably charge me double. He might even threaten to kill me. The last didn't worry me too much. I was still one of the best chefs in Athens. Still a man in demand.

And besides, I'd been killed before.